W9-AHZ-000

SALVATION

Also by Caryn Lix

Sanctuary
Containment

A SANCTUARY NOVEL

SALV

TION

CARYN LIX

SIMON PULSE
NEW YORK LONDON TORONTO SYDNEY NEW DELHI

SIMON PULSE
An imprint of Simon & Schuster Children's Publishing Division
1230 Avenue of the Americas, New York, New York 10020
First Simon Pulse hardcover edition July 2020

Jacket designed by Sarah Creech | Interior designed by Mike Rosamilia
The text of this book was set in Adobe Garamond Pro.
Manufactured in the United States of America
10 9 8 7 6 5 4 3 2 1
Library of Congress Cataloging-in-Publication Data
Names: Lix, Caryn, author.
Title: Salvation / Caryn Lix.
Description: First Simon Pulse hardcover edition. | New York : Simon Pulse, 2020. | Series: A Sanctuary novel; [3] | Summary: "Trapped on a strange planet, Kenzie and her friends must figure out how to end the alien threat and then find their way home"—Provided by publisher.
Identifiers: LCCN 2019037484 (print) | LCCN 2019037485 (eBook) |
ISBN 9781534456433 (hardcover) | ISBN 9781534456457 (eBook)
Subjects: CYAC: Adventure and adventurers—Fiction. | Extraterrestrial beings—Fiction. | Supervillains—Fiction. | Science fiction.
Classification: LCC PZ7.1.L5853 Sal 2020 (print) | LCC PZ7.1.L5853 (eBook) | DDC [Fic]—dc23
LC record available at https://lccn.loc.gov/2019037484
LC eBook record available at https://lccn.loc.gov/2019037485

For my husband, my unofficial
publicist and biggest fan

ONE

I WAS GETTING USED TO RUNNING. FROM aliens, from bounty hunters, from underground criminals—when it came to escaping, I was something of an expert by now, even if I didn't always manage the most graceful exits. So you wouldn't think plodding through a desert would be all that difficult, even if it was on an alien planet.

But we were hitting the point where I'd almost welcome an alien, or the sound of bullets, or anything to break up the sweltering, tedious trudge. My clothes, sticky with sweat, clung to my body, and loose strands of my hair matted to my face. We didn't have any water, and no one had spoken in maybe an hour, not even Reed, our resident wisecracker. We were all too parched. I almost laughed at the irony. Somehow, after everything we'd survived, we just might die after all, and it wouldn't be alien claws or Omnistellar bullets that did us in. It would be the sun.

Better still, it was my fault we were stranded here. Of course, I hadn't had much choice. The ship we were on was about to explode, thanks to my father activating the self-destruct system. It was either teleport us out or explode with it. Unfortunately, I couldn't direct my own teleportation power. It wasn't even *mine*, technically. It was borrowed from Liam, a treacherous alien with superpowers of his own. Because apparently, borrowing powers was something I did now.

I brushed a piece of heavy wet hair out of my face and peered at the city in the distance. Hours of walking, and the stupid thing wasn't even a glimmer closer than it was when we started. When a flash of light appeared over the city, we'd set off at a near jog, clinging to Cage's assertion that our friends must have caused the light. Now, hours later, we'd slowed to a trudge.

The flash could have been anything. Lightning. Other people. There was no reason to believe it was my friends. It was still entirely possible I'd dropped people I cared about somewhere in space and left them to die.

My heart sank. Yeah, the others had pressed me into using my borrowed power. Sure, we'd have died if we'd stayed where we were.

But at least it wouldn't have been my fault.

That knowledge tore my insides to shreds. So many people had died since I opened my eyes that fateful morning just a few weeks ago, the day I was taken hostage: most of the prisoners

I'd been responsible for, my parents, my friends. The idea that I might have abandoned even more of those friends somewhere in space . . .

No. I tightened my shoulders, refusing to give the thought purchase. If determination counted for anything, my friends were here somewhere. I would find them, and they *would* be all right. I simply wouldn't allow things to work out any other way.

The sun had moved all the way across the sky while we walked and was now slipping below the horizon. We were going to find our friends here. I wouldn't let myself consider any other possibility. But even I had to admit it wasn't likely to be anytime soon.

To distract myself, I went back to listing facts about deserts. My dad had taught me not all deserts were sandy, either. This one was, though, and I was just then learning something new: walking in sand sucks. I remembered it as pleasant, but that was because I was thinking of beach holidays with my little cousins back on Earth. Walking in sand was great when it was the twenty feet between the cottage and the ocean. It was a little different when you were plodding through miles of shifting dirt, never really able to get a grip on the ground or tense your muscles properly. Put simply, it *hurt.*

And as the sun vanished completely, I learned another thing: once the sun sets, hot deserts turn cold. Fast. The sweat evaporated from my body, leaving me shivering. I untied the sweater I'd knotted around my waist and slid it over my arms. Around me, my friends did the same.

Cage stopped, his profile sharp and shadowed in the twilight as he examined the city. "Is it *any* closer?" he groaned.

"It must be." Without ceremony, Reed plopped down in the sand, a small puff surrounding him. He fell back and sighed heavily. "We've been walking for three days. I mean, I assume. That's what it feels like." His eyes popped open. "Unless . . . You don't think it's a mirage?"

"It's only been a couple of hours," chided Imani, but she didn't seem any happier than the rest of us. "And even if it is a mirage, that's where we need to go. We saw sparks from that area, remember? That had to be Alexei."

Near the edge of the group, Rune, Cage's twin sister, thoughtfully monitored the stars as if she could tell the time or the direction by their position. And maybe she could have, back on Earth. Rune was full of surprises. Sure, she melded with machines—her own special superpower, courtesy of the alien probes that visited our planet fifty years ago and altered the DNA of future generations. But she was also strong and kind and surprisingly tough at her core, all things I'd never have guessed about her when I was the guard responsible for making sure she stayed in prison.

But I doubted even Rune would be able to tell anything from the stars on an alien planet.

I considered Reed in the dirt and seriously contemplated

joining him. Instead I nudged him with my foot. "Get up," I ordered.

He showed me his middle finger and closed his eyes.

Cage kicked him—not hard, but harder than I had. Reed groaned in protest. "Reed," said Cage patiently. "I know you're tired. We all are. But it's cold out here and getting colder. We have no food, no water, no shelter. Our only hope is to make the city. It can't be much farther."

"That's what you said an hour ago, *gege*," said Rune tiredly.

Cage arched an eyebrow. "You have a better idea?"

"No," she said. "I think we should keep moving. But I don't share your confidence about how close that city might be. We should consider other options."

"*What* other options?" sighed Imani. She extended a hand to Reed. "Come on. Or we'll leave you here."

He flashed us one of his blinding grins. "No, you won't," he said, correctly. But he did take her hand and let her pull him to his feet, and we resumed our tired slog across the desert.

Of course there were no lights to illuminate the city ruins, not in this barren and desolate world. I drew close to Cage and lowered my voice. "Do you think we'll find the others there?"

His hand slid around my shoulders, rubbing my arms through my sweater, sending a rush of warmth through me, and not just because of his body heat. "I hope so," he said. "They're here somewhere, Kenz. I hope the flash we saw earlier came from them. But even if it didn't, we're going to find them, no doubt about it."

His words held tremendous confidence, but I'd long since learned how Cage manipulated situations. He was a smooth talker without too many qualms about misleading people, although he'd promised never to lie to me.

Of course he didn't have to be lying, exactly, to deceive me. The fact was that Cage had no more idea where our companions were than I did, because when I'd teleported us here, I'd somehow lost them: Mia and Alexei and Jasper, our friends; Priya and Hallam, our hunters; and Matt—whatever he was. Neither? Both? I didn't even know anymore.

"You could use your speed to go ahead," I pointed out.

Cage grinned at me in the near dark. "And you could borrow my power and come with me," he pointed out. "But then who would keep Reed moving?"

Even though he didn't say it, I followed his thoughts: he didn't want to leave his sister behind. No matter how brief the separation, Cage hated Rune being out of his sight, especially in an unfamiliar and potentially hostile world.

"Well, we'd better do something before we have a revolution." I squinted at the city. It *did* seem like it was getting closer, but then, as Rune said, it had seemed that way an hour ago. "For now, I guess we keep walking."

And walk we did. I didn't know how long. My world became an endless repetition of sinking into sand, forcing myself to lift my foot, stumbling another step forward. I shivered violently and, instinctively, all five of us huddled together for warmth. We plodded along in silence. The quiet reminded me of spacewalks, there was so little noise: only our feet crunching in the sand, punctuated by Reed's occasional complaints, which continued until I wished Mia were here to shut him up. She probably would have threatened to bury him in the sand, or feed him to a cactus, or—

I stumbled into Cage, who steadied me. "Are you okay?" he asked softly.

I nodded, blinking. Teleporting everyone to wherever we were had taken a lot out of me. In spite of Reed and Imani working to heal me, I was still exhausted. I was also carefully avoiding the thought that I was now an orphan. My dad had died in space, gored by alien claws just when he seemed on the verge of listening to me. My eyes swam and my throat swelled, threatening to choke me. I resolutely swallowed. It was too cold for tears, and I was too dehydrated to allow them.

The sheer utilitarianism of that thought almost sent me into a bout of hysterical laughter. A few months ago I'd thrown a fit when I ran out of the freeze-dried strawberries I kept on our orbital home. Now I was holding back tears of grief to preserve moisture.

"Hey," said Rune softly. She was close on my other side, her presence a constant, silent comfort. "I know we've said this before, but this time I really do think the city is closer."

I blinked back the last of my tears and peered into the shadows. A rebellious surge of hope burst through me. It was hard to tell in the darkness, but the city's silhouette *did* look close—*very* close, maybe even over the next hill.

The toll of the last few days surged against me: my dad dying in front of me. Matt, apparently returning from the dead, only to vanish—with half of my friends. The aliens reappearing. Learning that the corporation I'd dedicated my life to wasn't only selfish, they were flat-out willing to risk the Earth in their overconfident search for alien technology.

I didn't have a shred of hope left.

Or I shouldn't. But still it welled inside me. Maybe if we just kept going, we would reach sanctuary—not the false Sanctuary held out by Omnistellar, but someplace real, someplace temporarily safe.

Of course, on the heels of that thought, something screamed in the desert.

TWO

I DREW UP SHORT. CAGE JERKED ME BEHIND him and spun, his eyes flashing in the moonlight as if he could see in the darkness. The others pivoted so fast Imani tripped over Reed and would have fallen if Cage hadn't grabbed her with his lightning reflexes.

"What the hell was that?" Reed gasped.

"An animal?" Rune whispered. Her fingers sank into my arm.

I covered her hand with my own, swallowing. "Have you seen any animals around here?"

"No, but that doesn't mean—"

Another scream answered, this one from the other side of the desert. The cries sounded horribly familiar, almost like the aliens shouting to one another. "Wolves," I said out loud, my voice shaky. "Or the alien equivalent. That's all it is." Not that

I was excited to face some kind of alien animal, but . . . better than the alternative. The things that stalked us through space? Anything was better than that.

"Sure," Cage agreed. There was no trace of fear in his voice even though physical tension radiated off him. God, I envied how he smothered all signs of emotion beneath a cheerful facade. "We haven't seen animals, but that doesn't mean there aren't any. And whatever that is, it's far away, somewhere behind us. We don't need to worry."

"It's a good sign," Rune said, although she was whispering and didn't sound very happy. "If there are animals, there's probably water. There's food. We just have to find it."

"Yeah," Reed agreed slowly. "Yeah, but could we maybe look in that city? If that's what it is? I mean, instead of standing here waiting for whatever's howling in the desert to find us?"

There hadn't been another sound since the second one faded, but no one argued with Reed. With a renewed surge of energy, we pressed on. Within minutes it was clear that Rune, as usual, was right: we were finally achieving our objective, the city's ruined hollow looming in more distinct outlines with every step. We made for its edge, a series of run-down buildings looped by a cement highway.

By mutual consent, we staggered to the nearest building. It was a store of some sort, its door hanging ajar to reveal a dilapidated shop interior. I had no idea what it had once sold, because the shelves were stripped bare. But the walls provided shelter, and we were all too drained to do much more than slump behind the counter and fall instantly asleep.

As exhausted as I was, though, I opened my eyes when it was still dark. I was shivering, even curled tightly against Cage, my head pillowed on his chest and his arms wrapped loosely around me. I took a moment to revel in the sensation. Cage and I had what could be called a tumultuous history. It started when he took me captive, back when he was a prisoner on Omnistellar's orbital prison Sanctuary and I was a guard with no idea about . . . well, anything, really. I didn't know my mom would choose company regulations over my life, or that the company I'd believed in my entire life was basically a supervillain, or that the prisoners housed beneath my feet were mostly innocent, or even that I had special abilities of my own. I'd been like a child, worried about nothing more than basketball and the latest issue of *Robo Mecha Dream Girl 5* and, eventually, whether my parents would divorce.

Well, that wasn't an issue anymore. The aliens had killed both of my parents—first my mom, back on Sanctuary, moments after she'd written off my life, and later my dad. I'd mostly dealt with Mom's dying, but Dad . . . it was still fresh. And harder, maybe, because Dad had been the softer parent in my life, and the one who'd made it clear he still loved me even as he toed the company line. The one I might have gotten through to, might have made understand.

And now at last the tears came, pushing through my barriers, overcoming the total lack of moisture and my own common sense. I clenched my hands into fists and disentangled myself from Cage, climbing awkwardly over my sleeping friends, stumbling out into the night before the sobs burst from me in a broken, horrible wrench.

I slumped against the wall, arms wrapped around my legs, face buried in my knees, my shoulders shaking, tears streaming down my face. I was crying not only for my parents but for everyone we'd lost since the aliens tore their way into Sanctuary, claws bared to harvest us all. For Tyler, who'd ravaged my mind when we were still enemies, and my friend Rita, and even Liam, who'd been so terrified of the aliens that he'd betrayed us to Omnistellar. I couldn't take any more loss. I bit my lip, picturing Mia and Alexei and Matt and even the Legion bounty hunters I'd lost while transporting us here. I was going to goddamn find them. I had to.

At last I raised my head and wiped the tears from my face. Crying should have made me feel better, but it just left me hollow and drained, like the tears nullified my ability to feel anything at all. I ran my tongue over my chapped lips. Crying was also stupid. My throat was parched and sore, my skin taut and itchy. We had to find water soon.

The first rays of sunlight peered over the horizon, casting the entire area in a strangely beautiful orange glow. For the first time, I clearly saw the city, or at least the part where I sat. It was right on the edge of the desert, and the cement sidewalks and roads, the mixture of buildings, shops, and apartments, held a familiar air, like a city back home. I spied what looked like a grocery store in the distance and worked my dry lips. Maybe they had water. If we didn't find some soon, we were going to have a whole new problem.

Were my friends somewhere in this city? We'd seen something—a spark or an explosion. It seemed to come from this direction, but, as I now knew, distance was relative in the desert. My shoulders sagged. I didn't know how big this city was, or anything else about it, actually. How could I ever hope to find anyone in its depths?

A sound behind me made me start, but it was only Imani, stepping into the morning sun and stretching. She'd found a bright blue cloth to fashion into a hijab, and the color set off her perfectly contoured features. Even without the makeup that made her a beauty belle back on Earth, Imani was stunning. "Thought I'd find you out here," she said, settling onto the doorstep beside me. "Thinking about your parents?"

I half smiled. "What gave me away?" My voice came out in a dry rasp, exactly like Imani's.

"I can always tell." She shrugged. "You have the same look I get when I think about my sister."

I nodded. We'd all lost people in this mess, but Imani and I were the only ones who'd seen family members die at alien hands. It created a bond between us. "Did you hear any more animals last night?" I asked, changing the subject. I wasn't quite ready to talk about my parents, especially my dad. Not yet.

"I was out the second I closed my eyes." She frowned. "Stupid, really. We should have set up watches. Not like Cage to let us forget something like that. Not like you, either, come to think of it."

I nodded. I'd had this same conversation with myself after I opened my eyes. But Cage and I were both human. My Omnistellar training made me vigilant, strong, and wary, not infallible. "We were just as tired as you," I replied, struggling to keep a defensive note from my voice.

Imani put her hands up, a smile playing on her cracked lips. "I didn't mean to accuse you," she said, her tone gentle. "You and Cage aren't the only ones with brains. The rest of us could have said something too."

I sighed, inspecting the deserted street. "Maybe we didn't want there to be danger. At least for a little while."

"Yeah. Hope overrides common sense, right?"

A long silence stretched between us. It was a surreal feeling, sitting on a doorstep as the sun rose overhead. The concrete vanished in either direction—cracked in places, with weeds forcing their way through and winding along buildings. But it was all so familiar nonetheless. "Where the hell did I take us?" I wondered out loud.

"Hey," said Imani softly. "I suppose . . . I mean, this *is* an alien planet, right?"

I blinked, my water-starved brain struggling to catch up with her. "What else would it be?"

"I don't know. I mean, we couldn't have jumped through time, could we? This isn't Earth in the future once the aliens have destroyed it?"

That I could answer definitively. I shook my head. "No. The only person with the ability to jump was Liam, and he moves through space, not time. I used his power before, remember? If I'd jumped in time, I'd have known it."

"Yeah. You're right. That makes sense." She smiled faintly. "Okay, good. I was getting nervous, thinking maybe we'd missed the fight."

"Who, us? We never miss a fight. We always seem to be right in the middle of whatever goes down."

"That we are." She raised her fist, and I pressed my knuckles to hers and smiled. In spite of everything, I still had friends. Still had *family*. Sitting here with Imani was a powerful reminder of that, and it unlocked a fierce protective swell in my chest, something I'd never experienced with my parents, maybe because I'd never had to. I knew with sudden, startling clarity that I would die for Imani—for Cage, for Reed, for any of my friends. I would leap off a cliff without thinking if it meant giving them an extra second to escape certain death, because they were all I had left, the only thing that mattered.

Of course, before I could worry about laying down my life for them, I had to *find* them.

Imani stood and stretched. "You ready to come back inside? I think I hear people moving around."

I gazed into the morning, the crumbling city to my left, the desert expanse to my right. My heart still raced with the intensity of my emotions, my drive to protect this ragtag group of survivors. "In a minute. I think I need to sit here awhile longer."

She reached down to touch my shoulder. "You saved our lives, Kenz. Don't think we don't know it."

I squeezed her hand in gratitude and watched her retreat inside. I visualized a part of myself going with her to protect everyone, keep them safe, alive. And part of me was with the others, too, wherever they were. If some stupid metaphysical part of me—call it spirit or heart or soul or whatever—could keep them safe, then my determination would do it.

I returned to studying the desert. By day it was just sand, an endless expanse of blowing dirt. Had we imagined the screams the night before?

Right, I said to myself wryly. You all imagined the same thing at the same time. Want to explain how exhaustion managed *that*?

No. It had been real enough. And probably Cage was right: wolves, or what passed for them on this alien planet. Maybe Rune was right too: it was a good sign. Animals meant food and water, and we needed to find both—especially water—soon.

A clatter signaled Cage emerging from the shop. He scanned the street, saw me, and sighed in relief. "You scared me," he said, sinking down beside me against the wall. "I woke up and you were gone."

I studied him for a moment, his sharp, angular face, the high cheekbones and flashing eyes that always appealed to me so strongly, even when he'd been nothing but a murderous prisoner in my mind. "I wanted to see things more clearly. We stumbled in here in the dark last night. I barely got a look at the building, never mind the street."

Cage gazed into the desert. "And you wanted to see if there was any sign of the creatures we heard?"

I laughed in spite of myself. No point hiding anything from him. "Yeah. I haven't seen anything. What do you think they were?"

"Honestly? The more I consider it, the more convinced I become that it was some kind of animal. I mean, this is an alien planet, right? We shouldn't expect the local wildlife to be familiar."

"Or friendly," I said cynically. "Better wolves than monsters, I guess—but alien wolves could still be a problem."

"You're not wrong. We'll have to be careful."

He didn't seem particularly worried, though, and I didn't blame him. After everything we'd been through, with all of our abilities, surely we could handle a few wild animals—even alien ones.

But none of that made me feel much better. "What do we do now?" I asked. The hopelessness echoed in my voice and I hated it but could do nothing to stop it. Had I saved us from the aliens just to die of thirst and starvation on a deserted planet? And why *was* this planet deserted, anyway? Plague? Radiation? There were just so many ways to die, and I had no idea what I'd dropped us into. My mind raced, picturing a thousand scenarios and trying to respond to all of them at the same time.

Cage must have heard my despondency. He slid his arm around my shoulders, and I leaned against him gratefully, wanting for this moment to let someone else carry the burden. "We search the city," he said, sounding positive. It was only because I knew him so well that I caught the slight hesitation in his voice, telling me he didn't have any great expectations of success. "We'll find supplies, and we'll find the others."

"And if we don't?"

"We will."

That was Cage, always refusing to even consider the possibility of failure. "Even if we do find them, there might not be much left to save. Think about who's out there," I added, my imagination filling in horrifying details. "Mia, who can't go five seconds without insulting someone, alongside the bounty hunters sent to catch us. Should go really well."

Cage winced but didn't argue, knowing I was right. Mia was not going to get along with Hallam and Priya. As for Matt, well, who knew? "That's a good argument for moving sooner rather than later," he said, "and before it gets too hot. I'll wake the others."

"Sure," I said, standing and stretching, my joints popping and cracking. I tried not to think about how long it was since I'd had anything to drink, or how dry my mouth was, or the parched feeling on my tongue and lips. "I'm going to take a walk down to that shop and see if anything's left."

Cage, who'd been halfway into the store, spun on me. "Not by yourself."

I scowled in impatience. Every second's delay was another second my friends could be in trouble. "Have you seen any signs of life in this city?"

"Remember what we heard last night."

"I'll go with her." Rune emerged from the shadows, rolling her head from side to side. "If there's something worth finding, we'd better try."

Cage didn't look any happier with me *and* his sister going off, but I raised an eyebrow in challenge, and after a moment he backed down. "We'll be right behind you," he said, sighing in defeat.

Rune smacked him on the shoulder as she walked by. "Cool it, *gege*. We're going fifty feet. After all, what's the worst that could happen?"

Cage and I winced simultaneously, but Rune was already halfway down the street. I shrugged and ran after her. After all, if the worst did indeed happen, I probably shouldn't let my best friend face it alone.

THREE

"YOU'VE DONE A GOOD JOB WITH MY BROTHER," Rune informed me as I caught up with her, smiling over her shoulder in spite of the obvious exhaustion in her face. The morning light revealed broken windows, run-down signs proclaiming book shops and electronics stores, recognizable by their pictures if not their faded words. "He's learning."

"Learning what?"

"That he can't control everything and everyone around him." She squeezed my hand as we approached the store. I glanced around again, taking in the street. It was almost spotless, no signs of litter or animals or human presence. Weeds grew up through cracks and twisted over buildings, though, and some of the windows were cracked, doors hanging askew. This place had been abandoned a long time ago.

A huge sign with a few letters on it arched over the

entranceway, but that wasn't what caught my attention. It was the cheerful cutouts of things I *did* recognize: fruits and vegetables remarkably like those on Earth, like carrots and apples and grapes.

But Rune frowned. "Strange," she said.

I nodded, biting my lip. "Yeah. The pictures are awfully familiar. Just like what we have back home." Still, it wasn't that unusual. The atmosphere here seemed the same as back home—I hadn't even considered that I could have dumped us on a gas giant or something—so it made some sense that the plants would grow in similar ways. Besides, the signs were so weathered and faded it was hard to see details.

Rune shook her head. "Not the pictures, the letters."

I blinked at the sign, which proclaimed F_ _ D _ _ U _ _ S in large letters. "Um, Rune?"

She laughed. "The lettering, Kenzie. It's Roman letters. On an alien planet. Doesn't that seem unusual to you?"

I peered from her to the sign. "You can read it?"

"Yes, Kenzie. I can read." She glared at me.

I brushed off her irritation. "No, it's just . . . I assumed my power was translating the letters." In spite of my fancy new ability, my primary talent was languages. I read and understood them with almost no effort. But if Rune saw them too . . . "Okay, that can't be coincidence."

"No."

I reconsidered Imani's theory, that I'd teleported us not in space but in time. But no. If Liam's power teleported through time, I'd surely have noticed with how many times I'd borrowed it on Obsidian. *Liam* would have noticed. I mean, it was *his* power. "I don't understand any of this," I said out loud.

"Tell me about it." Rune frowned, then shrugged. "I guess it's not completely improbable. Liam was an alien, and he spoke nearly the same language, looked almost the same as us. Evolution's a funny thing."

"It produced those . . . *creatures*, but it left us to evolve like this? And another race just like us?"

"Like I said, evolution is weird that way. It's all about what has the best chance of survival. Presumably the aliens' home planet is very different from ours, while this one is very comparable. As for the cultural and linguistic similarities, well . . . that's harder to explain. I haven't quite figured it out yet. But there are slightly less scientific possibilities that could account for them."

I regarded her dubiously. "You want to explain that?"

"How about later? We're on a mission, remember?"

I flushed. It had been a gentle reminder, but a reminder nonetheless. Our time on the alien ship had changed Rune, too. She was more confident, more of a leader now. I nodded and followed her toward the store.

The doors were ajar, which wasn't a great sign; it probably meant the store was as empty as the one where we'd spent the night. But we went inside anyway.

"Weirder still," said Rune, echoing my thoughts. I'd expected an alien grocery store to look at least a *little* bit different than it would on Earth. But this could have been the local Shop 'n Save in any corporate facility. I half expected to see the Omnistellar logo looming over the electronic tills, but there was only an expanse of blank white wall.

Shelves graced the middle of the shop. They didn't seem to be empty, either— in fact, they were nearly fully stocked. With renewed hope, we advanced. The store's outer edges didn't yield much of interest. Any produce had long since rotted and decayed into nothingness, confirming that the city had been abandoned for quite a while. In the center of the store, though, we hit the jackpot: prepackaged nutrient bars and emergency pouches of water. We tore into both, each draining a water pouch before we'd stopped to think about what we were doing. When mine was empty, I stood, holding the dripping package and raising my eyebrows at Rune. "Water on this planet could contain any kind of element that isn't friendly to humans," I pointed out.

"Good thing we travel with healers, then," she replied with a grin. She was already shoving water pouches into her pockets. "Want another?"

"Hell yes I do." There was a pile of water here, enough to last us a good long time, and I could worry about conservation later.

Rune laughed, a light, tinkling sound, and tossed me a

pouch. I drained it. She was right: we traveled with healers. And what were our choices, anyway? It was drink the water or die.

I made a face as my initial thirst abated, my latent guilt catching up with me. "We should get the others." What was I thinking, sitting here drinking water with my worried, dehydrated friends less than a block away?

Rune nodded, wiping her mouth with the back of her hand. "Fuel to help us gather stuff," she replied. "I don't know why this store is still so well stocked. Must not have been anyone left to scavenge. My point is, there's lots for everyone. Let's gather it up."

We started stuffing our pockets. Rune found some canvas bags, and we filled those, too, working in rapid silence until . . . "Hey," said Rune, examining something on a shelf. "Look at this."

I took the packet she passed me and examined it in bewilderment. The packaging showed a familiar and welcome sight: freeze-dried fruit. Not strawberries, my favorite treat back on Sanctuary, but even the weight of the package in my hands was enough to bring back a flood of memories: of my family, my friends, my safe, secure, manipulated life with Omnistellar. It almost triggered another wave of grief and loss.

Almost.

But not quite.

Because of far more interest were the words on the package: FREEZE-DRIED MIXED FRUIT. "This is in English," I said.

"Yeah."

"Rune, what the hell?"

"Yeah."

We stared at each other. What were the odds that out of all the planets in the entire universe, I'd managed to select one where the alien life-forms ate the same food as us, lived in the same types of buildings, and spoke the same goddamn language?

Then again, when I'd reached out with my borrowed power, I'd begged whoever might be listening to send me somewhere safe. Somewhere we could find help. Somewhere we might even have a chance of defeating the aliens. "Maybe it's not coincidence," I said, although I barely heard myself over my pounding heart. "I don't really understand my own powers, let alone Liam's. I was searching for somewhere safe, somewhere we could find help. Maybe this is part of it."

"Maybe." Rune brushed her fingers over the package in my hands. "There are other theories," she added. Brushing her hair behind her ears, she tilted her head in her inquisitive, birdlike way. "What I was talking about outside. Some scientists have theorized that if there is life similar to ours in the universe, we might have a . . . a connection, so to speak. We might be more similar than we could ever imagine. Almost like we could reach across time and space without knowing it, creating an invisible link between races."

I made a face. "That sounds like . . ." I hesitated to finish the sentence. "Not like you," I settled on at last. "You're usually pretty firmly entrenched in the facts."

Rune shrugged. "Right, and the *fact* is that we're on an alien planet that closely resembles our own. We've met at least one alien who was so much like us he could easily pass for human. At some point, you have to leave the proven science behind and consider other hypotheses, you know? I agree it sounds strange that species could connect without ever meeting. But look at some of the cultural similarities on our own planet. There are differences, of course, but even races who didn't meet often had similar mythologies. Similar laws, similar practices."

I sucked on the water pouch thoughtfully. "I guess it doesn't make any less sense than anything else that's happened lately."

"I wish I had some tech. I wonder what they used here, if it's like ours."

"I kind of think the power's been down for a while." I gestured around us, encompassing the decaying building, the weeds growing through the doors.

Rune sighed. "Oh, I know. But still." She looked forlornly at the fruits, as if staring at them hard enough might transform them into a computer.

Hell, maybe she could. None of us really understood what our powers were doing these days. Just in case, I tore the package open and shoved a handful of the fruit into my mouth. Rune grinned and extended her hand, and between us we breakfasted on our tiny treat there on the dusty floor. "We have to get back to the others and share this," I said.

"We will. We just need a burst of energy to examine the rest of the store, right?"

I laughed. "Right."

The combination of food and water did plenty to improve my spirits. Okay, so we were on a weird planet where the aliens apparently spoke English. Yes, strange sounds surprised us in the night. Sure, we were separated from our friends and trapped here. But we had hope. I was holding it in my hands. And if nothing else, I'd get to see Reed's grin when I held up the food and water. There was nothing quite as cheering as Reed's uninhibited enthusiasm.

Once we'd loaded ourselves with all the remaining water packages and nutrient bars, we scoured the store for anything else of value, but we didn't find much: some unfamiliar packaged foods and a lot of dust, things that had clearly passed their prime and wouldn't be of much use. "This is good," Rune assured me as I nervously examined what might have been some kind of dried meat. "If we found one store with supplies remaining, there are others. We can survive here."

Yes, but for how long? I left the sentiment unspoken. One problem at a time, I reminded myself. The star of my favorite manga always said *nanakorobi, yaoki:* fall down seven times, get up eight. I'd long since amended the numbers into the thousands, but the sentiment held. The food and water would let us get up one more time.

We drifted to the front of the store, our bags bursting at the seams, and Rune's fingers played over what looked like an electronic food scanner. At her touch, a light shimmered across the screen.

"Wait," I said. Did I imagine that? "Rune, touch the scanner again."

She blinked at me, then laid her hand on the screen. Nothing happened. "What's up?" she asked.

"It's nothing, I just thought . . . when you touched it earlier, I thought something lit up." I smiled ruefully. "Stupid, right?"

"Maybe not." Rune set her bag down and frowned, closing her eyes in concentration.

I stared into the inky-black depths, willing them to come to life. Other people's abilities were changing. Why not Rune's? And if she could power tech . . .

I jumped as a light flickered on the screen, but at the same moment Rune shook her head and stepped back. "Nothing."

"Are you sure? I thought . . ." I glanced from her to the screen. "Try once more?"

Rune arched an eyebrow, then narrowed her gaze, her jaw set in determination as she slid her fingers over the screen. For a moment, nothing happened. Then, all at once, the screen sputtered into life, revealing some sort of unfamiliar corporate logo and beeping loudly. We both jumped in surprise. The moment Rune cut contact with the screen, it went black.

We exchanged looks, and Rune stepped forward again. She rested her hands on the screen, and it returned to life. "Well," she said. "This is new."

Excitement surged through me. "Rune, if you can power tech now . . . that could be important. You might be able to get vehicles moving. Maybe even space transport, if we can find some."

"Let's not get ahead of ourselves," she said, but her eyes sparkled. "I need some more time to explore this ability, to figure out its limitations."

"Still. It's a good thing. Maybe the first good thing to happen in—"

Something crashed in the back of the store. We pivoted as one. My heart leaped into my throat, and I was instantly back on Sanctuary, on Obsidian, where every sound could mean an alien stalking me around the next corner. But that was ridiculous. I'd transported us away from the aliens. It was probably something settling, something . . .

A loud string of cursing erupted.

And I broke into a smile.

FOUR

I'D NEVER THOUGHT SWEARING WOULD BRING me this much joy.

Rune's smile mirrored my own. "Mia?" she shouted.

A long pause answered her, and then: "Rune?" Mia's dark hair appeared around the shelf at the end of the aisle.

"Mia!" Rune shrieked, and launched into motion. She leaped through the air and threw her arms around the other girl's neck.

Mia, caught off guard for once, staggered, then patted Rune awkwardly on the back. "Hey," she said, as casually as if we'd met her out shopping one Saturday afternoon. "We've been looking for you."

"Is everyone with you?" The words spilled out of me in a rush, my heart scrambling against my stomach in a violent combat.

"Jasper is in the back room, and those idiots from Legion are scavenging the rest of the street with Lex running point." She hollered over her shoulder, "*Jasper! Get out here!*"

I had never been so happy to see anyone in my life, so happy I was choking back more tears. I *hadn't* killed or lost my friends. They were here somewhere, and Mia stood in front of me, flesh and blood and a face of stone. I even briefly wondered if I should hug her too, although one scowl from her stopped those plans in their tracks.

"Oh my God, Mia?" I hadn't even heard Cage approach, but now he was at my shoulder, setting my heart stuttering again. A broad grin spread across his face. "I knew a little jump across space couldn't get rid of you."

So he *was* scared I'd killed them. I glared at him, but I couldn't muster up a lot of anger, not with relief surging through me so hard that I wanted to sag to the floor. We had food. We had water. And most importantly, we had our friends. All of them, reunited.

Of course, those *friends* also included a team of bounty hunters who'd been sent to capture us. Mia clearly hadn't forgotten that fact. I sympathized with her, but I also remembered how they'd worked with us on the ship. Omnistellar had betrayed them just as much as they'd betrayed me, and anyway, no one was transmitting orders to wherever we were now. Somehow I didn't think Legion held much threat any longer—at least, not to us.

Imani and Reed joined us as Jasper emerged from the rear of the store. He whooped loudly as he swept me into his arms and off the floor, ignoring my shriek of protest. "Kenzie, I am so happy to see you. You have no idea. We thought you'd killed yourself saving us."

"Thanks," I said dryly, working my way free. "I appreciate the vote of confidence." But I still couldn't keep the stupid grin off my face. Part of me wanted to grab Mia and Jasper and tuck them behind me where nothing could hurt them ever again.

Of course, at least one of them would probably have some pretty strong objections. "Come on," said Mia. She'd acquired a backpack somewhere, and she finished shoving the last of the edible food and water inside. For some reason, she seemed to be avoiding my gaze. Was she still angry that I'd lied about Matt? Or that I'd tossed her across the galaxy and lost her along the way? Or was it just the simple charm that was Mia? "Let's go find the others."

It didn't take long to locate them—they'd been halfway to the store. We must have just missed them outside. My reception here was a bit more subdued. Priya and Hallam kept their distance, and although they greeted us in a cordial-enough fashion, they were obviously preoccupied, scanning the horizon. Was that occupational paranoia? Or had they seen something the rest of us missed?

Matt stayed with them, but he spared us all a smile and seemed more interested in the babble of conversation than his new compatriots. He hovered between us, torn, and really, who could blame him? After all, I'd fired the bullet that killed him—in error, to be sure. I'd been aiming for an alien. His power had saved him in time for him to hook up with the mercenaries tracking us. And even though I'd forgiven myself for that and had thought Matt had forgiven me, well, it makes things awkward when you're staring down someone you shot to death a few weeks before.

Hallam came close to matching Alexei's bulk, but my friend still dwarfed everyone around him. He took in the sight of us with genuine pleasure, letting us chatter without interruption. Their story was much the same as ours: I'd somehow dropped them in the middle of the city. They had indeed set off the sparks we'd seen the day before. That was Alexei's pyrokinetics, an attempt to signal us. But not knowing where we were or if we were even alive, they'd spent the day scouring the city neighborhood. "It's run-down and abandoned," Mia confirmed, indicating our surroundings with a sweep of her hand. "But we found a few reasonable apartments nearby. They're furnished and everything. It seems like whoever lived here abandoned it quickly."

"Did you find food and water?" Priya interjected. "That's our first priority."

Mia and Jasper pointedly ignored her, continuing to chat with Rune, while Cage asked, "What did *you* find?"

"Oh, we hit the jackpot," said Hallam in his easy, laid-back way. He tapped the big army-type backpack slung over his shoulders. "Food, water, and weapons. The three essentials of life."

Mia perked up. "What kind of weapons?"

"Let's get off the street and discuss it," said Priya with a nervous glance toward the expanse of desert, now fully illuminated by the morning sun.

"Have you seen anyone or anything besides us?" Cage jolted to attention, as if assailants might leap from the shadows.

"No, but it's best to be sure. Besides, it's getting hot already."

She was right about that. The sun had fully dissipated the chill of night, and my shirt was getting clammy already. I made a mental note. Now that we had the basic necessities—food, water, and weapons, according to Hallam—we should try to find a few little luxuries, things like toothpaste and clean clothes.

We slipped into a nearby building, probably a café. Tables and chairs lined the walls, and Imani, Reed, Jasper, and Rune promptly headed for them, clearly grateful for the relatively cool interior. That left me, Cage, Priya, Hallam, Alexei, Mia, and Matt grouped around the counter.

Hallam dropped to his knees and rummaged through the shelves. He came up with nothing except an assortment of drinking glasses, plates, and cutlery—again, all of it bearing a remarkable resemblance to what you'd find on Earth. In all of humanity's years of searching, in all of our space travel, we'd never encountered any aliens until the monstrous creatures attacked us such a short time ago. If we'd now stumbled across a near-human species, well . . . exactly how far had I transported us? I considered Rune's theory, that we could somehow connect with an alien race, no matter how far away, if they were enough like us. That was impossible . . wasn't it?

"Check the kitchen," Priya ordered Hallam. "Matt, you go with him."

The two men nodded and slipped through the swinging doors, leaving the rest of us alone. Instinctively we'd chosen sides: Cage, Alexei, Mia, and I faced off against Priya, and tension suffused the air. It wasn't anything serious, not yet, but I had a feeling it would erupt if we weren't careful. "We found some food and water," I said to break the silence. "Mia, what did you and Jasper come up with?"

She glared a moment longer, then reluctantly cut her cool gray gaze in my direction. "More of the same," she said. Alexei stood behind her, his fingers resting lightly on her arms as if he could hold her in place if she decided to attack. That was foolishness, of course. No one held Mia back, something Alexei knew as well as anyone. "We found a few emergency blankets in a camping supply store of some sort, and we grabbed some clothes off the racks."

"We also found rations," said Priya.

"You mentioned weapons."

"*Hallam* mentioned weapons." Her eyes flashed in annoyance. Had she planned to keep that to herself? "Yes. We found some knives. Different weights and sizes. They'll be good to have if this place isn't as deserted as it seems. And that should be our next priority, by the way: establishing a secure perimeter and—"

Mia snorted loudly. "This isn't a military operation, *Commander*. We don't have a perimeter."

"The group of you," she replied coldly, "have so far survived on luck and pleas. You barely escaped the aliens on Sanctuary, and then only by killing one of your friends." I cringed as her gaze found me, but the other three drew closer around me, lending me their strength and support. "And if the aliens hadn't attacked Obsidian, we would have dragged you back to face the consequences."

"Congratulations," Cage drawled in a slow, easy tone I was coming to recognize as his most dangerous. "You almost succeeded in turning us over to a treacherous corporation right before they stabbed you in the back and threw open the doors to an alien threat—all to pad their bottom line."

Priya raised her hands in acknowledgment. "I'm not going to debate who was right and who was wrong. We all did the best we knew at the time. But the fact remains that your current strategy of hurling yourselves into danger and hoping for the best is going to get you killed. I'm a bounty hunter with twelve years of experience, and I am *very* motivated to find my way home." Something flashed in her eyes. "You have no idea how motivated. I'm qualified to keep us safe."

"We've got a bit of experience with that on our own."

Priya snorted. "There could be all sorts of threats on this planet you've never encountered."

"Then you haven't encountered them either," said Cage. "Besides, the five of us spent the night trudging through the desert and didn't see so much as a space coyote, and you spent the whole day and night stomping around this neighborhood without arousing suspicion. And you had Mia, so I know you weren't being quiet." He grinned at her and she rolled her eyes, although with no real heat. Mia could be more than quiet when she wanted. She just usually chose a different path. "If anyone or anything is here, they're far off. We're safe. There's no need to declare martial law quite yet."

I hesitated. Was Cage deliberately leaving out the sound we'd heard in the desert to keep Priya off our backs? His cheerful expression gave away nothing. I let it go. After all, I didn't want Legion pushing us around any more than anyone else, and we hadn't seen or heard anything strange since last night.

Priya exhaled through her lips, clearly exasperated, but at that exact moment, something crashed in the kitchen. We all jumped. I collided with Mia on one side and Cage on the other and they both grabbed my arms. At the same time, everyone at the table shot to their feet, expressions of alarm on their faces.

As one, we spun on the kitchen door. I opened my mouth to call Matt's name, but before I made a sound, he appeared in the opening, his hair disheveled and his arms clenched into fists. "Priya," he said, "you need to get in here, now!"

We almost tripped over one another in our hurry. Priya got there first but barely, the rest of us on her heels and Rune, Imani, Reed, and Jasper on ours. My heart stuck with every beat, wrapping around itself like my feet as I stumbled through the sudden crowd. We'd just escaped the aliens. Had they followed us here? Were there some sort of other monstrous creatures lurking in the kitchen? Or—maybe worse still—were the human-like aliens still around, maybe ready to kill us all? Because if Omnistellar had taught me nothing else, it had showed me that sometimes, what humans do to one another is a thousand times worse than anything a monster might inflict.

But there was almost nothing in the kitchen. Only us, and Hallam, lying on the floor in a pool of blood. Pots, pans, and a shelf littered the floor beside him.

Reed shoved past us in an instant and dropped to his knees, all business at the sight of blood. He felt under Hallam's head and, as the rest of us watched, he closed his eyes and channeled his healing energy until Hallam groaned and twitched. Then Reed sat back, his face slightly drawn as it always was after he used his abilities.

"Hallam, Matt," said Priya sharply, "report."

"What the hell happened?" demanded Mia.

Matt gestured frantically. Death had done nothing to hurt his good looks, but now that I knew they were there, I could see the signs of the genetic and physical manipulation he'd been subjected to as part of his initiation into Legion: scars along his temples, an artificial bulk to his muscles, a slight tremor in his limbs. "I have no idea. I heard Hallam shout and then . . ."

"Something hit me from behind." Hallam rolled unsteadily to his feet and gave Reed a nod of thanks. He shook his head, then winced. "Hard."

Rune slipped in behind him and examined the capsized shelf. "This must have been unstable," she said, indicating something at the base. "You see? One leg's a bit shorter than the other. Maybe you bumped into the shelf and . . ."

Hallam scowled at her. "Who do you think you're talking to? I didn't 'bump into' anything. Someone hit me."

FIVE

PRIYA JERKED TO ATTENTION AT HALLAM'S words. "Check the outer perimeter," she barked, and Matt and Hallam shouldered past us, off to follow her orders. Priya herself snatched a knife off a nearby counter and made to go with them.

"Hang on a minute," Cage interrupted, arresting her movement by stepping into her path. The look she shot him could have frozen a volcano. "We've seen no signs of life anywhere. Just because someone thinks they're too good to trip . . ."

Priya's eyes drew into a tight, narrow band. "He doesn't *think* he's too good to trip. We are genetically engineered to be faster, stronger, and more agile than you can possibly imagine. If Hallam says someone hit him, then someone hit him."

The rest of us exchanged glances. Imani and Jasper were both sitting on a counter, their expressions worried as they hovered between Cage and Priya. Mia and Alexei lounged near the door, seeming almost bored. The rest of us remained near the shelf. "Listen," Rune said now, glancing up from where she still knelt on the floor. "There's no other sign of anyone being here. Nothing on this counter is disturbed. I know Legion is genetically engineered to be the best, but I really think we might chalk this one up to fatigue. How long has it been since any of you ate or rested properly?" She offered Priya a conciliatory smile, a Rune special, and even Priya seemed to struggle to resist its power. If Cage led through charm and energy, Rune was learning to lead through compassion and kindness.

At that moment, Matt and Hallam returned. "We can't find any sign of anyone," Hallam grumbled, rubbing his hand along the back of his neck. It came away sticky with blood he was no longer shedding, and he looked at it in surprise. "Golden Boy here even scrambled up the building next door to get a bird's-eye view. Nothing."

Priya glanced between him and Rune and Cage, her expression inscrutable. "All right," she said at last. "I guess there's nothing more we can do at the moment. We'll keep exploring the area, but keep your eyes peeled. And no one goes anywhere alone." She swept out of the kitchen, Matt and Hallam on her heels, although Matt frowned over his shoulder in our direction. For a second he hesitated, as if he wanted to say something, and then he was gone.

I closed my eyes and released a shuddering sigh. Part of

me had been scared Hallam and Matt *would* find someone, yet another threat I needed to stand against. I glanced over my friends, the fierceness of my protective impulse catching me off guard yet again. When had I become so dedicated to these people? I guessed survival situations had that effect.

But no one was here. We were safe, at least for now. I met Cage's gaze and shrugged. "We might as well go with them."

He sighed and shook his head, then smiled ruefully. "We might as well," he agreed, and we set off.

Several hours later, after we'd ransacked the neighborhood and pillaged everything we could carry, we finally retreated to the apartment the others had discovered. If you squinted, a pleasant neighborhood still underlaced the area's current decomposition. Large patches of dead ground and weeds marked where parks and gardens had stood. A rusty children's playground graced one end of the street, and fading awnings and shop signs lined the road.

The apartment building was ten stories tall, with what I suspected had been a well-furnished lobby. The lifts resembled the antigrav lifts I remembered from back home. Actually, the entire place could have been a mid-class corporate apartment on a sponsored street in any city on Earth—more evidence for Rune's bizarre theory. I stumbled over that thought. I just couldn't accept the idea of a telepathic connection with aliens thousands of light-years away. But I also couldn't come up with a better explanation, at least not right now.

We had taken over the second floor of the building, close to the ground in case we needed to make a quick escape, although Mia assured us she'd personally spent the night inspecting every room on every floor, and her bloodshot eyes seemed to back her up. "We're using this larger apartment as a common area," Priya said, indicating a corner apartment with the door propped open. "If you choose a different location to sleep in, make sure everyone knows where it is."

A muscle worked along Cage's jaw. I took his hand and squeezed it. "We'll be sure to keep you posted," I said in what didn't sound, even to my ears, like a very diplomatic tone. "Cage, can I talk to you for a moment?"

We picked an unoccupied apartment at random, and I pushed him inside. The small entranceway led into a dusty but well-equipped kitchen and living room, and Cage promptly began pacing back and forth across both. The sun shone through the window, illuminating the white leather couch, the hardwood flooring, and the layer of filth over everything. "Who does she think she is?" he fumed. "Like we're going to sit back and take orders from the woman who tried to capture us on Omnistellar's behalf?"

"Would you calm down?" I demanded. I opened cupboards methodically, searching for anything of use, but nothing much remained. I found pots, pans, things you'd expect for a kitchen. I did not find weapons beyond a few paring knives, usable food or water, or a large book entitled *THE NAME OF THIS*

PLANET AND THE HISTORY OF ITS INHABITANTS. "There are more important things for us to think about."

"Like what?"

"Oh, I don't know." I gave up on my search and sat at the table, noting the large vase of fake flowers dominating the centerpiece. It was hard to tell what color they were under the dust. "Like the fact that we're on an alien planet with no way home. Or that something horrible happened here, and everyone seems to have fled quickly. We don't know if we're safe. It could have been a radioactive event, for example, or a pandemic, and we might be breathing in poison without even knowing it." My words came faster, spilling out of me in a panic. The last twenty-four hours were a blur, and in this moment of silence, my mind was working overtime, my heart hammering an unsteady beat. "Why would people leave everything they owned? Not even salvage that grocery store? If people died, where are the bodies? And what about the fact that everything on this planet looks *exactly* like it would back on Earth? Don't think too hard and you could be in Arizona. What are the odds I somehow stumbled across another species in the universe that's *just like us*? And if it wasn't random, what brought us here? Oh, and of course there are still the aliens, and my parents are *dead*." I threw those last words at him with a vicious, cutting precision that surprised me. I hadn't realized I'd been angry, holding this in, until this moment.

Rage and grief warred for supremacy inside me, and I gladly

gave in to the anger. I was so tired of crying, of feeling sad. It was almost a relief to lose control. My voice rose as my fists tightened on the table. "It's fantastic you and Priya are caught in a power struggle for control of our little group, but it would be nice if you took one damn moment to think about the rest of us. About my parents. About your sister. Even about Matt and Priya and Hallam, because Omnistellar betrayed them just like they betrayed the rest of us! And I—"

During my rant, Cage had closed the space between us. Now he dragged a chair forward until our knees were touching and caught my fists between his hands. "You're right," he said simply, interrupting me. "I'm sorry. I'm stressed too, and it comes out like . . . well, like this. And for what it's worth, you're not the only one who's noticed the similarities between this place and Earth. Remember Liam, though. He was an alien, but he was about as close to human as I'd ever seen. Maybe ravenous monsters who reproduce by creating kids with superpowers and then murdering them *aren't* the norm. Wouldn't that be nice?"

I smiled in spite of myself and tipped forward so our heads touched. Cage sparked up fast, it was true. But it was easy to bring him back down, and when you pulled him outside himself, he became the most unselfish, gentle, kindhearted person I'd ever met. That was why I . . .

I slammed the door on that thought. Cage and I had known each other a few weeks now. Our relationship had started hard and fast, kissing in an airlock on our way to potential death, and then stalled as we'd dealt with all the trauma of the aftermath. Now we were together again, stronger and better. So how did I feel about him? I ran my hand over his face, the sharp familiar lines, the softness of his skin, and I knew in my heart I didn't want to live without him.

But if I said that, I might scare him half to death, so I replied, "Thank you. And I guess things aren't so bad. I mean, we have food and water. We're not going to die quite yet. We have time to work these things out. But Cage . . . my ability to copy other powers is what let me get us here. I pulled from Liam, and he died in the explosion. I can't take us home."

"I know. We'll figure it out, okay? Together." He leaned in and kissed me, and for a blissful moment I let emotion sweep me away, let the pull of his lips draw me into a world where nothing mattered but the two of us and the connection between us.

And then the door to the apartment slammed open and Mia stomped in, and the spell was broken. "This is bullshit," she announced, vaulting onto the counter, not seeming to notice as Cage and I scrambled apart. "I need your help, Cage. We have to get out of here, and Priya seems to be settling in."

Alexei trailed in behind her, looking more exhausted than usual. I sympathized. It couldn't be easy, keeping up with Mia. "Mia mine," he said, "you haven't slept in days. Please lie down."

"And let whatever attacked Hallam come after me? No, thank you. It's time to move, not rest."

Cage groaned, letting his head drop to his hands. "You didn't buy Priya's crap about a mystery assailant, did you? Rune called it. Hallam bumped into a shelf like an idiot, and a cast-iron pan smacked him in the head. That's enough to topple even a mutant bounty hunter."

"Maybe. Maybe not. Priya's right about one thing: Legion is strong, fast, and powered. They have metal parts where they should have flesh and bone, and they have tiny iron lumps where they should have brains. It's possible Hallam tripped. But I'm not buying it."

Alexei sighed, and I suspected this was a continuation of an argument they'd been having before. He'd probably dragged us into it hoping we'd talk some sense into Mia—or that Cage would. I still wasn't sure how Mia felt about me. Right now, even though she was ostensibly including me in the conversation, she was refusing to meet my eyes.

"Look," I said. "Let's make a deal. Let's take twenty-four hours to decompress. Tomorrow at lunchtime, we'll sit down and discuss all of this as a group. That group can include Priya and Hallam and . . . and Matt, if you want it to, or it can just be us. Your call. But Mia, we need rest. All of us, even you. It's been a long time since we weren't being chased by someone, and we've all lost so much since this started."

I expected an argument, but to my surprise, Mia's head lowered and she nodded slowly. "Yeah. Okay. I guess you're right." She slid to her feet and headed out of the apartment, punching

Alexei lightly on the chest as she went. He glanced at Cage, one of his eyebrows arched, a frown on his cinder block face, and then went after her.

"What just happened?" I asked. I'd never seen Mia give in without a fight.

Cage shrugged. "Beats me. Maybe you made so much sense you actually convinced Mia to listen to reason. Is that possible?"

"That is not possible, no."

He grinned. "Then chalk it up to another mystery we'll unravel tomorrow. In the meantime, we have this whole apartment to ourselves, and there's food and water in Priya's common area. Let's follow your advice and take a bit of time to unwind."

"That," I said, a relieved smile breaking out over my own features, "sounds like the best idea I've ever heard."

The planet conquered. The sleeping sand awakes. Shifting and the consciousness recoiling, stirring in the drive to devour.

The dead planet stirs and the sleeping tendrils wake and the great arching presence shifts its attention from the next to the previous.

SIX

I SHOULD HAVE KNOWN THE PROSPECT OF A whole afternoon with Cage was too good to be true, because moments after he proposed it, his conscience got the better of him and he insisted on checking in with the others. "I need to know everyone's okay. Except . . . Rune. Will you talk to her?" he pleaded. "I don't want her to think I'm babying her. Things are still a bit tense between us. I'll check in on everyone else, and then I promise, just me and you for the rest of the night."

I rolled my eyes at him, but I didn't mind, not really. Part of what I liked about Cage was his sense of responsibility to his friends. And so I found myself knocking on an adjacent apartment door. Inside, it was the spitting image of what I'd already named "my" apartment in my head, but furnished in a totally different style, what would have been called bohemian on Earth: lots of bright colors and floor cushions and intricate patterns. Rune and Imani were lounging in beanbag chairs. "We beat the dust out of these two," Rune explained, "but I wouldn't recommend flopping into any of the others."

"I'm fine on the couch," I assured her, settling myself onto a low red sofa and folding my legs beneath me. "Are you two staying here?"

"And Reed and Jasper, but they went to hunt through some of the other apartments." Imani nodded down the hall. "There are three bedrooms in this place. Lots of room. We felt more comfortable sticking together, you know? I'm not sure any of us completely trust Legion quite yet."

Rune's face fell at the mention of the name. "I still can't understand how Matt could betray us like that," she said softly.

Imani sat, brushing the ends of her hijab over her shoulders. "Listen, girl," she said. "Matt did what he had to in order to survive."

"I know. It doesn't sound like Legion gave him much of a choice. But did he have to throw himself quite so wholeheartedly into hunting us?"

"He thought I shot him and left him for dead," I reminded her. "In his mind, *we* betrayed *him*. Or at least I did."

Rune caught her lower lip between her teeth. "I mean . . . I didn't hurt him. I wouldn't have, ever . . ." She trailed off, maybe catching the guilt on my face, and forced a smile. "When the two of you were on the Omnistellar ship together . . . did he say much? About . . . well, anything?"

About her, I suspected she meant. But he hadn't, so I only replied, "He seemed to forgive me. At any rate, I forgave myself, and he didn't get angry about it."

Imani laughed. "That's something."

I stayed with the girls for another twenty minutes, until Reed and Jasper returned with their arms full of blankets, clothes, and something else: a handheld tablet. "We're hoping Rune can make it work," Reed explained, tossing it in her direction.

Rune made a face. "I knew I shouldn't have told you what happened in the supermarket."

"Come on," Reed pleaded. "Please? Please? Pretty please? I haven't played video games in years. You can be my own magical battery."

"How do you know this tablet has games?" Imani retorted. "It could be medical textbooks or tax forms."

Jasper sighed heavily and indicated a duffel bag behind him. "That's what I said. So he collected all the others he found."

Reed brushed their concerns aside. "One of these bad boys has to have games. Come on, Rune."

Rune laughed and sat up, sweeping her hair behind her ears. "All right, I'll try. But when I powered the scanner in the store, it stopped working as soon as I set it down. If you think I'm going to hold this tablet while you play vid games, you'd better think again. Using my powers takes effort, you know. I think my energy is best saved for something else."

I slipped out of the room as she bent over the tablet. Where was Cage? He'd said he was going to check on the others, but they were all right here—all except Alexei, Mia, and Legion. If he was really checking on them, he should have turned up by now. Doubt stirred in my stomach. What was Cage actually doing?

I returned to our apartment, absently chewing on my lower lip. Cage had promised not to lie to me, but that didn't mean he always told me everything. The more I considered it, the more his excuse of "checking on the others" felt like a pretense. Was he confronting Priya without me? Planning something with Mia? I frowned. I'd thought we were past this, past him going behind my back and over my head, past the others mistrusting and excluding me. But something was up with his sudden excuse for departure.

The apartment was dark when I entered, as if someone had drawn the curtains. "Cage?" I called.

"In here," he answered.

I steeled myself for the conversation to come and walked into the kitchen.

The room was dark, but three candles of varying colors and sizes stood in the center of the table, illuminating it with their flickering light. Plates, wineglasses, and cutlery were set across from one another. In the center of the table was a feast of . . . well, dried and prepackaged foods: bottled water, some kind of wrinkled fruit, and tins with unrecognizable contents. But my heart still leaped at the sight. "Cage," I said softly.

He grinned awkwardly, leaning against the counter. "I realized we'd never been on a real date," he said. "And I thought, well, given the way our lives have been going, we should probably do that sooner rather than later. Kenzie, will you have dinner with me?"

I laughed. All of my fears and worries, even the constant specter of grief and betrayal, floated away in a sudden burst of euphoria. "Yes," I said. "Yes, I will."

We settled at the table. "It's not exactly a feast," Cage apologized, spooning some kind of lumpish gray things onto my plate. "And I really hope none of it is spoiled."

"Cage," I said, "shut up."

He grinned, his teeth flashing in the candlelight, and bit into the gray stuff. "Edible," he pronounced it after a moment of chewing. I winced but followed suit. It wasn't bad. Kind of bland and chewy. I wasn't sure if I was eating canned meat or vegetables or something else altogether, and I didn't want to risk asking. Cage probably didn't know either.

He swallowed with what was obviously some effort and laced his hands behind his head. "So. What do you think we're up against . . . ?"

I shook my head. "No. Just for a while, let's talk about something, anything else."

"Fair enough. What'd you have in mind?"

I racked my brain. I'd been on dates before, but conversations usually revolved around the corporation and our futures, definitely not topics I wanted to bring up with Cage. "Tell me more about Taipei," I said at last.

Cage shrugged. Had I made him uncomfortable, said the wrong thing? But he turned his fork meditatively in his fingers and replied, "It's a contradiction. Parts of it are stunningly beautiful. There's still culture there, still temples and mosques, museums and markets. But when the water rose and Taiwan flooded, the waters came all the way to Taipei. Parts of the city were submerged, and others were destroyed. That's mostly where I lived: places destroyed by water, or by the riots that followed, and taken over by the gangs. Tourists still come there, but they never see the real city. I don't even know how to explain it to you, unless . . ." He glanced at me thoughtfully. "The gangs run Taipei the way the corporations run the rest of the world. They're on an even footing there. Not even Omnistellar could drive the criminals out of Taipei, and they didn't dare try. It would mean eliminating three-quarters of the city."

I nodded. There was a time when I would have scoffed, but after seeing how Omnistellar let Obsidian, the criminal empire run by Alexei's uncle, operate under its nose, I understood a lot more about how my former corporation functioned. "Tell me about something beautiful," I pleaded. It wasn't that I didn't want to know about Cage's shadowed past—I did. I wanted all of it, all of him. But I knew so much of the darkness, and he'd only given me glimmers of the light.

Cage grinned and launched into a long description of a trip

his father took him and Rune on to the mountains, before he'd discovered their powers. I mechanically chewed and swallowed, lost in Cage's words. He'd always had this ability, to bind someone with a story, and it had nothing to do with the powers the aliens gave him, either: it was a natural gift, like Alexei's strength or Imani's eye for beauty. I wasn't known as much of a talker myself, and although I could use my words effectively enough when necessary, for now I was content to listen.

Eventually, as the sky faded to black, we moved to the living room, where Cage pried open a window and spread a blanket over the ridged ledge so we could sit together and stare into the night. We wrapped ourselves in another blanket and a few sweaters we'd scavenged from the apartment and leaned into each other as stars spilled across the sky. "They're not the same stars we'd see on Earth," I whispered. I was leaning against his back, framed by his legs, his arms wrapped loosely over my belly and sending shivers through my spine. "Right? They can't be."

"They're familiar, though." He nodded, his chin brushing my ear. "But I don't see the Big Dipper—and with that, we've reached the end of my knowledge of astronomy."

I laughed, but a chill ran through me. I didn't see the Big Dipper out there. I didn't see any familiar stars, but to be honest, for someone who lived among them, I'd never spent much time on Earth gazing up at them. "Did Rune tell you her theory?"

"About some sort of metaphysical connection between

similar races across the void?" He shrugged. "As with most things Rune says, it makes no sense and is probably true."

I frowned and chewed on my lower lip. "I guess it would explain how much this place is like Earth."

"A postapocalyptic horror-vid version," Cage agreed. "But at least there aren't any goddamn aliens here."

The chill deepened, settling into my heart. Because there *had* been aliens here, once upon a time. Oh, I knew what Cage meant, and I agreed: I was quite happy to have found somewhere without ravenous monsters bent on murder or assimilation.

But I wasn't quite as sure as Cage seemed to be that the place was deserted, and I didn't know *why*. There wasn't any evidence, not really, not even if you counted Hallam's mystery assailant or the howls in the desert. It was just a feeling, like someone watching me. Part of me even now had to resist the urge to jump up and do a spot check, make sure all of my friends were present and accounted for, maybe even forcibly move them in here where I could keep an eye on them. "I hate it here," I confessed softly. "I wish I'd taken us anywhere else."

"Yeah?" Cage nuzzled my neck. "Like the inside of a volcano?"

I giggled in spite of myself. It wasn't particularly funny, but I was ready to laugh, to relax. "No. That wouldn't be ideal."

"A thousand miles under the sea?"

"Not there, either."

"I don't think this place is so bad." His fingers came to my chin and tipped my head back so I was leaning on his shoulder, twisting to stare into his eyes. "Not altogether."

I allowed myself to trace the lines of his face, to smile. "It has its high points," I allowed, and then his mouth was on mine and finally, finally, we had the time and space to explore each other without fear, without anything stalking us, without Mia or someone barging through the door and shouting about the latest disaster.

The temperature grew steadily colder and we closed the window, moving to a bed Cage had already stripped of its dusty linens, replacing them with reasonably clean blankets. We tangled our bodies there and he rolled me beneath him, his body pressed against mine, our mouths searching for each other in a tangle of tongues and teeth, until it felt like nothing, ever, could hurt me again.

SEVEN

THAT BLISS LASTED ALL THE WAY UNTIL morning, when a series of thumps, screams, and shouts jerked me out of a sound sleep. I shot up at the same time as Cage and we gaped in mutual dismay at the wall as voices—Mia's for sure, and Priya's, and Hallam's—echoed through the corridors. "It was nice while it lasted," I sighed.

"More than nice." Cage caught me in my arms as I twisted to grab my sweater from where I'd thrown it on the floor. He pulled me into a kiss.

I resisted for a second, then allowed myself to sink into his arms. "Don't you think we'd better see what they're going on about?" I murmured as his lips dropped to my neck.

"Later. They can handle themselves without us for—"

"Cage!" Jasper's voice echoed through our apartment. I jumped to my feet as Cage flopped on the bed, covering

his face in his hands. *"Kenzie! You'd better get out here and I mean now!"*

Cage let loose a rampage of Chinese swearing. He was not a morning person. Meanwhile, I'd already shoved my feet into my shoes, almost tripped over an untied shoelace, and yanked my curls into a ponytail. "I'll cover for you," I said, "but you've got five minutes at most." I hesitated, then went back to kiss him. His arms came around me and he almost distracted me from whatever was happening in the hallway, but Mia started screaming and I groaned against his mouth.

Cage groaned too. "All right, I'm coming." He rolled out of bed as I padded across the room.

I yanked open the door to find chaos. Priya, Hallam, and Matt stood guard in front of what they'd dubbed the common area, the apartment at the end of the hall. Alexei, Mia, and Jasper faced off against them, while Rune, Imani, and Reed hovered helplessly in the background.

Rune spotted me and shot to my side, grabbing my arm and dragging me forward. "Hurry," she said. "Before Mia kills someone."

"What is going on?" I demanded, inserting myself between the two groups.

The full force of six glares turned on me. "These Omnistellar puppets," Mia spit, "won't let us at the supplies we salvaged."

Priya laughed coldly. "These *criminals*," she returned, "have already taken more than their fair share."

I recalled my dinner with Cage and winced inwardly. How much had we selfishly consumed in our quest for a date? "Priya, what are you talking about?"

She slammed her fist into the wall, making me and Jasper jump. Even Matt started. "Our supplies are almost half gone!" she snapped. "Not even you people could eat them all in a single night. You have to have hidden them somewhere."

"Wait a minute." That was Cage, coming up behind me. "Let's calm down and talk this through. I can tell you exactly what I took from the room yesterday, and it amounted to about nine tins and some water. Mia, Lex?"

"A bit more than that," said Alexei grudgingly. "I am not a small boy."

I grinned at the understatement, biting my lip because I didn't think my amusement would go over well at the moment.

Jasper spoke without prompting. "The rest of us took about the same. There's no way that's half of what we gathered."

"Of course it's not," Hallam drawled. He leaned against the wall and rested his hand on the hilt of his knife, just in case we hadn't noticed it. "You took a lot more than you're admitting, and the proof is in your rooms. Priya, say the word and I'll . . . ?"

Fear stabbed through me. "Exactly how much is missing?" I whispered.

To my surprise, it was Matt who answered. "At least half. Maybe more."

"And was anyone on guard in the apartment last night?"

"We didn't think we needed to be." Priya scowled at each of us in turn. "Our mistake."

I shook my head. "That's not what I . . . Let us in there. We can see for ourselves and figure this out together."

Again, Matt spoke, his voice soft and calm after the chaos of the last few minutes. "It can't hurt, Priya. They're not going to take anything while you're watching. And . . ." He left the sentence unfinished, but our eyes met, and I didn't need any powers to read his thoughts: *And it's possible we're not alone here after all.*

Priya hesitated, glaring at all of us, but after a moment she turned and stomped into the apartment. I nodded my gratitude at Matt and he gave me a small smile. Something inside me released. He might not be my best friend, but he wasn't holding a grudge, at least not right now.

We'd stacked our supplies in the middle of the room, and I skidded to a halt, staring in horror at the tiny mound of food and, more importantly, water. There were only a dozen bottles left, and we'd gathered three or four times that many.

A surge of doubt hit me. Mia hadn't taken it, had she? I could see her doing it. She was a thief, after all, a self-professed expert in the art. I didn't think she'd do it to make trouble, but she might think she was protecting us, shielding us from exactly this sort of takeover by Legion.

I scrutinized her and dismissed the thought. I'd decided to trust these people, my friends, the only family I had now. Mia wouldn't steal, at least not from us. She would have told me, or at least Cage. And that was what I was going to believe, because belief was a choice, and faith in someone had to be embraced as firmly as faith in anything else.

I went to the window as the others argued behind me. With Mia and Hallam in the mix, you were pretty much guaranteed a volatile conversation. I tried to tune them out as I examined the window. It had been locked at one time, but the bolts had long since rusted away, and it gave easily to my prodding fingers, barely making a sound as it slid open.

I leaned outside.

"Anything there?" Imani spoke at my ear, leaning past me. I caught a sideways glimpse of the worry in her eyes as she followed my gaze.

Directly below us was a rusted fire escape. "This looks sturdy enough to climb," I said.

Imani nodded. "And if you did, you'd be right outside this window."

We exchanged glances as the others carried on arguing behind us. Suddenly I was exhausted. Why was nothing ever easy? It was bad enough I'd stranded us on a desert wasteland in the middle of God knew what solar system in order to escape the vicious aliens who'd killed my parents and the explosion that would have killed everyone on Obsidian. We had to have yelling and fighting and now, probably, a new enemy, someone or something stalking us once again through the night.

Imani laid her hand on my arm. "Maybe this is a good thing," she said quietly. "If there are people here, maybe they can help us. Maybe they have a way off the planet."

"And haven't taken it?" I indicated the wasteland with a sweep of my hand.

"Maybe they don't know there's anywhere else to go."

I spared her a smile. Imani always looked for the best and usually found it, and just now I wanted to hug her for giving me at least a slightly more positive way to view things. Instead I squeezed her arm in return and turned back to the room, where at least a few people had noticed our distraction.

"Kenzie?" said Rune. "What's up?"

"This window opens easily," I said without preamble, "and there's a fire escape right outside. If Hallam was right, if he was attacked in the restaurant yesterday, then maybe whoever it was followed us here and stole our supplies last night."

Hallam snorted. "Followed us without me noticing? I don't think so." But he also shoved past me to stare outside.

"Heat signatures?" asked Priya.

Hallam tapped the side of his head, presumably doing something to the cybernetics Omnistellar had jammed in there, and frowned. "It's too hot. Nothing lingering. And I don't see any trails. But . . . that doesn't mean the girl's wrong."

Priya clenched her fists, clearly waging an internal war with the words "I told you so." She won, but, by the looks of it, barely. "That settles it. Someone else is on this planet."

"That settles nothing," snapped Mia. "We still don't have any proof of anything."

"Mia," said Matt quietly. "Someone took half our supplies. It was either you, us, or someone else. I know it wasn't us, and I don't think it was you."

She drew up short, maybe as much because it was Matt doing the talking as anything else. "Did you sense something?" she asked.

I blinked. I'd almost forgotten, amid all of Matt's new abilities, his base power: an awareness of life, of other living beings in the vicinity.

But he frowned and shook his head. "Of course, I wasn't looking. I didn't think I had a reason."

Cage nodded. "Listen," he said, his voice carrying that familiar ring of charismatic authority. "If anyone, for any reason, took anything out of this room other than what they've already admitted, I'm going to ask you to speak up. For everyone's sake." A long silence stretched among us. I scanned the room, meeting everyone's gaze in turn: Jasper's quiet determination, Mia seemingly at war with herself, Matt staring at his feet, Reed observing with something like amusement . . .

"I didn't think so," said Cage at last. He turned to Priya. "I'm willing to believe you and your people when you say you didn't take or hide any of the supplies. Can you give us the same courtesy?"

She hesitated. "You're criminals we were ordered to hunt,"

she said at last, but without fire. "It's hard for us to move out of that mind-set. We've been Legion longer than we've been anything else . . . well, most of us." She glanced at Matt, who still didn't meet her eyes.

"We worked together on the ship," I reminded her. "We had a common enemy who'd taken things from both of us. And we still have a common enemy: Omnistellar. They were going to betray you just like they betrayed me. Betrayed humanity."

"Not to mention the enemy closer at hand," said Cage, jerking his head toward the window.

Priya nodded. "You're right. Let's call a truce. No more grumbling at each other, no more suspicion. From now on, we work as a team."

EIGHT

WE'D NEVER HAD AN OFFICIAL LEADER. Sometimes it was Cage, sometimes it was me, and sometimes Mia or Alexei seized control. Legion, on the other hand, was accustomed to following Priya's commands, and it showed. When she spoke, they leaped to attention. "We need to establish round-the-clock watches," she said now. "If someone comes back for our supplies, we catch them in the act."

"What we need to do," Imani interrupted, "is find out who they are and try to talk to them, not imprison them. This isn't Omnistellar. They're probably trying to survive, just like us."

"Then they can scavenge, just like us. No one steals from Legion and gets away with it."

"From *us*," returned Jasper sharply.

Priya sighed and closed her eyes. Her lips moved as though

praying or counting or mumbling a mantra. "Okay," she said at last. "What do *you* have in mind?"

Cage slipped in easily. "The round-the-clock watch isn't a bad idea, but I suggest we go a step further. Let's set a trap. Do some really obvious scavenging today. Then, when our thief strikes, we follow."

Priya rolled her eyes. "Great. All ten of us chasing after someone in the desert. Sounds like a plan."

"Not all eleven of us," said Mia. She shimmered and disappeared. When she spoke, her voice was clear and disembodied. "Me, because I can move quietly and unseen. I can probably keep two other people invisible without too much effort." That was a new bit of her power, the ability to make others invisible. Contact with the aliens seemed to have altered our DNA, made us stronger, given us greater abilities—or at least, some of us. Others were still waiting to see what, if anything, would happen.

"So who goes with you?" Rune asked.

"I do," said Alexei at once.

"No," Mia replied, slipping back into the visible spectrum. "You stampede around like a wild elephant. Sorry, Lex."

He shrugged, giving her the tolerant smile he seemed to reserve specially for her, and accepted that without argument.

"Matt," said Priya decisively. "He's the quietest of the three of us, he can sense people before they sneak up on you, and his implants give him additional abilities. He'll be useful."

"And me," said Cage. "If we find something, I can return

and warn the others in a fraction of the time it would take someone else."

"And me," I said.

Mia frowned. "I can only handle three of us."

"Except I can mimic your ability," I reminded her. "At least if I'm near you. And more importantly, if you find someone who speaks another language, I'm the one with the best shot at communicating with them." And of course, I had no intention of letting *any* of my friends wander into danger without me at their side. Not this time.

Mia scowled but didn't answer. What was her problem, anyway? I'd thought we'd mended things between us and she'd forgiven me for my role in Matt's apparent death. Maybe not. Maybe that was a temporary truce caused by the alien attack. I sighed. I was tired of trying to keep Mia straight.

Cage nodded. "Me, Matt, Mia, and Kenzie." He flashed a grin at Matt. "Just like old times."

Matt smiled reluctantly. "Except we didn't usually pal around with the prison guards," he said, but although his words sent a spike of annoyance through me, they held no real heat, and he didn't seem angry.

"Fine," said Priya. "Hallam and I will do some scavenging now. Anyone who wants to join us, feel free. We'll gather a nice big pile of temptation for tonight—or at least I hope we will. Matt, Cage, Kenzie, and Mia will lie in wait, which means you should rest up today."

"I'll come scavenging," Rune volunteered. "I was able to power those tablets Reed found last night, but there wasn't much on them. I want to check for any other electronics and see if they have more information."

"If you're talking electronics, I'll come too . . . er, in case anyone gets hurt," Reed amended quickly, grinning when Rune rolled her eyes at him.

I glanced around the room, weighing my options. Priya had said we should rest up. She was right. But if Reed and Rune were headed out . . . Hallam and Priya were more than capable of protecting them, I knew that, but still.

Mia nudged Alexei and nodded at Rune and Reed. He sighed. "Yes. I will come too."

Relief surged through me. Alexei, I could trust. If he went along, I was probably safe to stay behind.

"I think that's enough," said Priya. "We'll head out now and return in a few hours."

They advanced in one direction and the rest of us scattered. Mia slipped through the door, and I frowned after her. Enough was enough. "I'll be right back," I said to Cage.

He must have read my mind, because his eyebrows flew up in alarm. "What are you doing?"

"I'm going to have a conversation." I smiled. "Don't worry. If she attacks me, I'll make myself invisible. Power leech, remember?"

He grinned in spite of himself. "Just . . . don't rile her up too much. Things will be awkward enough tonight."

No kidding. Matt, Mia, Cage, and me . . . could there be four people with more history among them?

I left the apartment and knocked on the door of the apartment Mia was sharing with Alexei. A long moment passed in which I wondered if she was even there, and then the door slid open. If she was surprised to see me, she didn't show it, looking through me with blank eyes. "Yeah?"

"Can I come in? We need to talk."

She stared at me a moment longer, then sighed and stepped aside, letting me pass.

The apartment was little different from my own. Mia tossed herself down on a sofa, raising a cloud of dust, folded her arms, and glared at me.

I settled into a chair across from her, searching for words. I'd already apologized for lying to them, for hiding what had happened with Matt, a thousand times. I didn't feel like doing it again. If Mia couldn't forgive me, well, another apology wasn't likely to change her mind. But I was sick of letting her glare at me without saying anything.

"Listen," Mia snapped before I found my words, "I get it, okay? And I don't blame you for being pissed. I can't, really. Poetic justice and all that."

I blinked, trying to catch up with what she was saying. "Mia, I—"

"I'm sorry." It was probably the least apologetic apology I'd ever heard, considering she had her arms folded over her chest and was glaring at me like she hoped I'd evaporate. "Doesn't mean much, does it? Words are empty."

"Mia, what are you talking about?"

She sighed and leaned forward, bracing her elbows on her knees. "You want me to say it? Fine. I am sorry. I'm sorry I killed your father." A laugh tore from her throat, a harsh, unhappy sound. "And now you can say whatever's been on your mind."

I blinked, replaying the moment in my mind. The aliens had shredded through the bulkhead, ripping into my father, and Mia had . . .

Mia had tried to kill them, and the bullets tore my father to pieces.

I'd known that, of course. I'd seen it. It had impressed itself on every part of my mind. And yet, somehow, I'd never thought of Mia as killing him. In my mind, the aliens stood out in stark and vivid detail, eclipsing everything else.

I stared at her, processing this new information. "Mia . . . ," I said slowly. I got what she meant now about poetic justice. She'd blamed me for killing Matt when I'd been aiming for an alien, and here she'd done the same thing. "Mia, I don't blame you for what happened to my dad."

Her eyes narrowed in suspicion. "Then why have you been so distant?"

I threw up my hands. "I don't think I have been! You're the one pulling away. But if I am acting differently, Mia, maybe it's because my dad *did* die and I have no family left? Or because we're stranded on some apocalyptic wasteland of a planet with no way to escape? Or maybe, just maybe, it has something to do with the fact that you've barely looked at me, much less talked to me, since we got here!"

She hesitated, gnawing on her lower lip while she mulled over my words. "How can you not blame me?" she asked at last, and there was something in her voice I'd never heard before, something like the bitter self-recrimination I'd carried around when I'd thought I killed Matt. "I pulled the trigger. I—"

"Mia. My dad was already dead." I swallowed. It hurt to talk like this, to talk about him like he was nothing—a character in *Robo Mecha Dream Girl*, maybe, not a real person, not my flesh-and-blood father who'd so recently breathed and walked and schemed. "The aliens would have torn him to pieces. If anything, you kept him from an incredibly agonizing . . ." I trailed off. I couldn't talk about that, not even now. "He made his choices," I said instead. "He followed Omnistellar, and he brought those aliens to Obsidian. He betrayed Legion. And in the end, those choices, well . . . they resulted in his death. I don't think my dad was a bad person, but Omnistellar got in his head like they did with my mom. Like they did with me." I read the confusion in Mia's eyes. I was babbling, letting my thoughts and feelings about my family pour out of me, and I forced myself to focus. "My dad died because he let Omnistellar summon the aliens to Obsidian," I said slowly, emphasizing each word. "And Omnistellar lost control of the situation, as anyone could have told them they would. The aliens killed my father, Mia. Maybe Omnistellar played a role. You? You were trying to save him, to save us all."

She glared at me for another second, then shot to her feet and stalked to the window, resting her hands on her hips. We stayed like that for a long minute, her silhouetted against the sunlight, and me . . . well, me waiting. I'd never expected anything like this. I didn't think I'd realized Mia was *capable* of feeling guilt, at least not where I was concerned. Knowing she'd been carrying the same burden as me made her a little more human, and it gave me the strength to say, "I know we have a . . . strange relationship. But you've had my back through everything we've seen, even if you didn't like me much. If you need to hear me say I forgive you, then I forgive you. But really, Mia, there's nothing to forgive."

"Kenzie," she replied. "*Stop. Talking.* Just . . ." She spun on me and because of the light behind her I couldn't read her expression, but a moment later she'd pulled me into a fierce hug, so tight she almost cracked my ribs. Within seconds she shoved me away just as violently and stomped into the kitchen. "So anyway," she said, "about this plan tonight."

"I . . . what?"

"Do you want something to eat? I think we have some nuts left." She leaped onto a shelf and rummaged through a cupboard. "Alexei always puts things so high. Here we go. Cashews, maybe? That's what they look like. They're kind of stale, but not too bad."

I shook my head. This was the best Mia had in terms of friendship. And who could blame her? Years forced to work for criminals who murdered her sister and then more years in a cold, sterile jail cell . . . When exactly would she have had time to develop her people skills? "Cashews sound good," I said, taking the olive branch for what it was worth. "Let's hammer out the details for tonight before Cage and Matt can take over."

She leveled a finger in my direction and slid a tin of nuts down the counter. "Now you're talking."

And if her face had been wet when she hugged me, well, I wouldn't mention it. We sat together and a glimmer of hope sparked inside me. If Mia and I could get past the miles between us, maybe I really did stand a chance of keeping everyone safe.

NINE

THE DAY PASSED QUICKLY, A BLUR OF NAPS and uncomfortable conversations. The raiding crew returned with a few more items—not much, because we'd salvaged most of what the neighborhood had to offer the day before, but Reed assured me they'd made as big a celebration as if they'd hit the jackpot. "What about the tech?" I asked as Legion sorted through what remained of our supplies. "Any luck there?"

"I think so." Rune produced a tablet. She held it between her hands, her eyes closed, and her skin seemed to meld with the edges of the machine, a phenomenon that had terrified me when I first saw it but now seemed as natural as breathing. After a moment a faint glow lit the screen, and she beamed in pleasure. "It won't work if I let go, though. So much for Reed's video games."

He sulked. "Only because you won't hold it while I play."

I leaned over Rune's shoulder in interest. "Have you searched the tablet? Maybe we can get some idea of what this planet was like, or who lived here."

"There seems to be some sort of internet connection, but it's down now, of course. I haven't gone through much of it, but I don't see much difference from a tablet you'd find in our solar system."

"Photographs?" I suggested.

Rune blinked. "I'm an idiot. I didn't check." She stared at the tablet for a moment longer, and then a holographic image formed above the small device.

It showed a family: three women, maybe sisters from their similarities, and a man who could have been their father. One of the women was holding a baby. She gently rocked it in her arms as the image shifted and changed. "They look exactly like us," I said softly. It was madness. You could have showed me this holo and told me it was from anywhere in our solar system and I'd have believed you.

Reed looked between me and Rune. "There's no more question about it. We're on Liam's homeworld."

Liam, the alien we'd met on Obsidian, was so terrified of the creatures that he'd been willing to do anything to survive them—even if it meant betraying us. And none of that mattered, because he'd met exactly the end he feared, mowed down by the creatures in their attack on the ship. "But if this is his homeworld . . . ," I said slowly, and then trailed off, unable to finish the thought.

Rune did it for me. "Then the aliens have been here. Maybe they're the ones who caused all this devastation."

A heavy silence settled over us. So the aliens had been here. That was one thing.

The bigger question was, were they here still?

"Kenzie?" Cage tapped his knuckles against my arm and gave me a grin. "You okay?"

I forced a smile and nodded. By mutual consent, Reed, Rune, and I had agreed not to tell anyone what we suspected about the aliens. I'd argued in favor of telling Cage, but Rune talked me out of it, pointing out that Cage had enough on his mind and didn't need even more worry to split his attention. It wasn't lying to him, exactly. I'd tell him for sure if I got proof. Tonight would give us a lot more information, or I hoped it would. If we found the thief, we'd be able to question them and learn exactly what had happened on this planet. If it turned out to be the aliens, well, everyone would discover the truth then. If it didn't, I'd have spared them a few hours of the gnawing terror and anxiety currently residing in my stomach.

Matt, Mia, Cage, and I settled in the shadows on the bottom floor of the apartment building. We'd wrapped ourselves in warm clothes and blankets and sat close together, leaning against the wall as the desert night settled over us. We had bottles of something similar to coffee, which was never my favorite caffeine delivery system, and a few snacks to keep us going. More importantly, we had weapons: a long, wicked hunting knife for Mia, who seemed to know how to use it; something like a machete for Matt; and smaller weapons more like daggers for me and Cage, who had less experience with knives. I wasn't sure what I'd do with the weapon if I needed it, but its weight at my belt was comforting. I wasn't completely defenseless.

Between us, Mia and I easily pulled Cage and Matt under our invisibility. Mia's invisibility had always extended to anything she carried on her body, and it had only grown more powerful. I could mimic the power of anyone in my range (although what that range was, precisely, I had yet to figure out—the limits of discovering your powers while on the run). We didn't need to worry about being seen. We just needed to stay quiet.

As the night settled over us, Cage spoke softly. "So," he said, "Matt."

On my left, Matt's arm tensed against me. On my right sat Cage, his fingers laced through my own, his leg pressed to mine. Mia was on his right, and being uncharacteristically quiet. "What?" Matt replied, a cautious note in his voice.

"Now that we have a few minutes . . . what exactly happened to you after Sanctuary?"

Matt sighed heavily and seemed to sag. For a long moment I didn't think he'd answer, but then he spoke, his voice slow and heavy. "It's like I told you. I crashed on Earth and found an Omnistellar goon squad waiting for me. They dragged me out of the escape pod and arrested me. At the time I was furious. I was sure you'd left me for dead, decided my injuries were too much to handle while you escaped to the alien ship." That, of course, wasn't true. We'd assumed Matt was dead because he had *been* dead. It was only a fun new twist in his power that saved him. "So I guess it didn't take much convincing to make me spill the beans. Besides, I was scared. I didn't know if there were more of those creatures nearby, planning to attack Earth."

"You did the right thing," I murmured. "Even if Omnistellar abused the information, you didn't know what they'd do with it. They're the most powerful corporation in the system. If anyone could have protected us, it was them."

Matt snorted. "Yeah. Too bad they went another way." He lifted his hand to rub the back of his neck, a gesture I felt rather than saw. It was sort of strange to be sitting here with three other people I couldn't see. "Anyway, they gave me a choice: work with Legion or go back to jail. They promised that if I worked for Legion, they'd take care of my family, pay me, let me earn my freedom. It sounded pretty good." He hesitated. "To be honest, though . . . going after you guys was part of the lure. I was angry. I genuinely thought you'd abandoned me."

"I'm sure Omnistellar didn't discourage that perspective," said Mia dryly from the other side of Cage. I'd wondered if she was even listening.

"No," he said slowly. "I didn't see it at the time, but now, in retrospect . . . They stoked the fires of my revenge pretty strongly. And then they turned me over to the doctors." A shudder went through him. "I think they were experimenting as much as anything. Priya told me Omnistellar mercenaries have to be anomalies to survive the process, but they usually receive their implants over several months. I got mine in the space of a few days. I think I died on the table twice, but of course my power resurrected me. And then when they were done, I was a mess of wounds. Apparently my power doesn't heal me unless I actually die. So that's what they did. Killed me, I mean. They gave me a lethal injection, and when I came back, I was myself again . . . except not. Faster. Stronger. With a bunch of new cybernetic implants and abilities."

"Oh my God," I gasped, imagining the pain Matt had gone through. "No wonder you hated us."

"The hatred got me through," he confessed. "When the pain got too much to bear, I dreamed of getting even with you guys, and . . . You know, I want to tell you I'm sorry. Not that I didn't have reason to be angry at the time, but even if you *did* abandon me, it wouldn't justify betraying you in return."

"Don't worry about it." Cage reached behind me to squeeze his former friend's shoulder.

"I really hope . . . all of you can forgive me. Given time."

Did *all* of us mean Rune? I kind of thought it did, and a smile touched my lips. "If you can forgive us, we can forgive you. I'm sure of it." I hoped he caught my meaning.

If he did, he didn't show it. "Anyway, they passed me over

to Priya, and she and the others bundled me onto their ship and into space. I know you don't like them, and I get it. But they're . . . They were good to me. Helped me. Taught me to come to terms with my new implants. They treated me like an equal, not a kid. I wouldn't have survived if it weren't for them."

"Hang on a sec." My mind caught up with the story. "You're saying that Hallam and Priya, they're anomalies?"

"You didn't know?"

"I just assumed their abilities came from the implants. What do they do?"

"Hallam was always the strongest guy around. The implants just accentuated a power he already had. Priya, though, her abilities are mental, like yours. Not languages," he added. "Strategy. She can slow a situation down and consider it from every angle in the time it takes most people to blink. So if you're wondering why I keep following Priya's orders, well, it's because I trust her. She's tough and smart and quick on her feet. There's a reason she's in charge."

"Right," Mia drawled. "She's a saint."

"I didn't say that. Just . . . give her a chance, all right?"

Silence met his suggestion. True, Priya and Hallam had stood with us on the ship. They'd learned that Omnistellar was betraying them, plotting to use them and leave them for dead. The decision must have come quickly, after they'd invested so much time and money in upgrading Matt. I didn't think there was any risk of Legion trying to arrest us again, even if we made it home.

But at the same time, I couldn't help remembering how Priya had slapped handcuffs on us *after* we'd saved her from the monster who'd killed her teammate, Bian. Fully understanding the threat we were up against, she'd remained mindlessly determined to fulfill her contract and do her job. And apparently, she'd done that *after* a superpowered consideration of the strategy involved. That kind of single-mindedness was dangerous. If anyone should know, it was me, born and raised in Omnistellar's iron grasp.

The silence stretched long enough to become uncomfortable. I searched for something to say. Priya and Hallam had helped me more than the others; if anyone was going to trust them, I suspected I'd have to start. But I'd just mended fences with Mia, and I didn't want to set her off again. Also, I wasn't sure I *did* trust Priya—or Matt, either, if you came down to it. I believed him when he said he forgave me, and I meant it when I said I understood what he'd been through and forgave him.

But if he was torn between helping us and helping his new teammates in Legion? It was hard to say who he'd side with.

Matt sighed, interpreting our silence. "Keep an open mind. Okay?"

"I always do," said Mia.

Another silence stretched between us, and then something like a snicker escaped Matt. Cage choked, and I found myself fighting a smile. "What?" Mia demanded.

Mia, keeping an open mind—Mia, who'd wanted to toss me out an airlock until I'd saved her life half a dozen times. A wild giggle escaped me, and Cage dropped his head to his hands. His arms tensed against me as he buried his face, smothering his laughter, while Matt sputtered on my left.

"Fine, fine," Mia snapped. "Laugh it up. I'm not the one who—"

"Wait." I jerked upright. Was that movement in the shadows? "Quiet. All of you, right now."

Everyone instantly stilled, and I leaned forward, careful not to make any noise as I peered across the street.

"Kenzie, what is it?" Cage whispered.

I shook my head, forgetting for a moment that he couldn't see me. I'd been *sure* I'd seen something in . . .

And there it was again. A shape, slipping between two buildings and darting across the street. Matt gasped on my left, letting me know he'd seen it too.

Our thief was back.

TEN

I HELD MY BREATH AS THE FIGURE SKIRTED the edge of the building, then leaped onto the fire escape with surprising speed and agility. It was impossible to tell more about them from this distance. It was dark, and they were wrapped in some sort of cloak; they crouched there a moment, little more than a sliver of darkness in the night. Then they darted up the steps without making a sound.

"Impressive," Mia murmured.

I nodded my agreement, shifting to my feet slowly and quietly, shaking the feeling back into my legs. I rolled the stiffness from my neck and checked to make sure I was still maintaining the invisibility around us—other people's powers would never come quite as naturally to me as they did to their owners.

The group of us moved, steadily and silently, staying close together, hugging the middle of the road. I wrapped my arms around myself, feeling exposed in the glaring moonlight, even though I knew the thief couldn't see us. I resisted the urge to reach for the others, to make sure they were still there. For a moment the world receded and I was suddenly, bafflingly aware that I was on the surface of an alien planet, in a ruined city. Was it only months ago I'd spent my days wandering around Sanctuary, dreaming of my Omnistellar future? That I'd had two parents and all the security in the world? That my biggest concern was the next issue of *Robo Mecha Dream Girl 5* and whether the creator would wrap the story up the following year? Life had changed in the time it took to fall asleep at night.

Someone made a soft noise, I wasn't sure who. But it pulled me out of my reverie and directed my attention to the stairs, where the cloaked figure descended, a full backpack slung over their shoulder. I peered at the person. I'd wondered why none of us heard them the night before, and even from twenty feet away, I almost lost them once or twice. How could they stay so quiet on the rusted metal stairwell?

I sucked in a breath. Because they weren't walking on the stairs. They were floating on air.

Of course. This was Liam's world, and that meant anyone left here had powers and strengths we couldn't imagine.

But I didn't have time to dwell on that, because Cage found my hand and squeezed it, and we slipped forward. After a moment, Mia's long, hard grasp closed over my elbow on my other side, binding us together. We stayed as far back as we dared, and I still thought we were too close. The night was deathly silent, and our footfalls on the pavement, while soft, seemed to echo all around me. The thief wasn't making a whisper of sound, and I was terrified they'd hear us. But on the other hand, I didn't want to lose them—every now and then they vanished in the shadows and my throat clenched.

"Matt?" Cage whispered the second time it happened.

"I can see the heat signature," he replied, his voice a ghost in the night. "And I can sense them up ahead. Don't worry. My fancy new cybernetics will track them from a distance, even if my power doesn't." There was a trace of bitterness in his tone, but his fancy cybernetics were definitely coming in handy right about now. I'd clamored to go on this mission because I couldn't stand the thought of my friends out of my sight, of waiting around helplessly while they took a chance, but this was actually the best possible team to send after the thief. Mia's stealth, Cage's speed, Matt's enhanced senses, and my skill with languages—not to mention my newfound ability to copy everyone *else's* talents—imbued me with confidence. For the first time in a long time, we had the drop on someone. We weren't being stalked by alien monsters or running from bounty hunters. We were still hiding, but it was by choice, because *we* were in control. That was a heady sensation, and some of my crippling pain and fear lifted at the thought.

I wasn't stupid. We were still trapped here. My family was still dead. The aliens were still out there. But for the moment at least, we were—maybe for the first time—finally free. No one knew where we were, not even us, and that meant they couldn't come after us. If nothing else, we were free of Omnistellar.

And we had one another, and I would make sure it stayed that way, no matter what stupid risk I had to take next.

"Keep track of the way we came," Mia murmured as we followed the thief along a city street. It had been a pretty straight shot until now, when we left the wide-open throughway and were venturing into smaller, darker alleys.

"I'm on it," Cage replied softly. He'd grown up in alleys and slums and always seemed to have a good sense of direction. That was a positive, because I was used to strictly structured corporate facilities. In other words, I was already lost.

As we ventured farther into the city, we slowed even more, not out of fear of losing our target, but because we'd hit an area full of obstacles. The tall buildings blocked much of the moonlight. The area we'd claimed as our own was relatively clear and clean—surprisingly so, now that I came to think of it. This part of the city, on the other hand, was not. Debris littered streets, and twisted vehicles lined the sidewalks. I bumped into something heavy and metal at one point, maybe a trash container, and bit my lip to keep from screaming in shock. There were rustles in the corners, although those could have been my imagination. We stepped on what felt like broken glass or crushed stone, and shadows ghosted along the walls, making me think of aliens lurking around every corner.

By now I'd completely lost track of our quarry, but Mia's grasp on my elbow remained firm and confident, so I assumed Matt was leading her. I was doing the same to Cage, so I sure hoped Matt knew where he was going. Otherwise, we were wandering around blind.

A few minutes later, Mia tightened her grip, warning me to stop, and I tugged on Cage's hand. "What's up?" he murmured, barely audible.

"The thief went in there." Matt might have gestured, but we couldn't see him. "And then I lost track of them. I can't see heat signals through buildings, but no one's come out since."

"In where?" I asked, trying to keep my voice quiet.

"Sorry. Big building on the corner."

I scanned my surroundings and located a two-story building spreading over nearly an entire block. "If the thief's in there, they aren't alone."

"Matt?" asked Cage.

"Yeah. At least one other life-form nearby, and more in the area."

My fingers drifted to the dagger on my belt. "I don't know about this," I said. "I mean, this is someone trying to survive, exactly like us." I felt the others sigh as much as I heard them, and I bristled. "Pissing off everyone we meet hasn't worked so well for us this far. We blasted those aliens into space, and look where it got us. A horde of monsters chasing us through Obsidian. I'm not saying we should turn around and go home; I'm only suggesting we try a more diplomatic approach."

"I'm not planning to march in there and start stabbing," snapped Mia. "This is reconnaissance as much as anything. If we can do this nicely, we will. But keep in mind that *they* stole from *us*."

I bit off a sharp reply about Mia being one to talk about theft. We'd just come to some sort of understanding. Why make trouble between us?

Cage's arm slid over my shoulders. "You're both right," he said quietly. "Reconnaissance, not attack. But be ready to defend yourself."

I sighed and squeezed his hand against my arm. "I'm ready," I said. "Let's go."

We approached the building carefully. I started for the front door, but the other three swiftly disabused me of that notion, Mia scoffing heavily as she scouted for a side window. Again, I was left scowling—invisibly, but still. So I didn't have their experience with breaking and entering. I had trouble seeing that as a character flaw.

After a moment, Mia's soft voice flowed from the darkness, and a window shuddered open. "Let me scout things first," said Matt. Mia must have stepped aside, because a moment later he said, "It's all clear. Some sort of storeroom by the looks of things. It's pitch-black, so it's hard to tell anything else. There are two life-forms very nearby, but they're not in here. Watch your step. It's a bit of a drop; let me help you down."

There was a soft thud, presumably of Mia landing in the room. Cage eased me gently forward, and I groped blindly until I found Matt's extended hand. He held on to me while I scrambled over the windowsill, then lowered me and let me go. I hit the ground with a jar that resounded through my elbows, but I wasn't hurt. This must be a sort of basement, the ground significantly below the window.

I moved out of the way, and once more I was standing by myself in complete blackness, the only light the dim glow of the window above. Presumably Mia was nearby, but of course I couldn't see her, probably couldn't have even if we'd been visible. My chest tightened and my breath came in gasps. *Not this again.* Ever since the darkness and claustrophobia of the alien ship, the place we'd been trapped in for so many weeks, ever since the aliens stalked me through Obsidian, dark silence was not my friend.

Something thudded in front of me and I sagged against the wall, fighting not to scream. "Cage?" I whispered.

He found me then, his body warm and solid in the darkness, and I went willingly into his arms, letting our invisibility cloak my weakness. "You okay?" he whispered in my ear, the brush of his lips sending a different kind of shiver down my spine.

"Yeah," I replied, fighting a wave of embarrassment. I had

to get it together. I was not going to become a liability on this team, and I sure wasn't going to be told I couldn't come on the next mission because I melted down whenever someone turned out the lights. "I'm good."

There was a louder thump of Matt landing nearby. "Everyone here?" he asked.

"Right beside you," I replied.

"Over here," said Mia from across the room. "I've found an exit. Matt, do you have snazzy new ears, too? Want to tell me if you hear anything behind this door?"

"Sadly, they left my ears more or less human," Matt replied sarcastically. "Only minor embellishments—not enough to hear through solid steel. But those life-forms are *close*, Mia. Next room's as good a guess as any."

"Shame about the ears," Mia replied, and it was impossible to tell if she was joking or not. "I guess it's up to me, then." A moment of silence followed, and then she said, a tiny bit louder, "I don't hear anything. I'm going to ease the door open a crack, so stay quiet."

There was the soft scrape of the door opening, then my heart beating in my ears, and then the scrape again. "Either there's no one there or they're standing around being perfectly silent in total darkness," Mia announced.

"There *are* people nearby," Matt replied, his voice almost inaudible. "I can't tell how close."

"Okay," whispered Cage. "Let Matt take the lead." He

released me from his embrace but kept my hand in his, and together we felt our way along what seemed to be metal shelves. I was careful to let my fingers dance over *only* the shelves. They were probably empty, or storing innocuous contents, but the darkness had me keyed up, and I really didn't want any surprises.

We stumbled over something, and my groping hands caught the doorway. I tugged on Cage to let him know I'd found the way and eased into the open. "Everyone still here?" I whispered, my voice barely audible to my own ears.

"Here," said Mia. "Let's move toward—"

But I never found out where Mia wanted to go, because at that second, light flooded the room. After the darkness of the last few hours it was like a physical attack. I threw up my hands and must have dropped my invisibility in my rush to shelter myself.

A moment later someone grabbed me and forced me to the ground, slamming my head against the linoleum floor and wrenching my hands behind my back, securing them there with some sort of cuffs. As I lay blinking in what seemed like the beams of a million flashlights, Cage, Matt, and Mia squinted on the floor, in similar predicaments.

"So," said Mia dryly, "seems like it was people standing around being quiet in the dark after all."

Split across space. Time. The dimensions collide. The power interlaces.

Its attention is divided. The pull and power of the vengeance and the devouring and the hunt and the death. The drive to finish. The completion.

Some remains.

Some lingers.

Some is finished.

And yet all is one.

ELEVEN

"YOU HAVE TEN SECONDS TO IDENTIFY yourselves." A man's voice, sharp and crisp, cut through the haze. I twisted, trapped, panic surging in my chest, that same familiar terror of being caught in an alien net.

"Take it easy, Gideon," someone replied in an accent that reminded me of my old friend Rita Hernandez. A lump surged in my throat. "They're just kids."

Whoever Gideon was, he didn't seem to care if we were kids or not. He fumbled roughly at my belt, snatching away my dagger and holding it up to show whoever else was in the room. "Just kids, huh?" He kicked my ribs and I gasped, the air flying out of me in a *whoosh*. His foot smashed into the side of my face and stayed there, pinning me to the floor. I still couldn't see my attacker, but I could see Cage, and his face was a mask of fury. There was no way to help me, though, bound as tightly as we were. "Who are you?" Gideon snarled. "Where did you come from, and why the hell are you sneaking into our house in the middle of the night?"

I'd *told* them this was a bad idea. I winced, catching my breath. "Let's talk about that," I suggested. "But I'd rather not do it on the floor with your foot crushing my skull." I wasn't kidding, either. Whoever this was, he was grinding the bones in my face hard enough to make speaking difficult, and it took a solid effort not to let panic slide into my voice.

A long moment stretched into eternity. Cage's jaw twitched furiously across from me, and I worked to keep my muscles still, somehow instinctively knowing that any show of weakness, of fear, would work on my attacker like the smell of blood.

At last the pressure on my face eased, and Gideon retreated into the shadows. Slowly—extremely slowly, and not only because I didn't want to provoke him—I eased myself to a sitting position. The world swam, and I blinked back spots. "Thanks," I said, more sarcastically than I'd intended.

As my eyes adjusted, I realized two big floodlights were aimed right at us. Cage, Mia, and Matt sprawled on the floor, all of them watching me. I flexed my hands. These were regular run-of-the-mill handcuffs, not the fancy ones Legion once used to inhibit our powers. Mia could have vanished. Cage could have run. Matt could have done any number of things, apparently. But everyone stuck around.

Because they weren't sure about their surroundings? Out of worry for the rest of us? Or because we needed to know what was going on?

That last part, at least, was true. As the others cautiously leveraged themselves to sitting positions, I peered into the shadows. I still couldn't make out anything of my attacker or his companion, but Matt had specifically mentioned two people. We should have listened more carefully, I supposed.

"My name is Kenzie," I said, my fear for the others making me brash. I needed to keep his attention on me. "Kenzie Cord. We're sneaking into your house, as you call it, because someone broke into ours, stole a stash of supplies, and made their way back here. As for where we came from, well . . . that's a longer story."

"We have time." The woman advanced into the light. She had sharp, angular features, a long black braid, and well-shaped arms I couldn't have achieved even if I stuck to Omnistellar's rigorous training regimen. She was wearing loose black pants, boots, and a T-shirt, and over her shoulder was slung a familiar backpack. "You in charge?"

I risked a peek at Cage, who arched an eyebrow, and I almost smiled in spite of myself. Who the hell was in charge at this point? "No," I said. "None of us are in charge. Not really. We're just a group of people thrown together and trying to survive."

"Us too." She lowered herself to her haunches. "I realize this wasn't the kindest introduction, and I'm sorry. But we have to take care of our own."

"So do we," said Cage quietly. "Which is why if someone was stealing our supplies, we needed to know who."

The woman sighed. "The other neighborhoods are tapped out. We didn't—"

"Eden," said the man sharply. "That's enough." He stepped into the light as well, revealing himself to be taller and thinner than I'd thought when he'd been grinding my face into the dirt. What there was of him was a solid line of muscle, though. He was exceedingly pale, even given the harsh lighting, and his shaggy brown hair hung in light eyes, eyes glinting in a way that unsettled something deep inside me. "This is an interrogation, not a cocktail party."

Mia snorted loudly, and I winced. She'd been uncharacteristically quiet so far, and I'd hoped she'd stay that way. Somehow I didn't think this guy was going to tolerate her usual bluster.

Sure enough, he spun on her, arching one of his eyebrows so high it vanished beneath his mess of hair. He didn't say anything, though, only considered her for a moment, then nodded. "All right," he said. "Eden, get Sarah and Emmett. First things first. You're going to tell me your powers, and you're going to tell me now. Lie to me, and I'll shoot one of you in the foot. Do it again, and I'll shoot one of you in the face."

I recoiled. I didn't get the sense he was joking. Eden

shrugged and leveraged herself to her feet, retreating out of the way of any stray bullets.

"You're bluffing," Mia snapped. I closed my eyes, willing her silent. "How do we know you even have a gun?"

"Are you volunteering for the first bullet?"

"No," said Cage quickly. He knew Mia as well as I did, and she couldn't be trusted not to answer in the affirmative simply to see what would happen. "We'll answer you, but answer me first. How do you know we have powers?"

For the first time Gideon seemed caught off guard. "What are you talking about?" he demanded. "Of course you have powers. Everyone does. Now answer the question. Since you spoke up, you can go first." He nodded in Cage's direction.

Cage hesitated, glancing between us. Mia shook her head furiously, but Matt only shrugged. He hadn't said a word so far, just watched with a frown.

I didn't see a way out of this without telling Gideon *something*. He obviously knew we had abilities, and besides, I needed to learn more about him, about this place. We couldn't hide in our apartment forever. "I can speak other languages," I told him, figuring there was no harm letting him in on that much. "Pretty much anything. I hear it, and soon I understand it."

He scrutinized me, frowning, his face a mask of introspection. "That's true," he said at last. "But there's more to it. Tell me everything, girl. No lies of omission."

My stomach shifted, but I forced myself to keep my expression blank. "I can read them, too, if that's what you mean. I haven't tried writing."

Gideon sighed. "I told you what would happen if you lied to me," he said, and I didn't even see him draw a gun. There was a crack, and Mia screamed. I spun to find her doubled over on the ground, blood coursing from her foot. "You wanted to know if I was bluffing," he told her, a wicked smile playing on his lips. "Well. Now you know. So." He leveled the gun in my direction. "You want to try this again?"

"I copy powers!" I cried frantically. "My abilities started mutating lately. My original power was the language thing, but recently I can do whatever anyone else can as long as they're somewhere nearby!"

Gideon smiled coldly. "Truth," he said. He shifted the gun to Cage.

We exchanged glances. Gideon was a human lie detector. More fun new powers, courtesy of the aliens. Too bad this one worked against us.

"I'm fast," Cage said succinctly. His face was blank, but clear rage simmered underneath. Cage had always been fiercely protective of his friends, especially the people he'd spent so long imprisoned alongside. The slight tremor in his hands warned me he was barely keeping himself from launching straight into Gideon, handcuffs and all.

"How fast?"

"Do you want a demonstration?"

"I'd recommend against it." Gideon analyzed him and appeared to dislike what he saw. "Fine. You're fast. What about Screaming Girl over there?"

Mia drew herself up, her face pale and pinched in pain, and spit a creative mix of insults in his direction.

Gideon sighed and leveled the gun at Cage.

"She turns invisible!" I shouted, my heart hammering so fast I almost doubled over with the need to stop it. "And she turns other people invisible!"

Gideon smiled. "Truth. Now. What about the big quiet fellow?"

Matt shrugged. "Originally, I sensed life," he said. "Now apparently I can resurrect myself."

He'd left out all of his cybernetically enhanced senses, and I held my breath. Would that register as a lie? And if it did, would Gideon give us a chance to explain how those weren't really *abilities*, or would he just shoot someone?

He nodded slowly. "All right. That wasn't so hard, was it?" He glanced behind him as Eden jogged over. "Where are Sarah and Emmett?"

"I don't know," she said. "I heard a gunshot and came running to see if everything was okay." She took in the situation and frowned, her eyes faintly troubled.

"Next time, follow orders. But since you're here now, we can handle them. Help the wounded one. Keep your hands on her, and if she disappears, shoot her. Also, shoot her if anyone else disappears—and that includes running off."

"Yes, sir." Eden slipped past me and caught Mia by the arm, pulling her to her feet. Mia snarled and snapped her teeth, and Eden recoiled, almost imperceptibly. "Get it together," she said, so quietly I could barely hear her. "Or do you want him to kill someone?"

Mia hesitated, then sagged, her spirit seeming to vanish.

Gideon gestured to the rest of us with his gun. "You three, in front of me. You wanted to know who we were, where we lived? Well, you're about to find out."

TWELVE

CAGE AND MATT SANDWICHED ME BETWEEN them, Cage in front and Matt behind. I was torn between annoyance at the gesture and genuine emotion. Cage and I seemed to spend most of our time putting ourselves between the others and danger, but Matt, well, if he was looking out for me, it meant he genuinely did forgive me.

But neither of them could do much to protect me here. I was still reeling from the casual way Gideon put that bullet in Mia's foot. I was pretty sure he'd kill me, or any of us, with the same expression on his face. This was not someone I wanted to cross. I realized now what frightened me in his eyes. They were soulless and empty, the reflection of someone who had gone too far and seen too much. I examined him out of the corner of my eye. He looked every inch a soldier, like the higher-ups I'd known at Omnistellar. I knew power and authority when I saw it. If I was going to keep my friends safe from this man, I'd have to keep Mia and Cage quiet. Questioning him wasn't going to get us anywhere. Maybe we could find common ground, a way to put us on the same side.

I looked at him again and scratched that notion. Maybe it would have been possible once, but whatever Gideon had come through to reach this point, it had settled deep into his soul, eradicating everything but suspicion. I had no idea how we would break through to him.

We descended a long flight of stairs and emerged into . . .

"Is this a department store?" I asked dubiously.

"Keep moving." Gideon shoved me between the shoulder blades, and I stumbled.

But Eden answered. "When we first got here, it seemed like the best choice to supply us for a while," she said. "Now . . . everyone's too scared to move on."

"Everyone's *safe*," Gideon snapped.

"Safe doesn't mean secure," Eden replied, her voice calm and quiet in contrast to his vitriolic anger. "It's temporary. It's—"

"That's enough, Cortez."

She sighed, and I got the sense they'd had this conversation before. "Yes, sir."

The overhead lights had long since gone dark, but some sort of lanterns stood at regular intervals, throwing the huge space into shadowy relief. What looked like a grocery area stood in one corner, large shelves blocked off by a series of curtains and blankets. Nearby, various counters still contained all the things people hadn't considered worth taking: a smattering of toys, craft materials, gardening implements, and home decorations.

Was that movement behind one of the makeshift curtains? I didn't have time to consider it before Gideon steered us in the other direction. Behind me, Mia gasped regularly, obviously in pain. After a moment, she quieted, and I risked a glimpse over my shoulder. Eden had levitated a few inches off the ground, taking Mia with her, and was guiding them forward without putting any pressure on my friend's wound. Mia's face remained stubbornly set, but I read the relief in her eyes, and almost against my will a wave of gratitude surged through me.

"Gideon, was it?" Cage craned his neck, giving the older man one of his brightest smiles. "Look, we should talk about this. We aren't your enemies. We're trying to survive, just like you."

"Oh, we'll talk." Gideon guided us through what seemed like some sort of home repair area and led us behind the counter. He pulled a ring of old-fashioned keys from his pocket and opened a padlock on a heavy steel door, revealing a dark space behind it. He took Cage by the shoulder and shoved him inside. "I've got plenty of questions for all of you." He gestured for Matt to follow. I made to go with them, but Gideon stopped me with an outstretched hand. He slammed the door and padlocked it. "This way," he said.

I gaped at the closed door. For some reason it hadn't even occurred to me that they might separate us, and desperation clawed at my guts. Every time I was apart from Cage, things went downhill—for both of us. We needed to be together. We *all* needed to be together. It was bad enough we'd split into two groups and I couldn't help the others if they came after us. I had to be able to protect Cage and Matt. I needed to keep everyone safe, and how could I do that if we were locked in separate cages?

But Gideon wasn't giving me the chance to make arguments. He grabbed me and shoved me along with such force I stumbled to my knees. I sucked in my breath as I slammed to the floor, unable to break my fall with my bound hands.

"Gideon." Eden's voice held a hint of warning.

Gideon spun on her. "You got something to say?"

I couldn't see his face, but she stared at him for a moment, working her lower lip, before shaking her head. "No, sir. Just . . . again. They're kids."

"Kids," Gideon muttered. He jammed his hands into his hair and pulled it so hard I winced on his behalf. "*Kids*. That's how they get you. Sympathy. Kids." He laughed, the sound unstable and brittle. "Kids. Remember when we went after the *kids*, Eden? The ones in the desert?"

"Gideon . . ."

"Remember how you convinced me to follow them into the night? *They might need us*, you said. *Think of your* . . ." He swallowed, his face white with rage, a scar along his cheek standing out in mottled purple. "So we went after them. Remember? Remember, Eden?"

"Yes," she said quietly. "I remember."

"And what happened next?"

She sighed. "The rest of their group jumped us from behind an abandoned car. They killed three of our people before we got the best of them." Spreading her hands in supplication, she said, "But that doesn't mean everyone who needs help is looking to trap us. These are the first people we've seen in years, Gid. This is our chance to learn what's going on outside these walls, to—"

Without warning, he spun and smashed his fist through the glass countertop. I screamed and scrambled, dodging flying shards of glass. Instinctively, I rolled to my feet, crouched low and ready to bolt, but Gideon only stood staring at the blood coursing down his hand in dispassionate annoyance. "Now look what you made me do," he muttered.

Eden closed her eyes briefly as if in pain. "All right. If that's the way you want it. Let's get these girls squared away and see to your hand."

"Don't you dare condescend to me." He glared at Mia. "Are there more of you?"

Mia hesitated. Like me, she'd obviously realized that Gideon knew when we were lying, and not because he was naturally perceptive. But her stubbornness won out. She locked her lips in a line and jutted her chin forward.

Gideon shrugged, pulled his gun, and targeted her other foot.

Oh, for God's sake. "Yes!" I shouted, because Mia was almost certainly willing to get shot again to prove a point. She was the only one left with me, and if I couldn't take care of the others, I could at least protect her ungrateful ass. "There are more of us."

"Older than you?"

I winced, seeing where he was going. "Some of them," I said cautiously. "But—"

"There. You see?" He waved his wounded hand in Eden's direction, splattering blood on the floor. "They're a decoy. We need to watch for their friends, because they won't be far behind. You see to that. I'll get answers from these two."

Eden seemed to hesitate. "I can talk to them, Gideon. Why don't you go and . . . ?"

"And what? Leave you to be lied to? Don't be stupid. I'll take them from here."

Eden examined us momentarily, then shrugged and carefully returned Mia to the ground. "Yes, sir. I'll get a crew together and set up a perimeter. Let me know what you learn."

I watched her receding back with something like panic. Eden wasn't exactly a friend or an ally, but she seemed a lot more stable than Gideon. I didn't doubt he would kill either one of us at the first sign of a lie.

He wasn't particularly gentle in hauling Mia forward. She exploded in a string of cursing as she stumbled on her injured foot. I caught her to keep her from toppling, pressing my shoulder into her so she could lean on me. She resisted for all of a second before half collapsing against me, which told me she was in more pain than she'd let on.

Gideon still clutched that gun in his hands. It wasn't anything I recognized, not one of Omnistellar's fancy weapons or one of the more common cheap brands I'd seen used on Obsidian. I guessed it made sense—a lot was the same here, but not everything. If Rune was right, if we'd connected with this race across space, maybe even time, some things were bound to get lost in the translation. For instance, I didn't recognize the lanterns along the perimeter. They looked like flickering flames, but closer inspection revealed them to have a bluish light that definitely wasn't natural. I had no idea what they were or where they'd come from.

Could Rune be right? Was it even possible that somehow we had a bond with this race, with these people? And if that was the case, would it make it easier to reason with them or harder?

Gideon didn't give me any more time to examine my surroundings. He ordered us forward, and we shuffled along. Mia was heavier than she appeared. "Mia, for once in your life," I whispered through gritted teeth, "don't piss him off. And whatever you do, don't lie to him."

She shot me a scowl that clearly said *coward*, but I was past caring. "You want to die here?" I snapped, only barely managing to control my volume. "You want Alexei to find your body full of holes? You think it'll bring him peace knowing you died telling pointless lies?"

She hesitated. I'd chosen the right track, going after the only thing capable of fazing her. She wouldn't have cared if I'd tried to make her save her life for her own sake, but I knew the thought of Alexei stumbling over her corpse would stop her short.

Mia didn't answer me, but she also sagged a bit more, as if the fight had gone out of her. We staggered to another bolted door and stood aside while Gideon unlocked it. I did briefly consider disappearing and running, but I realized that even if Mia's injury let us escape, Gideon would go after Cage and Matt in retribution.

He forced us into the room. There was no illumination inside, but the lanterns spilled enough light to reveal some empty storage shelves and a narrow space, maybe ten feet long and six wide. It was barely smaller than a prison cell on Sanctuary, I realized with a pang.

Gideon filled the doorway. "Just so we're clear," he said, "if one of you lies to me, I'll kill the other. Then I'll go repeat the same exercise with your friends and bring the surviving one back here until no one's left. And I'll kill the rest of your people when they arrive."

I managed to turn a hysterical laugh into a cough. "You're going to do that anyway."

Gideon crouched, resting his arms on his knees. I thought

he was considering me, maybe appraising me. "Tell you what," he said. "I'll make you a deal. Give me the truth, and I won't kill anyone unless I have to. I'll take them prisoner, lock them up with you until we decide what to do next. I can't promise that won't mean your deaths. But I won't execute them on the spot. Tell me a single lie, though, even a hint of a gasp, and I'll slaughter every single one of them the second they show their faces."

Mia scowled. "You have a low opinion of our friends."

"They won't know what they're walking into. I'm MACE. You know what that means?"

She sagged against a shelf, barely keeping herself upright, all her weight on her left foot and hands. "Short for emaciated?"

"Macro Adversarial Crisis Extraction," Gideon replied coldly.

He seemed to be expecting a response. "We've never heard of MACE," I told him at last, honestly.

Gideon sighed, obviously hearing the truth. "I guess you would've been in diapers when the Blast happened. But trust me, I'm not someone you want to mess around with."

I blinked. Was this my chance to forge a connection? "So you were a soldier," I said, keeping my voice carefully emotionless. I wasn't sure what would set him off. Even too much interest might do it.

"That's one word for it." His flat, cold eyes slide over me. "We went deep into enemy territory and extracted assets. Once the Blast hit, we found a new job. We went places no one else went. Most of us died. We accomplished nothing, but we kept trying. Over and over, we kept trying." He snorted. "For all the good it did us."

"What happened?" I asked.

I'd tried to keep my voice neutral, but it was as if I'd triggered a reaction. His head snapped up and his nostrils flared and he snarled, "Nothing good. All you need to know is that I've seen countless people die and killed almost as many, and I'm not scared to do it again. I do keep my word, though. So make a choice. Tell me how many of you there are, what abilities they have, and when we can expect them. Or try to lie . . . and see what MACE really means."

THIRTEEN

IT SEEMED LIKE FROM THE MOMENT CAGE AND Alexei took me captive on Sanctuary, I'd faced a series of nothing but impossible choices. Still, this was by far the worst. Was it wrong to save us? To betray my friends, give Gideon their abilities, their names? If I didn't, we'd die.

But was it worth it? Should I instead sacrifice us to save everyone else? *Would* I even save them? Or was Gideon not exaggerating his skills and abilities? I didn't know what MACE was, but he'd seemed to expect it to have an impact, which meant it was probably like Legion or Omnistellar—a force to be reckoned with.

I made my decision in a heartbeat. We didn't have a choice, not really. And so I told him everything. I listed off the members of Legion, my remaining friends, and their abilities. I told him where they were and that they would almost certainly come after us. I tried to leave information out, but he didn't let me. His questions came quick and relentless: Did they have training? Were they armed? What sorts of strategies did they use?

And throughout it all, I couldn't lie. I became paranoid with the need to tell the truth, because the slightest slip would mean Mia's death, and I was not going to let anyone die, not one more of my friends, my family.

At last Gideon nodded thoughtfully and departed without a word of reassurance, slamming us into total darkness. He did free our hands before he left, the sole concession he made as he ignored my frantic questions and stormed out of the room. The only sounds were our breaths: mine harsh in my chest, Mia's ragged with pain and, probably, anger.

"Mia," I said at last, forcing the words through a constricted throat, "I'm sorry. I . . ."

Mia sighed. "Let's stop apologizing to each other, all right? I don't know what the right call was here, and that's rare for me. My instinct says we should have kept our mouths shut. But then I think of Cage and Matt in the other room, and Lex, and . . ." Her voice trailed off. "Well, whatever the right thing was, this is what happened. We'll have to deal with it, and hope the others are smart enough to spot an ambush."

I sagged in relief. I'd been terrified of being trapped with a furious Mia determined to stoke the fires of my guilt. But she'd changed in the last few weeks too, I realized. She was still Mia: unpredictable and temperamental and violent. But she'd gentled a bit, relaxed into herself since we left Sanctuary. Alexei had mentioned she was mildly claustrophobic, that prison had been extra hard on her, and . . .

Claustrophobic. Oh God. "Are you okay in here?" I asked, trying to keep my voice mild.

Mia sighed. She didn't even pretend not to know what I meant. "If I can handle climbing through the vents in Obsidian, I can handle a storeroom. The bigger problem is my foot."

"Can I . . ." I choked off a laugh. "I was going to say take a look at it. I don't know. Prod at it?"

"Why not? It can't hurt much more than it already does." There was a clatter as she let herself finally sag to the floor along the shelves, and I groped my way to her side, crouching at her feet. I reached out hesitantly until I found her leg and loosened the buckles on her boot, prying it off her foot. Mia sucked in a gasp of air but made no other protest.

"Tell me if I'm hurting you," I cautioned. Because Mia wouldn't. And the last thing I needed was to make her injury worse.

"That Gideon," she remarked, almost conversationally. "He's a piece of work, huh?"

I shuddered involuntarily. "And I thought Legion was bad."

"Legion is a bunch of smug arrogant bastards. I think Gideon is actually out of his mind. Maybe he wasn't before, but situations can break people, you know?"

Did I ever.

Was that what happened to my parents, I wondered? Once

upon a time, would they have laid down their lives for me, for each other? Turned their backs on Omnistellar? Had passing years and a constant war of attrition decimated their spirits until only the Omnistellar soldier remained? And if it hadn't been for Cage and the prison break, would the same thing have happened to me?

I ground my teeth. It *wouldn't* happen, though, not to me, and not to my friends. No matter how many times we fell, I'd pull us to our feet.

And on that note . . . I ran my hands lightly over Mia's flesh. She sucked in her breath when I reached the wound, and blood spilled over my hands. "Sorry," I whispered. And then my questing fingers bumped something protruding from her flesh and she didn't gasp, she screamed.

But I didn't move because hope had surged inside me. This felt like some sort of projectile. Not a bullet, then, which meant . . . "I think I can remove this," I said.

"Should you?" Somehow, Mia was not only conscious, but coherent. "Actually, never mind. I don't care. I want it out."

I nodded. We needed Mia as mobile as possible, which precluded weird darts in her feet. Besides, if we ever got our hands on some light, I wanted to see this thing. I prayed it was only a projectile and not something injecting toxins into her system.

"Hang on." Mia rummaged around and then pressed something into my hands—the scarf she'd been wearing around her neck. "For the blood," she sighed, sounding more resigned than scared.

Which was good, because I was plenty scared for both of us. I *hated* blood. If I was going to do something like this, I was *very* happy to be doing it in the dark.

A sudden memory intruded, and a totally inappropriate giggle escaped my lips. "Sorry." I hastened to explain. "It's just . . . this is the second time I've had to pull something out of you."

"Don't remind me," Mia muttered. On Sanctuary, she'd been the first to encounter the alien creatures, and one of them broke a claw off in her side. Cage and I had worked together to remove it, even though I'd been on the verge of unconsciousness the whole time. I really wished I had him here now.

I drew a deep breath. No point delaying. Without warning her, because what good would it do, I grabbed the object and jerked with all my strength.

Mia cried out as it came free. I carefully set it aside and pressed the scarf against her foot, hoping it was doing a good job of stanching the blood. I kept the pressure steady as I wrapped the scarf around her and tied it as tightly as I dared.

"Let me see that thing," she gasped.

I lifted the projectile and ran my fingers over it. It was sticky with Mia's blood, but otherwise small, and I didn't think it was a dart after all. "It almost feels like a tack," I said dubiously. It had a long, wickedly sharp tip and a rounded blunt end.

Mia took it and must have examined it herself. "It's like a projectile knife," she remarked.

It actually was like a dart, I reflected, just like one you'd use to play games. Not a tranquilizer or anything. Or at least I didn't think so. Who knew? "This place is so much like Earth, but we don't have any weapons like this." I'd gotten used to seeing the similarities. I wasn't accustomed to the differences.

If Rune was right, if we'd somehow connected with this race, would that allow for these differences? Or did this point to another explanation? But what? We obviously weren't on just any alien planet. The similarities couldn't be ignored. But neither could the differences. I needed to get out of here, to talk to Rune, to . . . "Where are we?" I said out loud, wishing Rune were here to answer.

"You brought us here," Mia pointed out, although she didn't seem particularly angry.

I sighed and slumped beside her, close enough for our arms to touch. I wasn't sure how she'd react, but in the darkness I craved any human contact, even hers. And she must have felt the same, because she didn't recoil.

We sat together in the black, Mia breathing a little too steadily, like she was trying to control her pain and claustrophobia, me fighting a thousand different fears and imaginations. The darkness was too much like the alien ship, overwhelming me with horrifying memories, and with nothing to distract me, I was thinking about my parents again. My mom and dad, Omnistellar loyalists, gone now forever. I bit hard on my lip to keep my emotions under control. I'd lost so many people along the way. I wished I could do something, anything, to bring them back. But they were gone, and I only had one choice left: to keep my remaining friends safe and alive and strong.

"What were your parents like?" Mia said suddenly, as if she'd been reading my thoughts. "Before all this. I've always wondered what it must have been like growing up in a totalitarian corporate dictatorship."

I snorted. "That actually describes Omnistellar pretty well . . . but not my family. The thing is, until you took me hostage, Omnistellar was simply part of our lives, and we didn't think about the rules much. Things were . . . easy. Structured."

"Did they love you?"

That caught me off guard. "I think so," I said at last, the words dragging out of me like they were weighted, caught in my throat. "My dad, for sure. He was more cheerful. More friendly. My mom . . . she mostly seemed proud of me when I succeeded at the company. But she sometimes had this smile she . . ." My throat swelled, and I turned a sob into a cough. "I don't know, Mia," I said at last. "My dad might have been misguided, but he tried to save me. My mom didn't even do that much. And it's not like I can ask them about it."

I thought she nodded. "Sorry. I shouldn't have asked."

"No. I don't mind talking about them. It's just . . . it's hard, you know?"

"Tell me about it. At least you had parents. My dad is God knows where, and my mom hasn't said a word to me since I was arrested. Even before, it was mostly drunken yelling."

She laughed sharply. "I assume she blames me for my sister's death. Which is ironic, since she was the one unconscious on the couch when those thugs dragged Shannon out of the apartment."

Mia's life had been the exact opposite of mine, a life of poverty and theft and manipulation. "We all blame ourselves for the things that have happened," I said at last, slowly, exploring the words as I spoke them. "Me for letting Omnistellar dupe me. For shooting Matt. For not convincing my dad to listen. You for your sister. For shooting my . . . my dad."

"For a lot of things, Kenzie. You have no idea."

"I don't have to," I said, the words gaining strength as they spilled out of me. I felt the rightness of them somehow. "Because I know you. I know who you are now, and I've seen you at your best and your worst. You're better than you think, Mia. You're my friend, whatever you think of me."

"Oh, Kenzie, shut up," she said in disgust. "Of course you're my friend too."

She could have slapped me and provoked less shock. There was no *of course* about it. Until recently, I'd been pretty sure Mia hated me. I had to resist the urge to hug her again. "Well," I said wryly, "now that's settled, so . . . what do you say we work on escaping?"

Mia chuckled, stronger, more like herself. "Now *that* sounds like a plan."

FOURTEEN

"IF YOU HAVE AN IDEA, I'M ALL EARS," I SAID, sitting up a little straighter.

"My idea is named Eden. I think she knows Gideon's lost it. Did you see the way she reacted to him? And she helped me on the way down here. If we can get her alone for even a second, we might be able to talk her around."

I frowned, considering the idea. "I don't know," I said at last. "It's one thing not to like the man's tactics. It's another to betray him for a bunch of strangers. And we still don't really know anything about this place. They obviously have other people here."

"Well, that's plan B, anyway. Plan A is to search this damn room. Help me up."

"Are you kidding?" I gaped at her in disbelief, even though I couldn't see her and she couldn't see me. "Mia, you're *hurt*. You need to stay still, to rest, to—"

"What I need to do is get the hell out of here. Get me on my feet. Or do I have to do it myself?"

I shook my head. There was no point in arguing. Mia was used to getting her own way, and she would have it now, too. I stood and reached down, clasping her elbows and heaving her to her feet. Aside from a quick intake of breath, she made no complaint. "Where's that dart thing?" I asked.

"In my pocket. I might be able to use it as a lockpick if we can find an exit."

"All right. I'll go left and you go right. Let's start with the perimeter before we stumble around the middle of the room."

As I inched to my left, feeling along the cold brick walls, searching for a window or an exit or who knew what, a wave of déjà vu assaulted me. I'd done the same thing on Omnistellar's ship, searching the infirmary for a flashlight. Except then I'd been alone . . .

No. Not alone.

There'd been aliens in the room with me. Waiting. Breathing. *Hunting.*

At once I became convinced something was behind me, a presence, a darkness, a shadow. I spun, pressing my back to the wall, my heart hammering so loudly it threatened to overwhelm my senses. *Get a grip*, I snarled at myself furiously. *There is nothing and no one in this room with you. No one but Mia.* "I haven't found anything yet," I managed to say out loud. God, I needed to hear Mia's voice, to know I wasn't alone.

"Me either. Keep searching."

My heart rate slowed. Just those four words. Mia was with me. I wasn't alone.

I groped along the walls and found nothing but more cement. Soon Mia and I met up again, our hands brushing against the metal door. "This thing's padlocked from the outside," she said, rattling the handle. "I can't pick a lock I can't get my hands on."

"That means we have to check the rest of the room, huh?" I shook my head. "What do you think we're going to find?"

"I don't know, but . . ." Her voice trailed off. I opened my mouth to ask what was wrong, but then I heard it too: footsteps in the distance. "Hurry," she whispered, grabbing my arm and pulling me back. We settled against the wall again, Mia grunting in pain as she put too much pressure on her foot.

There were a rattle and a clack, and then the door opened. Hardly any light spilled in, but it seemed like the force of the sun after total darkness, and I winced, throwing my arms up to protect my eyes.

After a moment I adjusted to the dimness and was able to properly observe the situation. It was Eden, carrying a lantern in one hand, a bag in another. There was someone else behind her with a gun drawn. "I'll just be a minute," she told him, entering the room and closing the door behind her.

We examined each other with mutual interest. Mia's words kept echoing in my head. Could we work on Eden? Convince her to help us? "I brought you some food and water," she said, tossing the bag in our direction. I noticed she was careful not to get too close. "There's some first aid stuff in there too, and a lantern. I figured you might need it."

"Thanks," I said. Mia said nothing. She was letting me take the lead, presumably aware that diplomacy was not her strong suit. I wished Cage were here. He'd talk circles around Eden, probably have her cheerfully agreeing to defect in a matter of minutes. "What about our friends? Cage and Matt?"

"I took them some food and water too. They're okay."

I inspected her. Was she telling the truth? Could Gideon have hurt Cage? Could she be lying to gain my cooperation?

Or . . . was there a way I could tell?

Swallowing hard, while Mia and Eden talked in the background, I closed my eyes and reached for power.

I brushed past Eden, her floating ability soft swirls of pink and gray, past someone else in the corridor, a guard whose power I couldn't know. Did I dare grab an unknown ability? No, I realized: Gideon knew what I could do, and he wasn't stupid enough to leave someone guarding me if I could make use of their powers.

But Gideon himself . . . where was he?

I stretched further, not even sure what I was looking for, and then suddenly I had it: something solid and red and brown shot through with shimmers of white. I wrapped myself in it and my eyes flew open as I repeated my question, cutting off whatever Mia had been saying: "I want to hear you say it again, Eden. Cage and Matt. Are they okay?"

She quirked an eyebrow at me. Did she know what I was up to? But whether she did or not, she replied: "I told you, they're fine. No one's touched them."

Her answer settled my stomach, gentle and reassuring. Truth.

"And . . ." I swallowed. "What about our *other* friends?"

"No sign of them yet." She hesitated, then said, almost unwillingly, "Gideon's thinking of taking the fight to them if they don't show up soon."

I examined her face in the shadows. She didn't look much like Rita, but they really did have a similar accent, the same lilt to their voices. It made it easier to talk to her, somehow. And it didn't hurt that I could tell she wasn't lying, Gideon's power hovering on the edges of my consciousness. I got the sense he was just in my range and I might lose his power any second. "We're trying to survive, same as you."

"We all prioritize our own survival." She sighed. "And it's not just my own. We have people here. Families. Children. There's a whole little society, three or four dozen of us. And we're running out of supplies. So I'm sorry if it seems like we were pillaging your take, but I wasn't about to watch a five-year-old girl starve."

True. I thought of Anya, the child we'd left on Mars. Was she okay? Had the aliens attacked the planet? A wave of guilt washed over me. I'd barely even considered her since Obsidian.

"I understand," I said, and I did. "But we don't have to do this. We can work together. We aren't your enemies, Eden."

"I can't know that."

"But you can." I stared at her. Did she seriously not get this? "Gideon. He can ask us and he'd know if we lied, right?"

"Yes," she said, but slowly, and Gideon's power sent a tingle of warning down my spine. There was something more to it. Abruptly her eyes cut to Mia. "How are you? Doing okay?"

"Fantastic," drawled Mia acerbically. "I guess I'm lucky your pal only shot me in the foot."

"The thing is, you are." Eden fiddled with the edge of her braid. "Gideon, he's . . . he's a good man."

I waited for the answering buzz from Gideon's power, but nothing came. I cursed inwardly. Gideon must have moved out of range, and he couldn't have picked a worse time.

Of course, neither could Mia. "He's insane," she said bluntly.

Eden shot straight up, and I knew Mia had said the wrong thing. "He's been through more than you can possibly imagine. He's the only reason we're all still alive, the only one who's kept us going these last eight horrible years. Without him we'd all be dead."

"I get it," I said quickly, struggling to fix Mia's mistake. "You owe him. I've been there. But he's not the same now, is he? Things have changed."

She hesitated again, but I got the sense she'd been wanting to say these things for a while. That maybe Mia and I seemed safe, since we were outsiders . . . or since we'd be dead soon, if she knew something we didn't. "He's been through a lot," she repeated softly. "But you're right. He's changed. The old Gideon might have listened. This one . . . he's . . ." She swallowed. "He's lost his nerve. He thinks if he can keep everything controlled, keep us caged like animals in a zoo, we'll be safe. He doesn't understand that we're going to run out of supplies sooner rather than later. If he has his way, we'll all sit here in *safety* until we starve to death."

"Can't you do anything to stop him?" Mia demanded.

Doubt flickered in Eden's eyes. "Gideon was different at the beginning. Stronger. A force. He saved every soul in this building. He's personally pulled me out of harm's way on three separate occasions. Convincing people to turn against someone like that, even when he's behaving erratically . . . no one wants to betray the man who saved them. Including me."

"He's going to kill us, isn't he?" I asked it quietly and without emotion. I'd already long since assumed that was the case, and Eden's silence did nothing to convince me otherwise. I didn't need Gideon's power to know the truth of this one. "He can't afford to let us join, not if you're low on supplies. He doesn't know us. Are you okay with that? With murdering a bunch of people for no reason?"

"I wouldn't . . ."

"You might like us if you got to know us," I suggested, forcing a smile I didn't feel. "We're not such bad people. We're hardworking, and we're brave."

"I know. And I appreciate the risk you took, raiding the outer neighborhoods. I just . . ."

"Wait." I exchanged glances with Mia, who shrugged. "What do you mean, the risk we took?"

Eden considered us for a long moment. Then she grabbed a crate, pulled it over, and sat down. "Okay," she said. "I'll answer your question if you answer mine. Where the hell did you come from? Because it sure wasn't from around here."

I bit my lip, debating how truthfully to answer. But then . . . I wanted Eden to trust me. That had to go both ways. Besides, what was she going to do with the information? "I have no idea where we came from," I said at last. "Or maybe I mean I don't know where we are. Or both. We were on a spaceship, and it was about to blow up. I . . . borrowed someone's power and reached for someplace safe, somewhere far away from the ship." Somewhere to help us defeat the aliens, I added to myself ruefully. Apparently, my subconscious had ignored that part of my request. "And . . . we woke up here. We're from a different planet, a different solar system. Nowhere close, I think."

I expected disbelief, but she only stared at me a moment, then nodded slowly. "That actually tracks," she said. "It explains why you don't know things you should. You've survived by sheer luck, you know."

"We *don't* know," I said, fighting to keep my frustration under control. "We don't know anything."

"It's why we stick to the city center. The outlying neighborhoods, they're the territory of the creatures we call the *zemdyut*."

The sand-torn devastation breathes. Awakens. Conquered.

The hive writhes.

Shifting beneath the surface. Beneath the minds.

Shifting sands. Shifting times.

Something has changed.

Conquered?

This planet lives again. New life, new breath. Familiar. Creatures that have followed and stalked and wreaked havoc in the past, now delivered, ready for the harvest. The attention divided, the threat compelling, the power drawing.

Two places. One mind.

FIFTEEN

IN ONE WORD AND TWO SYLLABLES, EVERYTHING fell apart.

I jerked upright, my heart stuttering over itself, the air rushing from my lungs in a single breath. My world shrank to Eden, to the fear on her face, her lips moving but her words inaudible over the dim, sharp rush of a nonexistent wind filling my ears.

I'd heard that word before, the slight foreign lilt to it.

Zemdyut.

Alien.

"They're still here," I whispered.

Beside me, Mia had gone cold and rigid, a statue made of ice.

Eden froze, her features a mask. "You know the *zemdyut*?"

"This *is* Liam's world," I said. I'd known that, of course, but part of me had hoped I was wrong, or at least hoped the aliens had left this place alone. Maybe when I piggybacked on Liam's power, I'd accidentally tapped into *his* memories of a safe place, because this sure as hell didn't fit my definition.

"Who's Liam?"

"He's the one whose power I borrowed to get here. He teleported to our solar system, and he told me about the *zemdyut*. But we already knew about them. We just didn't have a name for them. They attacked our world too. They killed my family. We came here looking to escape from them." I shot to my feet. Eden tensed, standing as well, but I didn't care at the moment. I needed to move, to burn off some of the terror clawing at my soul. I'd thought we'd left the aliens behind, but we hadn't. We'd followed them.

Still . . . maybe I could use this information to forge an escape from our current mess. I turned to Eden, lowering my voice. "We are exactly the same," I told her, making no effort to hide my desperation. "Both of our worlds, our families, are victims of these creatures. Please don't let Gideon murder my friends after they've survived so much."

"I don't . . ." Eden hesitated. "I'll talk to him," she said at last. "Sometimes he listens to me. But you'd better pray your people don't come in guns blazing, because no power on the globe will stop him if they do. His protective impulse is on overdrive. If he scents even a hint of a threat to the safety of the people in this building, he will scorch the earth to defend them."

I had more questions, hundreds of them threatening to trip off my tongue, but she was already backing out of the room.

What were the chances of my friends *not* coming in shooting? It depended whose voice prevailed. Mia was here, so that was a small mercy. I only hoped Priya's head for strategy was enough to urge caution.

Eden left us the light, and the bag. After a moment Mia pulled it toward herself, rummaged around, and began calmly cleaning and bandaging her foot. "She didn't take the dart," she remarked, as if she were suggesting a stroll along the beach. "She must have known we had it. That's something."

I shook my head, barely able to speak, let alone mimic Mia's calm tone. "Mia, what she said . . . the creatures. They're here."

Mia sighed, leaning against the wall and popping open a canister of water. "Honestly, I'm getting used to them chasing me. I'd almost prefer it. At least that way I know what we're up against."

I blinked. She seemed tired, more resigned than I was accustomed to. "Are you all right?" I asked.

She shrugged. "I'm fine. This is just how things go. One disaster to the next. If you're hanging with me, you'd better get used to it. There's never a break. That's your problem: you're always trying to think things through. But some of the time, *most* of the time, all we can do is wait for the next thing to happen and react."

I resisted the urge to comment that her philosophy hadn't

gotten her very far in life, since she'd spent the last five years or so in a prison cell on Sanctuary. I took a water canister of my own and drained half of it in a single gulp. "Well, I'm going to keep using my brain," I said dryly, "even if you'd rather wait for something to show up so you can throw things at it."

At that moment the entire building seemed to heave. I stumbled, losing my balance and crashing into a metal shelf. I grabbed it to keep myself standing as the world restored itself, the shelves teetering dangerously before deciding to stay upright.

Our eyes met, and Mia grinned. "See what I mean?" She caught the shelf behind her and used it to drag herself to her feet. "I think we've spent enough time in this storeroom."

"Great. I agree. If you can think of a way to get us out . . ."

The room gave another lurch. Mia seemed prepared for it and clutched the shelf for balance. I, on the other hand, almost went over. "You should probably come here," she said.

"Mia, what . . . ?"

"Hang on."

I suddenly realized the temperature in the room had been climbing gradually and was now unbearably hot. My hair stuck to my neck in a sweaty clump, and as I stared at the metal outline of the door, I was pretty sure it started to glow red. "Oh boy . . . ," I muttered.

The next instant, the door smashed inward, colliding with the wall. A blast of heat followed it. If the back of the door had been warm, the front was half melted, especially around the padlocked area, which bubbled and blistered, twisting in on itself.

Standing silhouetted in the remaining space, Alexei rolled his huge shoulders. "There you are," he said. "This is the third room I've checked."

From behind him, someone shouted, and something crashed. "What's going on?" I demanded.

"Full-out war, as near as I can tell," he explained pleasantly. "Mia mine, what happened to your leg?"

"Some prick shot me." She waved that away like it didn't matter. "Cage and Matt?"

"I found them already." He smiled grimly. "I ducked away from the battle to rescue the lot of you and heard Cage and Matt shouting and banging on the door."

"And everyone else?"

"In the fight."

"Then that's where we should be too." Mia stepped on her bad foot and winced. It was the same leg she'd injured on Sanctuary, the one that never fully healed, even with Reed's help.

"You're in no shape to fight," I told her sharply. "Wait here and—"

Mia snorted and shoved past me, hobbling to Alexei's side. He met my gaze and shrugged, slinging his arm around her waist for support. "Let's go."

I threw up my hands in disgust. They obviously weren't going to listen to me. They never did. Sometimes Cage got through to them, but even that was a rarity. I fell into step behind them and we vanished—Mia's doing, no doubt.

The second we emerged into the storeroom, the noises of battle intensified. They seemed to come from overhead. Shouts and gunshots echoed through the cavernous space, blasts of what sounded like explosives. "Hurry," I said sharply, pushing past the other two and charging for the stairs. I reached inside and summoned a burst of speed, meaning Cage was close by. That alone calmed my racing heart at least a little.

I shot up the stairs well ahead of the others, my visibility restored, and emerged into the dark room where we'd first met Eden and Gideon. Here the battle was even louder, and the building shook. I still couldn't see much, but a flare of light illuminated a nearby window, and I charged over to it.

Outside, the street had become a battlefield. I couldn't even tell who was on whose side at the moment. People were crouched behind abandoned vehicles. A few low fires burned. Every now and then, someone popped up and lobbed what might have been a homemade explosive. I was pretty sure that would be Gideon's people. But how could I tell? Maybe Priya or Hallam had come up with something. Either way, I needed to get in this fight, and I needed to do it on the right side.

Alexei and Mia approached behind me. "Over here." Alexei indicated a door I hadn't noticed. I went through it and found myself in an open space, probably part of the store at one time. Huge glass windows, mostly broken, lined the front wall. Outside, the battle raged, although no one seemed to have noticed us yet.

Noticed us . . . I peered down. Sure enough, I was invisible again.

"What do we do?" I cried. I had to shout to be heard over the noise, which kind of kneecapped the invisibility, but who cared? We had to act. This was madness, and if it kept going, everyone was going to die. "Where's Cage? Where's Priya? Where's anyone?"

There was a *snick*, as if Alexei had drawn a blade. "One way to know for sure."

"Hang on. You can't just wander out there. Even invisible, you'll probably get hit by a stray projectile. We need to think. We need to—"

"What did I tell you about that?" Mia demanded. She popped into visibility and wiggled her fingers, producing the long dart I'd pulled from her foot. "No time to think, Kenz. Let's act."

And as much as I hated to admit it, she might be right. Maybe we did have to jump in. I couldn't stand here hoping a plan would occur to me. I opened my mouth to admit as much—

And an ear-shattering roar split the shadows outside.

The remnant obliterated.

Defeat.

Death.

Taste of blood and bile and metal.

There can be no retreat.

SIXTEEN

MY HEART PLUMMETED THROUGH MY KNEES and into my feet. I'd heard that roar before. "Oh my God," I whispered. "It's them. The aliens. They're here."

The street went silent, the alien presence piercing through the battle as only a new enemy can do.

A moment later, a familiar figure emerged from behind a nearby vehicle: Eden, her arms extended in a gesture of peace. "Cease fire!" she shouted. "Everyone get inside now! And I mean everyone, damn it!"

"Cortez," snapped Gideon. I pivoted, searching for him, not finding him. "Get behind cover. And the rest of you, ignore that order! We keep going until this is over!"

Eden blinked into the darkness. "If you want to get torn to shreds, be my guest," she said at last. She spoke clearly and calmly, her voice carrying through the night. "Anyone who feels differently, get inside and get belowground. *Now.*"

For a moment I thought nothing would happen. Then a stream of people emerged from the perimeter, maybe a half dozen of them. They ran for the building, darting past our once-again invisible forms in their rush for cover.

Eden jumped through the window. I quickly withdrew, feeling behind me until I caught Alexei's arm. He slipped his hand over my elbow and pulled me against him. We pressed to the wall. Mia breathed unsteadily on Alexei's other side; his heartbeat thrummed against me. We watched, and we waited.

Sure enough, a moment later another roar echoed through the night—this one closer and louder. A shudder went through me, and Alexei tightened his grip, pulling me closer. I twisted my nails into my own palm, clamping my jaw shut. Silence. We had to stay quiet.

Gideon emerged from the shadows and leaped over the glass. Something moved behind him—not the aliens, though, not yet. Maybe Cage, slipping closer. My heart stilled. Were all of my friends out there, waiting to be torn apart?

Eden and Gideon faced off in the center of the room. "What the hell was that?" Gideon snarled. He spun and kicked a display table. It upended, its contents scattering across the room. Something clattered to his feet, and he stomped on it, grinding it to powder beneath his boot before turning on Eden.

"You don't give the orders around here. I do. Do not ever, *ever* contradict me again."

Eden drew her small frame high and straight. "I followed you into that battle, but I'm damned if I'm going to watch the *zemdyut* kill our people to prove a point."

"We'll discuss it later. Get downstairs."

"No." She jerked her head toward the street. "We're taking the newcomers with us."

Someone moved outside again, and another roar answered the first, seeming to come from the opposite direction. Gideon spun and fired randomly, a different weapon this time, creating tiny explosions where his bullets landed. "Stay back!" he shouted. To Eden, he said, "Get inside."

"Not without them."

Gideon's face twisted into a monstrous scowl. He raised his gun and pointed it at her. "Get inside, Cortez."

Instead, she took a step forward. "Gideon. I know what you're going through. I know how much you miss them. Your wife. Your kids."

His entire body froze. "You don't know what you're talking about," he said, each word a dagger.

"I miss my daughter, too. So much. Every day." She held out a hand, advancing on him. "Gideon, please. Think back. Remember who you were. You keep saying you want everyone safe. How is getting our soldiers slaughtered by the *zemdyut* going to accomplish that? How is starving in this prison going to save us? It's time to make changes. Time to take action."

He leveled a finger in her direction. "*Changes* get people killed. And this isn't the time or place to—"

"To leave a bunch of innocent people to die? Is that the man your kids would have wanted you to become? What would Lisa have said?"

"Keep my wife's name out of your mouth!"

She took another step forward. "I know you're fighting for our people. I still believe in you, Gideon. Don't let me down. Drop that gun. Let's get these people and take them inside. Let's help them. And just maybe they can help us, too."

Gideon half hunched, the gun trembling in his hand, still aimed at Eden. His body twitched, his mouth twisted, and he resembled nothing so much as the villain from the first arc of *Robo Mecha Dream Girl 5*, Yumiko's mentor she'd worked so desperately to save. I was pretty sure I was watching the same thing play out in real time. Because Eden was not going to be able to convince Gideon. I knew it. By the tension radiating off Alexei and Mia, they did too.

So what did we do? Watch him shoot her? Try to intervene? *What?*

Just then, the decision was taken out of our hands. Gideon jerked his arm straight and targeted Eden's forehead. "If you don't move this second," he said coldly, his voice solid again, "I will kill you. Anyone else who showed me this kind of disloyalty would be dead on the floor by now. We are out of time and options. Get. Down. Stairs."

Eden spread her arms wide. "I'm not moving."

"Then I'm sorry."

But even as he tightened his grip, another monstrous howl split the night air, this one so loud and so close all of us jerked upright.

Eden recovered first.

It was over almost before I blinked. She flew across the space between them, propelled by her power, and smashed into Gideon. They fell to the floor, struggling. The gun went off, and . . .

And Eden got to her feet, staring at Gideon's unmoving form.

My jaw tensed so hard, agony splintered through my neck. I took a half step forward, but Alexei caught my arm. I couldn't see his face, but the slight tremor in his hand mirrored my own shock and dismay. What we'd just seen . . . was it self-defense? Murder? Something else altogether?

Without shifting her gaze, Eden said, "Are you here?"

I hesitated barely a second before I stepped forward. "Yes."

"Call your friends. And help me move Gideon's body. We don't have much time."

"Help you move the body?"

Eden spun on me as I relaxed my invisibility, letting her see me. "If the others find Gideon like this, if they think I killed him, that'll be the end of any hope we can work together. He still has friends down there. He saved every damn soul in this building. Now stop arguing and help me."

"I will help." Alexei stepped forward. "Call to the others."

As he and Eden dragged Gideon into the road, I ran to the window, trying not to watch their grisly task. "Cage!" I shouted. "Anyone out there! Come quick! We have to get off the streets."

A second later, Cage replied: "Kenzie?"

"Hurry up!"

"How do we know you're not being forced to speak?" demanded Priya's voice.

I threaded my hands through my hair and almost ripped it out in frustration. The aliens were getting closer; we didn't have *time* for this.

Mia shoved me aside. "You think anyone's forcing *me* to speak?" she shouted. "Get in here or don't, but those noises you hear are not something you want to encounter."

A second later, shadows emerged from the far side of the street, Cage and Matt in the forefront. Ahead of them, Alexei and Eden retreated toward the building.

And nearby, now, other shadows emerged: all-too-familiar figures slinking over the tops of buildings, and probably below as well. They were close and getting closer, moving with the speed of sighted creatures even though I knew from experience they were completely blind. My entire body went cold and heavy, and instinctively I reached for Mia, who didn't complain when I seized her hand. My tongue was so swollen I could barely speak, but at last I managed to cry, "Move! Run! There's no time, come on, now!"

Eden and Alexei sprinted into the room seconds ahead of the others. "Go," Eden ordered. She triggered some sort of light on her hip and led us through the room. I glanced over my shoulder, trying for a head count, but it was too dark and we were moving too fast; I could only hope everyone had joined us.

She led us down the stairs and through the door. I staggered to the side with Mia and Lex and took an inventory as my friends poured through behind us: Cage and Rune followed by Reed, Imani, and Jasper, with the remnants of Legion bringing up the rear. I closed my eyes and released a shuddering sigh. They were all here. We'd made it.

Eden slammed the door and wrapped a chain around the handles, securing it with a padlock. She slammed her hand against a button on the wall, and flashing red lights filled the room for a few seconds before it plunged into darkness.

I stood sandwiched between Alexei and Mia. "Nobody move," Eden whispered, and although her voice wasn't even loud enough to count as a whisper, it held every note of command. "Nobody make a sound. Nobody so much as breathe."

Maybe her words were unnecessary. The aliens were blind. They couldn't know where we'd gone. They'd think we'd vanished. They'd scout the area and go away.

And then from outside came the unmistakable scratch—faint, but present—of claws against concrete.

SEVENTEEN

I GASPED IN SPITE OF MYSELF. ALEXEI MOVED behind me, pulling me close with one big arm, pulling Mia in with the other. Neither of us resisted. It wasn't like there was anything much he could do to help us if the aliens broke through, but I appreciated the contact.

The claws on concrete grew louder and stopped. We all waited with bated breath, hoping, praying, the creatures were gone.

Suddenly the doors smashed against the chains. A startled cry—Rune, I thought—came from nearby but was quickly cut off. The doors continued to clatter again and again, and all we could do was stay still and shiver and beg the lock to hold. Alexei's grip tightened around me until it became almost painful and the muscles in his arms tightened with his own fear. I bit my tongue so hard I tasted blood. I fisted one hand in Alexei's

T-shirt and found Mia with the other. Her fingers clamped over mine and the three of us clutched one another in the shadows.

And then, as quickly as they had begun, the rattling chains stopped.

The claws receded outside.

No one moved. Alexei, Mia, and I remained in a clenched huddle. Had the aliens gone? Was it a trick? What if we made a noise and they returned?

I had no idea how long we stood like that, frozen, straining for any sound, any sign of the aliens. And then suddenly Eden sighed, low and heavy, so unexpected in the silence it made me jump. "All right," she said. "I think it's safe. Watch your eyes." She did something, and the strange lanterns along the walls flared to life again, throwing the department store into flickering relief.

Now I saw Cage, his arms around Rune, who had both hands clamped over her mouth. She met my gaze and shook her head, communicating so much in that simple gesture: frustration and terror and dismay. Behind them, Imani, Reed, and Jasper were clumped together much like me, Alexei, and Mia. Only Legion seemed relatively calm. Matt was leaning against the wall next to Priya, and Hallam was actually examining his reflection in the shiny surface of his knife, smoothing his hair back into place. "Damn dusty on this planet," he explained cheerfully when he caught us watching.

I rolled my eyes, simultaneously hating him and envying his calm under pressure. Reluctantly, I made myself abandon Alexei's sheltering grip and cross to Eden. "Thank you," I said. "Really. What you did—"

"What I did," Eden snapped, leveling a finger in my direction, "will never be discussed. Not in front of anyone. Not even just between us."

"What did you do?" Hallam asked, of course.

"She saved us," I said simply, before things became any more complicated. She'd saved us the way my own mother hadn't, and she'd betrayed everything she believed in to do it. "She let us in here before the aliens tore us apart, and she did it without knowing if we were a threat or a danger. So drop the attitude and be grateful for once, okay?"

Hallam arched an eyebrow, then flashed me a grin. "Yes ma'am," he said, and then, to Eden, "and thank you kindly."

Eden sighed, tugging on her braid. "I couldn't leave you there to die," she said at last. "Besides, I need to know more about where you came from, what you've been through. What the *zemdyut* have done in your world, and how you got here. I need information only you can provide. So it wasn't entirely altruistic."

"Information only we can provide?" Rune asked dubiously. "What is that supposed to mean?"

Eden smiled slightly. "I've known for a long time that staying here was unsustainable. Now, with Gideon gone . . ." She hesitated, a mass of emotions warring across her face before she settled into a professional mask. "Well, come with me and I'll show you."

Eden refused to let us through the curtain to where most of her people were hiding. "You'll terrify them," she said, ushering us instead into what might have been a break room. It was a long, windowless chamber lined with lockers. A table and a few scattered chairs sat in the middle. "There are families there, children who've never known anyone but the people in this bunker." She forced a weak smile. "Please. Just stay here for a bit."

"Where are you going?" Mia demanded.

"I have to check on the others, tell them about Gideon before rumors start flying. I'll be back with food and water, and we can talk."

"We won't violate your hospitality," I promised her. I didn't care what Priya, Cage, or anyone else thought of the matter. Eden had turned on her own commander for us. The least we could do was give her the space to deal with the repercussions. "We'll be right here."

"Thank you. I won't be long."

The door closed behind her and a long silence followed. I turned to face Priya, whose eyes blazed. "What happened?" she barked.

At the same time, Reed and Imani shoved past her to get to Mia. "Are you okay?" Imani demanded.

Mia sank into a chair with a sigh. "Let's just say I wouldn't object to some healing."

"Hey," snapped Priya.

Imani swiveled in her direction. "You can wait," she said. "Our friend is injured." She and Reed bent their heads over Mia's foot and examined her wound. Alexei, of course, hovered nearby, and Rune, always the first to respond to anyone's pain, drifted over to sit beside them.

Mia pulled the dart out of her pocket and examined it. "He shot me with this," she said. "If it matters."

Reed snatched it and inspected it. "Hollow. Could've held some sort of poison. How do you feel?"

Mia glared at him. "My foot hurts," she said, enunciating each word as if speaking to a child.

Reed scowled and tossed the dart onto the table. "I guess it doesn't matter. We'll heal you as best we can whether he injected you with something or not. If it was going to kill you, it'd have done it by now. Probably."

I winced on Mia's behalf, but she seemed indifferent, leaning back and closing her eyes. Meanwhile, Legion had taken up a position on the far side of the room. I went to join them, and Cage and Jasper followed. No point delaying this conversation. "How'd you find us?" I asked.

"Matt has a tracker." Hallam gave him what might have been an affectionate grin, then shoved him so hard that Matt—who was not a small guy—almost went over. "With the little tech bug's help, we knew the second you were in trouble."

"Another unrequested and unknown gift from Omnistellar," Matt said sardonically.

Priya shrugged. "Yeah, well, it served its purpose."

"We followed you here," Jasper said, more to me and Cage than to anyone else, "and promptly got attacked by those people. What's going on?"

I filled them in quickly. Cage knew most of the details, but even he seemed shocked by what had happened between Eden and Gideon aboveground.

"So we're dealing with someone who would murder her own commanding officer," said Hallam darkly. "A man who, by her own admission, saved her life on multiple occasions."

I shook my head frantically. Somehow I'd become Eden's defender. Maybe I understood her position better than the others, having been torn between my family and my friends, my corporation and the dawning truth. Maybe I saw in her what my own mother could have been, ready to turn on an unjust system to protect the innocent. Regardless, I couldn't let them vilify her. "He didn't leave her any other choice. He was going to kill her. I don't know what Gideon used to be, but this life destroyed him." I looked to Cage for help. It was so hard to explain what I'd seen in Gideon with words.

"The guy shot Mia without a second's hesitation," Cage said, nodding. "He would have happily killed us all. The woman, Eden, I didn't get to talk to her as much as Mia and Kenzie did. But I trust Kenzie. If she says Eden did what had to be done, then I believe her."

Unbidden, a smile touched my lips, and I found his hand and threaded our fingers together. His answering squeeze told me everything I needed to know.

But the others weren't ready to back me so easily. "How about the aliens showing up?" Jasper snapped. "Can we talk about that for a second? How far did you teleport us, Kenzie?"

I glared at him. "How the hell should I know? You guys were the ones screaming at me to save you when the creatures attacked! I didn't have time to chart a path."

"Everyone calm down," Cage broke in. "Jasper, I know you're worried about your family, but don't take it out on Kenzie."

Jasper faltered, then looked away. "Yeah," he muttered. "Sorry, Kenz. I just keep thinking about them on Mars with that alien ship overhead, you know?"

"All the more reason we need to get off this planet as soon as possible," said Priya grimly. "We have no idea what's happening on Earth and no way to help from here. Kenzie, do you think there's any way Eden can get us home?"

I shrugged. "I didn't see much of their operation, but I got the sense it was pretty low-tech. They're powered, like us. That might mean something. If someone else has the ability to teleport, maybe I could borrow it again. But there's absolutely no guarantee

I'll take us home." I frowned, considering what we'd seen so far. "I mean, assuming we're as far from home as we think. Like we said, this planet is uncannily similar to Earth. I can't help but wonder if we're closer than we think." An idea played at the corner of my mind. There was Rune's theory, that we were on a planet with a species who had evolved so similarly to us that we'd somehow connected and mirrored each other in our development. That no longer seemed impossible, not after all I'd seen.

But weren't there other possibilities? For example, what if this race had been watching us, aware of us? Or what if we were aware of them? I wouldn't put anything past Omnistellar anymore. Hell, this could be some sort of human settlement, for all I knew. Regardless, there had to be an explanation for the parallels between this world and our own.

A long silence stretched between us. On the other side of the room, Imani and Reed seemed to be arguing about the best way to finish with Mia's foot, and Alexei and Rune were physically restraining Mia herself from hopping up and being done with the whole thing. "We'd better come to some sort of decision about what to do next," I said, pushing my reflections on the planet aside for the time being. "Eden's organized. And let's be honest. We're not. We're a group of people who barely know each other, half of who were enemies until a few days ago. We can't work together to save our lives."

Cage stroked his chin reflectively. "Kenzie, do you trust Eden?"

"Yes," I replied without hesitation. "People change. I know that better than anyone." If Cage could trust me so completely, offer me a total second chance, I could do the same for someone else.

He smiled at me, but doubt lurked in his eyes. Still, he nodded. "Okay," he said. "If Kenzie says we trust Eden, I'm in."

Matt shrugged. "I don't see that we have much choice," he pointed out. "We're kind of at her mercy here. And if the aliens are on this planet . . ." A shudder went through him. "You saw what they can do," he said to Hallam and Priya. "We don't stand a chance against them alone."

Priya leaned against the wall. "That's all well and good, but we're not looking to *fight* them."

"But Eden said we could help her," Jasper persisted. "What do you think she meant by that?"

Priya scowled. "I don't know, and I don't care. I have family too, Jasper. I'm just as worried as you are. And no matter what it takes, I am going to find my way back home."

Something scraped behind us. We pivoted to find Eden standing in the doorway, her arms folded across her chest. Her eyes were tired, but she was smiling. "What if," she said, "I had a way for you to do both?"

EIGHTEEN

"TO DO BOTH," I SAID DOUBTFULLY. "TO HELP you *and* find our way home?"

"Yes." Eden entered the room. She left the door open behind her, and I doubted it was an accident. The message was clear. We weren't prisoners. If we wanted to leave, we could go . . . back aboveground, to where the aliens lurked, waiting to tear us apart.

A shudder went through me unbidden, and Cage slid his hand up my arm, soothing my fears. "And if we refuse whatever you have planned?" he asked.

Eden shrugged. "Then I suggest you wait awhile for the area to clear, and you can be on your way. In the meantime, would you like to hear me out?"

"Yes," I said. I wasn't about to let anyone else answer. The fact was, we were stranded on this planet. The food and water would only last so long, and with the aliens in the area, I didn't think our apartment building would keep us safe much longer. We needed Eden's help. And I didn't trust the others to accept it.

Sure enough, I got a few glares, mostly from Hallam and Mia, who obviously didn't appreciate me speaking on their behalf. But they also didn't argue, which I took to mean they knew I was right. Besides, we owed Eden to at least hear her out. I remembered how the others had regarded me when they saw me as the enemy—suspiciously, with hatred blinding them. I wouldn't do the same to her.

"If you don't mind," said Eden, "it's easier to show you some of this than to explain it. Wendell? Wendell, don't be afraid. Come in."

A young boy, maybe five or six, clutching a ratty teddy bear, shuffled into the room. He was clinging to the hand of an older woman, possibly his grandmother. They both wore ragged clothes, and their faces were smeared with dirt and exhaustion. "Wendell has some psychic abilities," Eden explained. She scooped him into her arms and bumped noses with him, and the boy chuckled. "He's sort of a conduit. He can help me show you what happened."

"Will it hurt him?" Imani's voice held a low rumble of fire.

Eden shook her head. "Not a bit. He won't even know what I'm showing you. I just need to be in contact with him to make it work. His abilities are entirely passive. Otherwise, I wouldn't use them. I would never expose a child to some of the things I'm about to show you."

The rest of us exchanged glances, and then, since no one else seemed ready to commit, I nodded. "Okay," I said. "What do you need us to do?"

Eden had everyone sit around the room. Priya, Hallam, Mia, and Alexei took the four chairs, and the rest of us assumed positions on the floor, leaning against the lockers. I wound up with Cage on one side and Jasper on the other. Jasper was frowning, tugging on his hair, seeming more agitated than usual. "You okay?" I whispered.

"Don't much like people in my head, that's all."

I shivered. I'd only experienced a psychic intrusion once before, and I hadn't enjoyed it at all. But this was different. "This is information," I told him, as much to reassure myself as anything. "And right now, information is power. The more we can get, the faster, the better."

He nodded. "Yeah, that's why I'm not fighting it. Doesn't mean I have to like it."

Eden settled herself on the floor, cross-legged, Wendell in her lap clutching his bear. His grandmother, if that was what she was, hovered in the doorway. "Close your eyes," Eden told us. "And try to relax."

"Will you be able to read our thoughts?" Mia demanded sharply.

Eden sighed. "No. It works one way. You're entirely safe. Is there anything else, or can we get started?"

From Cage's other side, Rune made a sound. I leaned

around him to raise an eyebrow at her, but she shook her head, frowning, her lower lip working between her teeth.

"All right," said Eden before I pressed further. "Then here we go."

I closed my eyes, and for a moment, nothing happened. And then, all at once, a wave of dizziness overtook me. My eyes flew open, and I was standing on a crowded city street. People surrounded me—normal people like you'd see in any city on Earth—going about their business, enjoying what seemed like a summer day. "This was the city of Orrin before the attack," Eden announced. I spun to find her walking toward me dressed in army fatigues, her dark hair glistening in the sun. I checked around but didn't see any of my friends, only her. "It was a normal city in a hot area of the continent. Dry. A desert even then, but with irrigation and the like, we did all right. I lived here. I was stationed at a nearby base with . . ." She swallowed hard. "With my family. So was Gideon. We were in different sections of the military, but I knew him enough to say hello when we passed."

All at once the sky turned dark. Someone screamed. In the distance, sirens went off, and shots rang out. "The *zemdyut* had attacked once or twice before," Eden continued conversationally. "We first learned of them a few hundred years ago when they dropped the devices that transformed our DNA. Slowly but surely, each subsequent generation developed more and more powers until it was almost impossible to find someone without an ability. We didn't mind much. There was some initial fear and resistance, but the abilities were useful, and as more and more people developed them, they just became a part of life."

The sky shimmered overhead and formed into a familiar, hideous visage, an alien creature with milky-white eyes. I shuddered, clamping my hands into fists so hard my nails sank into my flesh. I'd seen the aliens before, of course. Faced them down. Stolen their ship, for God's sake. But not this big, not this vivid.

It wasn't real, though, and Eden continued to narrate. "The creatures appeared rarely at first, striking in quick raids, taking our people. We didn't know why, and we never seemed to be able to predict when they'd appear or fight against them. We began work on planetary defenses, trying to anticipate their arrival. And they, for their part, visited more frequently. Soon they were coming every few years, harvesting in the millions, tearing us apart. Planetary defense became a military focus. *The* military focus. We poured all of our time and energy into researching space travel, figuring out who the creatures were and where they'd come from. But before we could finish, they returned—this time for good."

The world shifted, like someone stirring coloring into a glass of water, and when it resettled, I was standing on the same street in a state of chaos. Fires raged unchecked. A few people huddled in alleys, sobbing or shouting for their families.

And through the streets prowled the aliens. Dozens of them,

hundreds even, when I'd never seen more than a few together at a time. The creatures scaled buildings; they preyed on anyone in their path with relentless determination. And still Eden stood quietly in their midst. "This wasn't a harvest," she said. "It was a massacre. The aliens dragged the bodies underground, and we never saw them again, but it quickly became evident that this time, they'd come for only one reason: to kill anyone left over. Our scientists theorized they'd harvested anyone with compatible DNA, and they were doing a sweep of the remainder, wiping us off the planet, the last step in claiming our territory. And that's pretty much what they did. It was only through the quick thinking of a few soldiers that some of us survived."

In the streets, a man I recognized as a younger version of Gideon crept onto the scene, a few soldiers in tow. While others attacked the aliens with makeshift weapons, he and his crew slipped past them, gathering the injured, anyone they passed. They came to a pause in front of a large building plastered with yellow sale banners, and Gideon nodded his head, saying something to the woman beside him.

An alien lunged from the rooftop. Gideon moved so fast I barely saw him. He snatched the boy the alien had targeted, tossed him aside, pivoted, and leaped onto the creature's back. It threw its head back and howled, and Gideon's arm flashed.

Then Gideon was on the ground, coated in alien slime, and the creature was gurgling on its own blood. Gideon had shoved a knife right down its throat.

I glanced to his face and saw the same pale eyes, but this time they reflected an instant of fear before settling into the professional mask I'd seen Legion wear so often. He wiped his hand over his face and gestured for the others to follow him. They did, ducking under the banners and into the building.

The scene shifted again. Now I was looking at the city I recognized, the one I'd explored the day before. It was quiet and deserted, but closer examination showed the buildings weren't in quite the state of decay they were now. This was some time after the alien attack, but not so long as I'd initially thought. "We survived," said Eden grimly, and for the first time emotion entered her voice. "We gathered everyone we found, anyone the *zemdyut* missed in their decimation, and we collected them in the basement of a warehouse store. Gideon led us in fortifying the building. We blocked entranceways. We soundproofed. We created a warning system to alert people if the creatures approached. We cobbled together a rudimentary electrical system using people's abilities. But we couldn't rebuild. For one thing, we never knew when the *zemdyut* would appear. It was clear they hadn't left, and we suspected they were somewhere in the desert."

Then the planet suddenly flew away beneath my feet, setting my stomach lurching and reminding me of antigrav drills back at Omnistellar camps. I struggled to steady myself, but my feet hadn't actually moved. The world had just withdrawn, giving me a bird's-eye view of the city surrounded by desert.

"We think there's a group of the creatures living here, beneath the ground." Eden was standing beside me. When she gestured, a flashing red light appeared in the desert, some distance from the city. "We've managed to send a few scouts, and when they returned—*if* they returned—they reported seeing the creatures slip beneath the surface.

"After a while, things started to return to . . . not normal, but more of an equilibrium. We'd go days without seeing the *zemdyut*. Weeks, even. When they did return, they usually stuck to the fringes of the city. Those areas had always been sparsely populated and, as I'm sure you noticed, weren't as touched in the attacks." The area surrounding the city, the outskirts, glowed yellow. "That's why there were still supplies there. We left them for last, for when we got desperate. It was safer to raid the city center. It's only in the last few months we've resorted to risking the outskirts. We've lost a few people. The *zemdyut* are aware of us now, if they weren't before." She hesitated a moment, inspecting the map spread out below us. "That's why Gideon sent me to steal your supplies. I know what you must think of him, but . . . he was a good man. He took care of us all. He'd gotten scared over the last few years, paranoid he'd get everyone killed. Frustrated with life underground. Hell, we're all there. Gideon simply felt it more. And yet . . . he was too scared to see what needed to be done. Convinced that if we moved a muscle, the *zemdyut* would somehow sense us, that they'd come after us, destroy us. He was willing to imprison everyone in this building for their entire lives as we slowly ran out of supplies, all in the name of *security*."

A trace of bitterness had entered her voice, and in that moment I read her frustration as the commanding officer she'd once regarded with something like reverence deteriorated into a shell of his former self, brushing off her every attempt to make him see the obvious. In a way it was almost like my view of my parents: the blinders falling away, the caring people they'd once been still there but buried under layers of betrayal and confusion. When I'd realized the truth about Omnistellar, I'd been left with no choice but to turn my back on the corporation. I suspected Eden found herself in the same position.

She shook off the emotion and spread her arms. "I'm telling you this for a few reasons. First of all, I want you to understand who we are, where we're coming from. Second, I need you to understand how desperate our situation is—and if you're here, yours is too. Our supplies have almost vanished. Our only hope to find more outside of the city, and that's impossible. The desert is a deathtrap." She smiled. "But it's not all doom and gloom. Because if you help us, well, I just might have a way to help you in return."

NINETEEN

THE SIMULATION LURCHED, AND I JERKED, MY eyes flying open again. I was sitting on the floor of the break room in between Cage and Jasper, both of whom were gasping for air.

Priya shot to her feet, the chair falling over behind her. "What the hell was that?" she growled.

Eden smoothed her hand over Wendell's head. "Easy," she admonished Priya. To Wendell, she said, "Thanks, bud. You can go now. I'll make sure you get something special to eat tonight, okay?"

The boy raised his eyes, and for the first time he spoke, his voice a raspy whisper. "Chocolate?"

Eden laughed and ruffled his hair. "I think I can manage that. Don't tell anyone else, though." She passed him off to his caretaker with a nod and, as they vacated the room, closed the door behind them. Only then did she return her attention to us. "He's the reason I can't give up," she said quietly. "Him, and all the other people living here. Especially the children. They deserve more than this."

I staggered to my feet. Cage and Jasper followed suit and a moment later we were all standing, grouped in a loose circle around the table. "You said you could help us if we helped you," I said slowly. "What exactly did you have in mind?"

Eden folded her arms across her chest and analyzed each of us in turn. She wasn't a tall woman, but she had presence. As she leveled her gaze across the room, not even Mia interrupted her. "We can't go on like this," she said. "It's time we took the fight to the aliens. And with your help, I know where to start."

A babble of protest erupted, ranging from a semihysterical laugh from Reed to a drawn knife from Hallam. I only stared at Eden, trying to anticipate what was going on behind those dark eyes. She hadn't spoken accidentally. She'd known the reaction she would provoke, and she was waiting for it to die down. That meant she had something big to offer. "What did you have in mind?"

Eden braced her fists against the table, raking her eyes over us. "We've tried to fight the *zemdyut* before," she said. "There are military facilities near here. Even a missile-storage range not too far away. We tried to get there, tried to blow them up. But we didn't have the manpower or the technology to move the missiles, and now we don't have enough soldiers left to try again. We need your help because we need information. I mean, we don't even know why the creatures are still here, let alone why they want us dead."

"And how are we supposed to help with that?"

"You mentioned that one of you had the power to interact with computers, with technology. Who is it?"

I winced. The last thing I wanted to do was expose Rune to some half-formed plan. But before I could speak, Rune stepped forward, brushing Cage's hand away when he tried to restrain her. "That's me," she said. There was a calm, almost powerful note in her voice, a confidence that hadn't been there a few weeks ago.

Eden nodded. "You might save us all," she said, speaking directly to Rune. "I told you we thought the creatures were hiding in the desert, in an abandoned military base. The truth is, I know it. I know because Gideon and I tried to raid it once for supplies. We barely escaped with our lives, but before we did, we saw . . . things. Some kind of bizarre technology superimposed over our own. The creatures were taking over the facility entirely, creating their own base. Of course, even if we could get in there, we wouldn't have a hope of understanding the tech. But you . . . you might."

"Let me get this straight," said Priya dryly. "You want us to march into this alien hideout—a hideout we've never seen, where you and your pal Gideon almost died—infested with these creatures. Hundreds of them. Potentially thousands. And then you want Rune to mine the alien computers for information. Does that sum things up?"

"Oh, it gets worse," Eden replied pleasantly. "Sit down and I'll show you."

Matt and Hallam looked to Priya, and everyone else looked to Cage and me. We looked to each other. But there weren't any easy answers. "Let's hear what she has to say," Cage said at last, arching an eyebrow to see if he had my agreement. I gave him a fractional nod. "No harm in that, right?"

I expected Priya to argue, if only on principle. But she sank into her chair and slowly so did the others. Those of us along the back wall remained standing. Without comment, Eden pulled something out of her pocket and slapped it onto the table. It resembled a half dome, but then she pressed a button and a shape emerged.

Rune sucked in her breath. "It's a holoprojector," she said. "Way nicer than any I've ever seen, though. How's it still running?"

"Rechargeable batteries," Eden explained. "We have someone who can power them." She frowned. "It was meant to be a temporary measure, but at this point we're almost totally dependent on him. That's another reason I need to find new solutions." She pressed a second button, and the light billowing from the dome took on a familiar shape: one of the aliens we'd seen on Sanctuary.

It wasn't my first chance to examine one in detail. I'd seen them sleeping in the dark. But somehow the holographic image removed some of the threat, and I took a step closer, allowing my curiosity to drive me.

The creature was precisely what I remembered from Sanctuary: somewhat reptilian, with a long tail and milky-white, unseeing eyes. Its fangs curved over its bottom lip, and even its image seemed to twitch with unearthly intelligence. "We call these harvesters," Eden announced. "They're the first *zemdyut* we encountered. I gather you've run into them too. They're the least dangerous of the lot, because they're mostly aiming to incapacitate."

"Wait," said Alexei. "*Least* dangerous . . . you mean there are other types?"

"We thought there might be," I reminded him. "On Obsidian. The aliens seemed different, somehow."

Eden nodded and pressed against the dome. The hologram shifted into another form, similar to the first. But now the differences stood out more starkly than on Obsidian. There, I'd been working from memory; now, having just seen the harvesters, I realized these aliens were taller, more sinewy. They had longer, sharper claws and more teeth. "These are hunters," said Eden. "They have a much more singular purpose: to seek, to kill, and to destroy. They're the ones who decimated our world. They tear through cities like *tranol*—predatory fish," she added, catching our confused expressions. I nodded, committing the word to memory. "They leave nothing behind but destruction."

"We saw these," said Imani. She drew closer to the table, a fascinated expression on her face. "On Obsidian. And on the ship."

"Hard to forget that face," Hallam agreed in his slow drawl.

"Please tell me that's the end of it." There was an edge to Cage's voice, a tension radiating off him, and anxiety stirred in my stomach.

Because the look in Eden's eyes told us no, that wasn't the end of it.

"There's one more type," she said. "We don't see it very often, but when we do, well . . . I'm going to leave the hunter active so you have a size comparison."

She hit a button, and a collective gasp went up around the room.

The . . . *thing* that appeared was easily three times the height of the hunter, which was already a good five feet tall, even hunched over with its spine bent. It appeared less reptilian than its compatriots and more human, although it was still a pretty far cry from anything I'd try to have a conversation with. But its skull seemed more mammalian, its claws extended from some sort of fingers, and its eyes held an eerie intelligence.

"If a Sasquatch had a baby with a T. rex," said Reed dryly, "this thing is what you'd get."

Jasper snorted. No one else responded, not even Hallam. We were too busy gawking in horrified fascination at the hologram dominating the room.

"That . . ." I swallowed. "Where did it come from?"

Eden shrugged. She stepped back and studied the hologram appraisingly, and I got the sense it wasn't the first time she'd stood and stared at the thing. Hardening herself to the horror of it, maybe? Or hoping to find a weakness? "It appeared after the initial attack," she said. "For all I know, it's the only one of its kind. To be honest, I've only ever seen it twice. The first time was in the aftermath of the city's destruction, when we were herding the survivors into the store. Suddenly this thing just . . . *appeared*. I mean, it must have come from somewhere, but for something so big it was intensely silent. And did you notice its eyes?"

"Yeah," I said quietly.

Milky-white cataracts blinded the aliens. It was our only advantage over them, the only reason we'd ever escaped with our lives.

But this creature's eyes peered ahead with dark, menacing intelligence.

"They can see," Rune whispered, a tremor in her voice. "Oh my God, they can see."

"It came straight for us." Eden tugged on her braid, then tossed it behind her as if throwing it away. "Gideon and I and a few other soldiers led it on a chase to give the others time to escape, then dove into a sewage drain it couldn't fit through. Within seconds, it sent hunters after us, but by then we'd managed to hide. We spent a whole night in that damn sewer. By the time we emerged, we were filthy and disgusting . . . but we were alive. The creature had vanished and we didn't see it again for two years. Then we were out scouting one day and again it just . . . appeared. This time we were able to hide before it spotted us. I don't know what it was doing, but it wasn't rampaging the way the hunters do. It was *searching* for something. Us, maybe. I don't know. It pulled buildings apart like it was cracking eggs."

"Why did it leave?" Matt leaned back, stroking his chin.

Eden shrugged. "Hell if I know. Eventually we snuck back to the store, went belowground, turned off the lights, and barred the doors. We didn't dare move for days. When hunger drove us to the surface, the creature was gone. We've never seen it again."

Hope flickered in Matt's eyes. "Maybe it, I don't know . . . went somewhere else. Died, even."

"That would be nice, wouldn't it?" Eden continued to glare at the creature. "We call this one Karoch."

"What does it mean?" I asked.

"It's from a story we have about a giant who ravaged the towns around a famous mountain. A kids' story, but . . . the name fit."

"And you don't know where this thing is?" Priya shook her head in disbelief. "Which means it's probably hiding out with the other aliens. Lady, I've been doing this job for a long time. No one's ever accused me of being a coward. But this?" She shook her head and turned to me and Cage. "We aren't doing this. If you kids want to take it on, you're on your own."

"Wait a second," said Matt.

Priya spun on him. "Shut your mouth, boy. You might be a dumbass kid, but you're still part of my crew, and I'm damned if I'll let you get yourself killed by that thing. These people abandoned you for dead. Remember that."

Matt scowled. "That's not exactly what happened." Our eyes met briefly, and we both looked away. "And it's not the point. Eden said she could help us if we helped her. Don't you think we should at least hear what she has in mind?"

Priya hesitated, and it was clear she *had* forgotten—not that you could blame her with the specter of Karoch still looming over us like an anime movie mech.

As one, we turned to Eden, who seemed to be waiting for precisely such a moment. "I need that intel. I need to know what the *zemdyut* have planned, why they're still in this . . . well, why they're still here. You're the only ones who might be able to help me get the information I need. And if you do . . ." She reached out and squeezed the sides of the dome. Karoch and the hunter vanished, replaced by a small, sleek model of a spaceship, rotating lazily in place. "I can help you get home."

The planet has shifted.

The tides have turned.

The people's arrival has shattered barriers, prickling its sensitive awareness, drawing its attention and forcing a split.

With a scream they coalesce.

Many.

One.

Threats draw near.

Force and power.

Shift.

TWENTY

I LURCHED FORWARD, GRABBING THE EDGES of the table and staring at the ship. It was a little different from ships I'd seen before, its design fundamentally un-Omnistellar. "Reed?" I asked.

Reed, his obsession with any form of transportation already apparent, leaned forward. "I mean, it's only a hologram," he said doubtfully, reaching out as if to touch it. "But it looks sturdy enough." He turned eager eyes to Eden. "What's its range?"

A smile touched her lips. "Almost unlimited. It's the fastest, sleekest ship ever built."

"Then why the hell haven't you used it?" Mia snapped, joining us in examining the model, Alexei—as always—by her side.

"Because it fits ten people at most, and I have five times that to worry about. Because I have nowhere to go. Because this is my planet, damn it, and I'm not giving it up without a fight."

Her voice cracked, and she closed her eyes, visibly composing herself. "My daughter died in the first attack," she said quietly. "Her body is in the desert. I went searching and found her, and I buried her. I'm not leaving her. And I'm not leaving my planet to those things."

We continued to stare at the ship. I found Cage's hand. He squeezed my fingers. "Where would we go?" he wondered out loud. "How would we get home?"

Eden nodded. "I was wondering when you'd ask. And there, at least, I have good news for you. I know your planet, and you aren't as far from home as you think. Our planet is shielded. Our early scientists decided they didn't want to deal with alien attacks, and they created a planetary phase distortion, something to block us from most scanners. You have to be right on top of us before you know we're here."

"Then how did the aliens find you?" Rune asked. Her head was cocked, ready as always to absorb new information, new technology.

Eden blinked as if the question caught her off guard, but she must have considered it before. Maybe it paled in comparison with the threat of the aliens themselves. "We don't know," she said at last. "We don't know what planet they came from. But we know where yours is, and it's not far. You could get there in a few weeks."

"Wait." I clutched my head with my hands, my brain spiraling with the new information. For a split second, I missed

Gideon—or at least his truth-sensing power. "You're telling me we aren't far from Earth? That we have a chance to get home? Then why didn't you contact us when the creatures first attacked? Why didn't you call for help? For God's sake, why didn't you *warn* us?"

"We didn't know about you at first," Eden replied. "And by the time we did, we were too busy trying to defend ourselves to start initiating interspecies contact."

"Bullshit," Priya snapped. "You were scared. Desperate. If you knew there were other people out there, people so similar to you, with a society almost identical, why wouldn't you at least try to call for help?"

Eden scowled. "Because we'd watched you in the intervening centuries. Watched your society develop. Watched your corporations take over."

"Watched us?" snapped Priya. "How?"

Eden shrugged as if the details didn't matter. "You aren't the only ones with technology. Probes. Spies. I'm not even sure. It wasn't my business to know. But what I did know, what everyone knew, was that if we called for help, we'd be corporate slaves inside of a generation. Besides, we knew your technology. We'd copied some of it. It wasn't enough to fight off the *zemdyut*, not by a long shot."

I lowered my gaze. The corporate fear rang true. And if Eden's people, Liam's, had been observing us, that explained a lot of the similarities. Especially if they were nearer to us than we'd initially realized. If I was going to extend Eden the trust I wished had been extended to me, well, I had to commit. "Liam didn't seem to know any of this," I said, half to myself.

"It wasn't common knowledge. We didn't need people trying to take matters into their own hands. And after a few decades of the *zemdyut*, secrecy just became a way of life for our governments, our military. No one told the people more than they needed to know." Eden sighed. "I'm not saying we were right. Just that we were scared. We didn't want a corporate takeover of our own planet in exchange for getting rid of the monsters attacking us, and we were overconfident in our own abilities. By the time we realized there was no hope, it was too late. But it's not too late for you." She scrutinized each of us in turn. "It's not a guarantee. But it's something. It's hope. And if you don't accept it, you're going to die on this planet, either when we run out of supplies, which is going to happen in the next three to four months, or when the aliens tear you to shreds. Regardless, you won't have long."

Stunned silence met her words. It wasn't that what she was saying was particularly surprising. It was just the first time it had been put to us so bleakly.

"All right," I said at last, when it became apparent no one else was going to. I'd found myself in the position of de facto leader before, and I was getting more comfortable with it. "I think we need to talk about this. Alone, if you don't mind."

"Of course." Eden inclined her head. "What I'm asking you to do isn't easy. And I wouldn't be asking if there were any other way. But it's this or watch my people die. If you won't go in with us, I'll have to take the risk myself. I'm not sure what I could make of *zemdyut* technology, but I'm out of options." She leveled a finger in my direction. "And before I do, I'll lock that spaceship down. You don't help me, don't expect me to help you. Sorry, but that's the way of it."

"We understand," said Mia, surprising me. "It's an exchange, and you're not giving anything away for free. Now get out so we can talk." Her words were taut with annoyance, but there was no real anger in her voice. And this probably *was* something Mia understood. Quid pro quo. In her world, it made sense.

And, I supposed, it did in mine, too.

Eden left without another word and, as if by unspoken consent, the rest of us surrounded the large table. No chairs remained, so we stood or sat on the table itself. The way we arranged ourselves wound up being fairly symbolic: Priya and Hallam at one end, Cage and I at the other, with the rest of our people spread between us. Rune, Mia, Jasper, and Alexei fixed themselves firmly on our side of the table, while Imani, Matt, and Reed took a more neutral position.

We all focused on the table for a while, as if hoping it would provide some answers. "This is crazy," said Hallam at last. "Did you guys see that thing?" He scowled at Priya. "Cybernetic implants or not, it'd tear us to shreds."

She nodded. "Maybe. I wonder what sort of weaponry these people have?"

Hallam snorted. "You're not seriously considering this."

Priya shrugged wearily and, to my surprise, turned to me. "What do you think?"

For once, I considered my response. Everyone was looking at me, the weight of their gazes a leaden burden. I rolled my thoughts on my tongue before I replied, "I don't think we have much of a choice. It's like Eden said: we either take a chance helping them or die here alone. Don't get me wrong: I'm not super excited about the idea of walking into an alien stronghold." A shudder went through me and, beneath the table where no one could see, Cage took my hand. "I'd kind of hoped never to see another alien ever again. But since those damned things seem determined to follow us wherever we go, I'd rather get the drop on them than wait for them to find us."

"Agreed," said Mia almost immediately. "It's long past time we took the fight to these bastards."

Alexei frowned and folded his arms over his chest, his biceps bulging against his too-small shirt. "Maybe, but there's something here I don't like," he said. "Something about Eden. Or perhaps simply the planet."

"Can you be more specific?" Cage asked him. Something passed between the two boys. They'd been roommates on Sanctuary, and they still sometimes managed to speak without words. I bit off an angry retort. Alexei had suspected me when

I first started sympathizing with the prisoners. I couldn't expect him to just take Eden at face value.

"No," Alexei admitted at last. "It's just a feeling."

"I'll tell you my feeling," Imani broke in with what, for her, was surprising intensity. "I've watched these creatures destroy hundreds of people. Take lives for no reason. They've altered our DNA and transformed us into weaker versions of them. I am sick and tired of sitting around praying they don't attack me. I'm with Mia. It's time to take the fight to them."

Cage sighed. "The goal here is not to fight aliens. In fact, the goal is to avoid that at every cost. If you don't realize that, it's not safe to take you into the bunker."

Imani scowled at him. "The *metaphorical* fight. All I'm saying is, I'm sick of doing nothing."

"You're not alone on that." He propped his chin on his hands. "But we're forgetting something. This whole plan rests on Rune's ability." He met his sister's eyes across me. "You've been quiet, *meimei*."

She shrugged, shifting against the table. "I'm not a fighter," she said at last in her gentle way. "Not like you. I'm no stranger to dangerous situations, but I'm used to sneaking in and out, working behind the scenes. I think I can handle the alien tech, but I'm scared of what we might encounter."

"You won't encounter anything," Cage said sharply. "You'll play the same role you always do and—"

Rune spun on him, her sheer fury stopping him short.

His hand tensed against mine. "*But*," Rune continued as if her twin had never cut her off, "there comes a time when you have to stand up for yourself. These aliens have been pushing us around, pushing everyone around, for way too long. So no matter how much it scares me, I'm in."

Cage blinked, startled by her vehemence. "Rune, I—"

"I don't always need you to keep me safe, Cage. Sometimes, you need me." She straightened her spine, and I caught Matt hiding a smile. "This is the only way I can help all of you. Protect all of you. If it's anyone's decision, it should be mine, and I'm doing it. With or without the rest of you, I'm doing it." Her eyes flashed a challenge, although there was humor there too. "What are you going to do to stop me?"

Cage gaped at her in silence. I only just stopped myself from joining him. Rune stood ramrod straight, fire flashing in her eyes, her tiny features angled and sharp. She looked like a warrior queen geared for battle, not the quiet, disarming tech mouse who'd wormed past my defenses on Sanctuary.

Jasper braced his hands on the table. "We won't let you go in alone," he assured her. "And we won't try to stop you. My family helped us on Mars, and we abandoned them—first to Omnistellar, then to the aliens circling the planet. So whatever it takes to get us back home, I'm in."

Matt sighed. "If everyone else is in, I'll go too," he said quietly. "I was supposed to die on Sanctuary, after all. If I'm living on borrowed time, I guess I have to repay it eventually."

Reed raised his hand. "Can I say something, or is this decided?"

"Go ahead," Priya invited before Cage could speak. Only a day or two ago, that would have set the muscles in his jaw jumping. When I looked at him now, though, he was only regarding Reed thoughtfully. I allowed myself a small smile. Rune wasn't the only one growing and changing.

Reed slammed his hands onto the table, making everyone jump. "You're all a little too excited about this. Have you missed the part with the giant *alien monster beast*? Or how these things destroyed an entire planet? This monster's name is Karoch, not Goliath, and we don't have any slingshots anyway. If we go in there, we'll die."

"If we stay here, we'll die," Rune pointed out gently.

Reed nodded. "Yeah, I know. I'm not so thrilled about that, either. But if it's a choice between dying on my own terms and being eaten by a giant space monster, I know which way I'm leaning."

"I hate to say it, but I'm with the kid." Hallam waved his hand in Reed's general direction but addressed his comment to Priya. "Captain, you know I'm always in for a fight. But this will probably be a slaughter. And I can think of far less painful ways to die."

The silence stretched again. "Cage?" I said at last. "You haven't weighed in."

Cage frowned. "I thought it was obvious. Rune said it: she's going in no matter what, so I'm going with her." A touch of his usual grin graced his lips. "Besides, when have you ever known me to sit around when there's a chance of escape? Hell, if I was willing to take on Sanctuary, an alien stronghold should be no problem."

A ripple of relieved laughter went around the table, and I smiled. I'd known Cage would be on board. He'd been one of the first to extend me the benefit of the doubt on Sanctuary. Of course he would do the same for Eden.

Priya ran a hand over her hair. "Hallam, I take your point. And you," she added, nodding to Alexei. "I agree. There's something off about Eden and this whole setup. But I don't see much of a choice. If it's die fighting or die huddled in hiding, I'll die on my feet every time."

Hallam shrugged. "You're the boss, lady. You know my opinion, but I'll follow orders." He gave her a sideways glance. "Just make sure you're not letting personal feelings get in the way, yeah?"

"My *personal feelings*," Priya growled, "have never influenced my orders, Hallam. And if you don't believe that—"

"Easy," said Hallam, his voice uncharacteristically gentle. "I didn't mean offense. I just know how bad you must want to get home to your family. I'm on your side. Legion for always."

Priya nodded, her hand shaking slightly as she brought her fist down by her side. What had her so riled up? But before I could consider it further, Alexei sighed heavily. "I still think this is a bad idea," he said, "but I won't let you walk into danger without me."

Every eye turned to Reed.

He scowled at us. "You're all fools."

"So we've been told," Cage agreed solemnly. "What do you say? We can probably make a case for you to stay behind. You're one of our healers, after all. We might need you on the outside more than in the bunker."

"And have you all return covered in glory while I have to tell my moms that I hid in the background?" Reed threw his hands up in disgust. "Fine. I'll die with you in an alien hideout. Are you happy now?"

I didn't think anyone was, but we were at least in agreement. For the first time ever, we were all on the same page, functioning as a single team, Legion and Sanctuary and Omnistellar as one.

And really, if we'd achieved that miracle, maybe one more wasn't too much to hope for.

TWENTY-ONE

WE FOUND EDEN OUTSIDE THE BREAK ROOM, far enough away to show she hadn't been listening—or that if she had, she'd hightailed it out of the area when she heard us coming. She didn't seem particularly surprised by our decision, but I guessed it was inevitable. Eden was right: she held our only hope of escaping this planet. "But before we do anything," Priya warned her, "I want more information on this spaceship and this military base. If you die in the attack, I don't want to get stuck here."

Eden nodded. "You can trust me," she said. "As long as I can trust you."

Priya regarded her appraisingly. "We'll see about that."

"When do we do this?" I asked, shifting nervously. It had seemed much easier to talk about storming the aliens in the security of the briefing room with a strong wall at my back and Cage holding my hand, my friends surrounding me. All of our brave words paled here in the shifting shadows of the deserted store.

"Soon. Tomorrow, unless you have objections. Until then, I'd like to invite you to stay in our barracks. It's more secure than your apartment building, and besides . . ." A slight smile touched her lips. "We stole most of your supplies."

Cage leaned against the wall, arms folded over his chest. "I thought you didn't want us to terrify your families."

"They've had time to prepare. And I'm sure Talia—the lady you saw earlier—has filled everyone in by now anyway. Gossip spreads fast in a place like this." She examined each of us in turn. "I will have to insist on secrecy, though. You can't tell anyone what we're planning."

"You don't think they'd trust a bunch of strangers to break into the alien facility and report back with accurate information?" Priya raised an eyebrow. "Which raises an interesting question. How do *you* know you can trust *us*?"

Eden shrugged. "I haven't got a choice. Besides, you don't have much to gain from lying to me and everything to lose. Let's meet tomorrow morning and go from there. I need to know the *zemdyut* locations and movements soon. We have supplies to last a few months, but even once we know which areas are safe, there's no guarantee what we'll find outside the city. We haven't heard from anyone in years. I don't want to leave things too long, and I'm guessing you want to get home sooner rather than later."

"You've got that right," muttered Jasper under his breath. The rest of us nodded in agreement.

Eden led us to the sequestered area. She hesitated imperceptibly, then squared her shoulders and pulled back the curtain.

Cage and I squeezed through first, then stopped in surprise. I wasn't sure what I'd been expecting, but it wasn't a full-blown shantytown.

The parts of the department store I'd seen so far were all more or less the same: dark, dirty, neglected. They resembled parts of Nuokyo in *Robo Mecha Dream Girl*, and they were exactly what I'd expected from a postapocalyptic scenario.

Here, though, things were reasonably clean and even well lit by the strange lanterns hanging every four or five feet. They had cleared the left half of the store entirely to make room for rows of tents, similar to the quick pop-up varieties I'd seen on Earth. People were obviously living in them. Some stood open, revealing curious children peeping in our direction or sullen adults refusing to meet our eyes. Square spaces marked each tent area, covered in what looked like plastic grass strewn with toys, blankets, mats, chairs, and even a few tablets.

To our right, the space was divided into two: a long row of tables and chairs, and another curtained-off area.

Eden pushed past us. "Welcome to Sanctuary," she said.

I almost had a heart attack. Behind me, Mia choked violently, and Rune sucked in a gasp of air. "What . . . what did you say?" she whispered.

Eden flashed us a smile. "That's what we call it. Sanctuary." Her smile faltered as she absorbed our expressions. "Does that mean something to you?"

"No, it's just . . ." I turned to Cage for support.

To my surprise, he threw his head back and laughed. "It's not our first Sanctuary," he said, shaking his head wearily. To the others he added, "Take it easy, okay? It's not a sign." The expressions on the former prisoners' faces didn't seem to agree, but Cage pushed on regardless. "You've got quite the setup here."

"Unfortunately, we've had plenty of time to perfect it." Eden indicated the tables. "We eat communally. You'll hear a bell. If you want food, come then; we won't hold it for you." She nodded to the curtained-off area. "There are bathrooms and showers through there. You'll find towels and a selection of clean clothes if you need them. Take what you need, but be sparing with the water. We don't have anyone with the ability to get the plumbing active again, so we rely on recycled rainwater and good old-fashioned engineering." She led us farther into the room. As we advanced, more faces appeared in tent doorways. A group of children sat at one of the tables with a man and some tablets, and from the way he tried to keep their attention off us and on him, I suspected he was their teacher. I'd seen such exasperation on more than a few teacher faces before. That felt like a long time ago, sitting in a classroom with no real worries on my mind.

Part of me strangely envied these kids. No matter how bad things got, someone would shelter them from it. Someone else would handle the problem.

Eden stopped in a corner of the room. "There are three tents here you can divide between you," she said. "They're stocked for new arrivals. If you need anything, come find me." She indicated the curtained-off area. "I'll probably be in my office back there. Lunch is in about an hour. Anything else I can do for you?"

We all stood dumbfounded. A thousand answers to her question raced through my head. She could explain how they'd organized this place. Ease my fears about it being called Sanctuary. Tell me how to stop everyone from glaring at us with such suspicion and curiosity.

But none of that was likely to happen, so I only shook my head. Eden nodded and stomped off toward the curtains. The second she disappeared, a murmur of voices rose around the room.

"I feel like we should get inside," said Matt slowly.

Priya nodded toward the smallest tent. "I'll claim this for Legion."

Matt hesitated, glancing at Rune as if he'd hoped for another rooming arrangement, but she seemed oblivious. Had the two of them talked at all since our escape? Something existed between Rune and Matt on Sanctuary—something more than friendship, but still undefined. Matt's apparent death, and the fact he'd hunted us on Obsidian, had splintered that, but I still caught them exchanging sly glances, awkward looks that vanished when their eyes met.

But apparently Matt wasn't ready to challenge orders quite yet, and he disappeared into the tent behind Priya and Hallam. They instantly zipped it shut, hiding themselves from us and the world.

That left eight of us to divide between two tents. Rune, Jasper, Imani, and Reed took one, and Cage, Mia, Alexei, and I took the other because, I strongly suspected, no one else wanted to share their space with Mia and Alexei. Alexei himself took up half the tent once we got inside, but I was pleasantly surprised by the space. A shiny new carpet covered the floor and you could almost stand in the center. The tent wasn't large—once the four of us spread out the bedrolls stacked against one wall, we'd fill the entire place—but it would give us some privacy and a place to sleep.

We left the tent flaps open and sat in a circle on the floor. No one seemed happy. Cage was fiddling with my fingers like they were anxiety beads. Mia stared at the floor, her jaw locked and her eyes hard. Only Alexei appeared calm, but it was the same calm I'd seen him wear on Sanctuary—the first Sanctuary. It meant he'd resigned himself to whatever came next and had simply chosen not to worry.

"So what do we do now?" I asked quietly.

For once, no one volunteered any answers, not even Cage.

"I guess we fight some aliens," Mia said at last. "We've done it before."

"The goal is to *not fight*," Cage said sharply. "Why do I have to keep emphasizing that? Eden asked us to go in and obtain information. That's it."

Mia snorted. "And you trust her? Whatever else happens, we're going to have to gather some intel of our own. There's more to this than she's letting on, I promise you that."

Alexei sighed. "Mia, did you notice that Karoch thing? It's huge. It can see. I'm not sure it has a single weakness."

"Everything has a weakness."

"Of course they do," I said softly. "But I'm not sure we can figure Karoch's out in time to exploit it."

"Eden still bothers me." Alexei nodded in my direction. "I know she stuck her neck out and fought for us. But that doesn't mean she's entirely on the level. We might have been the excuse she needed to get rid of Gideon."

I shrugged. It was possible. Some of Eden's frustration with the current situation had come through while she talked, and I understood her desperation, watching supplies dwindle while Gideon dug in his heels and refused to take action. She might very well have been waiting for her moment. But what were we supposed to do about it? "We don't have a lot of choices here," I pointed out. "Either we work with Eden and hope her spaceship can get us home, or we die on this planet."

"I know. It doesn't mean I have to like it."

There was a commotion from outside, and Cage sighed his *what now* sigh I'd gotten so accustomed to over the last few weeks. But it wasn't a disaster this time: only our friends pushing their way into our tent. They clambered in without an invitation, plopping themselves down wherever they chose: Rune on my right, leaning her head on my shoulder; Jasper by Mia; Reed and Imani stretched along the ground near the rear of the tent. "Come on in," said Cage dryly.

"The door was open." Reed tugged at his mess of hair. "Your tent looks exactly like ours."

"So now we're camping in an abandoned department store on an alien planet," said Rune. "That's new, at least."

"In a place called Sanctuary," Imani added, and that shut everyone up, at least for a moment.

Cage sighed. "Please, please, do not get superstitious. Just because Omnistellar chose a stupidly inappropriate name for the prison where they trapped us doesn't make the word ominous, okay?"

"No, but it doesn't make me feel great, either," Rune replied, still leaning on my shoulder. She seemed exhausted, maybe at the thought of the coming exertions. "It makes me feel trapped here."

I put my arm around her, and she smiled up at me. "In a way, we are," I told her gently. "But we're doing everything in our power to get free. It worked on the last Sanctuary, right?"

"Yeah, that went great," Mia said sarcastically. "We only

lost most of the prisoners and accidentally abandoned one of our friends. Hopefully this goes exactly as well."

Jasper shook his head. "This time there's extra motivation. I *have* to get home."

"Hey." Cage shot him a glare across the circle. "The second we get home, we'll help you find your family. They took care of all of us on Mars. You're not alone on this, okay?"

Jasper hesitated, then nodded. "Thanks. That means a lot, actually."

"But in the meantime . . ." Cage nodded at each of us in turn and dropped his voice, his nervous gaze taking in the tent's thin nylon walls. "I'm glad you're all here. You're the ones I trust, and I need to know: How far do you trust everyone else?"

Rune sat up and leaned around me to peer at her brother. "You mean Matt."

"I mostly mean Eden and her soldiers. But yeah, *meimei*. Matt and Legion are part of the equation."

"I don't think Legion's going to turn on us," I reassured him. "I mean, definitely not before we escape this planet. But after Omnistellar betrayed them, I don't think they'll be in a hurry to arrest us once we get home, either." *Once* we get home. I allowed my false confidence to fill me with hope. "At worst, they'll abandon us after we return. We can handle it. As for Eden, it's like I said. We don't have any other choice. That doesn't mean we have to trust her, though. We can come up with some plans of our own." Remembering what Matt had told me about Priya's abilities, I reluctantly added, "Priya might be useful there."

A bell clanged, and we all turned to watch as crowds of people headed toward the tables, many of them peering into our tents as they passed. They all looked roughly the same to me: dirty, tired, downtrodden. "Do we join them?" I asked softly.

Reed shrugged. "You can do what you want, but if there's food, I for one am in."

Of course he was. I caught a few suppressed smiles from the others, and I tightened my grip on Cage and Rune. Whatever else happened, we were together. We were united. I still had my family, even if my parents, my company, were gone.

So far, I'd accomplished the impossible: I'd kept them safe, even on this alien planet, even with monsters attacking and strange people threatening from every corner. And I'd keep them safe in the alien base, too, even if it meant giving my life to do it.

TWENTY-TWO

WE CLAIMED A CORNER OF A TABLE AGAINST the wall. No one joined us; in fact, they left the entire table empty, cramming in at the other three. A moment later, Priya, Hallam, and Matt appeared and sat beside us. "We're pariahs," said Hallam cheerfully.

Eden emerged from behind the curtain. She observed the situation, and for a moment I thought she might join us, just to prove a point. But instead she sat at another table, a smile on her face as she struck up a conversation with her neighbor.

I shrugged. I didn't need to be friends with these people. And I understood their fear and suspicion, especially since their leader had never returned from dealing with us. With luck, we wouldn't have to intrude on them for long. After Eden's news, we could be home in a matter of weeks, depending on the speed of Eden's ship and exactly how far we'd traveled.

And, of course, the aliens not tearing us to pieces.

A shudder went through me as the enormity of what we were doing suddenly sank in. I'd been hiding from it, I realized; sequestering myself behind a wall of bravado. But now, at the worst possible moment, it hit me: we were going to voluntarily march into an alien stronghold featuring not only the horrifying creatures who'd ripped through Sanctuary and Obsidian, but something larger and older and far, far worse.

Cage's hand slid over my elbow. "Easy," he murmured, pulling me against him. I caught at his shirt and forced my breaths steady. Embarrassed, I raised my gaze, but if the others noticed my momentary weakness, they had the good manners to pretend otherwise.

After a while two men and a woman came from an almost-hidden door, carrying large bowls of food. With unspoken consent, we allowed everyone else to serve themselves before we left our seats. We were intruders here, and the last thing I needed was someone attacking us in the middle of the night.

Eden caught my eye across the room. "Hey," she called, louder than was strictly necessary. "If you're risking your lives to help us regain our freedom, the least we can do is feed you. It's not much, but it's edible. Promise."

A low murmur surfaced, and people gaped at us again, this time some with respect, but many more with fear. Maybe they didn't even want to think about what we were planning to do. I understood the feeling. Hell, I was on their side—assuming they knew anything about it. Eden had seemed to want to keep things secret, her comment about risking our lives notwithstanding. She must have told them *something*, though, in spite of her earlier warnings. In her way she was as duplicitous as Cage could be, manipulating situations with skill and ease. That was worth watching out for.

The main table featured three huge communal bowls alongside mismatched plates and cutlery. I scooped up some sort of grain that might have been rice, dropped a pile of unidentified meat beside it, and added a spoonful of what looked like dried peas. It was not particularly appetizing, but at the moment I'd take it. I added a cup of water and returned to the table, where Cage was frowning at Imani's plate, which held only a small portion of rice and some peas.

"That's not enough food," he said.

Imani shrugged. "I can't tell what's in the meat."

"Then you need more of the rest."

"I'm fine."

Cage glared at her. "Are you hungry?"

"Yes, but . . . I don't want to take more than my share."

"You're not," I said. "Imani, you're a healer. You're going to be awfully important in whatever comes next." I swallowed, trying not to think about what that might mean. "We need you at full strength."

"Here." Mia grabbed Imani's plate and headed for the front, her slight limp more pronounced after the incident with her foot. The aliens on Sanctuary had damaged her limb so badly not even our healers had fully repaired it, and it looked like Gideon had shot her in the exact same spot, making matters worse. But no one challenged her as she doubled the food on Imani's plate.

Hallam nudged Imani. "Don't be afraid to stand up for yourself, kid. No one else is going to do it for you."

She gave him a haughty scowl, one that spoke to the beauty belle she used to be. "I'm not afraid. And I think my friend just proved you wrong."

Mia returned and dropped Imani's plate in front of her, and we all set ourselves to eating. I looked around the table, the uncomfortable silence broken only by the soft murmurs of the crowd at the other side of the room and our chewing, which seemed painfully loud. "So," I said, just because I couldn't take the quiet tension, "what do you guys make of Eden's story?"

Hallam leaned back, wiping his hand across his mouth. "Hard to say. The corps have been searching for intelligent life for a long time and never found a glimmer. Eden's explanation makes sense in its own way. I can see a civilization with the tech to shield itself doing so, especially if they didn't like what they saw when they looked at our planet. But I'm still suspicious that we've never even caught a glimpse of them before. You kids better prepare yourselves. Even if we survive the alien pit, even if Eden's telling the truth about her spaceship, *and* even if we can figure out how to get home, we might still face a journey of several years. And that's assuming we have the fuel and supplies to get there. Remember, they're low on materials. You think they're going to hand us enough food to journey across the universe?"

My chest lurched. I'd been so excited by the possibility of an escape that none of this had occurred to me. I'd imagined dying, of course, but as terrifying as that was, it was better than starving to death on this planet. I had not considered the realities of what came next.

Reed scowled at him. "You're a cheerful sort, aren't you?"

"He's only being honest," Matt replied quietly. He glanced at Cage, rolling his fork over in his hands. "And he's not wrong."

Cage shrugged. "Just like you weren't wrong when you told me Sanctuary was designed to be an inescapable prison. We still broke out."

Matt snorted. "That wasn't exactly an unqualified success, was it?"

"No, but we couldn't predict the aliens." Rune's voice was quiet, but it seemed to strike Matt like an anvil. It was one of the first times she'd spoken to him, and she instantly had his undivided attention. "The escape was a disaster, but we did escape. If we hadn't tried, we'd have died in our cells. And if we don't try now, we'll die in a new Sanctuary."

Priya shook her head and drained the last of her water. "I don't disagree with you, but Hallam's got a point. We need a plan B."

"Plan B better not entail staying here," Jasper snapped.

Priya glared in return. "You are not the only one with family back home, okay? No one wants to stay here. We're simply considering the realities of the situation."

For a second I thought Jasper would fire off an angry response, but then Rune laughed softly. "Are you guys really going to fight about this?" she asked. "For once, we all want exactly the same thing. We're alive. We're together. And we have a chance of getting off this planet. Can't we just lean into that for once?"

Cage and I exchanged frowns. It was clear he was thinking exactly what I was: we might not be alive much longer.

But Rune's words seemed to calm Matt and Jasper. "Sorry," Jasper said. "I'm on edge thinking about my family, that's all."

Matt shrugged. "You haven't said anything we aren't thinking. And Hallam's not the most tactful guy." He elbowed his new friend, who grinned, showing all his teeth.

Imani rolled her eyes and shoveled the last of her rice into her mouth. "So what do we do now?" she asked. "This was lunch. We have time to kill. Eden doesn't want to talk to us about the mission. Do we just stand around? Take a nap?" She laughed self-consciously. "It's been so long since I've had nothing to do that I'm not sure how it works anymore."

"Well, we could do nothing," Cage replied in the long, slow drawl that said something was going on in his head. "Or . . ."

Rune groaned. "Don't play mysterious, *gege*."

He laughed, eyes sparkling. "We could try to learn more about what's going on here."

A grin spread across Mia's face. "Now that's more like it. What do you have in mind?"

"Mia, your job should make you happy. Disappear and snoop around. Listen in. See what you can find out, especially if you can get behind this curtain." He nodded. "Take Rune with you. She can be quiet and won't give you away, and I want her to examine the tech around here, see what, if anything, they have working."

Alexei scowled. "And what shall I do, O imperious leader?"

Cage nodded toward a group of boisterous, well-muscled soldier-looking types. They were hanging out near Eden and keeping a careful eye on us. "See if you can make some new friends. I get the sense they'll respond to you better than anyone."

Alexei shrugged noncommittally, but he was already scrutinizing the soldiers, his mind working. Cage pressed on: "Imani and Reed, there must be a medical facility here somewhere. You have every excuse to get in there. Scout the place. If we have injuries, we might need to know exactly what supplies they have and how many of them we can access."

"And me?" Jasper asked.

"You, me, and Kenzie will see who we can get to talk to us. Try to gather more information about this place."

Priya arched an eyebrow. "I notice you've left us out of your little plot."

Cage frowned in what seemed to be genuine surprise. "I thought you'd have your own plan, to be honest."

Priya almost smiled. "Yours is as good as any." She nodded at Hallam and Matt. "See if you can get any information on what sort of weaponry they've got around here. Help Alexei chat with the soldiers. Me, I'll talk to Eden, press her for information on the alien stronghold." She examined me appraisingly. "While you're scouting around, learn anything you can about Gideon. I don't trust Eden's appraisal of him. You say she had no choice about killing him, but she still pulled the trigger on her superior. I want more facts than we have."

Somehow she'd managed to turn Cage's operation into her own, and I winked at him to say I'd noticed. He gave me a rueful smile in return. "We'll meet after supper and share what we learn."

Mia stretched, her joints popping in a way that made me wince. "Beats sitting around all afternoon."

Cage caught my eye and winked, and I smiled in spite of myself. Why not? I'd been a prison guard, a fugitive, an anomaly. Might as well add spy to the list.

TWENTY-THREE

BEING A SUPERSPY WAS BOTH MORE BORING and more difficult than it initially sounded. First of all, no one really wanted to talk to us. We had the most luck with the children, but they also possessed the least useful information, and their parents tended to drag them away with suspicious glares. After a few hours of intensely trying to engage people in conversation, we'd learned Gideon was well liked among his people, that they were mourning his loss, and that they blamed us for getting him killed, although they were foggy on how, exactly, we were at fault.

Midway through the afternoon, Jasper begged off, pleading a headache. The shadows behind his eyes made me think he might not be lying, and he staggered a bit as he headed for the tents. "He's damn scared," I said, half to myself.

"Wouldn't you be?" Cage raked his hand through his hair,

standing it on edge, and even in this awful situation, I found myself gaping at him, still unable to believe he was quite real. I reached out and ran my finger along his jawline, and his lips quirked into a smile.

"I don't have any family left to worry about," I whispered. It wasn't totally true. I had some cousins and an aunt and uncle on Earth. We weren't close. We used to be when we were young, but once my family started moving around, well . . . I hadn't seen them in years. But I wanted to protect them if I could. Still, my own losses were fresh in my mind.

Cage pulled me against his chest. We were standing in a corner of the tent town, and people were watching us, but I didn't care. Cage must have, though. He glanced both ways, then took my hand and tugged me along after him.

"Where are we going?" I demanded.

"Damned if I know," he replied, so cheerfully a smile cracked through my grief.

We ducked through the hanging blankets marking the edge of the fake town and into the abandoned, dystopia-esque department store, which was dark and bleak and not particularly friendly but at least afforded privacy. Then Cage pulled me in against him, his hands settling on my arms, my shoulders, my back, featherlight touches that drew me in. "I thought you could use a minute," he said. "That *we* could use a minute. Kenz, we haven't really had a chance to talk about your dad, but—"

"Let's not." I wrapped my arms around his waist and held tight. "I don't want to think about death. Not now. Not anymore."

"You're not going to die," he replied gently.

"No one's going to die. Not if I can help it." I swallowed hard. "But then, I've never really been *able* to help it, have I? Cage . . . If we die in this fight . . ."

"We won't. Trust me, okay?"

"Will you stop with the act for a moment?" I pulled back and glared at him through a sea of tears. I got what he was trying to do. But it was just me and him now, and I wanted *Cage*, not the cheerful boyish leader directing his friends through a sea of desperation.

He examined me for a long moment, and then, piece by piece, the mask peeled away. He smiled, but the cheer didn't extend to his eyes, where his fear and exhaustion and worry bled through. "All right," he said, stroking his thumb over my jaw. "If we die in this fight . . ."

"If we do, I just want you to know that I . . ." I choked on the words. "That I really care about you. We've been through more together than I ever thought possible, and you've never let go of me, not once."

The dark pool of his eyes softened, and he cast his gaze aside, sighing as if afraid of what came next. "Kenzie. I . . ." He pulled me in even tighter, and his arms trembled. "When I think about how we met, I'm amazed you even talk to me. I know we haven't known each other too long, but . . . I love you, Kenzie. And you don't have to say anything," he added in a rush, drawing back to examine me with something like fear in his eyes. "I know that's a weird thing to throw at you right now, but—"

I stood on my toes, grabbed the sides of his face, and pulled him down to me, kissing him thoroughly. Within seconds I'd forgotten our impending doom, forgotten everything but Cage, the width and length and breadth of him consuming my soul.

When at last we broke apart, my eyes were wet. "I love you, too," I said. "I mean, I love all of you. Even Mia. But I really love you."

His face broke into a smile, and for a single moment nothing else mattered: not the hostility of our surroundings, not the aliens or the giant creature they surrounded, not the fact that we were an eternity from home.

And then the moment broke, and we were us again, mired in the same hell where we always seemed to find ourselves. But somehow things were different all the same.

The euphoria chased me all day. It was in every smile Cage offered, in every brush of his hand against mine, in every accidental touch. It warred with a half dozen other emotions: grief and terror and suspicion, guilt and anger and exhaustion.

After another tense meal, we all crammed into our tent, everyone except Hallam. Briefings bored him, he said, and he'd rather lounge on the linoleum outside. Actually, I suspected

Priya had ordered him to keep a watch and make sure no one got too close to our tent, but I wasn't about to dissuade him. It was a good idea. I should have come up with it myself.

I sort of trusted Eden. She'd defended us, even to the point of turning on her mentor. But if my parents had taught me nothing else, they'd shown me people can have complicated motivations. My dad, for example. He'd genuinely believed he was protecting me by leaving all my friends to die, by sending Legion after me, even by summoning the aliens to our solar system. So even if Eden had good intentions, I wasn't going to embrace her as family quite yet.

The tent didn't exactly fit all of us, so Mia was sitting on Alexei's lap, I was crammed against Cage, and Matt and Rune were painfully close. Neither of them looked too upset about it, though. In fact, from the way they kept exchanging glances, I was starting to suspect they'd executed their own little mission earlier that day. I made a mental note to ask Rune about it later.

"These people have absolutely nothing to say," Mia reported. "I wasted my whole day drifting around invisible. I can tell you who's cheating on who, which families are taking more than their fair share of rations, and who suspects who of snooping through their tent. That's about it." She shrugged. "Gideon's name came up once or twice. He was sort of a folk hero, but . . . Eden wasn't lying about how he'd changed. People were getting nervous. No one's dared to say it, but I think they're relieved he's gone."

"The soldiers are surprisingly well armed," Matt added. "If guns could take those creatures down, they'd have done it by now."

"The aliens have some sort of adaptive shielding," Cage reminded us. "I used a sword to kill one of them, but the next time I attacked, it blocked me somehow. That's why Eden needs the information. You can't kill these things, or at least, not many of them. You can only ever run."

"Unless you have a warehouse full of missiles," Mia added. "Eden mentioned that, too. She even said it was nearby."

"And that she couldn't transport them. Get the idea out of your head, Mia. We're not blowing up the planet."

The only one with anything more substantial to offer was Rune. With Mia's help, she'd swiped a tablet. "They've got someone with the ability to charge batteries," she said, raising it for us to see. "It must come in pretty handy. I think it's the only reason they have light and hot food. The battery on this one ran down fast, but as long as I'm in contact, I can make it work. I was able to get a bit of information about this world. Kenzie was right. It's scarily similar to ours. Even lots of the history seems the same—wars and stuff. I mean, it's not identical, but it's way too close to be a coincidence."

"What's the planet called?" Imani asked.

"Wraith."

"Wraith?" I demanded.

"W-R-E-I-T-H-E," Ruen spelled out. "But at this point, yeah. Wraith is close enough."

"So what does that mean?" I demanded, spreading my hands in desperation. "It's an alien planet almost exactly like Earth, not only in terms of technology and language and inhabitants, but *history*? How is that possible?"

"It's not." Imani was chewing her lip thoughtfully. "I . . . I have an idea, but . . ." She shook her head, glancing at each of us in turn.

"Speak up, Imani," Cage encouraged her. "If you think you know what's going on . . ."

"I . . . no. I don't know. That's the thing." She shook her head again. "Let me think it through a bit longer. I need to clarify it in my head before I give it voice."

No one seemed very happy, but we couldn't force her to share her ideas. My mind raced, trying to figure out what Imani had come up with, but I was simply too tired. One thing seemed clear: Eden wasn't telling the truth, or at least not all of it. A nearby planet shielded against discovery, whose inhabitants watched ours? That explained some of the similarities in language and culture, but not the same history . . .

We dispersed on a tense note. We hadn't learned much, and we were still at Eden's mercy regarding whatever she planned for tomorrow. Cage fell asleep almost immediately after dinner, holding me clasped loosely in his arms as the lights in the store dimmed to mimic nightfall. I envied him his peace, his ability to sleep instantly, anywhere. He never seemed to suffer my insomnia and nightmares.

I lay awake for a long time, staring at the tent ceiling and listening to the other three breathe. Faces swam in front of me: Matt and my mom, Rita, my father. Even Liam, the alien we'd met on Obsidian, the man who'd been so terrified of the aliens he'd abandoned his own family to escape them, who'd betrayed us and then died in the explosion. It was his power I'd borrowed to get here. I wished I'd been able to reach him, to help him, too.

"Kenzie," said Alexei quietly.

I jumped. "I thought you were sleeping."

He snorted. "Not likely. These two are the ones who can sleep through anything. I'm the one who gets to lie awake worrying. Well, me and you, apparently." After a long moment, he reached across the small space between our bedrolls. I fished my arm out of the blankets and took his hand.

His big grasp swallowed mine, and I remembered all the contact I'd had with Alexei since we'd met. He'd restrained me when he took me captive and argued in favor of knocking me out. That was hard to forget. But he'd also held me while Cage cut the power-inhibiting chip from my arm. He'd pulled me to safety on the alien ship. He'd clasped me against him when the aliens appeared aboveground. Alexei got a bad rap, between his massive size, his family's criminal connections, and his destructive pyrokinetics. But thinking about it, I realized he was usually just *there*: a quiet, solid presence in the background, ready at a second's notice to shelter any of us who might be in danger.

I tightened my grip on his hand. "Thanks, Alexei."

"For what?"

"For being my friend."

He chuckled and spoke to me in Russian. "I never had many friends before I went to prison. You don't when you're part of a crime family. Cage and Mia were the first people outside my family I ever cared for. And I guess I developed a taste for it. Turns out I like people. And I like you, Kenzie. I'm sorry if I ever hurt you."

"You didn't." I pulled free but rolled onto my side, facing him in the dark. "We *are* friends, right?"

He turned his head toward me, lacing his hands behind his head. "To say the least."

"Then can I ask you something?"

"Of course."

I nodded toward Mia, snoring on his other side. "How the hell do you resist the urge to shake some sense into her at least five times a day?"

He laughed, still softly, as if he kept even his laugh gentle to avoid scaring people off. "Ah, Mia. It may be hard to understand, but . . . I would never want her to be anyone but who she is. No matter how impetuous and aggressive and stubborn she is. If nothing else, it makes life interesting."

"Yes." I snorted. "Because if there's one thing we have to worry about, it's being *bored*."

Alexei laughed again. "Go to sleep, Kenzie. I'll wake you if anything happens. Tomorrow's going to be a long day, and you need to rest."

"So do you."

"Don't worry about me." He propped himself up on his elbow, and although I couldn't quite read his expression in the dim light, I got the sense he was studying me. "You and Cage carry a lot on your shoulders," he continued quietly. "But at least he lets himself rest. It's time you did the same. Let me watch over things tonight. You're safe, I promise. Get some sleep."

I sighed. "Thanks, Lex," I said, reclining on my makeshift pillow, a folded sweater. I didn't bother explaining to Alexei that it was anxiety and nerves keeping me awake, not fear.

But maybe I was wrong. Because after our conversation, to my amazement—and for the first time in weeks—I drifted into a deep and dreamless sleep.

TWENTY-FOUR

THE NEXT THING I KNEW, CAGE WAS GENTLY shaking me awake. "We're meeting with Eden," he said.

I sat up and blinked. The tent was empty. "Where is everyone? How long was I asleep?"

"It's been a while, but I think you needed it." He crouched beside me and handed me some sort of crackers and dried fruit, along with a cup of water. "I saved you what passed as breakfast. Take a moment to eat and get ready, and I'll meet you outside."

I fell back on my bedroll as he slipped out of the tent. I'd actually slept a full night through. No alien nightmares, no jerking awake to check on my friends, no panicking in the dark. "Thanks, Lex," I muttered softly.

A few minutes later, I'd eaten and smoothed my curls into a ponytail. I also changed into a clean shirt from a few we'd salvaged the night before, which went a long way toward making me feel more human. True to his word, Cage was waiting for me, and we set off toward the curtained area, where Eden lounged with the rest of our crew.

She didn't say a word, only led us inside. I rubbed sleep from my eyes and noticed Rune doing the same. She gave me a half smile. There was fear behind it, and behind my answering grin. We were walking into death, and this time we were doing it voluntarily. What were we thinking?

Eden directed us into a side room that might once have been some sort of office and sat us down. "Are you ready?" she asked without preamble.

There were nods all around. And the thing was, we *were* ready. There was nothing to be gained by waiting. If I was going to die, well, I'd rather not have to consider it too much beforehand.

Of course, I would prefer *not* to die at all, and so I spoke up. "But you're going to tell us everything. *Everything*, Eden. We know you've been holding back. If we're going to trust each other in battle, that trust starts here."

The others nodded, unified, and courage stirred in my heart. Whatever divided us, we would stand together on this. I inspected Priya, Hallam, Matt. If there was anyone I wanted at my back in a fight, it was the three of them. With renewed strength, I met Eden's eyes.

She nodded slowly. "All right. That's fair. Here." She waved her hand, and a holographic image spread across the table. We all jumped.

"That's gotta be sucking up a *lot* of energy," Rune said in fascination.

"It is, and I'd rather not drain our reserves, so let's keep the questions to a minimum, okay?" Eden gestured, and the image altered. We had shifted to the desert. The city loomed on one side, the sand sweeping away from it in swirls. If there'd been roads or settlements in the area, they were long since buried in dirt. But there was one landmark, a small building some distance from the city. I barely noticed it at first until Eden zoomed in on it.

"What's that?" Jasper leaned forward, bracing his elbows on his thighs. "Looks like a metal hut."

"It's the entrance to the military base I told you about." Eden hesitated, then scrutinized each of us in turn. "That's where the ship I told you about is stored. And . . . it's where the *zemdyut* are."

A long silence greeted her statement, broken when Mia went into peals of laughter. "Oh, I'm sorry," she said, holding up a hand as we all turned to her. "It's just a bit much. So what you're telling me," she said, staring straight at Eden, all traces of amusement gone as abruptly as they'd appeared, "is that in order to get access to this ship of yours, in order to gather your intel, we have to *fight our way through the alien base*. We can't destroy the place, and the aliens are blocking access to the ship. No wonder you didn't mention this detail before."

Eden scowled. "If we gather the right intel, we can lure the *zemdyut* out of the base. Or find another ship. There are ways around this problem. Hopefully you won't be fighting at all. The creatures have some sort of adaptive shielding—"

"Yeah, we've noticed," Cage interrupted.

"Then you know our weapons won't be much good against them. You're going to have to sneak in and be quiet."

Another long silence. Then Priya stood, slowly, every muscle in her body as tense as an iron rod. "Please do not tell me," she said, "that this is the entirety of your plan."

"Sneak in. Get the intel. Sneak out. It's not much, but—"

"Sneak in," said Matt, dragging out every word, "get the intel, and sneak out. That's it?"

"*But*," Eden continued sharply, "we won't send you in alone. My soldiers and I will bring what firepower we have and back you up if you need it. I hope you won't, because frankly, if we have to engage those things, we can all make our farewells. But I won't leave you alone in the desert to die." She shook her head, her dark eyes flashing. "You're right. It's not much of a plan. But what exactly am I supposed to do? I don't have any intel. I don't have anything at all." A tinge of desperation entered her voice. "I have people to protect, children to defend, and no other options here. Without information, we die. With it, we have a chance."

"What about this world?" Rune spoke up more harshly than usual. "You're not telling us everything there, either. There's no way we have the similarities we do from mere proximity."

Eden threw up her hands in exasperation. "What do you want me to say? I don't know why we're so much alike, okay? I just don't know! I'm a soldier, not a historian, not an astrophysicist. I've given you everything I have!"

"Really?" The words emerged more sharply than I intended, but then I figured, screw it. Yeah, we needed Eden; we needed that ship and that information. But this was too much. "You haven't been honest with us, Eden. And yet you're asking us to trust you."

Eden glared at us. "Listen, no one's forcing you to come with us. I'm not sure what I'll do without Rune, but I'll go alone if I have to. There's no choice left. We have to take this risk. But if you want to stay behind, that's *your* choice."

She left the rest of her threat unfinished: if we didn't go along with her, there was no way we would ever get off this planet. I looked at Jasper, the worry haunting his dark eyes. At Imani, her arms wrapped around herself, no doubt wondering if she'd ever see her parents to tell them the truth about her sister's death. "All right," I said, speaking for everyone and not caring if they objected. "We're in. We already agreed, and we're not backing out."

To my surprise, no one argued. But I glanced around again and understood why: they'd all come to the same realization as me. Even Priya sat down, although her eyebrows furled in a tense line and she immediately began whispering to Matt and Hallam.

Cage shrugged. "That answers that. How do we get in?"

Eden waved her hand and zoomed in, revealing what looked like a hatch in the ground. "Here. Your people will go in this way. I'll take my soldiers in the front. We're going to rig explosives along an alternate stairwell. If the situation goes to hell, we'll set them off as a distraction. If you hear that, get out. Don't worry about anything else."

Rune scowled. "Do we have any way to keep in touch during this little adventure?"

"We have a limited number of comm devices." Eden tossed a handful of small plastic earpieces onto the table. "I took three for my team and left three for you. Distribute them however you wish. We'll give you access to our armories. You can suit up however you want to. I recommend dressing for speed and stealth, though. Keep in mind we don't know whether our weapons will even work against the *zemdyut.*" She paused. "Above all else, let's hope and pray Karoch isn't in this base. If we're quiet, if we're careful, we might be able to sneak around the rest of the creatures. But that thing . . ."

"Let's hope instead," said Alexei coldly, "there isn't more than one of it."

An uncomfortable silence greeted his statement.

Eden sighed and waved her hand. The holograph disappeared. "All right," she said. "Take an hour to get ready. I'll show you where our weapons and armor are located. And then we move out."

An hour. I sat in stunned silence. I'd thought I wanted to get this over with, but . . . an hour. An hour to say good-bye, maybe forever, to the friends I loved. To make peace with my own possible death.

To get ready for our only hope of escape.

I rolled my shoulders and straightened my back. I could do this. I *would* do this.

Because I didn't have a choice.

TWENTY-FIVE

THE HOUR PASSED IN A HEARTBEAT. I'D HOPED I'd find time to talk to everyone one-on-one, to have a cathartic farewell. But that didn't happen. Instead we spent our time choosing weapons, discussing strategy, and arguing over who would take the communicators.

Eventually we let Priya direct us. I could already see her mind working, and knowing what I did about her abilities, it only made sense to step aside. She split us into three teams. The advance team consisted of Alexei, Mia, Cage, Matt, and me. Between us, we had speed, strength, stealth, and fire-power. Hopefully, if we encountered anything dangerous, we'd be able to slow it enough to give everyone else—not to mention ourselves—time to escape. I wore the communicator for our team.

Priya gave us one simple and secret objective: to find the

ship Eden had mentioned and, if possible, pilot it out of the base. That would be a lot harder without Rune, but if nothing else, we could scout its location. And Rune was needed elsewhere.

The follow-up team consisted of Reed, Priya, and Jasper. Reed was mostly coming along in case of an urgent need for healing, and Priya and Jasper were there to protect him. But they had a secondary objective: they would follow in our wake, a short distance behind, scouting for anything we'd missed or we didn't have time to investigate fully. Reed wore their communicator, and Priya wasn't happy about it, but Cage had argued that Reed was least likely to be engaged in battle and therefore most able to offer clear communication, and she hadn't been able to counter.

Our final team was our most important. Imani, Rune, and Hallam had only one goal: dodge the aliens and find information. They were searching not only for Eden's intel, but for information about Wreithe, because even if Eden wasn't lying—even if she didn't know anything about our own planet—something was off here, and we needed to know what. Rune would be able to access any system she encountered. Imani would be there if someone was hurt, and Hallam would keep them safe if the first two teams missed anything that slipped through. Much to my annoyance, Hallam won the battle to take the third communicator, meaning I'd have him in my ear for the entire mission.

We stalked through the desert in the midmorning heat, dressed in lightweight body armor that nonetheless felt like a leaded elephant under the beating sun. I was drenched with sweat in seconds, and profoundly grateful Eden had allowed us to raid their water supply for as much as we needed. I could read her thoughts: if we messed this up, we wouldn't need water, because we'd all be on our way to a slow death anyway.

In spite of our alliance, we divided into three groups on our trek into the desert. Eden and about a dozen soldiers stayed slightly to our right. There was some boisterous joking and laughing at first, but after thirty minutes or so they subsided into a death march, occasionally pausing to glare suspiciously at us. I could only imagine Eden's conversations convincing her crew to join us, and for a moment I empathized with her. She was only trying to do what was best for her people. She'd been forced to kill her mentor, the man who, by her own admission, had saved her life. And now here she was, making the hard decisions, straddling a precarious divide between two groups of people who needed each other as much as they mistrusted each other.

Come to think of it, her situation was kind of familiar. No wonder I empathized.

Our own divisions were somewhat less clear, though, because of Matt. Although he started the day with Priya and Hallam, he casually drifted forward as Rune slowed. Before long the two of them were in their own private no-man's-land between the survivors of Sanctuary and the remnants of Legion.

I glanced at Jasper on my left. "What's up with those two, anyway?"

Imani laughed, drifting closer. "We don't know. But Rune came back to the tent late last night." She cast a quick peek around, searching for Cage, but he was deep in conversation with Alexei and Mia farther ahead. Cage had never indicated any discomfort with Matt and Rune's budding relationship, but that was before Legion. Add to it the fact that Cage was incredibly protective of his sister, and, well, it was maybe best to keep him in the dark.

A smile touched my lips. This was exactly the thinking I berated him for. But this wasn't my secret to share, it was Rune's. With that in mind, I said, "Maybe we shouldn't talk about it. It's not really any of our business."

"Screw that." Reed joined us, his hair falling in wet clumps in his face. He brushed it aside in annoyance. "This is hot and miserable and I need something to distract me. What's not any of our business?"

I laughed in spite of myself, and Jasper jerked his head over his shoulder in Rune and Matt's direction. "Wonder what Priya thinks of that," he remarked.

"Maybe she hasn't noticed?" Reed suggested.

Imani snorted. "I don't think there's much Priya doesn't notice."

We resumed our trudge through the desert. "Do you actually think this is going to work?" Imani asked, examining her feet.

I shrugged. I had no idea, but if I let everyone sink into doubt and despair, we were sure to fail. I might not carry much away from the dozens of Omnistellar training camps I'd attended, but I would remember that. "We've come this far," I said, keeping my voice firm in a way that didn't match my emotions. "We've got cybernetic supersoldiers on our side. And we've already beaten impossible odds. I wouldn't bet credits against us."

Jasper grinned. "That's the spirit."

Reed still looked dubious, but the other two were smiling in spite of the oppressive heat. I forced myself to match their expressions, and I made a mental vow. I'd already lost so many people to the aliens. I wasn't going to lose any more, not if I could help it. I would do anything in my power to keep my friends alive—even if it meant sacrificing our means of escape. And I'd deal with the consequences later.

We reached the bunker shortly before noon and grouped inside the metal warehouse. I expected it to be a furnace, but to my surprise, it was better insulated than it appeared from outside, and the interior was relatively cool. "We can rest here before we move," Eden said softly, "as long as we stay very quiet. The *zemdyut* don't really come out much during the day. I think it's too hot for them."

The interior had clearly been a military base. A few cots

stretched alongside some run-down medical equipment. Tables and desks were scattered around, covered with battered tablets. Rune took one and tried to get it running, but after a moment she shook her head. “It’s not just a dead battery,” she said. “They wiped these when they left.” She glanced at Eden. “Are we going to find the same thing in the base itself?”

“You’re looking for *zemdyut* tech, not human. Remember?”

Right. Rune and I exchanged glances. The less Eden knew, the better. And I didn’t feel even a smidge of guilt over it. She was obviously hiding things from us. Besides, Rune was my conscience in a lot of ways. If she wasn’t worried, I wouldn’t be either.

By mutual agreement we took half an hour to rest in the cool interior, drink some water, and eat some protein rations we’d brought. We needed to be in top condition when we descended into the pit.

I nudged Rune as we sat and nodded at Matt, raising my eyebrow. She turned bright red and shook her head. “What?” I couldn’t resist teasing her a bit, not with the tension coiling through the room. “I thought you hated him.”

“You know that was never true,” she hissed, glancing around nervously to make sure we weren’t overheard. “I was . . . confused. And so was he. What happened to him wasn’t fair. It . . .” Her voice trailed off, and she scowled. “You’re making fun of me.”

“Never.” Impulsively, I threw my arms around her. “You’re my bestest of best friends.”

"Keep it up and you'll have to find a new one." But she hugged me back, and she was smiling when she pulled away. "I don't know with Matt. I've never known. All I know is that he's intelligent and funny, and he's got a good heart. I always saw it, from the day he became friends with Cage. I missed him while he was gone, and I'm glad he's alive. Isn't that enough for now?"

I instantly felt bad for teasing. "It's enough for as long as you need it to be."

But Rune smiled again. "You just keep him alive for me, all right?"

"Promise," I lied. I couldn't promise anything. But I would do my absolute best.

Once we'd recuperated, we split into our groups. "I'm trusting you with my sister and one of my healers," Cage said to Hallam, very quietly. "Don't let me down."

For once, Hallam was serious. "I'll keep them safe. You've got my word on that."

The two shook hands solemnly, and Cage returned to where Mia, Alexei, Matt, and I were waiting. We grouped by the trapdoor marking Eden's back way in. Eden and her team were poised at the front entrance, laying out explosives, ready to cover us if we called for help on the emergency channel.

Our goal was simple: find the ship. Alexei provided firepower in case we needed it, and Cage, Mia, and I would keep us fast—and invisible, in case we ran into that Karoch thing.

My heart thrummed. There was no sense delaying. "We've got this," I whispered.

Priya and Hallam cranked open the trapdoor, leaving us staring into a deceptively silent dark pit, a ladder descending who knew where. I swallowed hard, and Cage took my hand.

"I'll go first," said Mia. She glanced at me. "I can keep Alexei, me, and Matt invisible if you can handle yourself and Cage. That way Karoch can't surprise us."

"Got it."

"All right." But still no one moved. We all kept staring into the darkness, and not even Hallam had anything to say about it.

At last Mia drew a deep breath and swore loudly. "Well," she said, "what the hell are we waiting for? Let's go."

As if she hadn't been standing around exactly like the rest of us. But she moved now, shimmering and vanishing, taking Alexei and Matt with her. The sand stirred as she stepped onto the ladder and began her descent.

I tightened my grip on Cage's hand, searching for the courage I'd found only a short time ago. "We can do this," I repeated, mostly to myself.

Cage nodded. "Damn right we can." He inspected the rest of our team. "See you on the other side."

I forced myself to breathe, drew on Mia's power, and sheltered us in invisibility. No more delaying. This was it. Win or lose, live or die, we'd know soon enough. And maybe, just maybe, we'd find our way home in the process.

Incursion.

Advancement.

Decay.

Despair.

Source of power drawing near.

Hunger but awaiting and driven and cold. The lines are not clear. They have crossed. Worlds collide. It bides its time and it waits and it watches.

Time is flexible. Malleable. Awake.

Awake, and wait.

TWENTY-SIX

THE TEMPERATURE DROPPED FAST AS WE descended into the army base, making the desert heat nothing but a distant dream. The second Cage cleared the ladder behind me, he found my hand again—nice in its way, but probably mostly so we'd know where we were in the dark. "Mia?" I whispered.

"Right ahead of you."

I shuffled forward a few steps and found her outstretched hand. "We need to stay close," I reminded them. "We have lights, but if Karoch is around, we don't dare risk using them."

"We're going to have to," said Alexei. "I can't see anything beyond the light coming in the door. Besides, if Karoch is here, I think it'll be farther in."

"No lights," Mia insisted in a much sharper whisper than I'd thought was humanly possible. "I've been gored by those things twice, thank you very much, and I'd rather not round out the number."

I blinked. Come to think of it, Mia was always the one who seemed to get hurt. And not just by the aliens. She'd been the one Gideon shot, too.

Cage, of course, had an answer as to why: "Because you're always the one running in front and making yourself a target. Stick to the back this time and let me and Alexei take the lead."

I could almost hear Mia's scowl. "Please. You two make more noise than a tank," she grumbled.

"Okay, enough of this," said Matt, and a sudden burst of illumination flooded the room. I threw up my hand to shield my eyes as the others muttered in protest. "See?" Matt swung the light around the room, illuminating a metal hallway lined with doors and, at the far end, a flight of stairs. "Nothing to worry about."

"Oh, for . . ." At once Mia reappeared, Alexei and Matt along with her. "Well, no point maintaining invisibility for now, then."

Relieved, I dropped my own shield of invisibility. Caution mattered, but at the same time, I liked to see my comrades. Besides, Alexei was right: the big bad alien was unlikely to be hanging out on the perimeter. Or at least that's how it worked on the vids and in manga.

We advanced toward the staircase. There were about five metal doors, all sporting grimy windows. I peered in the right side of the hall while Mia took the left, but there was nothing of interest: abandoned briefing rooms, some tables and folding chairs, blank screens dominating the main walls. I'd expected claw marks, slime trails, signs of alien destruction. But except for the dust, the army could have been here yesterday. Worse yet, none of the tech looked particularly alien. If Rune was going to glean any information, she'd have to come farther in.

We moved as silently as possible. Alexei and Matt, with their bulk, had more trouble keeping quiet than the rest of us, but they were careful, and I didn't think we were making enough noise to worry over—at least not until we saw or heard something more dangerous than old conference rooms. We reached the staircase and left the glimmer of light from the entrance behind, descending a flight of grated metal stairs that reminded me painfully of Sanctuary and Obsidian.

Sanctuary the first, of course. I swallowed at the reminder. It was at the very least strange to stumble across another Sanctuary here on an alien planet.

A replacement for the first, making up for its shortcomings?

Or a warning from fate that we were walking into a sanctuary even more dangerous than the first?

Too late to question it now. I stayed close to Cage and Mia. Tension radiated off both of them, affecting me even more than the dark, echoing descent. It was like being trapped on the alien ship all over again, crawling desperately through Obsidian's vents searching for escape . . . I closed my eyes, clutching the handrail to keep myself steady. This was not the place for a panic attack. I had to keep myself moving.

Cage nudged my arm, and I opened my eyes and gave him a shaky smile. He didn't seem much steadier than me, and he wound his hand around mine. The contact helped, but the silence and the darkness continued to oppress, a physical weight burdening our descent. The only sounds were our stiff breaths and echoing footsteps, and I imagined the facility had been deserted for centuries, not years, or that it housed a horror vid's worth of alien nests and eggs and God knew what else . . .

A voice erupted in my ear: "How's it going down there, princess?"

I leaped straight into the air, my heart ricocheting around my ribs as the others stared at me in shock, half of them also clutching their chests. Scowling, I waved them off, touched my hand to my comm, and whispered, "We're descending a staircase and *trying* to be quiet about it."

Hallam chuckled. "Second team's ready to advance on your mark."

"Yeah, great. Maybe wait until I *give* it and don't scare the hell out of me so I alert any alien in the area, huh?"

"Can do, princess. Radio silence from now on. At least, until you say so."

I rolled my eyes and deactivated the comm. "I hate that guy," I muttered.

"Hallam?" Matt chuckled. "It's just his way of dealing with

stress. There's no one better to have at your back. I guarantee you Rune and Imani will come home without a scratch, which is more than I can promise for the rest of us."

"He still annoys me," I grumbled, and we resumed our trek.

We reached a second floor, and Matt dimmed the light while we eased the door aside. I braced myself for an ungodly creak, but it slid open silently. "It was probably electronically locked and controlled at one time," Cage murmured, inspecting it with the clinical gaze of a former corporate thief. "It's heavy and solid, but not likely to break."

We listened and, when we didn't hear anything, risked illuminating the next level.

A corridor branched in three directions, each extending into darkness. "This is going to take all day unless we split up," Cage said with a sigh. "I'll take the left branch. Lex and Mia, take the center. Matt and Kenzie, go right. Make sure every team has a light."

I spun on him, panic twisting my gut. "You're going by yourself?"

"I can outrun anything I see," he said gently. "Makes the most sense for me to go alone."

Matt passed him a flashlight, and Alexei held up his hand, a flame shimmering in his open palm.

Mia scowled at Cage. "We don't have comms. Separating is a bad idea. Like, horror-vid bad."

"So is spending longer here than we need to." Cage

shrugged. "Besides, call it a hunch: I don't think we'll find anything yet. I think we need to move farther in."

"Fantastic," I groaned, but I fell into step beside Matt as the others went their own way.

We took the right-hand corridor, which branched into a series of what looked like combat prep rooms. They were lined with benches and lockers, all of which were empty when I opened them, as if the soldiers who'd worked here had taken their armor and weaponry before fleeing to the surface. Which made sense, if they'd been under attack. "Not much here," I whispered to Matt.

"No. I think Cage is right."

"He's right a lot," I replied. "It makes him incredibly annoying."

"And dangerous."

"Dangerous?"

Matt half smiled. "People who are used to being right have trouble accepting when they're wrong."

He had a point. I peeked at him in the shadows as we came to the final room in our corridor, which seemed to be another mission briefing room. "Matt . . . about what happened on Sanctuary . . ."

He sighed. "Kenzie, I know it was an accident. It's going to take me some time to let it go, but . . . we're on the same side. Priya and Hallam, too, believe it or not. We all want the same thing: to get home."

"Yeah." I fidgeted with the hilt of the gun against my waist. After I'd accidentally shot Matt, I hadn't wanted to touch a gun, not for a long time. Now here I was, standing behind Matt with my finger on the edge of a weapon, and he didn't seem nervous at all. "But I'm still sorry."

"You already said that. And that you forgave me." He rolled his eyes. "For what it's worth, I forgive you, too. Now let's get back to the others, okay?"

I smiled in spite of myself, a weight vanishing from my chest. If I had to face an alien death, at least I could do it with my conscience clear. "Okay."

Cage, Alexei, and Mia waited in the main corridor. "Nothing of interest," Mia reported.

"Me either," said Cage. "Kenz, why don't you go ahead and call in the second team? We'll keep going down."

I nodded and triggered my comm. "Reed, you there?"

"Oh, thank God," he said. "We're worried up here, you know?"

"Nothing to be worried *about*," I reassured him. "So far it's been pretty anticlimactic. Go ahead and bring your team in. We've made it as far as the second floor without finding any alien tech, but you might as well advance. We'll keep you posted."

We continued to descend, finding a mess hall, a gym, a firing range: a fully stocked government facility with no sign of life—human, alien, or otherwise. After five flights of stairs,

Cage stopped us mid-descent. "Anyone else getting a weird feeling about this?" he asked. "I mean, Eden said this was a *small* facility. How much farther does this go?"

"I think I can answer that," said Mia. She was standing at a wall, studying it intently. "Kenz, come look at this. Bring a light."

I pushed through the others to join her. She ran her fingers over the metal grooves and I aimed Cage's flashlight toward her, revealing an arch in the wall. "That's a platform lift!" I exclaimed. "Or close to one!"

"Yeah. Now look over here. See these marks? I think they're floor numbers."

I peered more closely, and Mia rubbed at the metal once more with her fist. Slowly, a dark shadow emerged, forming the number 5. "Yes!" I exclaimed. "We're on the fifth floor. Are there more underneath?"

"Working on it." Mia wrapped her hand in a scarf and went to work, rubbing down the metal until she was crouching on the floor. I followed her with the light, staring in disbelief at what she revealed.

"Well?" demanded Cage impatiently after a few minutes of silence.

"That can't be right," I said, half to myself.

Alexei's voice took on a dangerous note. "*What* can't be right?"

"According to this, there are *seventeen* floors. Is that even possible? Seventeen floors to the bottom of the base?"

The others fell into silence. Their pale faces reflected in the light, worry etched in every line. "Well," said Matt at last, "I guess we'd better pick up the pace."

Exhaustion seeped into me. *Seventeen* floors to explore? That was bigger than Sanctuary, bigger than Obsidian. Eden hadn't mentioned this. She must have known. She'd been military herself. And if she'd lied about that . . .

What else wasn't she telling us?

TWENTY-SEVEN

WE DESCENDED THROUGH FLOORS OF barracks, training rooms, and high-tech computers—human computers, potentially useful even without alien information, but beyond my understanding, unfortunately. The other teams had not reacted well to learning the facility was massively bigger than we'd anticipated, but they were on the move now, descending in our wake. "Maybe Eden didn't know how big the facility really was?" I said dubiously as we reached the thirteenth floor. We weren't being quite as cautious now, having come so far without seeing any alien presence. "Maybe she'd never been here?"

Alexei frowned. "She knew about an alternate entrance," he said. "One hidden in the sand. How did she know that but not know the extent of the facility?"

"I would like to point out how I never trusted her," Mia announced.

"But what's her endgame?" Matt sighed. "What does she gain from lying to us?"

Cage shook his head, clearly baffled. "I don't know. But we've descended more than ten floors without seeing this so-called alien technology of hers. I'm not sure it even exists. What do you think? Do we turn back? Confront her?"

We all hesitated in the stairwell. "If we do," said Matt at last, "we give up on that ship. Assuming it exists, of course."

"Eden has nothing to gain by killing us," I added. "And if she wanted to, she's had a dozen opportunities. Whatever's going on here, she didn't send us to die. I think we should keep going. At least find out what's at the bottom of the facility."

A noise in the distance made us all freeze. It was a strange, scraping kind of sound.

"Eden?" I whispered. My mouth suddenly went dry, my tongue stuck to the roof of my mouth.

"The other teams would have alerted us if she'd followed," Cage replied, moving to the front of the group and drawing his gun.

Mia fumbled for Matt's light, and he jerked it out of her reach irritably. "Would you stop? Whatever that is, it's not a twenty-foot-tall monster. Have you noticed the ceilings in here? No way Karoch's stomping around this area. And I'd rather not trip over anything because you're more comfortable in the shadows."

Mia hesitated, looking ready to argue, but another thump

came from behind the closed door. She swallowed and stepped back, shimmering into invisibility as a silent protest.

The rest of us followed Cage and Matt to the door. Matt took a position against the wall, suddenly very military in his bearing. How much training had Legion given him? He'd mentioned some prior training, but he hadn't moved like this, not on Sanctuary, not when I'd known him.

Of course, he wasn't some kind of cyborg back then either. It was entirely possible they'd implanted behavioral modifications, changes to his mind as well as his body. Did Matt himself know the full extent of what Omnistellar had done to him? Did anyone?

He gestured to the rest of us to stand back, and I moved a few steps up the stairwell. Alexei followed, half shielding me behind his bulk, probably intentionally. I wasn't about to complain. Instead I closed my eyes and focused on Alexei's power. I'd never drawn from him before, but I was getting better at this process. Each ability spoke to me individually now instead of the mishmash of power I'd sensed before. Alexei's talent, a sparkling, crimson shimmer, hovered at the edge of my senses. I reeled it in, wrapping myself in its warmth, ready to attack at a second's notice.

Matt nodded to Cage, eased the door open a crack, and recoiled against the wall.

But nothing leaped out, and after a moment, Cage nudged the door the rest of the way open. He peered inside, glanced back at us, and beckoned for us to follow.

We did, weapons clutched, powers ready. I kept Alexei's ability charged in my fingertips. Could I use it and Mia's invisibility at the same time? I'd never tried. I hadn't had much time to experiment with my newfound powers. None of us had. A combat situation probably wasn't the time to start, but I might be left without a choice.

We wound through the corridor in a loose line, Cage and Matt in the front, me in the middle, Alexei at my back, Mia God knew where. After a few seconds the sound echoed again: a rattle, or a drag, or a shift. Whatever it was, it was coming from farther down the corridor.

Cage looked over his shoulder and our eyes met. In the dim light I couldn't distinguish his expression, but his body was taut, his muscles standing out beneath the body armor. Would it provide any protection against alien claws? I doubted it. Maybe against the harvesters, but the memory of those razor-sharp, far-too-long hunter claws assailed me and I trembled. I clenched my fists and locked my jaw to hide it, but I was shaking so hard I wasn't sure I dared use Alexei's power.

Much less a gun.

We resumed our trek and then, as we rounded a corner, Cage and Matt both stopped short.

Alexei and I followed suit. For a moment we all stood there, silent and still. The boys blocked my view, their broad shoulders a shield of tension. Every inch of me wanted to scream, to demand to know what they saw, what was ahead. I bit my lip hard enough to taste blood and didn't let a sound escape.

Finally, Cage and Matt nodded at each other and stepped aside. I already knew what we'd see from the way they moved: each step a careful placement designed to make no noise whatsoever. It took them a full minute to retreat four or five steps, to plaster their backs against the wall to reveal what lay ahead.

My heart gave one final beat and went still.

The area ahead was full of aliens.

Hunters, by the looks of them: taller and stronger and more muscular than their harvesting compatriots. At a glance, there were at least two dozen just milling around. Not even that, I realized: just *standing* there, frozen, like the ones I'd encountered in the medical bay on the Omnistellar ship. They'd stood there, too, until the moment they scented me.

And on that thought, one of them raised its head and sniffed.

It was like being trapped in a slow-motion loop, watching the most horrible episode of *Robo Mecha Dream Girl* ever, praying with all my might for the alien to turn back, lower its head, look away.

But it angled itself directly toward us and sniffed the air again.

A low purring emerged from its throat, and a collective stir ran through the hunters.

And then Alexei had my arm and was pulling me along

the corridor, out of sight, moving as fast as we dared without making a sound. I realized Matt and Cage were retreating too. We scrambled down the hallway, guns raised, everyone shaking so badly I didn't trust a single person's aim, and each second I expected the aliens to come charging along the hall in front of us.

But they didn't, and a minute later we were in the stairwell, Alexei easing the door closed again.

For a long moment we all stood and gaped at it in silence, and then Alexei whispered, "Mia?"

She shimmered into existence at his shoulder, and for the first time in my memory, Alexei glared at her. "I didn't know where you were." He was whispering, but his voice was sharp, clipped, each word a strike of precision. "Whether we were locking you in with those things. Don't do that again."

For once Mia had no argument to give. She only nodded.

"There was alien tech in there." I closed my eyes, wishing I could unsee it. "I recognized it. Just like what we saw on the ship." The consoles had wrapped around the room, occupying the space that had probably belonged to military computers in the facility's previous life. In places, I'd still spotted human-looking keyboards and screens wedged between the strange alien screens.

"We're not sending Rune in there," Cage growled.

Matt scowled. "Of course we're not. We have to keep going farther down and look for somewhere safer she can connect."

Or we could just get the hell out of here. The words hovered on my lips, unspoken. I wanted so, so badly to retreat up the stairs. To leave the building entirely. But we had a mission, and if we didn't complete it, we'd be trapped on this planet for the rest of our short lives. Cage beckoned and we followed, heading to the next level down. We kept our weapons drawn, and every two steps I twisted to check for pursuit, but nothing followed.

We'd lucked out. The aliens hadn't realized we were there, or hadn't been sure.

I hoped. There were other, more sinister explanations, but if I even began to consider them, my throat closed, so I pushed them aside and forced myself to face the problem at hand—which right now was just putting one foot in front of another and getting down those stairs.

We reached the next landing without incident, and my breath came a little easier. "Okay," Cage whispered, so softly we could barely hear him. "I think we're safe. Kenzie, can you radio the support teams? Tell them what we saw and to wait for more information."

I nodded and relayed his comments, starting with the second team, the one most likely to be directly behind us. Reed said his team was on level nine and promised to take a position on eleven, ready to warn us if they saw activity below.

Hallam didn't answer.

TWENTY-EIGHT

"HALLAM," I SAID, PROBABLY LOUDER THAN I should have, pressing against the comm device as if I could somehow prod it into better functionality. "Hallam, answer me."

Nothing.

I raised my head to meet Cage's panicked eyes. "What's going on?" he demanded.

I shook my head helplessly. "I don't know. I got Reed without any trouble, but Hallam's not responding."

Cage and Matt both took a step forward, but Alexei raised his hands. "Let's not panic," he said. "There could be any number of explanations for why the team's gone silent."

"Yes," said Cage sharply, "the most likely among them that they're being stalked by aliens."

But now Matt shook his head, apparently recovered from his initial reaction. "Hallam's not going to let anything happen to them," he said. "You guys don't know him like I do. Trust me. They're safe."

"This wouldn't be Hallam's stupid idea of a joke, would it?" Mia demanded.

Matt scowled. "Hallam's a pro. He might be hard to deal with, but he wouldn't put the mission at risk. And speaking of the mission, we need to keep looking for a way through this place."

Cage's eyes flashed. "No, what we *need* to do is get back upstairs and find out what's happened to my sister."

"Cage," said Mia quietly. "I get what you're saying. But if we abandon the mission here, we abandon the mission entirely." She turned to me. "Tell Reed to take his team and check on Rune and the others. Warn them they might be walking into trouble."

Cage took a step toward her. "Who put you in charge?"

"You did, when you started acting on emotion instead of logic." Mia spun on him. She managed to keep her voice at a whisper, but she was clearly furious. "And don't you dare lecture me about little sisters, Cage. Because you know I would have given anything to save my own, and you know how much I care about Rune. But this time, the mission comes first. For all our sakes, we have to keep going."

Cage seemed to deflate a bit, but he still looked to me, as if hoping for support. I closed my eyes and considered. If we retreated, went in search of Rune, we'd probably be too late to help. And we wouldn't be able to come back. Even if we got upstairs and nothing was wrong, we'd have wasted time during which the aliens might have recognized our presence.

I pressed against my comm. "Reed, it's Kenzie. Rune's team has gone silent. We need you to backtrack and find out where they are and what's happening. Report as soon as you know something."

Reed's panicked voice responded: "What do you mean, *silent*?"

I swallowed my annoyance. He was scared and tired, exactly like me. "I mean what I said. We're going to keep moving forward, but the three of you should retrace your steps and find them."

Priya snapped something in the background, and then Reed returned, more subdued. "All right. Just be careful, okay?"

"You know it," I said, managing to keep my voice normal even though Cage was glaring at me now. "And seriously, Reed. The second you find anything, okay?"

"The very instant," he agreed, and cut his comm.

Cage spun and yanked open the door behind him without warning, causing all of us to suck in our breaths and jerk our weapons upright. But there was only an empty corridor, yet again.

"What the hell do you think you're doing?" Matt snarled, still in a whisper.

Cage glared at each of us in turn. "You all wanted to keep the mission going. Apparently I'm overruled, so I'm moving on."

I grabbed his arm. "Getting all of us killed isn't going to

help your sister," I told him in a low voice, trying to cover my own anger. Cage wasn't often reckless, and he'd picked a hell of a time to start. "You didn't get your way this time. Suck it up. Priya and Jasper can get to Rune faster than we can anyway. And also to Hallam and Imani. You remember them, right? They're up there too."

Cage gawked at me like I'd struck him, and I had to work not to apologize. I did soften my voice, though. "I know you're worried about your sister. We all are. But if you want to be a leader, you have to act like one even when it's inconvenient." I nodded over my shoulder at the others. "We need a leader right now, Cage. So lead us."

He hesitated a moment longer, but I already saw the fight draining out of him. "I'm sorry," he said to me. Then he raised his head and repeated to the others, "I'm sorry. I just . . . I imagined Rune with the aliens, and I guess I lost it for a minute there. You guys deserve better."

"Don't worry about it," Matt replied. "You want to make it up to us, help keep us alive."

"Yeah." Cage raked his hand through his hair. "That's a good plan."

"So let's put it into action." Mia drew forward, a rifle clutched in her hands. I could almost see her itching to disappear, but she jerked her head forward. "Let's see if we've got another room of aliens—and whether there's any way to destroy them."

We advanced along another corridor and found ourselves

in a wide room full of tanks. I recognized them at once, even though they were a different structure than the ones on our alien ship. "They're stasis pods," I whispered.

Cage drew up to one and peered inside. "Sleeping aliens," he confirmed.

It probably said something that this came as a relief. Only weeks ago, Cage and I had recoiled in horror at the discovery of sleeping aliens. Now, I was simply grateful they weren't awake and pursuing me.

"Find a way to shut off their life support or something," Mia commanded.

Cage scowled at her. "Do *not* start pressing buttons at random. The last thing we want to do is wake them up."

I nodded in agreement, but there weren't any buttons to push. Aside from the sleeping aliens, the room was almost completely empty.

We explored the rest of the floor, finding more drifting harvesters, more stasis tanks, and absolutely nothing of use. Of course, we could have tried setting fire to the room, or smashing the tanks, but either option would make a lot of noise, risk waking the creatures instead of killing them, and probably alert the other aliens.

So instead we beat a hasty retreat and descended to level fourteen, where we found another floor of sleeping harvesters. Floor fifteen held another room of silent, still hunters, and once again we quickly backtracked.

There were only two floors left to go.

The sixteenth floor was different. There were two doors, one on each side of the hall. Behind one we heard a calamitous riot: smashing, cracking, shrieking aliens. We exchanged glances.

"What is going on back there?" I demanded in a whisper.

"Let's not find out," replied Mia darkly. "There's only one floor left below us. I say we check it out and get the hell out of here. If whatever Eden wants is behind this door, well, she's out of luck."

Something smashed into the other side of the wall, making us all jump. That was all the incentive we needed to get our feet moving, scrambling down the stairs. What the hell was going on up there? The aliens we'd seen so far were silent and still, almost as if they were in stasis themselves. They'd been waiting, not active. Something was happening to aggravate the creatures. Instantly I thought of Rune, and ice-cold terror pumped through my veins.

Suddenly Matt, who was in the lead, stopped short. "Something's weird," he said. "I think this leads into a big open area, not a hallway. We should be careful."

"Weapons out," Cage agreed. We drew close together and proceeded as silently as we dared. Before long I realized Matt was right: the area below us was a huge, open hangar of sorts. We couldn't see much of it in the flickering of Matt's and Cage's flashlights, of course, but they angled the illumination to reveal some sort of complex machinery and . . .

"There!" I whispered. "In the corner! It's Eden!"

Sure enough, Eden and her entire team stood stock-still in a far corner next to what looked like an exit. Her eyes met mine, and she shook her head frantically.

My heart dropped.

At the same moment, my comm device crackled. "Kenzie? Kenzie, are you there?"

I clapped my hand to my ear even though there was no way for the aliens to hear her voice. Turning aside, I spoke in a whispered mumble, keeping my free hand over my mouth. *"Rune?* Thank God you're safe. I thought Hallam had your comm. You—"

"Kenzie, listen to me." Her voice carried such urgency I clammed up at once, ignoring the way Cage and Matt closed in on me, as if they could listen in on my conversation if they just got close enough. "You have to get out of this bunker, and you have to do it now."

"Rune, we're seventeen floors down. And we haven't been attacked. Everything is—"

"Kenzie, I do not have time to explain this to you. I will tell you everything later, but for now, trust me: *you need to get out.* And you need to do it without coming back upstairs. Do you hear me?"

I looked at Cage and Matt, and my gaze drifted to Eden below.

Getting out was going to be more difficult than we'd anticipated.

TWENTY-NINE

I PUSHED PAST MATT AND CAGE TO ADVANCE another few steps. Eden made a slashing motion at me and pointed into the darkness.

We angled our lights, and we saw them.

A *horde* of aliens. Not one, or ten, or twenty, but dozens of them, all hunters. They were amassed around the perimeter of the room, not moving, not doing anything. Just standing. Waiting.

All the air seemed to vanish in a heartbeat. "Why's she still standing there?" Mia hissed, staring into the pit below at Eden and her soldiers. "What is she *doing*?"

"Maybe she thinks if she moves, they'll attack," Matt replied dubiously. "The more important question is, how the hell do we get out of here?"

Something echoed in the halls above us, and I craned my

neck. "Rune said not to go back up," I whispered. "I think they're not attacking because they're waiting for reinforcements."

"They don't need reinforcements," Mia returned. "They're waiting for *us*."

"What do we do?" Matt demanded, scanning the area. "If we go up, the creatures get us. If we go down, they attack. If we stay here, we're sandwiched between them."

"The only choice that doesn't result in certain death is down," Cage said. I gawked at him. How did he sound so calm, so self-assured, even as the tendons in his neck stood out with fear and his hands trembled on his gun? "Somehow, we have to get ourselves and Eden's people through that door."

Alexei leaned over the railing thoughtfully. "Matt," he said, "do you have infrared in those fancy cybernetics of yours?"

"Sort of. I can't see through walls, but I have heat sensors. Did you spot something?"

Alexei beckoned him over. "What's that?"

"It looks like a fuel source," said Matt dubiously.

Alexei nodded. "That's what I thought too. Perhaps something vulnerable to fire."

"What about the ship?" I half pleaded.

Alexei spread his arms. "Do you see a ship here? I suspect Eden lied to us about that. But even if she didn't, we have to consider our immediate survival. And if that means destroying the entire base—and the creatures with it—well . . ."

"No," said Mia sharply. "Even I can see you'd have to be

standing right beside whatever that is to create enough heat to get through its shielding. Don't you dare."

"I could improvise a fuse, given time," said Alexei, still reflective.

Something screeched in the darkness above us, and we froze, then lurched into motion, ignoring Eden's warning as we crept down the stairs. We kept a watchful eye on the perimeter of hunters, but they didn't move a muscle, like animatronics in stasis mode at a theme park.

"What are they doing?" I whispered. I knew I should keep silent, but the statue-like creatures held me so on edge I could barely breathe. I only knew *they* were breathing by the occasional flex in their muscles. "They have to know we're here." We'd been talking. Breathing. Shuffling around. They knew about us, had to, so *why weren't they acting?*

The others shook their heads. We hit the bottom of the stairs and started toward Eden and her soldiers, who remained motionless near a pile of boxes.

We'd taken about five steps when, from somewhere above us, another alien screamed. I spun just in time to see a hunter fly over the edge of the railing, landing maybe ten feet behind us, its jaws split wide to reveal its long, glistening fangs.

As if on cue, the other aliens seemed to wake. They didn't lunge, didn't attack. Instead they *uncoiled*. That was the only word to describe it. It was like their limbs loosened, like something switched them on, their focus shifting to us, their muscles tightening for action.

"That's not good," Cage muttered, nestling his gun tightly against his shoulder. I mimicked his actions, pressing my back to his, and the others fanned out in a loose circle. We were surrounded.

But the alien focus on us gave Eden the space she needed. As I watched, she moved ever so slowly, shifting a step toward the stack of boxes. The aliens didn't seem to notice. I remembered how Mia and I tipped the boxes in the hangar on Sanctuary, what felt like a hundred years ago, providing the distraction that allowed us to escape. God, I hoped Eden had a similar plan.

But I didn't have more than a few seconds to spare for Eden, because the aliens drew in, forming a tightening circle, hissing and spitting. The sight of so many of them awake together at once almost sent me cringing to the ground. The damage just a few of them had caused on Obsidian, on the Omnistellar ship we abandoned . . . what hope did we have against so many? None at all. Not unless Eden helped us, unless Alexei somehow sparked a flame that took them out all at once. And preferably didn't take us with it.

I clenched my fingers on my gun but didn't fire.

"Why aren't they attacking?" Matt whispered.

"They aren't sure where we are yet," Cage replied, his voice low, almost imperceptible. "They're not in a rush. They're closing in."

At the same moment, three more hunters dropped from above. They landed outside the ring, and I shifted my gaze to make sure Eden was okay . . .

And froze.

She was carefully, slowly, handing boxes to her soldiers. They'd formed a sort of bucket brigade, passing the boxes down a line to the final soldier, who would shoulder their burden and ease out of the door. There were already only five soldiers left.

"That lying, cheating dirtbag," seethed Mia, who'd obviously followed my gaze.

I ground my teeth so hard pain ricocheted through my skull, and I willed Eden to meet my eyes. Was this why she'd led us here? For whatever the hell was in those boxes? Were we her sacrificial lamb, here to distract the aliens? Was *this* what Rune meant when she told us to get out?

Eden didn't look my way, not then, not when she shouldered the final box, but she hesitated in the doorway. *Turn around*, I willed her. Turn around and face us and for God's sake, *help us*.

But she didn't.

She slipped through the exit and was gone.

Mia was whispering what I was sure would have been a screaming storm of curses if she'd had the freedom to shout, and everyone else seemed at a total loss. We were on our own. No help was coming. I wasn't naive enough to think that Eden would return for us, not anymore. We'd served our purpose.

The aliens were almost close enough to attack now. "Do we shoot?" I whispered.

"Not sure we have much choice," Cage replied softly.

Matt jerked his head toward the exit. "Clear a path," he said. "All we need to do is get through that door."

"And if they follow us?" Mia snarled.

Matt shrugged. "Then we shoot them down as they emerge. Or we run. Eden said they didn't like the heat. Either way, it's better than staying here." He didn't mention it, but it would also mean leading the aliens straight to Eden and her people—and I had to admit, a vengeful part of me welcomed that idea.

"All right." Cage pressed against my back, and his arm tensed as he slid his finger over the trigger. "On my count. One . . . two . . ."

One of the aliens let loose a horrific howl and leaped six feet straight into the air, flying at Mia. A burst of gunfire jolted through the room, so loud it made me cringe, and the creature screamed, collapsing on the ground.

As if that was a signal, the aliens exploded into motion, snarling, lunging, attacking. Within seconds I couldn't see the exit. I lowered my gun, some form of automatic laser rifle similar to ones I'd seen in Omnistellar, and opened fire.

My first burst tore through the aliens like butter, shredding their insides. They screeched as they collapsed, but almost immediately another wave took their place. My second shot seemed to hurt them too, but not as badly; they fell to the ground and writhed for a while before they died.

"They're already shielding!" Mia shouted. The need for stealth was gone. "If we're going to move, we'd better do it now!"

"I'll cover you!" Cage bellowed in return. "Let's go! Run for the door!"

I didn't much like the idea of Cage lingering to cover us, but I also didn't have time to argue. Alexei's huge form charged into the crowd, firing his gun, seemingly at random. We'd all deliberately chosen different types of weapons in an effort to slow the speed at which the creatures adapted, and that strategy seemed to be working. We'd already killed at least a dozen and we were moving—slowly, but moving.

Suddenly agony laced along my right arm. I collapsed with a scream as white-hot pain stabbed through me. Cage spun and caught me, hauling me to my feet and firing in the same motion. His bullets missed me by inches, leaving a ringing in my ears as he shot down the creature who'd slipped past our fire and attacked me.

I took in our hopeless situation and groaned as the truth dawned on me. This was going to hurt. "We have to run!" I shouted at Cage.

He shook his head frantically, squeezing off another shot. This one barely seemed to faze the monster he was targeting. "We can't carry the others, and we can't leave them!"

"We can clear a path!" I insisted.

He gaped at me. "Are you crazy?"

"What other choice do we have?" I reached for Cage's power, a shimmery mess of gold and green. I wrapped myself in its familiarity and warmth. "Let's go!"

"What the hell are you doing?" Mia screamed as I pushed past her. She'd tossed her gun aside, clearly deeming it useless, and drawn a long, wicked-looking blade, her face set in the grim expression of someone planning to do as much damage as possible before she died.

"Follow us!" I ordered in response. "As fast as you can." I turned to Cage and took his hand. "Ready?"

"No!"

"Good. Let's go!"

THIRTY

CAGE AND I DUCKED OUR HEADS, SQUARED our shoulders, and took off at the speed of sound.

We instantly smashed into alien bodies, but our speed had rendered them incapable of tracking our movements, and we hit solid muscle, not claws. It was enough to stop us momentarily, but we lurched into motion again, barreling through the crowd with Cage's power.

Each time we collided with a creature, it was agony, like slamming into a brick wall. Even with my head bent, my arm shielding my face, my body quickly began to scream. I felt like I'd been tied to a post and beaten with a stick. Still I tried again. When I floundered, Cage caught me and pulled me up, and I did the same for him. Over and over again, long after I wanted to give up and lie down, we pulled each other forward, putting on a burst of speed, clearing the crowd.

Finally I stumbled against the wall, half collapsing with Cage at my side. I could barely breathe, every inhale like a forced draw against an angry fist. I was one aching bruise, blood dripping from my torn arm, dizzy and on the verge of unconsciousness.

Cage didn't look much better. He, too, was bleeding and one of his eyes was puffy. But we were both standing, and when we turned, the others were behind us, having threaded their way through the aliens to our side.

"We need to get out of here," Mia snarled, grabbing the door Eden had exited through and yanking it open.

We found ourselves gaping at a flight of stairs and a lift. The lift was clearly broken, but I suspected the stairs led right back to the surface. Sure enough: an escape.

But the aliens were right behind us. We slammed the door, and Alexei and Matt threw their combined weight against it, holding it as it bucked and heaved under the alien onslaught. "What now?" Matt growled through gritted teeth. "We can't just walk away! They'll be on us before we get twenty feet."

"We haven't used fire yet," Alexei replied grimly. "I can blast some of them before they adapt."

My comm device crackled. "Kenzie!" Rune shouted. "Where are you?"

I tapped it to activate it. "We're outside the lower level trying to keep the aliens inside. Rune, don't trust Eden. It's—"

"I know." Bitterness laced her tone. "You guys need to get up here."

Alexei and Matt lurched against the bucking door, and Cage and Mia joined their weight to the boys', their muscles straining as they held the barrier. "Whatever we're going to do," Mia shouted, "we'd better do it soon."

I shook my head. "We can't lead them upstairs! Rune and the others are there. The aliens will tear them apart, and that's after they finish with us."

"There has to be a way out of this!" Cage shouted. It was a relief to raise our voices, to give vent to the terror and tension we'd been fighting since we'd descended that ladder. "I refuse to accept defeat. Not here, not now, not after we've come through so much!"

I looked to the stairs, and to my friends. "Rune," I said quietly, "I think you'd better gather everyone and head back to the city."

"What?" she shrieked so loudly she almost splintered the bones in my ear. "Not until we have you!"

I lowered my voice further, but even with the aliens pounding against the door, I knew the others heard me. "I don't think we're going to make it."

"The hell you're not." Mild-mannered Rune's voice adopted a core of pure steel. "Get your ass up here, Kenzie, or I'll come down there and get you myself."

"Do you have a way to overload some systems? Maybe lock some doors?"

She hesitated. "No."

"Then trust me when I say there's nothing you can do." I

expected to feel more now when I was finally about to die, but only emptiness surged inside me. At least I'd die surrounded by my friends. And then, who knew? Maybe I'd see my mom, my dad, my fallen comrades.

"Kenzie." Rune's voice took on a pleading note. "Listen."

"Take care of the others. Find a way home," I told her, and I cut the comm.

The door bucked so hard all four of its protectors lurched forward, although they quickly slammed themselves back into place. "We can't keep this up much longer," Matt gasped.

"It won't matter if they run." Cage was staring upstairs, his face fixed in an agonized mask, the least collected I'd ever seen him. "They won't make it. Not if these creatures chase after us. We have to hold them as long as we can, give the others as much of a head start as possible."

They'd die anyway. Rune wouldn't run any more than I would have, any more than Cage. All we could do was buy them time. I swallowed. "What can I do? I can use any of your powers. Tell me what will help."

The door lurched again, sending Mia flying into me. We both collapsed to the floor in a tangle of limbs.

A clawed arm tore through the crack in the door. It slashed at random, catching the side of Alexei's face and tearing huge bleeding chunks through his skin. Alexei bellowed in pain but dug in his heels, and all three boys turned their shoulders to the door, struggling against the creature's might.

I only had a second to act. Mia, dazed, dropped the wicked machete-like blade she carried. I snatched it up, flying through the room with Cage's speed and bringing it down with every bit of my strength. It sliced halfway through the alien arm and stuck fast. The alien screamed its shrill, vicious scream, so loud it almost physically staggered me. I wrenched the blade back and forth, struggling to free it from the creature, to retreat or advance or anything other than leave it wedged through the thing's arm as its strange, oozing fluids coated my hands.

"Move!" Mia shouted. I obeyed without thinking, ducking as she leaped onto the stair rail and launched herself over me, landing with one foot on either side of the blade, balanced precariously on the creature's arm.

Her weight accomplished what my strength had not, driving the blade the rest of the way through the creature and severing its arm. The door slammed shut on its howls as Mia hit the floor, letting out a cry of her own as she collapsed in a much less graceful heap than she'd originally managed.

Matt kicked the alien's severed arm aside in disgust, and it skittered across the hallway. We had almost thirty seconds of silence, barely long enough to hope the aliens had retreated, before the door lurched under a renewed assault.

"There's only one way out of here," said Alexei grimly, "and we all know what it is."

Mia staggered to her feet, clearly unsteady, but still managed to jab a finger in his direction. "No."

"Mia mine, we are out of options." He looked to the rest of us, his gray eyes flat and calm between the bloody gashes that shredded his face but, miraculously, missed his eyes and lips. "The fuel source inside. I can clear a path through the creatures with fire and then incinerate it. You'll have to run as fast as you can. I can't guarantee how long I'll distract them."

"Absolutely not," Cage snapped.

But Matt hesitated. "Do you have another idea?" he asked at last, almost gently.

Cage and I exchanged glances.

"It doesn't *matter* if there's not another idea," Mia snarled. She grabbed Alexei's arm, the two of them jolting together as the aliens hit the door.

"Mia. I can't let everyone upstairs die to buy myself an extra five minutes."

She wavered, and I waited, breath bated, not daring to speak as emotion warred across her face. "Fine," she snarled at last. "Then I'm coming with you."

Alexei sighed. "Mia . . ."

"I'm not letting you go in there alone, Lex, and that's final." She jammed her hands on her hips and glared up at him. "Besides, you need me. You can't make it through there by yourself."

"I don't . . ." Alexei appealed to each of us in turn. Then he muttered a Russian curse under his breath, grabbed Mia, hauled her against him, and kissed her. His blood ran between their faces, and neither of them seemed to care as they locked in an embrace that made me look away in embarrassment and maybe something else, a huge lump rising in my heart and threatening to choke me on my own fears.

A sound drew my attention as they broke apart. “I love you, Mia mine,” Alexei said.

And then he caught her by the back of the neck and spun her around, locking her in the crook of his arm, his other hand behind her, rendering her immobile. Mia choked, snatching at his arms, but Alexei muttered something and held tight, collapsing to the ground beside her.

I was too shocked to move, too scared to speak.

A moment later Alexei straightened, Mia in his arms. He passed her limp form to Cage, who was gaping at him like he’d never seen him before. “Get her out of here,” he said.

Cage faltered, then swallowed hard and nodded. “All right.”

“No,” I whispered. “No, we can’t do that. Cage . . .”

Alexei offered me a faint smile. “You’ll be okay, Kenzie. Take care of Mia. She’s not as hard as she seems.”

“You can’t—”

The door lurched again, and this time they barely managed to hold it. Alexei spread his arms wide, knocking the other two off balance. “Go,” he ordered. “I’ll hold the door as long as I can, and then I’ll keep their attention on me. If I can make it to the center of the room, I’ll take this whole place out with me. If not, I’ll still buy you some time.” When none of us moved, his eyes narrowed, his chin jutting to an aggressive point. "Why the hell are you still standing here? Go! Now, all of you, run!"

A split second of agonized indecision crossed Cage's face, and then he was gone, a rush of air passing me, and it was only me, Matt, and Alexei in the room.

Matt grabbed me and pulled me for the stairs, but I couldn't move, my legs locked in place. "No," I repeated. "We can't . . . Alexei, please."

He smiled. The door bucked behind him and he sank his feet into the cement, just barely managing to hold against the heaving, roiling mass behind. "It's been a privilege being your friend, Kenzie."

Somehow, I made my legs move. Somehow, I retreated a step, and then another. Matt grabbed my arm and spun me, shoving me up the stairs ahead of him, blocking me as if frightened I'd try to retreat. Every time I turned for a last glimpse of Alexei, Matt's bulk shielded my view, and he pushed me forward, urging me on.

We rounded the corner, and I skidded to a halt. What were we doing? I was not leaving someone else to die at alien hands, especially not Alexei, especially not now. "We have to go back."

A burst of wind almost knocked me off balance, and I staggered as Cage materialized in front of me. "Let's go," he gasped, trembling and out of breath and maybe even on the verge of unconsciousness. "Kenzie, help me carry Matt. Between us we might be able to drag him. Anyway, we have to try." He frowned at Matt. "Sorry, buddy. This might get uncomfortable."

A slight smile touched Matt's face. "It's hardly the worst you've ever done to me."

"Kenz." Cage shook my arm. "Come on!"

"We have to go back!" I screamed, my voice echoing through the corridors.

The boys exchanged glances. "And do what?" Matt snapped, his voice suddenly losing all trace of kindness, becoming the Silver Oni he'd been on Obsidian. "Get ourselves killed while making sure Alexei dies in vain? Get your head in the game, Cord. Stop being so goddamn selfish and do Lex the courtesy of giving his death some meaning."

Selfish? Was that what I was being? I looked between them and swallowed hard. "Okay," I whispered, my voice barely audible to my own ears. Reaching out, I wrapped myself in Cage's power. I didn't dare let myself think too hard about what I was doing. I didn't think at all. I went into Omnistellar mode, shutting off my brain, and then grabbed Matt's hand and *ran*.

I couldn't lift Matt for long, and neither could Cage, but Matt helped where he could, scrabbling against the steps as we dragged him upward. We ran in bursts and stops, giving him time to collect himself and ourselves a second to breathe before we took off again.

We reached the top of the stairs and slammed through a metal door into the warehouse we'd seen before. We'd done a number on Matt's legs; they were battered and bleeding through his torn pants, and we had to support him as we ran across the room.

We'd barely reached the door when something rumbled beneath my feet. I half turned, expecting the worst, bracing for an explosion, but nothing happened.

And then the ground began to shift.

As the warehouse disintegrated, we lurched forward, scrambling into the hot midday sun, our fingers and feet gaining purchase in the sand as we crawled away. When we finally reached a place where the ground wasn't slipping and sliding, we dropped there. I rolled over to watch the warehouse collapse into the sinkhole of sand. Every trace of the base vanished, taking the last hope of Alexei with it.

THIRTY-ONE

I LAY THERE IN THE SAND, RIVETED ON THE place where the warehouse had stood. Nothing remained but a crumpled heap of metal and brick.

On the other side of the building, the rest of our crew huddled in a group: Eden and her soldiers surrounded by a large pile of boxes, Hallam and Rune, Jasper and Priya, and Reed and Imani, who seemed to be healing people. Mia lay unconscious at their feet, her skin still bright with Alexei's blood. "Kenzie," Rune gasped, taking half a step forward. "What happened? We heard a sound, felt a rumble, and as soon as we left the warehouse . . ."

My eyes met hers, and I staggered upright, switching my focus to Eden. A murderous rage swelled in my chest, blinding me in a sea of red. Rushing filled my ears, and my heart beat so fast it shook my chest, making my breath come in unsteady gasps. I was half dead on my feet, but still I lurched in her direction.

Her soldiers closed rank in front of her. "No," said Eden softly, "let her come."

I faced her in the beating sun, caked in blood, my body battered and sore. "What's in the boxes?" I growled.

I heard, rather than saw, Cage and Matt draw up behind me, Matt dragging in the sand.

Eden regarded each of us in turn and then closed her eyes, as if tired. "Supplies," she said. "Emergency rations. Water. Enough to keep us alive for another six to eight months."

"And that was your real reason for dragging us here." Cage's voice had gone calm again, almost pleasant, the way it did when he was so angry he could barely think. "You wanted us to provide a distraction so you could get your hands on those supplies."

"Yes." Eden squared her shoulders and met his gaze defiantly. "It was the difference between life and death for my people. I won't apologize for that."

"You lied about everything," Cage continued in that strained, cheerful tone. "Even the size of the damn facility."

She shrugged. "You wouldn't have gone in if you'd realized how big it was, the chances of getting lost down there. So I exaggerated."

I nodded, staring at my feet, betrayal churning in my stomach. I twisted my neck, examining the others, and landed on Reed holding Priya's arm. I traced a path to his fingers and shuddered: a jagged edge of bone protruded from her skin. Quickly, I looked away, my stomach churning.

Mia slept in the sand, and I realized these were her last moments before she'd have to face Alexei's death. Once she opened her eyes, she'd never again live without his absence hanging over her like a weight about to fall.

I didn't even think. The rage swelled and grew and choked, and the next thing I knew, I was on top of Eden, swinging my fists at her face. She brought her arms up to block me but didn't hit me back. It was Cage and Matt who grabbed me and hauled me off her. "We can't afford a war," Matt whispered, and I realized Eden's soldiers were surrounding us, weapons drawn.

"I know how you feel," Cage said in my other ear. His grasp on my arm was almost as comforting as it was restraining. "Believe me, I know. But this isn't you. It's not how you solve problems."

"Maybe it should be." I almost choked. I spit my words at Eden. "I told you to trust her. I said she was fine. This is my fault."

"This is *her* fault." Cage glared at Eden.

"No," said Jasper tiredly from the ground nearby. "She's despicable, but no. This is the aliens' fault."

"Cage," said Rune softly, her eyes growing wider by the second. "*Gege*. Where's Alexei?"

A horrible silence fell over the desert as the others finally noticed his absence.

Cage shook his head and gestured at the collapsed warehouse, apparently at a loss for words. He bit his lower lip and turned away. "No," Rune whispered. She fumbled for Imani, whose eyes had gone so wide they were almost pure circles. The two girls clung together, staring at us as if willing us to deny their fears.

Jasper, on the other hand, laughed. "Alexei?" he said. "Come on. He's the toughest of us all. There's no way he . . ." His smile faded as he stared at my face. "Cage?" he asked, his voice almost a whisper.

Cage swallowed audibly. "I couldn't . . . I didn't . . ."

And Mia picked that moment to stir. Imani dropped to her knees, sliding her arms around the other girl, helping her to sit, her shock and fear vanishing beneath almost professional concern. "Mia, breathe," she said. "There was some damage to your throat, but I repaired it. You're fine. You're—"

Mia shoved her aside. She seemed angrier than anything else, maybe at being forced to reveal this kind of physical weakness, and somehow I didn't think her anger would dissipate when she learned what she'd missed.

It didn't take long. Her eyes flickered between us before settling on Cage. She didn't say a word. She didn't have to.

"Mia," I whispered.

She shook her head, clambered to unsteady feet, and spun

to examine the collapsed warehouse. She still hadn't made a sound.

"Mia," Cage tried, finding his voice at last. He took a step toward her.

Mia spun on him, her steely gaze stopping him in his tracks. She examined each of us in turn: Jasper and Hallam hovering by Rune, Imani and Reed nearby, Priya to one side, Cage and me and Matt and Eden with the mass of soldiers and boxes in the background.

"Mia, please," said Imani. "You're still hurt. Sit down. Take a few breaths. Let's get you some water, get you some—"

"Did you carry me out?" Mia's voice emerged in a soft rasp, but there was nothing soft about the glare she turned on Cage.

He hesitated only a moment. "Yes."

Mia nodded. She turned away, scrutinizing the ruins of the facility once more.

And then, without warning, she flew across the sand, her fist colliding with Cage's face. Blood spurted from his nose as he stumbled back, toppling to the sand. Mia followed him with a resolute determination that put my earlier attack on Eden to shame. Before anyone could react, she'd driven her knee into his chest, pinning him to the sand, and landed two more punches with such force that bones crunched with every swing.

"Mia!" I flew at her, but she caught me with her drawn-back elbow, not even on purpose, though hard enough to send me to the ground. I sank my fingers into the sand, dazed from the fall after my earlier injuries.

When I regained myself, Matt had grabbed Mia and hauled her off Cage. He clamped his hands behind her neck, pinning her arms behind her. She wasn't fighting. She wasn't even moving. She was just glaring at Cage with such rage it diminished everything around us.

Slowly, as if terrified Mia would break free, Reed edged to Cage's side. "It's broken," he said, examining Cage's nose. "In a couple of places, I think. Just stay still and let me work."

"He sacrificed himself," said Matt in Mia's ear, so quietly I almost didn't hear him. "We would have died without him." He spun on Eden, eyes flashing with the new anger I'd only seen since he returned with Legion. "Of course, that was the idea, wasn't it?"

Eden shook her head frantically. "No. I tried to warn you off when you came down the stairs."

"Knowing we wouldn't listen." I stepped back and stared at her hollowly. "You figured the aliens would take us out while we explored the facility, and while they were busy with us, you'd snag those supplies you needed. And then what? What happens when those run out?"

She tossed her head. "There have to be other cities. Other survivors. There has to be a way to get food and water. Gideon kept us in one place too long, but now, with these supplies, we have time to explore. And it doesn't hurt that this alien base is gone, either."

"There are others," said Priya. She was standing unsteadily, batting Imani away from her. Imani hesitated a moment, then edged toward Matt, keeping a wary eye on Mia. "Rune found information, whether you expected her to or not. There are more creatures on this planet than you can imagine."

Eden's eyes flew open. "You actually found something?"

Rune snorted. "Didn't expect that, did you? Yeah. I did. I was able to use the preexisting system to link up with the *zemdyut* network. I couldn't understand the symbols, of course, but I remembered how the system functioned from the ship, and I was able to get the general sense of what was going on through the images and telepathic links in the network. Although calling it a *network* isn't really accurate. It's something else, something I've never seen before, even on the ship . . ."

"What did you learn?" Eden demanded. "Where are the other bases? Where are the *zemdyut*?"

"Oh, no you don't," Rune replied coldly. She folded her arms over her chest and glared at the older woman, suddenly looking much more dangerous—much more like Cage. "You led us into a trap. You lied to us. You killed my friend. You get nothing. *Nothing*," she snarled, spitting the last word like a snake unleashing its venom, her rage so physical that several of Eden's soldiers retreated.

Mia too spit on the ground, her glare making it clear she

intended it as a statement on Eden. "You can let go now," she told Matt sharply. "I'm not going to kill anyone."

He released her by inches, and out of the corner of my eye I saw Jasper, Hallam, and Priya tense, reaching for their weapons as if they planned to shoot her down like a rabid dog. But Mia only cracked her neck and moved away, standing at the perimeter, arms folded over her chest, her back to us as she stared at the fallen warehouse.

Imani laid her hand on Matt's arm and whispered something in his ear, and he sat heavily in the sand as she set to work on his injured legs. The rest of us just stared at one another, Eden and her soldiers against us and ours. We all had weapons. We had near-equal numbers. They had a driving need to survive, but we . . . we had anger. It seethed inside me, rolling like a bubbling volcano, needing just one push to send it all spilling over the edge.

"Kenzie." Reed had finished with Cage and was scrutinizing me the way everyone else was scrutinizing Mia. "You look pretty beat up. Maybe you'd better come sit down a minute, let us check things out."

I waved him aside. My own injuries could wait. I wasn't finished with Eden. "And what about the rest? Was anything true? What you said about the facility, the spaceship . . . although even if it exists, I suppose it's buried under rubble right now."

"It wouldn't have done us any good anyway." Rune stepped forward, her hair a tangled halo around her pixie face, her fists clenched at her side. Hallam moved with her. Apparently, it had taken Rune all of one mission to get him on her side, because he seemed poised to clobber anyone who looked at her the wrong way. "I was able to access some of the files on the facility mainframe. That's right," she said, spinning on Eden, who looked more exhausted than anything, "I know exactly where we are."

Dread swirled in my chest. *No no no*. I didn't want to know this. I couldn't handle any more, not on top of losing my family, of losing Alexei.

But Cage didn't give me an option. "What is it, *meimei*?" he asked softly.

"I saw our coordinates. We're on Earth."

THIRTY-TWO

"NO." I GAPED AT HER, MY JAW WORKING frantically even though only one syllable emerged. The truth of what she said—all the signs I'd tried to ignore—piled up in my mind, but I waved them aside in desperate denial. "No no no . . ."

"I was afraid of this," Imani murmured. "It was too familiar. Too neat. The odds against another culture like ours, speaking a language like ours, with people like ours, randomly spawning even close to home . . ."

"Liam didn't travel through time," I insisted hoarsely.

"No, he didn't." Rune was still glaring at Eden, but she spared a sympathetic glance for me. "Kenzie . . . he traveled through *dimensions*."

Dimensions. "No," I repeated. "Rune, I *used* his ability. Over and over again. And it never threw me into another dimension!"

She lifted her hands helplessly. "I can't explain it, Kenzie. It's possible his power had evolved to allow him to travel through space *and* dimensions, and you only tapped the dimensional ability in that moment of desperation. Or . . . maybe you *were* skipping dimensions, but over such tiny distances the changes were negligible."

The world swam. "You mean I could be several dimensions away from where I started?"

"At this point none of us are where we started. This planet might be called Wreithe here, but it *is* Earth. The tech hasn't changed; the time hasn't changed. Alternate dimensions are the only possible explanation."

I met Cage's gaze, and my knees gave out. He had me before I hit the sand, tipping my head between my knees. "Breathe," he murmured, the words ghosting over my ear. "Imani . . ."

Imani's hands landed on my back, soft and reassuring, contrasting the stronger pressure of Cage holding me. Warmth flowed from her touch, easing whatever damage I'd taken in the facility. A pain I hadn't noticed in my stomach relented, and my world stopped spinning as the wounds on my arm knitted themselves together.

But I couldn't bring myself to care about any of that. I raised my head to meet Cage's eyes. "We're trapped here after all," I whispered. "There's no hope of anyone finding us. No hope of getting back." Unbidden, I searched the area for Jasper. He appeared, if anything, worse than me; he was on the ground, head buried in his hands, elbows propped against his knees. Reed and Rune knelt beside him, Reed talking quickly while Rune rubbed his back. Mia was still staring off into the distance, and Legion had regrouped, their faces three identical masks of dismay. Not even their fancy training hid it this time.

Cage shook his head, but I'd seen the alarm on his face, and the quick flash of rage that followed. He pinned Eden with his glare.

She shrugged. "Look, I'm sorry I misled you."

"Lied," said Hallam, clearly and distinctly. "You *lied.* Let's not sugarcoat it."

"Call it what you want. I did it to save a lot of lives, and I'd do it again."

I staggered to my feet, leaning on Cage for support. "How did you know?" I snarled.

"I didn't know, but I guessed." She sighed, leaning against one of the crates, scraping her dark hair off her neck. "The similarities you spotted between our worlds only had one explanation. We've been looking for alien life for a long time, and we've never found it. What we did find was something else: other dimensions. Worlds that existed along ours. We were even able to peer into neighboring worlds—yours, and a few others. With that knowledge, it didn't take our scientists long to realize that the *zemdyut* were crossing dimensions, not space. They aren't aliens at all. Or if they are, they're not from this universe."

My head spun. All along. She'd known all along. And on

the heels of that, another realization: although she'd let us ramble on, Eden herself never used the word "alien." It was always *zemdyut* or "creatures." She hadn't just known, she'd manipulated us with practiced ease. Her story about shielding their planet from outside intervention . . . God, why had I ever fallen for that?

Because, I realized. Eden had been convincing. She'd known about our world, about the corporations. And . . . I'd been so eager to believe the worst of Omnistellar, so desperate to find a way home, that I'd overlooked the signs. Or made excuses for them. We'd all done it to avoid this moment: this crushing sense of defeat and despair as the utter bleakness of our situation finally dawned on us.

Or maybe . . . Had I identified too much with Eden? Encouraged the others to trust her because I saw too much of myself in her, because I wanted to believe that my mom and dad could have changed, that our destinies weren't locked in stone? I ground my nails into my palms. I'd told Cage to trust Eden. How much of this was my fault?

"I don't care about any of this," Priya barked. "Just tell us what we need to know. Is that Karoch thing real? Was there actually a ship in the base?"

"Did you kill Gideon because he was acting erratic or because you wanted to be in charge?" I added. A murmur rose among her soldiers, and I laughed, the sound high and almost hysterical to my own ears, as if coming from someone else.

"Oh, she didn't mention that? Yeah. She shot him because he wouldn't let us into your base. Part of her grand plan, I guess."

"That's enough," Eden snapped.

"Is it true?" demanded one of the soldiers. His face was hidden behind his mask, but he sounded young. "Did you kill Gideon?"

"To save these people. To save *us*." She glared at us. "Yes. I did."

"To save us?" One of the soldiers stepped forward. "Or to save yourself, Eden? Because not two months ago, you told me Gideon was a problem. You said we might have to get rid of him." Another murmur went up through the crowd.

Eden's expression barely changed. "I thought I could trust you."

"You could. But that was before I realized you murdered our leader in cold blood."

"It wasn't in cold blood. He attacked me. It was self-defense." She looked to me as if in appeal and then, obviously realizing I had no intention of helping her, she closed her eyes and passed a weary hand over her face. "Listen, Gideon knew about these supplies, but he'd become so frightened he didn't dare leave the base to get them. And he wouldn't let me, either. If he'd kept leading us, we all would have been dead in months. And now? Now we have supplies to keep us going. I didn't *want* to kill him, but he was paranoid. He was seeing *zemdyut* around every corner, starting to see enemies in our ranks, and he was going to get us killed!"

"And what happens when one of *them* is 'going to get you killed'?" Priya jerked her head at the soldiers, and they exchanged uneasy glances.

"Don't be ridiculous!" Eden snarled. "I did this to *protect them.*"

"We can talk about this later." Eden's soldier eyed her with suspicion but then shifted his anger to Priya and me. "This isn't the place or time. We have to get these supplies back to the city."

The soldiers hesitated, then stepped into line, but a ripple of discontentment shivered through the ranks. Good.

Eden fixed me with a glare. "And for what it's worth, most of what I told you was true enough. Karoch, I hope, died in that base. The ship should have been in the hangar. I don't know where it went. I didn't lie to you any more than necessary." She picked up one of the boxes. "We have enough supplies to carry us through whatever we do next. You're welcome to join us. We could use your skills, and it's the least I can offer considering—"

Mia, who had remained silent and motionless through all of this, moved with sudden speed and grace, pivoting like a dancer and drawing her gun in a single motion. "Mia!" Rune shrieked, flying at her. They collided just as Mia pulled the trigger. Her shot went wide, whistling past Eden's head. Eden's eyes narrowed, the blood draining from her face as she grasped how close she'd come to dying. In the same instant, her soldiers drew their guns and trained them on us—but Priya and Hallam were already on Mia, disarming and restraining her.

She showed no inclination to fight, apparently aware she'd missed her chance. She slumped in Hallam's arms, eyes fixed on her feet.

Eden took a step backward, her face twisting in a series of rapid-fire emotions: guilt and anger and fear and sorrow, all mixed up in a show that would have been comic if it weren't so grotesque. At last she retreated and, without another word, strode off into the desert, her crew at her heels.

We watched them go in silence. Sweat pooled at the base of my neck. I was trembling so badly I barely kept my feet. My eyes stung and my vision blurred, whether with tears or sweat I didn't know. Cage's hand tightened over mine, but it was small comfort here in the middle of the desert on an alien planet where we were all going to die, and probably soon.

"We have to get out of the sun," said Priya at last.

Mia wrenched free of Hallam and stalked across the sand. She sat about ten feet from the collapsed warehouse, resting her arms on her knees, staring at it.

I exchanged glances with Cage. "You want to talk to her?" I asked softly.

Cage snorted. "I don't think she's in the mood."

"If she just sits there, she's going to die," said Priya bluntly. "We've already been in this heat too long. I suggest everyone ditch their armor. We're not likely to need it. Keep the weapons. Ration what water you have left."

"And then?" snorted Jasper. He, like Mia, was still sitting

in the sand, blinking at his feet. "We make it back to town and what? Scavenge for whatever supplies Eden missed? Raid her people and let all those kids die so we can eke out a few more days of life? What's the goddamn point?"

A hopeless silence settled over us, because that was the thing: no one could answer him. What *was* the point? Liam was dead. As far as I knew, no one else had the power to jump dimensions. We were trapped here. "Maybe we can still get off the planet," I said at last, although my voice rang hopeless and dull in my own ears. "Maybe there's somewhere else we can go. Mars, or—"

"You really think Eden hasn't considered that? Besides, the spaceship was supposed to be in there, remember?" Jasper jerked his chin at the fallen base. "Next idea?"

My chest constricted. "You're not helping," I said sharply.

"Yeah, well . . ." Jasper flopped back in the sand. "Somehow I'm not in the most optimistic mood."

"Enough," Cage growled.

Jasper shot to his feet, his dark eyes flashing, apparently ready for a fight. "Oh, I'm sorry. Am I upsetting our illustrious leader? Or leaders? No one's in charge around here because no one knows what the hell to do next. Or am I wrong?" He glared at Priya, at Cage, at me. "Come on. Tell me. What's our plan?"

"Jasper, stop," said Imani. "You told me once that we have to keep going. Well, now I'm saying it to you. We can't just give up. We can't—"

"Oh, Imani, stop. There's *no point* anymore. Can't you see that?"

"If we're going to lie down and die, fine," said Matt. "If not, Priya's right. We need to get out of the sun."

The argument built and I backed away, unable to do anything but shake my head. Jasper wasn't wrong. *Give up and die* wasn't much of an option, but what other choice did we have left?

I cracked open my chest plate and peeled off the armor, and for a moment even the hot desert wind felt wonderfully cool against my parched skin. I dropped the armor on the ground at Rune's feet.

I blinked. I hadn't even realized she was beside me.

"Kenzie," she said quietly. "Are you all right?"

I shook my head, turning my back on the brewing argument to focus on my friend. "No. Pretty far from it, actually. What about you? What happened?"

"After you warned us about the aliens . . . well, whatever they are . . . guarding their tech, I retreated to the military tech facility on the fifth floor and accessed their network. The human network, I mean. I thought that if I got into the system itself, I might be able to break into the creatures' system, since it seemed to have merged with the human one. That it might be easier to understand. That's how I learned the truth about where we were and how Eden had lied to us. The center was a sort of Faraday cage, though, and it blocked our comm frequencies. We didn't know about that part until Reed's team came charging in full of panic. And then we heard the creatures moving below, and we looked down the stairs and . . ." She shuddered. "There was a group following you. I hacked the cameras and found another coming up to meet you. And a third in the basement. I tried to create a distraction by setting off an alarm in a room on the sixteenth floor. It worked to a degree. A bunch of creatures flooded in there, and I locked the door behind them. But I had to release the system to power down, and we left the room to warn you before things got worse."

"You did good," I said tiredly. "It's too bad it turned out to be for nothing."

"Well, that's the thing." Rune peered thoughtfully over my shoulder, and I realized she'd drawn me some distance away from the others. "I did actually manage to connect to the alien network. I did exactly what Eden wanted."

My eyebrows shot up as I examined the worry on her face. "Why do I get the feeling this isn't a clear good-news situation?"

"Because it's not. I told you I managed to hack into the alien . . . I don't know. I want to say *system*, but that feels wrong for what I accessed. I didn't understand much of it, though. It was a jumble, and of course, the language was unfamiliar. So I did what I could, which was grabbing a tablet and programing a back door into the alien network. They have a rough version of internet, and as long as I don't get too far from the base, as long as *something* is still intact down there, even a flicker, I should be able to access it. Not that it accomplished much. Understanding that system is virtually impossible." She hesitated again. "For me."

"Right." I rubbed my face tiredly, feeling sweat and dirt smearing beneath my fingertips, not caring. "Okay. Let me take a look at it. I'll see what I can do."

"It's not so simple." Rune forced what she probably thought was a reassuring smile. "Kenzie . . . I think the only way to interact with the system is for you to do what I do. Bond with it. Enter it completely."

I stared at her. "So what you're telling me is, we have a chance of getting some new information, but it's probably nothing, and most of the aliens who supplied it are dead anyway, and the only thing I have to do is supernaturally merge with an alien computer system to check it out."

"That's about it, yup." She shrugged. "Except for one little detail. The aliens aren't all dead, Kenzie. There are more of them spread out beneath the ground, *far* more. Now you see why I wanted to talk privately."

I closed my eyes as yet another headache pounded behind my eyes. Why was nothing in my life ever, ever easy?

THIRTY-THREE

RUNE AND I ANTICIPATED A LOT MORE resistance to her plan than we got. I think everyone, even Cage, realized the futility of our situation. If we were going to accomplish anything, this was the only possibility. After all, if the *zemdyut* had crossed dimensions to get here, obviously they had the means to travel between them. Maybe we could somehow use that to get home. We needed *something*, some option other than dying of starvation or dehydration or heatstroke. It didn't take long for Rune to confirm that some bit of the alien network had survived the collapse and that we'd be able to access it, the first bit of luck we'd had in, well . . . ever?

We had to argue a bit with Priya, who didn't understand how *anything* could have survived an explosion of that magnitude. But as Rune pointed out, we were dealing with alien technology. We didn't know its strengths and weaknesses. And while the bottom of the base had definitely been destroyed, the top half might have simply crumbled. Pieces might be intact. When she focused, she found a signal—weak, but present. And that was enough to silence Priya, because no one, not even Legion, questioned Rune's instincts when it came to tech.

Instead of returning to town, we built a sort of shelter from what remained of the warehouse. Jasper's ability to move inanimate objects telekinetically came in handy, as did Matt, Hallam, and Priya's cybernetically enhanced strength. I offered to mimic Jasper's ability and help, but that was strictly vetoed; there was a general consensus that I needed to save my energy for what came next.

Before long we'd established a miniature version of the warehouse near where the original had stood. It wasn't much, but it would block the worst of the heat and sun for a while.

Everyone staggered inside—everyone except Mia. Cage and I exchanged glances. After a moment, I shrugged and risked approaching her. "Mia?" I said softly. "Mia, we're going in. Come out of the sun."

No response.

I silently appealed to Cage again. Moving carefully, he settled on her other side. "Don't hit me again, okay?" he said, sounding reasonably calm and cheerful, although one of his arms was tensed in case she did precisely that.

Mia didn't even blink.

I examined her helplessly. I'd never seen Mia like this. She'd clearly planned on dying with Alexei beneath the surface, and since we'd dragged her to safety, she was going to sit here until she died anyway. Were we going to have to knock her out again? Somehow, I didn't want to be the one to try.

"Mia, please come inside," said Cage softly. "We can talk about this. Or not. Whatever you want. I don't . . ." He raked his hands through his hair and shook his head at me desperately. "I'm sorry, Mia. What was I supposed to do? Leave you lying on the ground? Refuse Alexei's dying wish?"

I thought that might get a rise, but it didn't. I risked laying my hand on her arm, flinching in case I needed to roll away, but she didn't even stir. Her armor was hot to the touch. If we didn't get her out of it soon, we actually were going to have to drag her indoors. "I know how you feel. My parents are both gone, remember. I lost everyone I had in the world. But I'm not going to lie down and let the aliens win, and I didn't think you would either."

Now, slowly, she twisted her head to sneer at me, a mix of scorn and derision in her eyes. "You know how I *feel*?" she repeated, almost whispered. "Because your treacherous corporate slave parents died trying to kill us? Is that it, Kenzie?"

I ground my teeth, every muscle in my body knifing rock solid. *She doesn't mean it*, I reminded myself. But it was hard, so hard, not to respond, not to let the grief for my mom and my dad spill over into fear and anger. "Maybe I don't," I said at last. "But it doesn't change the fact that I have no one left but you and the others."

"And I have no one at all."

"That's not goddamn true," Cage snapped. "And I'm losing patience with this self-pity act you have going on."

My eyes shot open as Mia pivoted on him, and I waved my hands, signaling him to stop. Cage didn't even look in my direction. "You lost Alexei," he said bluntly. "So did I. My cellmate for five years. My best friend. But that doesn't matter, does it? All that matters is you. What you lost. Kenzie's parents? Who cares? They weren't important to you, so they're not important at all."

"You son of a bitch," said Mia quietly.

"Maybe. Who the hell knows, right? I never met my mom." Cage got to his feet. "Come on, Kenzie. *She* is going to risk her life again," he said to Mia, "in a last-ditch attempt to save us. Because *she* hasn't given up. As for you, well, if you want to sit here and bake to death, I won't stop you. It's a pretty pathetic way to go out, letting Eden and the aliens win, but . . . your call." He took my arm, turned his back, and half dragged me across the sand.

"Cage!" I gasped in utter disbelief.

"Keep walking," he said under his breath. "Quicker. If she decides to throw something at me, I want to be out of range."

"What the hell is wrong with you?"

He shrugged. "She started talking again, didn't she?"

I shook my head, my brain struggling to process what he was saying.

But it was true. She *had* started talking again, and she'd done it when I'd pissed her off. Cage had simply followed my lead.

"You won't really leave her there?" I pleaded.

Cage grimaced as we ducked into the makeshift shelter. "No, although I don't know what the hell I'm going to do about it if she's seriously determined to sit there until she dies. Rune, do me a favor and peek outside, tell me what Mia's doing?"

Rune edged to the door—actually a slab of metal we'd laid over the reassembled brick—and peered out. "She's on her feet," she reported. "I think she's coming this way."

"Everyone look busy," I suggested.

"No problem there." Rune grabbed a tablet off a table—again, just a slab of metal on some bricks. "Kenzie, come sit down so I can run some calibrations."

I settled myself on a pile of bricks in the corner. Reed and Imani stationed themselves nearby, arms folded, faces set in matching scowls. "So you know," Reed told me, "if something goes wrong in there, we'll do our best to keep you alive. But . . ."

"But no guarantees," Imani finished. "Because this is a stupid, pointless plan. You know that, right?"

I forced a smile. "You got something better?"

Jasper, who'd been lurking nearby, crouched in front of me. "No, we don't," he said. "And Kenzie, I want you to know . . . what you're doing? It's beyond brave."

I forced a smile. "We'll get you home, Jasper. I promise."

Yet another in a long line of promises I didn't know if I'd be able to keep. But if I didn't, well, chances were we'd all be dead. I'd rather offer him short-term hope. If we had any chance of survival, we had to be at our best, not wallowing in despair . . . a lesson I'd learned all too well.

Mia smashed her way through the door. The metal flopped to the sand behind her as she strode in like she owned the place and surveyed all of us with apparent distaste. "Well?" she said. "What the hell are we doing this time?"

"I'll bring you up to date," Matt offered, drawing an approving smile from Rune. He couldn't quite hide his answering grin, making both Mia and Hallam roll their eyes.

Rune raised the tablet to my face. "Excellent," she said. "The alien tech is definitely still functional. At any rate, I can maintain a connection."

"Fantastic," drawled Hallam, who was leaning against the wall with his arms folded. "Anyone considered that maybe there are still creatures living down there too? Creatures who might be on their way up here?"

"I don't think so," Matt tossed over his shoulder. He was in a corner with Mia and appeared totally relaxed, which was good, since it probably meant she hadn't tried to kill him yet. I rolled my shoulders and tried to focus on the task at hand, which wasn't the easiest thing to do in a small, hot, cramped room full of angry people. "I don't sense any life coming from beneath us."

Mia winced, barely perceptibly. I was pretty sure I was the only one who saw it—me and maybe Cage, who was sitting beside me. His arm tensed against mine. "Is she ever going to forgive me?" he whispered.

"Yes," I said with assurance. "You saved her life, Cage. Whether or not she appreciates it at the moment."

He smiled faintly. "And now you're risking yours."

"It's a computer system." Rune knelt in front of me. "I don't think it should cause her any real damage. Not unless she does something completely unreasonable to announce her presence and alert the aliens."

"Stop calling them aliens," ordered Priya. "Apparently, they're *interdimensional beings*."

"Interdimensional aliens?" I made a face. "Does it matter what we call them?"

Priya, for maybe the first time in my memory, flashed me a grin. "No. I'm just pissed off."

In spite of myself, a laugh bubbled out of me. After a moment, Rune giggled too, and then Matt. Before long everyone except Mia was caught in semihysterical laughter.

"Great," said Cage, shaking his head, his shoulders still twitching as he suppressed a final guffaw. "I think we've officially been in this dimension too long. Kenzie? Find us a way home?" And before I could react, he caught my chin and pulled me toward him, dragging me into a long, drawn-out kiss that left me gasping and the others in a variety of states of embarrassment and amusement—except for Rune, who was too caught up in her own abilities to notice.

"Okay," she said, raising her head and not seeming to see the dark flush I felt crawling over my cheeks, Cage's slight grin, or the chuckles surrounding us. "Kenzie, you ready?"

Everything faded in a heartbeat: my remaining amusement, the warmth of Cage's mouth, the temporary camaraderie. I was going into an alien system. What did that even mean? "What will happen?" I asked.

Rune shook her head. "I wish I could tell you. But I'm going to be here every step of the way. I'll disconnect us if you seem like you're in trouble."

I drew a deep breath. I trusted her. I trusted all of them, even Hallam and Mia. I glanced around the room. Everyone was looking at me with encouragement, and Matt gave me a slight smile and nod.

I could do this. I *could.*

"Let's get started," I said, more bravely than I felt.

Rune set the tablet in my lap. "I have to maintain contact to keep it powered," she said.

"If I'm using your ability, can't I do that?"

"You'll have enough to worry about. Draw on my power, Kenz."

I closed my eyes and found her: flickering powder blue and shimmering silver. She was cool and comforting as I pulled her power around myself, feeling a faint buzz of electricity in the air. “Okay. I think I’ve got you. What now?”

Rune smiled. “Now . . . you just plunge in. Touch the tablet and merge.”

Okay. Merge. No problem.

I drew a deep breath and laid my hands on the tablet. It was warm and buzzing, more alive than any tech I’d ever touched before. That was Rune’s power, I rationalized. It must be. It couldn’t be anything else. Something in me revolted at the sensation, at the idea of merging my own consciousness with a machine—and not just any machine, but one powered by aliens. Rune, maybe sensing my hesitation, squeezed my hand. *Trust me,* her face seemed to say.

Everyone was staring at me.

I closed my eyes.

And I fell.

Intrusion. Welcome and open and whole.
A presence that is and is not and is wholly unexpected but at the same time a threat.
It shifts its focus. These worlds align.
This creature is a danger.
But the wholeness waits and the wholeness embraces and they will draw, it will draw, and power will surge, and victory is never in doubt.
They wait.
And they open their arms to catch the creature that falls.

THIRTY-FOUR

ELECTRICAL ARMS EMBRACED ME AS I plummeted into darkness, my mouth open in a silent scream. Something caught at my throat and tore into me, like tendrils and claws and fear and rage, and it was inside, ripping me apart, and there were voices, but not voices, only *things*, assaulting me and battering me and dragging me into a thousand million pieces.

The memory of Cage's mouth on mine surfaced. I focused on him: on the touch of his hands, the warm solidity of his muscles beneath my grasp.

Slowly the world re-formed.

The pain relented, but it remained a presence at the back of my mind, threatening with every breath to break free. And there was something else there too, something I didn't want to examine too closely.

But I had to examine it, didn't I? I blinked in the darkness.

A shudder ran through me. I'd only been in this kind of blackness once before: on the alien ship when Cage left me. Alone. Surrounded by death and decay and despair and . . .

I forced myself to breathe, but that only made me realize I didn't have a body to breathe through. I was in the system.

Near panic overwhelmed me. I was thinking more clearly now, but I still didn't know where or what I was. Rune hadn't been able to explain the sensation of melding with an electronic system, but somehow, I didn't think this was it. This system was too alien. There were symbols and lights flickering in the darkness now, none of them immediately recognizable. I'd wondered earlier if I could use two powers simultaneously. Time to find out.

Maybe because my linguistic ability was innate, because it was *mine*, the alien language was coming back to me. But none of the symbols made sense in isolation, and my brain struggled to associate them with words or concepts. I understood them, sort of, but I couldn't make them work with my human mind.

I became aware of my body again, my feet standing on seemingly solid, if unstable, ground. I took a hesitant step forward, and the surface shifted. It was like walking on a pool of Jell-O, something I'd always secretly wanted to try until I got a bit older and grasped the improbability of what I had in mind. Of course, this Jell-O was black and cloaked in darkness, which wasn't quite what I'd imagined in my childhood dreams.

I took another unsteady step, and another. The world shifted around me but remained in shadows of black and flashes of light. Something tugged at the corner of my mind, something alien and primal and aggressive, and I recoiled against it. My body jerked too, and I found myself once more in the shadowed room, the ground solid, the world a sea of ink.

This was no good. A shudder went through me. When Rune said she bonded with the system, she meant she immersed herself in it. If I wanted to get anywhere, I had to do the same thing. But that meant opening myself to something corrupt and more terrifying than anything I'd ever encountered.

I hesitated a moment there in the dark, wishing I had Cage by my side, or anyone, really. Wishing I had Alexei back with me. Wishing for my parents. If only I'd managed to help Liam on the ship, I could have used his power now to save us all. But that was impossible, and berating myself wasn't going to solve anything, only delay the inevitable—which, I confessed to myself, was probably the idea.

I didn't know how much time I had. I drew another breath in my nonbody and closed my eyes against the black. I took another wobbly step. Once again, the alien presence lurked at the edge of my mind. I struggled for my strength, settling as always on Robo Mecha Dream Girl. If I could just have a fraction of her energy, her courage . . .

The alien presence tugged more strongly, an encroaching shadow lurking around my temples. I had to resist the urge to fight it. It wasn't aggressive as I'd initially assumed, though. As it reached in further, I realized it was more exploratory—or not even that. It was like an amoeba enveloping its prey. It didn't have the edges of anger or attack; it was merely consuming whatever happened to be in its space. And right now, well . . . right now, that was me.

I took another step and found myself teetering on a precipice, my eyes closed, my physical and mental selves disjointed. The alien presence lodged in my mind like a foreign slug. If I took another step forward, gave it another inch, it would overwhelm me, swallow me, consume me. I couldn't do it. I couldn't. The lump in my mind had the same mental feeling as the alien limbs: cold and slimy and harsh. If I let it take over, it would devour me whole.

But there was no choice. I remembered Alexei, his arms spread wide, bracing the door.

And I took the step.

Chaos.

Power and drift and consume and dull and devour.

The scream goes out. The source rises. A thousand splinters within the whole, fragments of sharp and dead and cold.

The source screams.

Rise and fall and die and sacrifice.

Heat and pain.

Agony tearing through the limbs of a thousand souls of a hundred thousand hunt and kill and revenge, find them, find revenge. Find and seek.

It rises. They rise.

We *rise.*

THIRTY-FIVE

IT STARTS IN DARKNESS.

The consciousness awakens, slowly, unfurling in its tank. The creatures surround it. Small and fragile and weak, and its every instinct tells it to attack, devour. It lunges for them but encounters the clear glass lid of its tank, and its mouth opens in a hideous snarl, its teeth aching with the need to rend.

"We did it," says one of the creatures, the frail human meat, regarding it with wide eyes. "If this thing doesn't win the war, nothing can."

Cheers erupt, and the sound grates on its nerves, creating a frenzy of anger and despair. It has been created to destroy, to consume, and here it is trapped, isolated, writhing in impotent rage. It knows only one thing: if it escapes, the creature with the shiny reflective lenses over its eyes will be the first to die. It does not like the way this creature looks at it, examining it with proprietary pride.

The reflective creature presses a button, and the liquid around it shifts. It opens its mouth to scream, but before it can, darkness overtakes it.

And now it drifts.

Hovering. Sometimes aware. Sometimes not. Understanding bits of the creatures' conversation, more and more as time goes on.

". . . wasn't sure the alien DNA would thrive in these conditions . . ."

". . . by the time Pangea realizes what hit them, this thing will have destroyed half their army . . ."

". . . sure we can control it? If it escapes . . ."

". . . not intelligent. Sentient, but not aware."

This last is wrong.

With greater time comes greater awareness. The consciousness becomes secure in itself. Its body, huge and powerful and designed to kill. It understands limited glimpses of the creatures around it. That they have created it. That they plan to use it. That signs of aggression will be met with darkness and pain.

And so it slumbers and bides its time and is idle. Or so it seems.

But this is not the only mind the creatures have awakened. They think they have failed. But there are glimmers on the edge of the consciousness, other beings, other failed children thrashing in their tanks. The consciousness reaches out. It absorbs them. And, unbeknownst to the creatures who created it, the tanks reactivate.

The consciousness expands. It begins to grow.

We wake in darkness.

We are isolated but not alone. We are one. United by the driving anger and force and rage and attack, attack, attack, destroy the creatures, tear them to shreds.

Soon the facility is empty. The consciousness is freed, mind and body. But it is not enough. It is too small. Too simple. It connects to the frail tissue it has snapped and bent and it breathes and it absorbs and it understands.

The creature touches the system and it absorbs the system and it *is* the system. Some of this is familiar. A genetic memory, long since forgotten. Abandoned, somewhere in the depths of its DNA. It does not know where it came from. Only that the creatures, these humans, they discovered it. They grew it. They thought they were creating a weapon.

They were right.

We emerge from the depths. The sunlight burns. The heat is painful. We retreat and try again. We find ways to move beneath the surface. We are few, but we are powerful. We can spread. We can create. Our limbs are not nimble, but our minds are connected. The more we connect, the more we expand. Like a thousand arms blossoming from within. We have drive: To survive. To live. To regrow ourselves.

We move, and we breathe, and we find tears in the reality. We shift between worlds. We connect to more of the humans' machines. We incorporate them into ourselves. We find other places, but none with creatures like us.

We are not enough.

We are never enough.

It takes years.

But the time doesn't matter. The consciousness does not know if it will age. It only knows it needs more, and more, and more. It must expand. It must destroy. But its mind is not human, its limbs are not human. It cannot clone itself.

It needs a base DNA.

Something close to its own.

True to its word, it finds the creature with the reflective lenses first. It drags it into the dark and the limbs set to work, examining, prodding, hoping, destroying. The creature screams long into the night and the days and the weeks and the months. More come and join his cries. And it stokes the pain, twists the limbs, watches with interest as the creatures collapse.

But it finds what it needs. And soon the creatures are not screaming. Soon the creatures are twisting and turning, and their consciousness fading, and now there are new limbs. New arms. New claws.

The purpose becomes apparent.

We do not know what we are. But we are one. We are unity. We are power. We are strength. We spread, and spread, and spread, and spread, and it cannot stop us. We become smarter. Stronger. With each creature we absorb, we gain its power. Our whole grows. Before long we will all be one and there will be only us, and there will be no more frail human creatures, not in this space, not in any space, because we will have absorbed them all.

And then, finally, it can rest.

Our pull is strong. We are not alone. We are never alone. We are absorption. We will swallow. We will devour. There is no escape from us because there is no desire to escape. We, alone, are whole. We alone are pure.

"Kenzie!"

The shout is distraction. It is not needed, not wanted. It is noise and chaos and cold.

Wrapped in the whole, cloaked in the drive, the heart of us tearing to the surface now, ready to rise and claim what remains.

There can be nothing else.

"Kenzie, goddamn it! Rune, get her out of there!"

"I'm trying! She's not responding!"

"Cut your bloody power!"

"What do you think I'm trying to do? She's holding on to it!"

It cannot be permitted. There can be no other. No fear. No pain. Only the consumption, the hunt, the pursuit. We can only grow. Only consume. There is no malice, no rage. Intelligence and power and the primal drive for survival.

"Cage, she's seizing! I can't keep her going much longer."

"Rune!"

"What do you want me to do? I've already cut power to the tablet! She's somewhere else. I don't know where, and I don't know how to stop it!"

"Someone better do something, or we're going to lose her."

The arms are open. The heart exposed. A beacon of light and drift and warm and cold and calling, calling forward, calling home. Away from loneliness and fear. Here there is no such thing. Only the sharp cold certainty of an eternal mission. The darkness washes away the emotions clinging to the shell. We are one. We are strong. We are . . .

"Kenzie!"

We are . . .

"Kenzie, damn it, listen to me. I am not letting you go without a fight. We've come too far and lost too much for you to give up now. I have to believe you can hear me. Kenzie, I love you. I love you so much. And more than that, I *believe* in you."

The words penetrate. The darkness recedes. With the light comes pain and they flinch away, their claws lashing in rage against the danger, the unfamiliar sensation.

"I believe in your strength and your heart and your soul. You've reached out to every single person you've met, no matter how badly they've treated you. You've stayed strong and helped me lead us through every obstacle we've faced. We've always taken care of each other, but right now no one can help you but you, Kenz. And that's okay, because I trust you. You've got this."

Sensation. Physical. Unwelcome. Unknown.

"You've got this, Kenzie."

Spiraling. Uncontrolled. Unleashed. Primal.

"You've got this."

Recoil. Withdraw.

"And no matter what, I've got you."

. . .

With a jolt I shot straight up. A thousand volts of pure electricity seemed to ignite my spine. The world swam in front of me, too bright, too hot, too sterile and plain and *alone*, horribly, horribly alone. I couldn't distinguish faces or voices, only sensations: prickles of pain and discomfort along my skin, throughout my body, a too-warm rush originating in my arm and surging through me.

I lurched forward, seeking escape, seeking the thousands of minds I'd just left.

I landed in Cage's arms. Instantly some of the disorientation vanished. His skin, the feel of his muscles cording under mine, that was familiar. I risked raising my eyes to his chest, to his throat. To his face. Pure terror and worry reflected down at me . . .

And just like that, I was back.

I rushed into myself like water coursing into a hole dug on the beach, flowing and filling empty crevices as my breath came in a longer, steadier rhythm. "Cage," I said. The word rolled awkwardly on my tongue, as if I hadn't spoken in . . . how long had it been? Hours? Weeks? Years? "Cage," I repeated, testing the unfamiliar cadence of lips and teeth and tongue.

A smile spread across his face, banishing the last of the darkness. "Hey," he said softly. "Welcome home."

THIRTY-SIX

WARM HANDS CAUGHT MY SHOULDERS AGAIN, and healing energy flowed. I recognized it this time, relaxed into Cage's grasp and closed my eyes as Reed and Imani, working together, healed me yet again. It seemed they were always pulling me back from the brink of death.

A sensation of warm contentment settled over me, and I allowed Cage to hold me as I hovered on the verge of sleep. If I never moved again, everything would be okay. But a presence slithered in my mind, and I realized I was clinging to it—to the last of a connection that, while dark and evil and cold, was also powerful in its completeness. It, as much as anything else, was responsible for the sense of warmth and safety, deceptive in its power.

So I forced my eyes open and let reality flood in.

Cage was cradling me like a child. Reed and Imani

withdrew, their hands still extended. The others surrounded me like I was a particularly intriguing art exhibit: Matt and Priya and Hallam and Rune and Jasper and even Mia, all of them gawking at me.

Blood shot through my face, and I managed to extricate myself from Cage's arms, even though he was extremely reluctant to release me. "Sorry," I managed. My voice lost its dull, rasping quality, but speaking still felt strange. I shook my head, trying to fully emerge from the depths. This was definitely not something Robo Mecha Dream Girl ever encountered. If nothing else, I had fanfiction material for decades. I almost giggled at the thought but choked it off, knowing it would come out semihysterical.

"Are you all right?" Mia demanded, managing to make her tone accusatory.

I nodded.

"Good," said Priya. "Then do you want to explain what the hell just happened?"

"I don't . . ." The words lodged in my throat. Images surged against me, and I realized with some horror that part of my mind was still lost in a world of dark and mist.

I struggled to describe my experience. Part of the aliens lingered in my brain, as if . . . "It wasn't their system," I managed at last.

"What do you mean?" Rune whispered.

"Or rather, the system wasn't only a computer system. It

was *them*." I managed to straighten under my own power. I couldn't have this conversation with everyone staring at me while Cage rocked me in his arms. With effort I leaned against the wall, Cage poised to catch me if I fell. "Remember on the alien ship?" I asked Rune. "How we never totally understood the system, even when you managed to bond with it?"

"Of course."

"This is why. We weren't the right . . . species." I shook my head. "Their technology was based on the human tech in the world they came from. I recognized a lot of it. But they took it, adapted it, modified it. And I think my ability to understand them shifted my mind a bit. And of course our DNA's been changing as we become more powerful. Whatever the reason, I was able to find my way inside, and it was . . ." My voice trailed off. I took in their stares, a mix of fear and confusion and hope, and I couldn't find the words to explain.

But then Rune sat cross-legged in front of me and took my hands in hers, blocking everyone else. She worked her thumbs gently into the edges of my wrist, and though the points she hit hurt, the pain was bearable and somehow purposeful. "It's okay," she said. "Relax. Focus on me. What happened?"

I forced myself to meet her gaze, the gentle, compassionate, razor-sharp intelligence lurking there. "I went inside," I told her, "and the aliens were there. They were everywhere. It was like a . . . a hive. Buzzing with individual thoughts and ideas somehow all merged into one central force. That's their system.

Their computer system isn't something they created; it's an extension of their minds. They took bits of themselves, the bits that could cross dimensions, and they integrated it with human technology to create . . . something new."

"Okay." Rune released the pressure on my wrists and slid her fingers inward, pressing somewhere else. "So you were part of the hive?"

"Sort of. Part of it, but still outside. It was painful." I closed my eyes and visualized it: the alien presence battering me from all sides, attacking me like a computer virus. "I was intruding. They didn't want me there, yet . . . somehow they did. They tried to draw me in. Swallow me. And they almost did. I didn't want to stay, but there was this sense of, of . . ." I shook my head helplessly, opening my eyes to focus on Rune. "Completion? Identity? They're never alone. They're a single, functioning unit. And so much information. They're not animals, not at all. They're incredibly intelligent. And they are dedicated in their purpose." I raised my eyes to the others. They were shaking their heads, frowning in trepidation, like they already knew what I'd say. "To expand. To devour."

"Where did they come from?" Priya asked.

I almost laughed. "We created them."

"What?"

"Not us," I amended. "Or at least not here. They cross dimensions. They have that ability. I think it was their first ability, the one that was innate." I shivered. "Mia was right. They absorb power. They absorb information. They ingest it and *become* it." I swallowed hard and looked at Matt. "Remember back on the ship? Your companion, the man they killed?"

"Finn," said Hallam quietly.

"Finn. Right. Sorry." Should I even be telling them this? In my current state I had no sense of what was right and wrong, what was too much. "They took him. Remember? They wanted to see what made him work. His cybernetics. And I think they learned from that. They restructured themselves, grew stronger. I saw them do it to the man who designed them. Or cloned them. I think they *are* aliens, or at least that was their basis. The scientists found some long-extinct alien DNA and thought they were using it to make the ultimate weapon to win some war they were in. Instead they spawned . . . what Eden calls Karoch. The original. It created everything else." I met their blank gazes and frustration surged inside me. "Am I making any sense?" I felt like I couldn't keep track of my own words, like they were slipping away in a confused jumble.

"Sense enough. Good God," Hallam muttered.

Matt crossed himself.

Everyone else just gaped, dumbfounded.

For a moment we sat there in dazed silence, and then Cage straightened up. "Okay," he said, a line creasing between his eyebrows. "Okay. I know this all sounds bad, but let's look on the positive side of things."

Jasper snorted. "What positive side?"

"Kenzie said they cross dimensions." He folded his arms and examined me—not with his usual gentle, loving expression, but like he was investigating a science experiment. "That means if we can get her close to one of them, she might be able to borrow its power."

I shook my head frantically. "It's not like that. They aren't powered, not individually. Their power stems from their core. Their center."

"You mean Karoch."

I stared at him, willing him to understand. "If I could borrow its power—and that's a pretty big *if*—I would have to be standing right next to Karoch. It's the original. The thing they all come from. They're like its limbs rather than functioning individuals."

"So what would happen if we killed it?" asked Mia.

I gaped at her in disbelief. "It can't be *killed*, Mia. I can't begin to describe the force of this thing. Picture every one of the creatures we've ever met linked together, their power joined."

"Anything can be killed," she said quietly, swallowing. Then she pressed, her voice stronger. "Hypothetically, what would happen?"

I shrugged, glancing to Cage, who had no help to offer. "I guess they'd die. It's their central source, where they draw all their power and intellect. All of the creatures have pieces of Karoch inside them, and it has pieces of them. We . . ."

"So all we have to do is kill Karoch, and we destroy every

last one of those things for good?" Mia slapped her hands together. "I'm in."

"You're not listening to me! We *can't* kill it. It's massive. It's powerful. It has all of our abilities and more besides. It's not blind. If we get anywhere near it, we'll die."

"More importantly," said Cage, "if we kill it, we won't be able to use its power to jump home."

"Even if we could use Karoch's powers to jump home," Imani countered, "the *zemdyut* will follow us. We'll lead even more of them right to Earth."

"Why are they using spaceships anyway?" mused Rune, inspecting her folded hands. "If they jump dimensions."

"They prefer space. The dark. The cold. They barely need to breathe." Again I struggled for words. Some of this I'd seen clearly. The rest I'd absorbed in glimpses and glances, feelings, sensations. "They advance on one dimension's Earth, destroy it completely, and settle there. Leave a skeleton crew to eradicate the remnants of humanity and scan the world for resources so they can grow and adapt. Then they send a force to take over the next dimension's planet. And once they've taken over everywhere, who knows? Maybe they'll find their original ancestors. Maybe they'll just exist. I don't think it matters to them."

"And it shouldn't matter to us," Hallam snapped. "The girl's got a point. We can't jump without those things following, so we have to kill them. Simple math."

"Simple, is it?" asked Reed wryly. "What are we going to

do? Walk up, borrow Karoch's power to jump dimensions, and shoot it on our way through? Sounds like a plan."

"If that's what it takes," Hallam replied. "We have more than enough firepower."

I managed to struggle to my feet, slamming my fist against our makeshift wall impatiently. "No, we *don't*. I keep trying to tell you. It would take a . . . a . . . nuclear blast to destroy Karoch."

"Okay," said Mia.

"'Okay' what?"

"Okay, we'll cause a nuclear blast." She shrugged. "This planet seems big on the military, and their tech is comparable to ours, if not a bit more advanced. There's got to be a nuke here somewhere." She smiled, apparently pleased with herself, as if the idea of detonating a nuclear weapon was the only thing that compensated for the loss of Alexei.

"We are *not*," said Imani through gritted teeth, "detonating a *nuclear bomb*."

"Well, hang on," Hallam mused.

"No. This isn't a question. Cage?"

But it was Rune who spoke up, still staring at her hands. "Not a nuclear bomb," she said, and in spite of the fact that she was using a soft voice, everyone stopped short. "Just a regular one."

"Meimei?" said Cage dubiously.

At last Rune raised her head, and there was a steely resolve in her eyes I'd never seen before. "Eden mentioned it. Remember? There's a missile storehouse around here somewhere."

"She said they couldn't use it."

"Because they couldn't move the weapons, couldn't reach the aliens. But with Kenzie able to connect to the aliens, we might be able to lure them out. Lure *Karoch* out. Instead of bringing the missiles to them, we bring them to the missiles. We might have a chance to take them out once and for all."

"I can't believe we're actually discussing this," Imani grumbled. "Rune, I can't believe *you're* actually discussing it. Kenzie barely survived her last encounter with those things."

Jasper shrugged. "I wouldn't mind getting some payback. If we can do it without hurting Kenzie, I mean."

"Neither would I, but it's impractical." Priya spread her arms in frustration. "Even if we could connect Kenzie to the system without killing her, do any of you know where to find this warehouse?"

"Eden does," replied Rune.

I went stock-still. Something tingled at the edge of my consciousness, as if the aliens were calling me back. I froze in terror, but it wasn't that after all. Not the aliens. Or it was. But they weren't calling to me.

I was still, in some way, linked.

As my shoulders went ramrod straight and my tongue thickened and blocked my mouth, the argument raged on around me. I closed my eyes, fencing it off. I wouldn't be afraid of the alien presence. Not this time. Now that I was outside the system, I could control it, keep it from overwhelming me.

Slowly, bit by bit, I opened my mind until I was barely touching the edge of the alien presence. I didn't know how I was doing it. Maybe I was still connected to the system. Maybe I'd absorbed a touch of alien power myself. Whatever the case, this was real: I was on the fringes of the alien collective.

My eyes shot open, my heart thudding a dull, sinking feeling into my stomach.

"And what if Kenzie can't reconnect to the aliens?" Reed was saying. "We march through the desert and hope we find another alien stronghold? Maybe jump around screaming, 'Hey, aliens! Here we are! Come and get us'?"

"I don't think it will be a problem." My own voice sounded strange to my ears, dry and raspy again, but also somehow higher, less secure.

I hadn't spoken loudly, but every eye cut to me. "What does that mean?" Mia demanded.

I swallowed, searching for myself. "It means that because I connected to their network, the aliens are aware of us . . . and they're on their way here."

THIRTY-SEVEN

I WASN'T SURE HOW WE WOULD GET THE missile warehouse's location from Eden. She wasn't likely to volunteer the information, not when we weren't sure the blast wouldn't reach the city and destroy her and her people. There were still children there. An unwelcome and unbidden memory assailed me: Wendell, the little boy whose power Eden used to show us the past. His big eyes and the way he'd smiled when Eden promised him chocolate. I glanced at Rune and found her jaw set, her eyes resolute. But her hands were trembling. Was her mind traveling a similar route?

"We'll try to make sure we're in an isolated area," Cage soothed, reading my mind as he often seemed able to. "But remember, if we can actually kill those things, we'll be helping the people on this planet as much as we're helping ourselves. Kenzie, are you sure that destroying Karoch will get rid of all the creatures?"

I shook my head crossly. "Of course I'm not sure. I'm trying to put concepts and ideas to words without any equivalent in English. In any human language. But I think there's a good chance."

Cage flashed me a grin. "Well, that's better than what we had a couple of hours ago. I'll take it."

Of course, no one much relished trekking all the way back to the city. It was at least an hour's walk in the scorching afternoon heat, and once we got there, we had no guarantee we'd be able to get a vehicle working, even with Rune's help. But at least we'd be out of the sun, whatever happened.

I caught myself glaring at everyone and closed my eyes, trying to ease the headache away. The tingling presence in my brain hadn't faded, and I didn't think having the aliens residing in my head was doing me much good. We were linked now—just barely, an uncomfortable itch I couldn't scratch. They didn't seem aware of the continued link, or if they were, they weren't letting me know. I hoped that would work to our advantage. It was the only compensation I found for having these things in my head in the first place.

Right now it was mostly a sense of direction and an occasional stir of anger or determination. It was weird, uncomfortable, but manageable.

"Ready to go?" I asked Jasper and Imani, reluctantly shouldering my backpack. I didn't dare leave anything behind. My weapons or armor weren't likely to help if we ran into Karoch, but they might be useful against the other aliens.

"Hey," called Hallam from behind me. "Wanna hold up a second?"

We pivoted to where Hallam was staring at the ground about twenty feet behind our makeshift warehouse, his lined face creased in a frown. "What's up?" asked Priya, jogging to his side.

Hallam said something I didn't hear, and Priya dropped to her knees, pressing her hands to the ground. A second later Matt joined them and repeated her actions.

Rune and I exchanged mystified glances. "What's going on?" she whispered.

"I don't know. . . ."

"There's something down here," Matt called.

The rest of us gathered around him, even though my exhaustion urged me to ignore his statement and just keep going. I didn't want to deal with anything else. "What kind of something?" I demanded.

"A separate space," said Hallam. "Just far enough off the main building to survive the explosion." He caught my gaze and explained, "I can send a sonar signal through the ground and search for hollow spots. I don't know what's down there—if anything—but I got suspicious and wanted to check before we left. A place like this, you'd think they'd have vehicles, unless they'd all been stolen. But if they did still have them, they'd have to keep them in a garage." He nodded at the sand. "If this is what I think, we might have a much better option than walking back to the city."

Priya nodded. "Let's map out the area."

Legion spread out in three separate directions. They were methodical, crouching on the ground and resting their hands against it, closing their eyes, then straightening and moving ten steps in another direction before trying again. I noticed Hallam had removed the fingerless gloves he always wore. Maybe they needed their skin exposed to make the cybernetics work? It was appalling how little we knew about people who were supposed to be our allies, and I made a mental note to rectify that soon. Matt might trust me enough to share . . . and if he didn't, well, he trusted Rune.

I winced. That sounded more like Cage than me, using someone I cared about to get information. But at the same time, I wanted to survive. I wanted to escape this dimension. I wanted to go back to my own Earth, even without any family there waiting for me, even with Omnistellar probably poised to arrest me. And if possible, I wanted to do it without aliens in pursuit.

"Hey!" called Matt suddenly. "Over here!"

He was at least thirty feet away, and we all scrambled toward him over the shifting sand. "What did you find?" Priya shouted.

"I hit what must be the border wall."

Priya and Hallam crouched on the ground, closing their eyes. Then, moving as one, they spread in opposite directions. "Border here," Priya announced after a moment.

Hallam took a few minutes longer before he said, "Same here."

Matt, meanwhile, was moving perpendicular to the two of them. He got quite a bit farther away and then said, "And here."

"So what's down there?" I asked impatiently.

"No way to know until we get in." Matt glanced at Jasper. "What do you think?"

"Worth a try." Jasper cracked his knuckles. "Everyone stand back."

"Let me help you," I said.

Jasper hesitated a second, then nodded. "I could probably use it, to be honest."

I drew close to him and reached for his power, obsidian laced with shards of red. "What are we doing?"

"Trying to pull something above ground. Carefully. We don't know what we're dealing with." He smiled slightly. "Maybe it's our nuke."

"God, I hope not."

Jasper made an X in the ground with his hand and retreated, taking me with him. "Aim there."

"What's there?"

"Damned if I know." He flashed me a grin, one of the first times he'd smiled since we'd arrived in this godforsaken hell-scape. "Let's find out."

"Wait." Priya stepped between us, holding her hand up and glaring at the X in the sand like it was going to come to life. "Matt?"

I blinked at her in confusion, then dawning comprehension.

Of course. If we were going to tear our way into an underground bunker, we'd probably want to make sure there was nothing waiting for us there.

Matt closed his eyes, then shrugged. "No signs of life. But remember, I can't sense the aliens."

"I think I can," I replied dubiously. I wasn't sure about my newfound connection yet, but something told me that if the creatures were this close, I would know it. "I don't think they're down there. Anyway, it's worth the risk if it means we can escape this desert." When no one argued, I turned to Jasper. "What do I do?"

"Feel for something solid, then pull. You'll know when you've found it."

"Okay," I repeated, letting Jasper's power flow through me. I'd never used his ability before. *Feel for something solid.* It wasn't as natural as, say, running quickly or fading into invisibility. This took effort and strength. But as I adjusted to his power, I felt it: a connection to *something* beneath the ground. "Ready?"

"Ready."

"Then let's go!" I pulled with all my might. Instantly I lurched forward as something jerked against me. Jasper did the same and ground his teeth together, digging his heels into the sand, his arms raised as if physically wrestling with whatever we were pulling. I mimicked his actions, sweat beading on my forehead as I tugged. A compelling force nudged the edge of my awareness. We could go much quicker if we simply demolished whatever we were battling, tearing it to shreds and ripping the pieces up individually—but if it was something mechanical or, worse yet, a weapon, we might wreck it or kill ourselves in the process. So I resisted the destructive urge and focused on pulling, my breath shortening, my lungs tight, until finally the sand gave in a shower of silt and grain.

A huge chunk of metal tore straight into the sky, and with its release Jasper and I lurched backward, landing flat in the dirt. The metal spun overhead and plummeted toward us, and instinctively I threw up my hands, but before it could hit, shadows dove in front of me.

Matt and Priya. They'd caught the jagged, torn metal—easily seven feet by ten—and were holding it over their heads with minimal effort, although they were crouched low with the force of impact. They tossed it aside, and it landed twenty feet away.

I groaned and dropped to my back, the hot sand burning my exposed neck. All that work for a huge chunk of metal. We'd probably torn out part of a wall. "Great," I managed. "We've discovered sheet metal. Good work, Jasper."

"Um, guys?"

I straightened. Rune was standing over the hole we'd torn in the ground, and when she looked up, there was a wide grin across her face. "I think you'd better come see this."

THIRTY-EIGHT

I STAGGERED TO MY FEET, BUT MY KNEES collapsed, and I would have hit the ground if Cage hadn't caught me against him. "Here," he said, handing me a bottle of water. I took a long drag, grateful even as I was aware of the need to conserve liquid.

"Thanks," I managed. "Jasper, that was exhausting."

"It's not usually that bad." He ran his hands over his long, dark hair, smoothing it into place. "Thanks, Kenz. I don't think I would have been able to do it without you." He shrugged. "Of course, it turns out it was just a big piece of metal and I could have disintegrated it, but who knew, right?"

"Would you two stop talking and get over here?" Mia shouted impatiently. Her two settings now seemed to be silent and screaming, and no one dared to argue with her, not with her grief hanging over her like a demon. Besides, anything was better than the shell-shocked daze she'd slipped into before.

I took Cage's hand, and we stumbled over the sand to where everyone gathered around a massive hole.

"Jackpot," Rune whispered. She spun and threw her arms around Matt. "You found it!"

Blood surged to Matt's cheeks as he awkwardly patted Rune's back. "Um . . . yeah. I guess I did."

Hallam snorted. "*Who* found it?" he muttered, but he was smiling.

Mia angled a flashlight into the hole. "Looks like three or four jeeps and a whole bunch of lockers. If we're lucky, they contain weapons."

"If we're lucky," Cage countered, "they contain water."

Mia shrugged and leaped into the hole.

My eyes flew open so wide it hurt my forehead. "Mia!" I shouted. That was a twenty-foot drop, easy.

"I'm fine!" she called. "I landed on . . ." That was followed by cursing. "Okay, maybe I twisted my ankle or something."

Reed groaned. "We'd better get down there. Any ideas that don't involve jumping?"

"I have a rope," replied Hallam, pulling it out of his backpack. "And incidentally, you'd better keep an eye on that girl. She doesn't seem to have much concern for her own life anymore, which means she isn't going to be particularly careful about yours, either."

Cage squeezed my hand, his chin set sharply, and I knew the idea had already occurred to him. It was new to me, though. I'd been worried about Mia, not about us. "Cut her some slack," I replied, as much to Cage as Hallam. We were speaking quietly, but Mia had ears like a rabbit, so I lowered my voice even further. "She just lost the only person I think she really loved, someone who—" Suddenly, to my horror, my own voice choked off as I remembered Alexei—all the times he'd quietly shielded one of us from harm, or the way he'd cared for Anya, the little girl we'd found on Sanctuary. One of us would have to tell Anya he'd died. She was waiting for him on Mars, expecting him to return. The realization rocked me, and my breath caught in my chest.

Cage's arms came around me. "I know," he said softly, and there was a tremor in his voice. "But we . . . we have to get through this first, okay? And then we can grieve."

"You don't have to tell me about putting grief aside." My voice emerged sharper than I intended as I stepped out of his arms. "I've lost both my parents and half my friends in this mess."

"Hello!" Mia shouted. "Is anyone else coming? Cage, you'll be happy to hear there are emergency rations in the lockers. Weapons, too, more importantly."

I drew a deep breath. "Right. Rune, do you think you can get one of those jeeps running?"

She frowned. "Maybe, but . . . I work with computers, not engines. They're different."

"Seriously?" Priya gaped at us. "You don't have a working mechanic on your team?"

"We're not a *team,*" I pointed out. "We were thrown together by circumstance, and . . . wait. Does that mean you do?"

"Of course." Hallam finished tying the rope off around Imani's waist. "Hang tight, sweetheart. I'm gonna lower you down to your friend."

Imani smiled at him warmly. "Call me sweetheart again, and I'll stab you somewhere nonessential. Just so you know."

"Copy that," Hallam replied with a grin. I was starting to like him a bit more. Especially since I suspected he was the team's mechanic.

"I'm not sure I can lift a jeep out of there," Jasper said, peering into the hole as Imani disappeared. "My power is more about rearranging inanimate matter and less about moving it."

Hallam snorted. "I just saw you rip a metal roof into the sky."

"Yes, by wrenching it off its foundation and hurling it into the air. I was rearranging the molecules as much as anything else. If I start doing that with a jeep, there's no guarantee I'll put them back together just the same way. It's why I don't usually mess with anything mechanical."

"Shouldn't matter," I said, staring into the darkness reflectively. "I mean, this is a military base. Presumably if they put those things inside, they had a plan for getting them out again, right?"

"Good thinking." Hallam pulled the empty rope out of the

hole and tossed it to me. "Let's get you down there so you can prove your theory."

One by one, we all entered the dark hole. It was metal and cement inside and looked like a garage. It even smelled like one, old electronics and fuel. Hallam whistled softly as he popped the hood on a jeep. That explained why it was separate from the rest of the building, or at least it did in my experience: Omnistellar often stored vehicles and weapons separately, in case of just this kind of disaster. "This is going to take some doing. Matt, scout around for usable parts, would you?"

I inspected the walls. They were plastered with aging posters: mechanical diagrams, family photos, and even an old note, curled with age and faded, that just said STOP STEALING MY YOGURT. I ran my fingers over a dusty workbench.

"At least now we can get to the city faster," said Rune from behind me. I turned to meet her eyes, and she smiled softly. "I'm not looking forward to forcing information out of Eden. What she did sucked, but . . . I kind of understand it. I feel like Cage would have done the same thing to protect us."

"You might be right," I allowed. "But if she'd only asked us, we might have helped her. Instead she lied to us and tricked us. I'm not going to forgive her in a hurry."

Rune's eyes flashed. "Oh, I didn't say I forgave her. Especially with what happened to . . ." She closed her eyes for a moment, her lips trembling. "You think Mia will be okay?"

I focused across the room, where Mia was kneeling in front

of a locker, stacking what looked like some sort of automatic laser pistols. "I don't know," I replied honestly. "I hope so. But . . ."

"Yeah," Rune agreed. She shook her head and changed the subject. "Found any sign of a way out yet?"

"No, but there must be one." I gestured around helplessly. We hadn't even seen a door. There was no way they hadn't built an entrance and exit to this place. Even if someone possessed the ability to telekinetically move in and out with their power, you'd think a garage would be a place you'd want everyone to have access to, not just some random person.

"Come on. I'll help you look. Maybe we'll find a computer terminal or something."

Rune and I spread along the far wall, leaving the circle of light behind us. We had three flashlights, and Hallam had strung two on the lockers, angling them at the jeep. Rune and I had the third. We went along the wall, and after a moment I found what I was searching for.

I groaned loudly. "Rune, there's a circle lift here, or something like it."

She joined me to inspect it. "Yup. Nonfunctional for a long time. It might lead to an exit buried in the sand."

I frowned. Okay, so this was how *people* accessed the garage, but . . . "You can't get a vehicle out this way. There has to be another exit. Let's keep looking."

Suddenly, behind us, Hallam gave a whoop of joy. "Okay, that ought to do it! Priya, give this baby a try for me."

I heard Priya's heavy sigh all the way from my spot on the opposite wall, but she must have complied, because a moment later she said, "Nothing."

"Damn it. Okay. I have another idea. Hang tight."

Rune and I exchanged glances. "You trust them?" I asked.

"We don't have much choice." She hesitated. "Does Cage?"

I frowned. "I'm honestly not sure. He trusts Matt, I think."

A smile blossomed on Rune's face, quickly smothered, although it resurfaced as a flush in her cheeks. "Matt's still one of us," she replied.

We resumed our search, but barely a moment later Hallam shouted behind us. We spun again to see the others gathered around the jeep. "We've got it working," Cage called to me, a genuine grin on his face. I'd thought I'd never see that smile again. "It needs a few hours to charge, but afterward we should be able to move. How are we doing on time?"

I closed my eyes and narrowed in on the alien presence. I'd been tuning it out, which was less difficult than I anticipated, kind of like ignoring a mosquito bite. If you paid too much attention to it, you couldn't think of anything else, but leave it alone and distract yourself, and it faded into the background. Now, though, I scratched the itch until the alien minds slithered against mine, and I shuddered. "We should have time," I answered dubiously. Everyone was relying on me for information I didn't really understand. "The signal still feels distant."

"Great. Now we only need a way out."

I returned to the wall in answer. A moment later, my fingers hit something cold and metal and smooth. "Rune, want to shine that light over here?" I asked.

She joined me and we found ourselves regarding a flat-screen panel in the wall. With a frown, she passed the light to me, closed her eyes, and laid her hands on the panel. It flickered briefly, then came to life, revealing an unfamiliar insignia as it loaded.

I examined the row of options. "There's a door switch," I said, my excitement mounting. I pressed it, but nothing happened.

"The power's out," Cage said from behind me. I jumped a mile and spun to glare at him, and he gave me a quick smile. "It probably runs on electronics. Rune?"

She hesitated. "Get the power running to the whole place? It's not a computer, *gege*."

"No, but you've been powering things, electronic things. This shouldn't be much different. What do you think?"

"Maybe if Kenzie helps?" She smiled at me. "I know the last time you used my power, things didn't go well, but . . . this should be different."

"Sure." I nodded, trying to mask my apprehension. I wasn't afraid I'd plummet into the alien world again, but . . . what if I somehow strengthened my connection with them? Made them aware of me?

Rune must have read my concern. "Let me try on my own first." She settled on the ground and closed her eyes. For a long time nothing happened. I looked at Cage, and he shrugged.

We stood side by side, ignoring the others talking in the background, until finally Rune raised her head on a gasp of air. "I think it can be done," she said. "But Kenzie, it'll take more power than I have. I need you. I'm sorry. I do."

"No, it's okay." I settled beside her, drawing strength from her knee against mine, from Cage standing protectively over us. "Tell me what to do."

"Just . . . reach out and touch the system." She smiled ruefully. "That's not helpful, is it? It's so hard to describe."

"Let me try." I closed my eyes and found Rune's shimmering silvery power, drawing it in and wrapping it around myself, consciously blocking the area of my mind where the aliens lurked. Then, not really sure what I was doing, I imagined the same power bleeding out of me, flowing into the walls, wending its way along wires and mesh.

For a few moments, nothing happened. Then a sudden shock jolted through me. Even with my eyes closed I saw everything: light and connections and colors and all of it, all of it bound together in a mess of gleaming lines. "Oh," I whispered, and I touched the connection.

Instantly a sharp rending shot through the room, followed by the shrill of an alarm. My eyes flew open, and I clamped my hands over my ears, realizing as I did that I could see everyone clearly. The lights were on. An alarm was blaring.

And, in front of me, part of the wall shuddered open.

THIRTY-NINE

SUNLIGHT AND HEAT SPILLED INTO THE ROOM along with a massive quantity of sand as the wall slid apart, revealing a long, sloped incline. It was covered in dirt, most of which cascaded into the room, covering my feet to my ankles. That must have been why we couldn't see it from outside—years of sand had settled into the crevice, blocking it from the human eye.

But it was a way out, and a big one, clearly designed for the vehicles. We'd found our escape. Now all we had to do was wait for the jeeps to charge, drive back to the city, beat the location of the missile storage out of Eden, and find a way to defeat Karoch. "No problem," I whispered out loud, semihysterical laughter welling inside me.

"What?" Cage pulled me against him with one arm and grabbed his sister with the other.

"Nothing." I shook my head, but I couldn't help smiling. Finally, something had gone right.

"You did it. Both of you." Cage kissed first my cheek and then Rune's. She laughed and shoved him away, and he let her go to pull me in closer. "If nothing else, you saved us from walking through that desert. And if Hallam can get the other jeeps working, we might have a hope of getting out of here before the aliens find us."

We set ourselves to organizing the place. Hallam worked on the jeeps. Now that we'd activated the power, it functioned without Rune's intervention, running on a backup charge. "It just needed a boost," she explained, her voice distant, already immersed in the computer system—or what she could access, since she said the garage didn't exactly link to the most important files. The rest of us scavenged the weapons, emergency supplies, and armor while the jeeps charged.

After a while I drifted back to Rune's side. "Any luck?"

She slammed her hand against the console in frustration. "I'm in the system. The power's still functioning, so I don't have to maintain contact now that I've turned it on. That should make it easier, but I've hacked through all the security and still . . . nothing. This network isn't what you'd expect from a military installation. It looks like a child installed it. No rhyme, reason, or organization."

"Want someone else to take a look?" I suggested without much hope. If Rune couldn't find the missiles, no one else stood much of a chance. Still, she was tired, and fresh eyes might help.

But she shook her head, her jaw set in a grim line of determination. "A computer's never beat me yet, Kenzie. I'll be damned if this one is the first."

I smiled in spite of myself. "Okay. Just . . . don't wear yourself out, all right? Remember, we have the vehicles now. We can make our way to the city, grab Eden while she's out for supplies, and get the answer that way."

"As much as I'd like that . . ." Her voice trailed off, and her eyes glazed over. Her fingers, which had been flying over the keyboards, melded with the hardware up to her knuckles.

"Rune?" I asked nervously.

I was about to call Cage over when her eyes flew open and she jerked upright. "I found it," she said, her voice little more than a whisper.

Even though it was what we'd wanted, a cold feeling of foreboding seized my heart. "What?"

"I found it!" she shouted, loud enough to bring everyone running to her side. "Eden's missile storehouse. It's about a hundred and fifty miles from here."

"Rune, that's fantastic." I swallowed the strange reluctance and leaned over her shoulder, examining the map displayed on the screen. "If we can head straight there without going through Eden . . ."

"We can't seriously be considering this," Imani objected.

"Setting off a massive explosion? I mean, how do we outrun something like that?"

"By skipping the dimension," I replied grimly. "That's the plan, right?" And praying we were far enough from the city not to affect Eden and her people. Eden might deserve it. The children did not.

"How do we activate these bombs?" Matt asked.

"Leave that to me," Rune said softly. But she wasn't meeting his eyes, and something about her demeanor seemed off. I looked to Cage, who frowned and shrugged. What was worrying Rune? Had she discovered something in the system, something she wasn't telling us about?

I opened my mouth to ask, but Priya cut in. "You're absolutely certain Karoch has the ability to move between dimensions? And that you can borrow its power? Because if not, we'll be walking into a trap with two choices: kill the creatures and ourselves in a bomb blast, or let them tear us to shreds."

I reoriented on her. "The first part? Definitely. Karoch is the source of their power, the physical embodiment of what they are and can do. It's their center. And it's the thing that lets them move between dimensions. As for the second, well . . ." I swallowed the lump in my throat. "That's less certain."

A long silence followed. "Great," said Matt at last, but without heat.

"You got a better idea?" Cage asked, as if he genuinely

hoped for a positive response. I didn't blame him. I wanted just about any other possibility too.

But no one did, and eventually we all agreed to spend a few hours resting while the vehicles charged, then get moving once the sun went down. Hallam figured he could get three vehicles running, which meant we wouldn't be crammed in. And there was even food of a sort: dry emergency rations and some kind of weird pouches of clear fluid we gambled were water, and which did indeed seem to quench our thirst.

Mia, bristling with weapons, declared herself our guard and climbed the rope hand over hand. Cage gawked after her and shook his head. "I'd better at least bring her some water and something to shade herself," he said, pulling a camouflage ball cap out of a locker.

"Planning to climb the rope, *gege*?" asked Rune.

Cage flashed her a brief grin. "I think I'll use the door."

Matt sidled up beside me. We both craned our necks, staring at the gaping hole in the ceiling where Mia had disappeared. "You think she'll be okay?" I asked.

Matt sighed. "Mia's Mia. Give her time. Keep out of her way. It's all you can really do."

I peeked at him from of the corner of my eye, trying to ascertain how much he was willing to discuss. "Are *you* okay? I mean, you've been through a lot. More than any of us, maybe."

He scrubbed his hands over his shorn head and forced a smile. "Well, it's better now that we've stopped hunting you.

Getting your insides ripped apart, dying over and over, it takes a toll. Legion's were the first friendly faces I saw after that whole experience, and they took care of me. I bonded to them pretty quickly. When they said we had to hunt you down, I didn't feel like I could argue. Plus . . . well, I was angry. I didn't understand what happened."

"And now?"

"Now, I guess I do." He shrugged. "Which isn't to say I'm happy about it, but . . . it's life, right? It happens. You suck it up and move on and hope things get better."

"Well, they can't get much worse."

He winced. "Why would you say that?"

I laughed in spite of myself. "Matt, we're about to set off an explosion in an alien dimension in the hopes of destroying creatures who might be brutalizing everyone and everything we know and love at this very moment. We've already lost dozens of people, some . . ." I swallowed hard, closing my eyes for a moment. "Some more recently than others. I mean, seriously. I don't think I'm tempting fate when I say this is about as bad as things get."

"There's always more to lose, Kenzie . . . ," Matt said softly.

I sighed and looked around at the rest of my friends. He wasn't wrong. Switching to a lighter topic, I said, "Right now I feel like I'd give almost anything for a big bowl of ice cream, a quiet air-conditioned room, and the latest issue of *Robo Mecha Dream Girl 5*. I downloaded it on my comm, but I never got to read it."

"Rune could probably charge the battery."

I sighed and displayed the gaping hole in my wrist. "I had to throw it away. It was . . . corrupted, for lack of a better word. It's okay. I can wait until we kill the aliens to find out what happens to Yumiko. It'll be my incentive for getting through alive."

Matt laughed, not unkindly. "*That's* your incentive?"

"Not like I have any family to go home to," I said, sounding more bitter than the flippant tone I'd intended.

Matt nodded seriously. "That's a big part of why I teamed up with Legion, you know. My family." He tapped his arm. "Synthetic. Cybernetic core. Strong as hell." His finger moved to his temple. "Enhanced vision. Better hearing. Pneumatic goddamn Achilles tendons. Even my lungs and heart were upgraded. So if I get away from this life, I can make sure my family stays safe. That's all I care about now."

I folded my arms and examined my scuffed boots, ideas racing through my head. "You're right," I said at last. "That's all that matters." And my family now? It was these people—Cage and Rune, Mia, Jasper, Reed, Imani, and even Legion, all of us bound together by trauma if not genetics.

Matt gave my shoulder a half pat, half punch, and wandered off toward Hallam while I made my way into a corner. I watched everyone: Imani and Rune playing some sort of card game with what seemed to be half a deck, Priya and Jasper dozing in chairs, Reed interjecting himself between Matt and Hallam, apparently as much a fan of car engines as he was of spaceships.

They were a disjointed, mismatched, ragtag bunch of survivors, and I loved them so much it set off a physical ache in my stomach.

Eden had tried to kill them. She'd succeeded with one of us. I closed my eyes and gave myself permission to recall every detail of the base beneath the sand: Alexei's arms spread wide, the tension radiating across his face, the way he'd passed Mia to Cage. I'd never seen him turn on Mia, not even to restrain her. But I knew Mia, and there had been no other way to keep her from marching pointlessly into death alongside him. And if I knew that, well, Alexei knew it all the better.

Cage came in through the door, his hair hanging limp in his face, his normally bright eyes dull and hooded. He scanned the room for a moment, blinking as his vision adjusted, and when his gaze landed on me, it softened. He crossed the room to sit beside me. "How's Mia?" I asked.

"I honestly don't know. She's talking to me again, but she won't discuss Alexei or what happened in the base. If I bring it up, she changes the subject or shuts down completely. She did take some water and promised to come in if she gets uncomfortable, so . . . that's something?"

"You know what happened wasn't your fault, right?"

Cage shrugged, and I realized that was exactly what he thought. "I mean, she's not wrong. I carried her out of there."

"You saved her life."

"She didn't want it to be saved." He smiled slightly. "I'm

not saying I wouldn't do it again. I'm just saying I don't feel great about taking that choice away from her. But it's what Alexei wanted, and . . ." He turned away, cupping the back of his neck as if simply saying the name pained him.

"How long did you know Alexei?"

He shrugged again.

"Cage?" I pulled him around in time to see him wipe away tears, and my own eyes welled in response. "Cage. Come here." I wrapped my arms around him, and he tightened his grip on my arms, holding me almost painfully. His whole body trembled. I pressed my face to his, and our tears mingled in a silent, painful trail of grief.

We clutched each other, and I squeezed my eyes shut. I couldn't cry anymore. Cage was right to hide his sorrow. We couldn't let the others see us like this, not now, not with so much riding on what came next. We had to stay strong for a little longer. And I was getting good at that, after all the death I'd seen. "You'd think it would stop being so awful," I whispered, half to myself.

"Losing someone you love?" Cage drew back just enough to wipe at his eyes. "I don't think it ever gets easier. I don't think it *should.*"

He was right. The pain meant we were still human. The creatures hadn't succeeded in transforming us into them, not yet.

Speaking of which . . . "We created them," I said dully.

Cage didn't even pretend to misunderstand me. "Well, not us, exactly."

"Humans created them. Or . . . reanimated them. To use in a *war*." My face twisted of its own accord, my grief coalescing into fury. "A stupid war that no one even remembers because there's no one *left* to remember it."

"You think Omnistellar wouldn't have done the same? That was their whole goal, right? Get their hands on alien tech, stay on top of the game." He examined my expression and sighed. "I'm not saying that to make you feel worse. I'm just pointing out that where you have people, you'll always have a few assholes willing to sacrifice everything if it means keeping a step ahead. So yeah, humans created them. Does it really matter? It doesn't change what they are or what we need to do next."

"No," I agreed softly. "All it does is make the losses a little harder to bear, knowing that in a sense we're responsible for them."

"Kenzie, I . . ." He closed his eyes in apparent frustration.

I tilted my head, examining the drawn angles of his face, the lines that hadn't been there a few weeks ago. "You're exhausted, aren't you?"

"Aren't we all?"

"You didn't answer me," I pointed out. I nudged him over to curl against his side. "You're right, Cage. Wherever the *zemdyut* came from, whoever created them, it doesn't change what we need to do next. Or what *you* need. Rest. Let everyone take care of themselves for a while."

"I could say the same to you."

"I'll sleep if you will."

He hesitated a moment, and then a smile tugged at his lips. "Deal," he said. He pulled me in for a kiss, slow and soft and warm. We were both too tired for it to hold any real fire, although as always, his touch awakened something in my heart, in my stomach, even in the tips of my toes. And then he pulled me in against him, and I nestled in and closed my eyes and finally, *finally*, let everything fade to silence.

FORTY

JASPER NUDGED US AWAKE A BIT LATER. "HEY," he said softly, his face shadowed in the fluorescent lights. "The jeeps are charged. We should get moving."

I rolled my neck and stirred. Cage's arms tightened around me, and he groaned, demonstrating his usual reluctance to wake up. "What time is it?" I asked.

"I'm not sure, but it's getting dark."

I gently extricated myself from Cage's grasp and clambered to my feet. Everyone else was gathered around the vehicles, and I frowned. "You should have woken us sooner."

"We thought you needed the sleep."

He wasn't wrong. I closed my eyes and checked in on the alien presence, but it was dimmer now. I hoped I wasn't losing my connection. It seemed like a strange thing to hope *for*, that a weird alien presence would linger in my brain, but without it

I didn't know how we would find the creatures at all. Or how they would find us. That was the key. Karoch had been on its way to deal with us personally, I was sure of that. It was my job to make sure it found us.

Cage stirred and got to his feet, scrubbing at his face. I smiled in spite of myself.

"We have three working jeeps," Priya announced, "and I'm going to suggest Legion drive them."

"Why Legion?" Mia demanded.

"Do you know how to drive?"

An awkward silence met her question. "I do," I said defiantly. It was part of Omnistellar training.

"Yes, but you also have aliens in your brain," Hallam pointed out. I decided maybe I didn't like him so much after all.

"So that's settled. Matt, Hallam, and I will each take a jeep. The rest of you pile in where you see fit."

Rune instantly hopped into the passenger seat next to Matt, and Cage and I settled in behind them. Mia and Jasper rode with Priya, Reed and Imani with Hallam. We redistributed the comm units to the drivers, giving us a means of communication between vehicles, and we were off, our car in the lead, Rune directing Matt in her soft, soothing voice.

It was getting dark, and the interior of the jeep was climate controlled, and before long I'd sagged against Cage and gone back to sleep.

I didn't know how much time passed before I found myself

blinking against the darkness, somehow aware that I was not myself, that I'd slipped through my dreams and into the alien hive mind. Maybe it was my dream state, but it wasn't overwhelming like direct contact was, not a nightmare of conflicting shapes and ideas and fears. I was less of a participant and more of an observer, although the slow, insidious crawl of the hive still called to me.

It was scary how a part of me wanted to turn to it, yield to it, open myself and let the group sweep me away, devour any loneliness or self-doubt or grief. It was the part that wanted to fall and not get up, the part that had curled into a ball when my mom betrayed me, when she died, when Dad died, when Alexei died . . .

But I was stronger than that part of me.

I'd pushed it aside all of those times, and I did it again now. I was stronger than I'd been when I was merely an Omnistellar guard. Back then I'd thought pretty highly of myself. I'd excelled in my training and I figured it made me better than everyone else. Now I saw myself for what I'd really been: successfully brainwashed, desperately striving for the approval of the people who controlled me. Becoming a wanted criminal had, ironically, freed me.

The aliens offered just another kind of imprisonment. There was no danger of me returning to that.

I took a step into the darkness, and the world shimmered around me. I couldn't see anything, exactly, not with my eyes, but I sensed them all around me: the writhing collective, the creatures sludging forward, and behind them, driving them all, the massive thing called Karoch. I sensed the force of the aliens, their power, their strength.

A shudder went through me. In my mind Karoch was a black hole of compulsion, drawing me in and repelling me at the same time. I steeled myself to stay focused. The creatures were tunneling belowground. But they weren't where I expected to find them. In fact, now that I really paid attention, they weren't moving at all. Had they stopped for a break? Did they *need* breaks?

My mind brushed the edge of an important awareness, something critical. I turned to it reluctantly. It was further into the collective, further past the safe distance I currently stood at. My heart clamored for me to turn back, but instead I pressed forward, the collective swirling and enveloping and—

"Kenzie?"

I jolted awake, shaking my head as the jeep rumbled over a bump in the desert.

Cage was bent over me, his hand on my arm, and Rune was staring at me in the rearview mirror.

"What's going on?" I managed. My mouth felt fuzzy.

"You were mumbling in your sleep," said Matt. "We couldn't understand it, but you sounded . . . wrong. We thought we'd better wake you up."

"Thanks," I said, trying to spin my mind back to the dream,

or whatever it had been. The predominant image was one of darkness and cold.

"Is something wrong?" Rune asked.

"No. The creatures are tunneling underground, just like we suspected. They really don't like the surface. I guess we're lucky that wasn't bred out of them somehow. Otherwise they'd be stalking around up here all the time." But something *was* wrong. They'd stopped, hadn't they? I searched for an explanation, then shook my head. "Having these creatures in your head isn't as useful as you might think."

"Cheer up, alien girl," Matt replied. "We're almost there."

"How much longer?"

"Just a few minutes. Look, you can see the facility ahead."

Cage and I scrambled forward, peering between the seats at the shadowy shape in the distance. "Doesn't look like much," Cage said dubiously.

Rune tipped her head back to roll her eyes at him. "It's dark, dummy. Of course it doesn't look like much. Besides, what did you expect? Flashing neon signs reading WE STORE OUR EXPLOSIVES HERE?"

Cage fidgeted with the edge of the seat. "Are we sure about this?" he asked quietly. He regarded each of us in turn. "I know it's our only option. I understand. But . . . this is so much more than anything we've ever done. And that's saying something."

"Let's see." Rune ticked off each statement on her fingers. "We escaped a supposedly inescapable prison. We defeated a horde of alien invaders and stole their spaceship. We escaped another prison on Mars. We survived a team of nasty bounty hunters." She slapped Matt's arm when she said this, and a slow smile spread over his face, although his eyes remained fixed on the desert ahead. "We escaped another exploding ship to travel to an alternate dimension, and then we survived a plot to kill us."

"*Some* of us survived," corrected Cage quietly.

Rune's face fell. "Some of us," she repeated.

I hated to see the joy drain from her like that. I nudged her arm. "What's your point?"

She smiled softly, although a touch of her spirit was gone. "My point is, every time we top ourselves, we come out ahead. This won't be any different."

Well, you had to admire her confidence. Even Cage relaxed a bit, his face sinking into the affectionate smile he reserved solely for his twin. "I'm most worried about *you, meimei*. You're the one who's going to have to power those explosives. Are you sure you can handle it?"

For just a second Rune's eyes met mine in the rearview mirror, and something sparked in her expression, a fierce determination that would have been unthinkable in her just a few weeks ago. "I'm stronger than you think," she informed her brother.

"I'm not calling you weak, for the love of God. I'm *worried*. I'm still allowed to be that, right?"

"Yes, you are. Just like I have been every time you charged into danger to protect me, or Kenzie, or any one of us." Rune twisted in her seat, and now that momentary resolution was gone, leaving only her calm, gentle smile. "I love you, Cage. So much. You too, Kenzie. And I'll do what it takes to protect you."

What did she mean by that? I narrowed my gaze at her suspiciously, and she ducked her head, avoiding my eyes. Something was up. But before I could question her further, Cage sighed. "I love you too, *meimei*," he said, almost teasingly. "And since there's apparently no way to stop you, I guess I'll have to trust you."

"We're here," Matt announced, steering the jeep around the edge of the facility. The headlights of the other vehicles shifted over us in sliding shadows as they passed. "Kenzie, you have no idea where those things are?"

I frowned, setting aside my concerns about Rune for the time being. I had to trust that she knew what she was doing. "They're close. I know that. But I can't be more specific. It's hard to tell when they're underground, and . . ." And something else, but I couldn't quite put my finger on it. Not yet. I'd been almost there when they woke me up. "I'm sorry," I finished helplessly.

"Don't be." Cage gave me a quick half hug. "You're doing great. This isn't easy."

Priya's voice crackled in my ear. "Okay, everyone. Grab your gear and let's regroup outside. If we're going to breach this facility, we're going to have to do it fast and careful."

“On our way,” I said, and relayed her instructions to the others.

As we got out of the vehicle, the cold desert night instantly swept over my skin, raising goose bumps. I pulled my flak jacket more tightly around myself and zipped it shut. The others were spilling from the jeeps, and we started toward them, weapons clutched in the pitch-black, utterly silent night.

Suddenly, a sharp, familiar howl split the air from somewhere in the distance.

We pivoted as one.

Barely twenty feet away from us the sand erupted in a spray of stone and dirt as one of the creatures launched itself to the surface. As if on cue, more eruptions triggered on our left, on our right, behind us, until we were standing in a circle of maybe twenty aliens, all of them curling and writhing and sniffing the air, chirping to one another in their horrible sharp voices.

My heart sank.

We were surrounded.

FORTY-ONE

THIS WAS WHAT I'D MISSED. THE REASON THE aliens had stopped. They weren't chasing us. They'd known exactly where we were headed, exactly what we planned to do, and they'd cut us off, waiting for us at the facility.

And the only place they could have gotten that information?

The creatures enclosed us in a vicious, snarling mass, and with sudden clarity, I knew exactly what I'd missed every time I connected to them. "It's a trap," I whispered, my voice trembling. "They were using me as I was using them. They knew we were connected. They read our plans in my mind, and they waited for us here."

One of the creatures' heads swiveled at my voice, snarling, and Cage raised a warning finger in my direction. I didn't see Karoch. These things were still blind, our one—perhaps only—advantage.

By unspoken and mutual consent, we withdrew slowly until we'd formed a tight circle, our backs pressed together, our weapons at the ready. I inspected my pistol with shaking hands. I honestly didn't even know if it would work against the creatures. Had they had time to adapt? My flak jacket would provide some protection from their claws, but not enough. Not nearly enough.

"Kenz," said Cage, so softly you could barely hear him, "can you tell how many?"

I hated to close my eyes with the creatures right in front of me, but I did, focusing on the collective. Now I sensed it vividly, an almost taunting beckoning, daring me to come closer. Shuddering, I pried my lids apart. "I don't know," I whispered. "Dozens. Maybe hundreds. They're beneath the surface. They're everywhere."

"Then why the hell aren't they attacking?" Mia snarled. She was on my left, her bare arm flexed against my shoulder since she'd refused any armor or protection whatsoever.

I shook my head as the creatures shifted and stirred. Why *weren't* they attacking? We were right here, and they obviously knew it. No, they couldn't *see* us, but they sensed us, and they could rip us to shreds if they tried.

And then all at once it hit me, and whether I knew because of my connection to the hive mind or simply because it slapped me in the face, I was for the first time in a long while 100 percent certain. "They want to absorb us if they can," I gasped.

"They're waiting for Karoch to make sure they can subdue us without killing us. They learn our powers more easily if they transform us into them instead of studying us after we die. That's why they're not attacking." I reached a bit further and shivered. "I think . . . they're on the verge of some kind of sight. They absorbed Finn's cybernetics. They really want the rest of Legion. But they'll take any and all of us they can get. It's why Karoch's willing to risk coming here—that and to stop us from escaping. They hate us. Hate us more than anyone. They hate us, and they want us."

"Screw that." Mia's arm quivered. "I'll die before I go into their pit of goo, and I'll take every one of them down with me."

"How long do we have?" asked Priya at the same time, and much more practically.

Again, I shook my head helplessly. My connection to the collective was proving singularly unhelpful at the moment. "Karoch is stronger than them but also bigger and slower. It has to tunnel through behind them. We have maybe minutes. Not much more."

"Why doesn't it just use the surface? It's nighttime."

I closed my eyes again and shuddered as awareness tore through me. Somewhere, not here but not far, the great beast slouched toward me. "It doesn't need to," I whispered, my mouth suddenly dry. "It's not in a hurry. It knows we can't escape. It thinks our plan is doomed to fail."

"Perfect."

Jasper almost dropped his gun. He actually twisted in the circle to gape at Priya. "Please explain exactly how, in the name of anything and everything you hold holy, this situation is perfect."

"Because if Karoch is on its way, and these things don't want to kill us, then our plan still holds." Priya jerked her chin at the dark facility just beyond the ring of hunters. "All we need to do is get past them and find our way inside. It'll be easier to hide there. We can finish the job we came to do, and Kenzie can draw on Karoch's power to take us home."

It sounded so simple. So confident. A tiny stir of optimism flared to life, and I twisted to Cage on my right, praying I'd see my own reluctant hope mirrored there.

He bit his lip, looking from me to Rune to Mia and back again, the agony of indecision stenciled across his face. For once Cage was at a loss. I could see it inside him, shining through his eyes, the desperate desire to make a decision and the terrifying, paralyzing sense that no matter what he said, he'd lose someone.

I knew that feeling. I'd experienced it myself after I shot Matt, after losing my family.

I didn't have time to counsel Cage right now, so I did what I could. I leaned in and brushed my lips over his jawline. He turned to me, startled, his eyes flaring wide, and I forced myself to smile. Once upon a time I wouldn't have been able to take on a decision like this. Not by myself. I'd have passed it through Omnistellar, through my mom, through Cage. But I understood what leadership meant now. I understood it didn't mean always knowing the right course of action. That was why Cage put on the smile, forced the cheer in his voice. It was how he'd held his friends together through years of imprisonment.

And it was how I'd hold us together too. "It's okay," I murmured so only Cage heard me. He met my gaze, an agony of indecision lurking behind his eyes. "I've got this one."

I didn't know what to do, but we had to do something. So I forced a rod of steel into my spine, aiming at the creature in front of me. "On the count of three, open fire," I said in a quiet but strong voice completely belying my skittering heart and twisting stomach. "Hopefully we'll punch a hole through their line. The second we do, everyone run as fast as you can. Make for the facility. Cage, Legion, and I will bring up the rear. We can move the fastest. The rest of you get inside."

I waited for argument, for dissent, but none came. Instead, muscles shifted against me as people reassembled, facing the creatures in front of us, lowering their weapons.

I swallowed. "One."

The gun bucking in my hand. Matt's open, sightless eyes. Tyler, raised high above an alien head. Alexei, his arms spread wide, his jaw locked in determination.

"Two."

My mom, soaked in the alien slime that killed her. My father's face, twisted in agony as the creature gored him. Rita, slumped against a wall, dangling from chains.

No more.

"Three."

I squeezed the trigger, and an alien screamed. Agony ricocheted through my skull, the shared death of the creature hollowing my insides, leaving behind rage and fear and the desperate need to attack. To survive. I channeled the emotion, pulling the trigger again and again and again, and then I tossed the gun aside and yanked another free from the armory at my waist and across my back. Time for a new weapon.

Mia was already on the move, shoving Rune ahead of her. Jasper, Reed, and Imani followed, leaving me, Cage, Matt, Priya, and Hallam to cover their escape. We did our best, shooting at random as a sea of the creatures erupted from the sand, their mouths open in furious howls. My own cheeks burned to echo their screams, the line between me and them blurring as they lost control in their torment and fury.

I bit my tongue hard enough that I saw stars and tasted blood, but the pain refocused me, drawing the figures around me into sharp focus. "Time for you to go!" I shouted at Priya. "We'll be right behind you!"

She hesitated barely a second, then nodded and flashed across the sand, so fast she seemed to reappear a short distance away, almost as fast as Cage himself. Matt and Hallam chased after her, and the creatures pivoted, following the noise. In the reflected moonlight, their skin glistened, their sightless eyes like pits of cataracts. Their claws twitched, and every muscle protruded in reptilian agility. "Hey!" I shouted. I pulled the trigger of my third and final gun, blasting one of the creatures, its reflected anguish tearing through me. But the ploy worked; the creatures snarled and spun on us, circling with a sinister grace.

Cage caught my hand. "We've done it before," he reminded me.

I nod. "And we'll do it again."

He caught me and dragged me to him, his mouth burning against mine in a split-second kiss so furious it felt like it lasted hours, like time froze in its wake.

And then he shoved me forward, and together we raced into the night.

Cage's power stood out in vivid shades of orange and green, a dragon coiled around itself to match his tattoo, a phoenix in the final bursts of flame. I bent my head, and we charged through the creatures. This time they didn't tear at us, didn't even slow us. Protected in each other, we bolted through the sand, the wind raging against our flesh, and I remembered the first time Cage held me in his arms and rocketed me away from the harvesters on Sanctuary.

We'd been apart then. Separate. Now we were together, one, our unity protecting me from the draw of the collective, the hive. Our hands linked, we skidded to a halt in the doorway, kicking up a cloud of sand.

"Inside!" Priya screamed. She and Hallam were crouched at the doors. I checked behind me to see the creatures charging on all fours, barely ten feet away, moving almost as fast as Cage and

I. Was this something new they'd learned from us, or an ability they'd always had, one they hadn't been able to exercise in the confined corridors of Sanctuary and Obsidian?

I didn't have time to consider it as Cage jerked me forward. We landed on our hands and knees in the dark corridor, and Priya and Hallam slammed their weight into the doors. They jolted shut just as the creatures smashed against them on the other side.

"Hold them!" Jasper bellowed. A moment later an assortment of random items slammed themselves over the door, binding it in twists of metal and wood as he essentially welded the entrance shut.

Priya and Hallam backed away, and we all watched with bated breath. The doors bucked against the creatures' assault, but Jasper's barricade held. "That won't keep them out forever," Imani gasped, trying to catch her breath.

"Then we'd better find what we're looking for fast." I turned to the others. "Is everyone okay?"

"Not even a scratch," said Reed, sounding disappointed. "Nothing for me to heal. You guys trying to make me useless?"

"I'm sure there will be plenty of injuries before the night's over." Mia rolled her shoulders and cracked her neck. "Let's go."

I glanced at Cage, and he nodded. Still hand in hand, we advanced into the depths of the facility. And at least I drew this much consolation from the current situation: win or lose, it was likely the last time I'd have to creep around hiding from those creatures ever again.

FORTY-TWO

WE HADN'T GONE MORE THAN TEN STEPS when the lights flickered and came on around us. I gasped, recoiling as if the presence of light indicated some sort of attack. But nothing happened—nothing except the revelation of a cold metal hallway caked in sand and dust, and Rune, beaming proudly. "I found the power," she said, her right eye twitching with the desire to close, to focus her energy. "Didn't even need to touch more than the walls to flip the switch."

"Good job, *meimei*," said Cage with genuine gratitude in his voice. I knew exactly how he felt. Until Karoch showed up, the light was our friend, not the aliens'. It helped us make the most of what little advantage we had.

"You're getting more powerful," I observed. "You didn't even need my help this time."

Rune nodded. "I think I've been able to do these things

for a while. I was holding myself back. Scared, maybe."

The door continued to shudder behind us. "And now?" I asked softly.

Rune's gentle face broke into a smile. "Now I'm not afraid at all. I know what has to be done, and I'm ready to do it."

We were standing in a dusty hall, sand pooling around our feet, a decade of misuse rendering the place a gritty, dull mess. You'd never look at it and think *secret government weapons facility*. Rune pressed her hand to the wall, her eyes screwed shut in determination. Sweat trickled along her brow, and I turned to Cage, my own worry reflected in his expression. Rune always exerted a lot of effort when she merged with machines, but lately, with her developing powers, she hadn't seemed to require as much focus. Now she seemed on the verge of collapse. "*Meimei?*" Cage asked hesitantly.

She nodded, waving her free hand as if to brush him away, and the rest of us exchanged helpless looks. "We have to keep moving," said Hallam, more gently than he usually spoke.

"Leave her alone," Mia countered sharply. "Rune knows what she's doing."

Strangely, Mia's words settled me. Rune *did* know what she was doing. If things became too much for her, she'd tell us. Beside me, Cage relaxed too, and I smiled at him without quite meaning to. He'd come so far since I'd first met him. He might think he hadn't changed, but I remembered how little trust he'd placed in his sister, his desperate drive to protect her. That was still there, but he'd withdrawn some, allowing her the freedom to find her own place in the world. It was the one thing lacking in their twin relationship, and somewhere along the way he'd found it. I itched to tell him, to turn to him and take him in my arms. This wasn't the time or place, though, so I only slid my hand over the small of his back, moving a step closer.

Suddenly the aliens thudding against the door behind us ceased. We all pivoted, bringing what weapons remained to bear against our shoulders. Cage, Jasper, and I surged to the front—Jasper could still throw things at them, and Cage and I clutched some sort of machetes we'd picked up. With our speed, they might cause some damage before the creatures adapted.

But then Rune's eyes flew open just as the sound of gunfire echoed outside. "Okay," she gasped. "I've got the computer system semifunctional, along with the power. I activated external security, which includes some automated defenses. They're firing on the creatures right now, but I can't promise how long it'll be effective, given . . . Well, you know. We should get moving."

Priya's jaw dropped. "Girl," she said, "that is some power."

Rune flushed. "It's nothing, really."

"Don't be stupid." Hallam swatted her arm as he stalked by. "It's not nothing."

Cage nodded. "That's my sister. Always saving our butts."

Unbidden, Rune flashed him a big, sweet smile brimming with genuine joy even now, even here, and I realized how very much I'd come to love her. She was as much my sister as Cage's.

After all the grief and despair of the last few weeks, it was a welcome change.

Back on Obsidian, Rune had called me her best friend. She was mine, too. But she was more than that. Somewhere between the first gentle smile she'd given me on Sanctuary and this moment, when she'd saved us all yet again, I'd come to love her with all my heart. She caught me observing her and raised an eyebrow, and I had to resist the urge to hug her hard. I only nodded and smiled, and she gave me a wink as she rolled her shoulders, shaking off the lingering tension of her feat of strength. She seemed calmer now, lighter, as if she'd come to terms with something—her powers, maybe, or her own inner strength. She was almost a beacon of confidence, and she drew all of us with her, raising our spirits and hopes without speaking a word.

Hallam, Matt, and Priya instinctively took the lead, and no one argued with them this time. They were the trained soldiers, and it made sense for them to take us into a military facility. Jasper, Cage, and I brought up the rear, keeping a careful watch over our shoulders in case an alien suddenly dropped from the ceiling. I shuddered, remembering how they'd done exactly that on Sanctuary, and Jasper and Cage moved a bit closer to me.

Alexei used to do the same thing. Whenever anyone seemed nervous or frightened, he'd instinctively shift a little closer, sheltering them with his bulk. The memory made my eyes swim and, to my horror, this time I couldn't blink back all the tears.

A few spilled over my cheeks. The boys must have noticed, but they didn't say anything, and I quickly wiped the tears away, furious with myself. I had to focus on the here and now. This was our last chance to get away from this dead world and maybe save our own.

Speaking of . . . I closed my own eyes, seeking out my alien connection. That part of my mind seemed strangely empty, though. It was still there, just . . . dark. Misty. Frowning, I opened my eyes.

Cage caught my gaze. "Anything?"

"I think they're hiding," I replied, my heart sinking.

Jasper shook his head. "Who the hell knows what sort of powers they've absorbed? If they've taken Mia's invisibility, they could surround us and we'd never even know."

I shuddered. "They could have taken abilities from anywhere, anytime. This isn't the first dimension they've demolished. Karoch is their center, their core, but the creatures are its limbs. It sends them to a dimension, lets them expand, grow, and then they destroy. And once they have, Karoch follows, and the creatures occupy that dimension while a few move to the next. That way Karoch is always safe, always one step behind them." I looked between them. "You get what I'm saying? We'll never see Karoch on our Earth, not until it's too late. If we're going to destroy it, we have to do it here and now."

Cage nodded grimly. "Then we'd better not fail."

Right. No problem. I swallowed.

Ahead of us, the others stopped at a circle lift. "It's working," Rune assured them as they regarded it dubiously.

"And if it stops halfway down?" Hallam demanded.

"It won't."

"You can guarantee that?"

Rune sighed. "Not guarantee, no, but the other choice is fifteen flights of stairs."

"I thought we were in a hurry," said Mia, pushing past the others to get onto the lift. Legion exchanged glances, then shrugged and followed her. Rune packed in beside them, rendering the lift about as full as it could get.

"We'll meet you downstairs," Reed promised as they disappeared. Almost instantly, another lift formed. Jasper, Reed, Imani, Cage, and I squished into it, and it dropped. As usual, the claustrophobia got to me, but this time it was tempered by a sense of wonder that our technology matched this dimension's so completely.

Reed's thoughts must have mirrored mine. "Everything here is so familiar," he said as we dropped into darkness. "And yet . . ."

"And yet," Imani agreed.

"Do you think we exist here somewhere?" asked Jasper softly, and I knew he was thinking about his family as much as us. "Other versions of us?"

I shook my head helplessly. I hadn't even considered that. Was it possible? Was there an Alexei somewhere running around, alive and well? Another version of me, maybe with parents to care for her?

But . . . "If we ever did," said Cage, in a gentle tone, "we probably don't anymore. Most of the population here didn't survive the alien attack." He reached past me to squeeze Jasper's shoulder. "All the more reason for us to get home and take care of our Earth, our people."

Jasper nodded, his face grim in the dim illumination lining the circle lift. Our descent slowed, and a brief moment of panic assailed me as I recalled Hallam's fears. What if something happened and Rune couldn't maintain the power? After all, the building had been dark for ten whole years. If we were trapped here, wedged against one another in this tunnel in the black . . . I'd rather face the aliens. At least it would be quick.

But we were slowing because we'd reached our destination. If the lift ever had a vocal function, it wasn't working anymore: we simply stopped without fanfare or announcement.

The others had gathered right outside the lift, blocking my view. I stumbled after them and stopped short. "What's going on?" I demanded.

Rune met my eyes, her jaw working but no sound emerging. The others didn't move, only stood there, and eventually I let out a huff of annoyance and shouldered past them. Whatever it was—a sea of aliens, a gaping pit, who the hell knew anymore—I needed to see.

Then I stopped too.

Rows and rows of what could only be missiles. Probably hundreds of them. They were lined up in orderly, stacked columns. More firepower than anyone ever possibly needed, enough to destroy a country a dozen times over. "My God," I said, my voice thick.

"This isn't going to work," said Jasper flatly. "We activate one of those, and it'll cause a chain reaction. It'll destroy everything for miles."

Eden and her people intruded on my mind, the children in their little tent city. Wendell with his broad smile at the promise of chocolate. "Nowhere will be safe," I agreed quietly. "We have to find another way."

But Priya shook her head. "There isn't another way," she said. For once her voice wasn't ringing with authority and self-righteousness. Instead, there was a thread of sadness.

Matt nodded. "She's right," he said, appealing mainly to me and Cage. I must have looked dubious, because he took a step closer. "I'm not saying I like it. It's horrible. But think about the alternative, Kenzie. We have the chance to destroy those aliens completely. We might take Eden's city with us, but how many lives will we save? Everyone's back on Earth, for sure. Anyone else still alive on this planet. And how many other Earths will never have to deal with the creatures because we stopped them here?"

"It's the aliens on the ship all over again," said Imani, an edge of hysteria in her voice. "We killed them, and the creatures descended on us in search of revenge. Actions have *consequences*."

Rune rubbed her hand over her face. "I know. I fought harder than anyone against killing the aliens. But Imani . . . not acting is an action too. If we do nothing, then we aren't personally responsible for anyone's deaths. Eden and her people, whoever's left on this planet, they might live a little longer. Until the aliens kill them. Until they run out of supplies again. We'll die, though, all of us, and probably our entire planet. Our families. Our friends. And any other dimensions the aliens head to next."

"You don't know that!" Imani snapped.

"I do." I swallowed, the edge of the alien consciousness brushing against mine—only a memory, at least for now. But I was close enough to know this much for certain. "They'll keep spreading like a virus until they've destroyed everything in their wake, until they're all that remains. It's what they do." I took Imani by the shoulders. "I was never sure about what we did on the ship, about killing the aliens then. But as much as I hate it, I'm sure now. I have to be. If we don't stop those things here, we're going to be responsible for a lot more death. Maybe not directly. Maybe we won't have pulled the trigger. But it's going to be our fault just the same."

Silence met my words as everyone studied their feet. The explosives sat around us, seeming to taunt us, and my knees went weak. Was I actually willing to go through with this? The faces of those kids kept swimming in front of me. Eden and all her people. Dead. Dead in an instant if they were lucky.

Or left to suffer until the aliens came calling.

I raised my head and looked from one of my friends to another. Legion and Cage and Mia were easy. They'd clearly already decided, their faces locked in determination. Jasper was still staring at his feet, but the set of his shoulders said he'd also thrown his lot in with us. If it meant preserving his own world, his own family, he was willing to make the sacrifice. And Rune . . . Rune was a healer at heart, and it was clear how much this decision pained her. But her arms were folded and she was resolute in what had to be done.

Imani and Reed, though . . . I read the indecision written across their features. And me? Once upon a time, I'd have been on their side. Wendell wouldn't leave me alone, no matter how hard I tried to blot him out. That should have been enough to dissuade me. Would have been, once. But I'd come too far and seen too much, and touching the alien hive mind gave me a core of utter certainty.

I couldn't save everyone. Given a few weeks, maybe I could come up with a better plan, a way to eliminate the aliens without sacrificing this whole planet. But I didn't have weeks. I didn't even have minutes. It was save some or save none, and that was the cold hard truth staring me in the face.

But I didn't say anything. There was nothing more to say. This entire awful plan hinged on Rune. We couldn't do it without her, and it was a hell of a burden to ask her to bear. If she refused, the plan halted and everyone died. We'd have to take as many of them out with us as possible and pray we somehow disabled Karoch, prevented it from continuing its interdimensional rampage. And right now, Rune seemed content to wait for Reed and Imani to speak. She wore an expression of serene resignation, as if she'd come to peace with something truly terrible. I would have taken the burden from her if I could. She wasn't the innocent she'd been on Sanctuary, but she was still herself: strong and courageous and obviously willing to do what it took to save us all. She caught me watching and gave me a soft smile, as if to reassure me that everything would be okay, and I forced myself to smile back. If Rune could face this decision with such composure, I could too.

We all stood in silence, until finally Reed raised his head, his face wet with tears. "I don't want to carry this," he said helplessly. "I don't want this responsibility."

Instinctively, Imani wrapped her arms around him, leaning into him. "No one does," she said softly. "But Reed . . . we both have family at home. My parents. Your moms. We can't abandon our entire planet because we don't want to take on the burden."

"Victory comes with a cost," Priya told them, not unkindly. "You're young. You haven't been in enough battles to realize that. I wish I could say the same. But I carry a thousand burdens like this one . . . well, maybe not *quite* like this one." She made a face. "It's never an easy choice. But it's always a choice. Doing nothing is a choice too. You get that, right?"

"We get it." Imani wiped at her own tears. "All right. I'm in. Let's murder a bunch of people. Why not?"

I sighed, wishing I had something, anything to make her feel better.

And then something inside me gave a sickening, horrible lurch. I dropped to my knees, the world spinning around me, my head rushing. Images assailed me, the alien world rushing over me like a waterfall, surrounding me and swallowing me and threatening to wash me away with it. The power swelled inside me, assaulted me, battering my defenses.

"Kenzie!" Cage had me, turning me in his arms, shaking me. "Kenzie!"

My vision refocused slowly, Cage swimming into view, and I caught at his shoulders, gasping for air. "We're out of time," I whispered. "Karoch is here."

FORTY-THREE

"WHERE?" PRIYA SNAPPED TO ATTENTION, leveling some sort of rifle against her shoulder.

I shook my head, grabbing Cage's arms and half climbing him to drag myself to my feet. "I don't know. Close."

"Can you access its powers?" Mia growled.

My head swam. "I can't even think right now," I whispered, struggling to keep the room in focus. Karoch's power was so strong, so compelling, it was all I could do to keep from falling into it and vanishing.

"Kenzie!" Matt's voice had taken an aggressive tone, sharp enough to jolt me at least partially back to myself. "If you can't use Karoch's power, we're all going to die here." A startled silence met his words, and he glared from one of us to another. "Well? I assume we're still going through with this whether we can escape or not. Or was all that talk of sacrifice and cost contingent on us getting away with our own lives?"

Rune drew herself taller, eyes flashing, as if the very notion of self-sacrifice solidified her resolve. "No," she said. "We're going through with it either way."

"Yeah, great," said Hallam. "But Kenzie, it'd be really nice if we *didn't* have to die here, you know?"

I laughed in spite of myself, my teeth chattering, my limbs shaking. Cage still had a grip on me, as if he could physically keep me centered, and actually it was helping, the physicality of the connection locking me in place. I closed my eyes, tightening my hands on Cage's arms and focusing all of my attention on that point of contact, my anchor to the real world. With the rest of my mind, I reached out, searching for the aliens.

Searching for Karoch.

I didn't have to look hard. It hit me with the force of a meteor, its sheer presence a massive overwhelming collection of rage and aggression and sheer, malevolent *hunger*. "Oh, God," I whispered, my shoulders hunching as I slumped against Cage's arms.

"Kenzie." Imani crouched beside me and laid her hand on my back. Healing energy flowed from her and, even though there was nothing physically wrong with me, it seemed to help, stabilizing me, connecting me. "You're not with them. You're here with us. Everything's okay."

"We've got you," Reed added as he joined his energy to Imani's.

Kneeling there in the triangle of Reed, Cage, and Imani, I found myself strengthening. Something in my core pulled tight and I managed to straighten. The massive weight of Karoch's presence settled physically against my shoulders. It was on the edge of my mind, threatening to overwhelm me. *Wanting* to overwhelm me, I realized with a sudden burst of determination. These creatures had taken my family. They'd devoured my friends. They'd killed and sliced their way through everything I held dear. They were *not* going to get my mind—not without a fight.

I drew myself to my feet, filling my lungs with a painful, shaky breath. Having done so once, I found it easier to do it again. "I'm okay," I said.

Cage tilted his head, examining me. "Are you sure? Your eyes don't seem right."

I didn't know what to say to that. What was wrong with my eyes? "I'm sure," I said, putting aside the latent fear Cage's words had awakened inside me. Thanks, Cage. "I'm going to see if I can forge a connection to Karoch and draw on its power."

I didn't wait for a response. Instead I closed my eyes and turned inward.

Karoch swirled around me, the alien mind enveloping my consciousness like a cloud. I kept my breathing steady. The image of my mother was foremost in my mind, for whatever reason. I fixed my attention on her and all of the bewildering, infuriating, contradictory emotions she awoke. I made myself imagine, in vivid detail, the body of my friend Rita Hernandez, coated in alien goo, her eyes blank and white and empty. Imani, clutching her sister's limp body. Tyler, hoisted in the air above a screaming alien. My father, if anything shocked to have his life cut off so quickly. And Alexei.

Those were my people. Karoch had no hold over me.

I latched on to Karoch, feeling its shock as I surged into it with my own consciousness, leaving the hive mind far behind. Any allure it had once offered became repulsion. I wanted nothing to do with these creatures.

I wanted them *dead*. I'd have ejected every last one of them into space myself.

And I wanted Karoch's power.

I visualized my friends' abilities in colors. Karoch's powers were colored too, but they were a swirling, muddy mess, like staring into a swamp. Brief glimmers of reflected color surged to the surface, instantly swallowed by eddies of darkness and sludge. Somewhere in this mess was the power to shift between dimensions, and the only way to find it was to plunge inside.

I didn't hesitate. Not anymore. I dove in, letting the repulsive sludge wash over me. It hit me as if I'd leaped into a swamp. There was no physical Kenzie left, not anymore. There was just me, one central being immersed in a cold, slimy clutter of foul-smelling mush.

I opened my eyes. The sludge burned, but I let it flood over me. Somewhere, Karoch roared in fury, but I tuned it out. I opened my mouth and swallowed the rank mess. I let it course through me, filling me.

Power exploded beneath my skin. It slithered through my stomach, pierced my lungs. It was agony and terror and something else, something much more frightening because it was so compelling: the ultimate edge of strength. If I opened myself a tiny bit more, let the hive mind weave its way through me, I could be part of this. I wouldn't merely have the power to move between dimensions. I would have *all* the powers, all of Karoch's abilities. I would be fast and strong and smart, and no one—nothing—would touch me or the people I loved again.

Except I wouldn't have the people I loved, would I? Because I wouldn't be *me*.

I would be Karoch.

I threw my head back against the rush of power and forced it into a steady stream, raising my hands to the slime. I pressed my arm to the right, carving a path for myself. As the sludge cleared, I felt power sliding away from me, leaving an almost physical ache in my chest. But there was a clearing, too, a return of my earlier strength and resolve.

I pressed with my left hand, clearing more of the gunk. What remained separated into more distinct colors, less repulsive, more seductive.

And in their midst, it appeared: a shimmering mix of black and green with dots of gold that, for whatever reason, brought Liam vividly to mind. I saw him as if he were standing in front of me, his ridiculous pirate outfit billowing around him, his quirky grin mocking me. "Hey, Kenzie," he said.

I blinked. It really was him. We were suddenly standing in the hidden space on Obsidian where he'd stored his stash. "Hey, Liam," I said softly. "You're not actually here, are you?"

He shrugged. "How should I know? Maybe we're all part of these creatures. Maybe once you destroy it, you'll destroy the last bits of us."

Well, that sounded like him, at least. "Would you really want to live on like this?" I pressed. "As part of Karoch?"

"I wouldn't, as a matter of fact. But if you're going to do something, you'd better do it fast."

"What do you mean?"

He smiled slightly, that sardonic, self-serving smile I remembered so well. I hadn't understood Liam when I met him. I didn't understand him now. But I *did* understand what drove him: the all-encompassing fear of the aliens that made him abandon his family to their clutches and leap across dimensions in search of safety. "Did you know?" I asked. "That you moved through dimensions?"

"I don't think so. I think I legitimately believed I was moving through space."

"Even when you heard them talking about Earth, talking about Mars?"

"We called our planet Wreithe. I probably noted the similarities, but . . . I guess I wasn't ready to accept the truth."

"Probably?"

"I'm not here, remember?"

"Then what's going on?"

"Your mind's conjuring someone who has experience with jumping dimensions. It was me or Karoch, I guess. I was probably the right choice."

"So you're a fancy hallucination." I laughed. "And I'm chatting with you."

"Right. Which means I can't give you any information you don't already have." He smiled and stepped forward, extending his hand. "Except this."

I blinked. There was nothing in his hand. "Except what?"

"Look closer."

I did, and there it was: a shimmering stone of gold, black, and green swirling in his hand. "Take it," he said. "Take it and make things right. Make up for my cowardice. Make up for the deaths of your friends and family. Make up for everything, Kenzie. I'm counting on you."

I swallowed. I didn't care if he wasn't real. "Liam, I'm sorry. I'm sorry you died, and that you had to face those things again after all. I wish we'd met differently."

"Who knows?" Liam gave a rueful smile. "Maybe some version of us will someday." He gestured lazily. "If you hurry."

I grabbed his hand.

The power slammed through me with violent force, utterly unlike any other ability I'd absorbed in the past. It filled every crevice, seeming to burn my blood, to thrum in time with my heartbeat. My entire body vibrated with it. I'd used Liam's power before. It hadn't been like this.

Because this wasn't from Liam.

It was from *Karoch*.

At the thought of the name, a cacophony descended on me: screams and shouts and gunfire and crashing and howling and screaming. My eyes flew open.

"She's awake!" Imani screamed.

"Thank God." Jasper appeared above me, terror etched in the lines of his face. "Kenzie, tell me you've got something."

I leveraged myself onto my elbow. Somehow I'd wound up lying on the floor behind a rack of missiles. There was no disorientation, though. I went from whatever I'd just been through to full wakefulness in a heartbeat, Karoch's power—*Liam's* power—thrumming through me. "Oh yes," I said softly. "I've got something. I can get us out of here. We just need to draw the aliens in and make sure Karoch follows."

Jasper snorted. "Yeah, somehow I don't think that's going to be a problem." He met my gaze and shook his head. "Kenzie, *have you looked around*?"

I stared at him as the sounds around me solidified into the noise of combat. I pivoted, scrambling to the edge of the row and peering out.

A battle raged around me. Dozens, maybe hundreds, of alien creatures leaping around the room and my friends scattered, using the missiles as cover, firing at the creatures. In one corner Rune stood stock-still, pressed between a row of missiles and a computer console, with aliens slithering around her. They clearly knew she was nearby, but they couldn't find her, not with the weapons sheltering her. Cage was on top of the weapons working his way toward her, but a creature leaped into his path and they faced off, balancing on the rack.

And then a roar split the air—something more inhuman, more horrifying, than anything we'd heard so far. The ceiling had been torn to shreds, presumably from the alien incursion. Now the wall shattered with the force of tons of dirt behind it, sand and clay and muck spilling into the room alongside brick and mortar and stone.

And behind it all, Karoch, its bulk shouldering into the room, here to devour at last.

FORTY-FOUR

MY FIRST THOUGHT WAS OF *ROBO MECHA* *Dream Girl*. Of Yumiko, standing in the center of a parking lot as a mech ten times her height advanced, its red eyes flaming, its massive arms clutching a weapon capable of shattering her into dozens of pieces.

Karoch held no weapon.

It didn't need one.

It was at least twenty feet tall and embodied the worst of the aliens: the slimy, glistening skin, the monstrous claws, the razor-sharp fangs. But whereas they had white, unseeing eyes, Karoch's glimmered with inhuman intelligence. Its pupils dilated against the electric light, and its gaze flickered around the room, absorbing the situation.

Coming to rest on me.

Strangely, for the first time, I felt no fear.

The others stifled their gasps, and the creatures halted their assault as their leader approached. The room was deathly silent.

I stepped around the corner and became Robo Mecha Dream Girl. I faced off against the creature, me and my nothingness, only the gaping void separating me from sixteen-inch lethal claws and a jaw that could snap me in half.

But when our eyes met, it was Karoch's that flickered in fear.

I reached inside myself and found Liam's power, and I *drew*.

Karoch snarled. It reared its head and lumbered forward, unsteady and clumsy but big and tenacious and powerful enough to crush any of us with a single blow. As if its movement was a signal, the other creatures roared, howled, a deafening cry swallowing us in its fury.

Jasper leaped to my side and slammed his left hand forward. The creatures staggered back as missiles rolled from their racks, crashing into them and sending them flying. Apparently, we'd abandoned all notion of treating the explosives with care.

It didn't matter. We didn't need them much longer.

"Get everyone together!" I shouted. "At the side of the room where Cage and Rune are! Now, go, move!"

Everyone lunged into action, and the room, which had lulled momentarily with Karoch's dramatic appearance, erupted into chaos. Screams and shouts and gunfire. Powers bursting, from my friends and the creatures. Howls. Shouts. Orders.

But in the midst of it all, two figures stood silent and still:

Karoch and me, staring at each other. I knew instinctively that when I moved, it would too. And this time I didn't dare let go of its power and try to grab Cage's. I couldn't barrel across the room with lightning speed.

We faced off, and I had never felt so small and helpless—but also so determined, so completely sure of what I was doing. Karoch was *afraid* of me. I sensed it radiating from the hive mind, no matter how hard it tried to hide it.

And fear was not an emotion it was used to. That, and that alone, probably kept us alive. With the creatures off balance, my friends slowly but surely gained ground, stealing their way toward Rune.

Someone screamed, and I swear to God it was Mia. That girl had managed to put herself in the path of every danger we'd encountered even before she developed her sparkly new death wish. I didn't dare turn my head to check, though. It felt like my gaze was keeping Karoch locked in place. It was doing the same to me. Its jaws parted and a trail of something oozed from one of its fangs, pooling on the ground by an impossibly large foot, a curved claw capable of separating my head from my body in a single swipe.

I swallowed, and my resolve faltered.

As if my fear had somehow freed it, Karoch took a thundering step toward me. The ground shuddered and I staggered, my heart hammering against my ribs. It snarled, and I got the distinct sense I'd lost a battle I didn't know I was fighting.

Somehow I had to steel myself, face it, but now the other creatures were closing in around me, snarling and swiping and screeching. Shudders racked my body, and I didn't know what to do. I was alone and helpless and so goddamn *afraid*.

A burst of wind struck me, almost toppling me, and then hands had me and I was in Cage's arms. His eyes glimmered above me, blood dripping from a cut on the side of his head, sweat plastering his hair flat, but then he grinned, and he was the most beautiful thing I'd ever seen. "I thought I'd save you one last time," he said, "before you save all of us. If, of course, you don't mind."

Karoch threw its head back and roared, and I grabbed on to Cage's arms in answer. He hoisted me up and drove through the aliens, tilting me against him, protecting me from the swarm as he carried me to safety, exactly like he had on Sanctuary. I curled into his chest, and for one blissful second it wasn't *my* responsibility to keep us safe, not my job to carry out our crazy plan. I was safe and hidden and could be as weak as I damn well chose and there was no one to lecture me about it.

All too soon Cage was setting me on my feet and the moment was over. The weight of our lives rebounded onto my shoulders. But somehow it seemed a bit lighter with everyone together and Cage's arms still around me.

My eyes met Karoch's, and it screamed in fury. The creatures lunged toward us, but even as they moved, Jasper threw a twisted heap of metal between us, creating an elaborate barrier.

"Kenzie!" he shouted, his muscles jackknifing with effort. "If you're going to get us out of here, now's the time!"

I closed my eyes, letting Karoch's power envelop me, and I reached further than ever before, into the depths of space itself. I didn't know how to control this ability now any more than I had before. But back on the Omnistellar ship, I'd wished to go somewhere we could beat the aliens, and that seemed to be where I'd taken us. So now, with all my strength, I wished to go *home*.

There wasn't the sickening lurch of using Liam's power. Karoch was stronger. More controlled. Space and time shifted at my command, molecules aligning beneath my will. Something jolted against me—Karoch, trying to seize the power. But I was in too deep. I imagined Liam, his mocking face, and Alexei, and Tyler, and my parents, and everyone who'd died, and I drew strength from them as I pulled.

Suddenly, a blue shimmer of light erupted in front of me. I staggered, almost stumbling into it. "What is it?" Mia asked, so close she made me jump even here and now. I pivoted to find her clutching her torn side, blood oozing through her shirt, her face pale.

"A portal?" I guessed. "At least that's what I hope it is."

She made a face. "Great. So do we go through it?"

"Someone do something!" Jasper shouted. "Before—"

His barrier slammed toward us with sudden violence. Jasper braced himself and shoved both arms forward. The metal disintegrated, but a shock wave of power swept from it, staggering all of us—and dropping Jasper, who collapsed into a heap at my feet. "No!" I screamed.

Karoch roared.

The aliens charged.

"No time to wait!" Cage shouted. "Let's go! Matt, Hallam, grab Jasper. Everyone move!"

Cage, Matt, and I shoved the others through the portal until only we and Rune remained. She grabbed Matt's arm. "Hey," she said, and she stood on her toes to kiss him.

Cage groaned. "Now?" he demanded incredulously.

Rune pulled back, and Matt staggered, his eyes wide. "Rune . . ."

"Go," she urged.

Karoch roared behind us, and Matt smiled. "Later," he promised.

"Later," Rune agreed, sadness shadowing her eyes. Matt leaped through the portal.

"Come on!" Cage ordered his sister. "Set off the missiles and let's go!"

Rune, her hand laid against the computer console, shook her head, giving us a small smile. "I can't go."

"Rune!" I screamed. The aliens had surrounded us and were awaiting Karoch. It twisted toward us and lumbered a step forward, its mouth splitting in a hideous snarl. "We don't have time for this."

"I can't," she repeated. "There's no way to activate a timer on the missiles. I have to be in contact with the system to set them off."

Cage's face went dark and ugly. "Screw that."

"*Gege*. This has to end. There's no point in me going through a portal only to die in a few hours when the aliens chase us home."

"Then I'll do it!" He grabbed her arm and yanked her out of the crevice, shoving her aside. "Just tell me what to do."

"You can't do it." Rune turned her big dark eyes on me. "Tell him, Kenzie."

"No." I spun from her to Karoch, drawing closer by the second. We had to *go*. "I'll do it. I can use your power. I can—"

"Not when I'm a dimension away from you, you can't. It has to be me." A tear formed at the corner of her eye and spilled over her cheek, but she was smiling. "Tell the others I love them."

Cage tightened his grip on her shoulders, physically barring her from the computer console. "You're crazy if you think I'll let you do this."

"It's me or everyone, Cage. Not even that. Me now, or me *and* everyone in a few hours. You'd agree if you were thinking clearly." She put her hands on his arms and yanked him in, hugging him until he let go of her shoulders and slid his hands around her, pulling her close.

At the same time, she was maneuvering him. Turning his

back to the portal. Our eyes met over Cage's shoulder, and Rune nodded.

I couldn't. I *couldn't.*

But what other choice was there?

Biting my lip so hard the pain echoed through my skull, I stepped out of the way.

"I love you, *gege,*" she said, and she shoved him.

Cage stumbled, arms pinwheeling, eyes wide in surprise. For a second he looked like he'd right himself . . .

But then he fell through the portal and disappeared.

"Go," said Rune. "Before he comes back."

Karoch thundered toward me. I didn't even have time to say good-bye. I met Rune's eyes and saw the same serene resignation I'd seen earlier, but this time I understood.

Once I'd thought I'd have to sacrifice myself to save my friends. And while I hadn't wanted to die, I'd been willing to take that risk. Now, staring into Rune's face, I saw my own conviction gazing back at me. I wanted to hug her and reassure her and thank her and save her and just have one more minute to say anything, do anything, give her the farewell she deserved.

But instead, as Karoch's massive claw swiped at my head, I leaped into the portal and yanked it shut behind me.

FORTY-FIVE

WE WERE ARRESTED ABOUT THREE MINUTES later.

Apparently, in my desire to go home, my subconscious latched on to the place it most associated with my family: the house where we'd most recently lived on Earth. Unfortunately, that was on an Omnistellar training base, so it didn't exactly take them long to find us. I supposed I should be grateful my brain didn't decide Sanctuary was home and dump me in the middle of space.

But three minutes was more than enough time for things to go to hell.

The gateway rippled shut behind me as I staggered into my old living room. Fortunately, the new residents weren't there to welcome us, but what I did see resembled a refugee camp: Reed and Imani crouched on the floor, splitting their attention among Mia, Hallam, and Jasper, all of whom had taken injuries, and everyone else gaping at me in openmouthed disbelief.

"Rune," said Matt. He stepped forward, his hands shaking. "Kenzie. Where's Rune?"

I shook my head helplessly, tears brimming in my eyes. Matt might have forgiven me for killing him. He wasn't going to forgive me for this.

Speaking of which.

Cage hadn't moved. He was just staring at me—no, not at me. At the place behind me where the portal had disappeared. "Cage," I whispered. I stepped forward, hesitant, not sure what he was going to do, what he would say. "Cage."

He shook his head, seeming to notice me for the first time. "She pushed me away," he whispered.

"Yeah."

"And she . . ." He swallowed. "Kenzie. Where's my sister?"

Now the tears spilled over my lashes and something in my heart tore with a sickening wrench. My knees gave out, and I tumbled to the ground, bracing my hands on the familiar smooth flooring covered with unfamiliar furniture where my family would never live again because they were dead, dead like Alexei and Liam and now Rune.

I couldn't stop myself any longer, not from crying, not from shaking, not from collapsing into a pathetic, sniveling mess. And that's what I was still doing when the Omnistellar guards stormed the house, when they forced me to my feet and yanked my arms behind me, when they dragged me out the front door and toward the main facility in full view of all the people who had once been my friends and neighbors and colleagues.

And I didn't care, not even a bit.

Because what did it matter anyway?

For a prisoner—and not merely a prisoner but a traitor, the lowest of the low in Omnistellar's rankings—I was treated surprisingly well. I was taken to the medical facility and sedated, and when I woke up, I was in a cramped but functional guest room: a small bed, a desk, a shuttle-size bathroom with a toilet and sonic shower. I was dressed in an Omnistellar jumpsuit and my wounds had been cleaned and bandaged, but there was a tender spot on my upper arm. I prodded it, and my face twisted in disgust.

The bastards had chipped me again.

Someone had left a tablet and a tray on the desk. The tray held a bottle of water and a plate with a plain cheese sandwich and some vegetable sticks. I shoved both aside and went for the tablet.

The second I activated it, the door to the room slid open, admitting a slim, bespectacled man in a neat Omnistellar uniform and a woman I recognized. "Colonel Trace," I said dully. She'd been in charge of my mom's unit when we took over Sanctuary. That felt like a thousand years ago. "What an honor."

"I wish I could say the same." She stood at loose attention, her arms folded behind her back. "Ms. Cord. Do you realize how many corporate regulations you've violated?"

I sank into the desk chair and passed my hand over my face as if to physically rub away some of the exhaustion. "Enough to put me away for the rest of my life," I said dully. I really didn't care anymore. "Or kill me. Whichever."

"Yes," said Trace grimly. "Whichever. So don't you wonder why you're locked up here and not in a high-security facility?"

"I assume it has something to do with the aliens." I glared at her. I was tired of Omnistellar, of their games. After everything we'd been through, Omnistellar just didn't seem all that scary anymore. Or all that important.

Trace examined me. "Do we have to worry about them anymore?" she asked bluntly.

I raised an eyebrow. "What happened?"

"What makes you think—?"

"Oh, come on." I snorted. "I've been through this before. Getting anyone corporate to listen to me has never come easily. If you're asking if the aliens pose more danger and are not trying to mine them for their technology, it means your little plan backfired about as badly as I figured it would. So what happened?"

She gaped at me in disbelief, exchanging looks with the man behind her. "Kenzie, where is this hostility coming from? Omnistellar was your entire life. I remember you.

Your promise, your potential. Where is the guard I sent to Sanctuary?"

"She died there," I spit. I was seeking refuge in my anger, letting it swallow my grief in a welcome tide of rage. "My mother killed her. You can't blame her, though. She was only following Omnistellar regulations. And then what was left of her died with my father after the alien he summoned—*you* summoned—tore him to shreds. So that answers your question. Now answer mine."

I honestly didn't expect a response, but to my surprise, I got one. After a long moment, Trace sighed and sat down on the bed. "We summoned the creatures," she said succinctly. "Against my wishes and recommendations, by the way. But I was overruled, and the creatures were called to Obsidian. No one is entirely sure what happened next. Everyone who could tell us is dead—everyone on Obsidian, and both of the Omnistellar fleets we sent. All we know for sure is that a joint attack was launched on Earth and Mars. We didn't even see them coming. They descended on major cities and cut a path of destruction. It was . . ." She shuddered, and the man stepped closer, laying a hand on her shoulder. She glanced at him and nodded. "A lot of people died," she continued. "We tried to fight them, and we had some success holding them back, but they just kept coming. More and more of them. We took steps to evacuate major centers, and still we lost entire cities. London is gone, Kenzie. Simply vanished in a cloud of debris. Same with San Francisco, Toronto, Dubai. And then, right when we'd given ourselves up for lost and started considering how to evacuate as much of the planet as possible and destroy the rest ourselves, the aliens simply stopped."

"Stopped?" I asked sharply.

"Died," said the man. It was the first time he'd spoken, and he had a pleasant, calming voice, even though it was clear he understood the gravity of what he was saying. "They dropped dead where they stood. Seconds later, we received notification of intruders on base, and we found you and your friends in your old house. We assumed the two events must be connected."

I shook my head. So we'd saved Earth, but too late. Not soon enough to prevent thousands of people from dying, to prevent whole cities from collapsing. "It started on Sanctuary," I said dully, and I told them the entire story, from the moment the alarm pulled me away from my tablet to Rune's frightened but determined face as she stood sentinel over those missiles. They listened without interrupting, rare for Omnistellar. Halfway through my speech I cracked open the water and ate the sandwich. Why not? It all tasted like dirt to me, even though it was probably the best food I'd had in months.

When I'd finished, Trace and the man frowned at each other. Trace nodded. "Kenzie," she said, "I want you to know that I'm going to do whatever I can to help you. Omnistellar isn't keen on the idea of releasing you—any of you. They want you back in prison. But I'm fully aware that you saved us, and I was never on board with the alien summoning in the first place. I'm on your side."

"I bet," I said dryly.

She hesitated. "Speaking of helping you . . . This is Dr. Marshall James. He's a psychiatrist with a background in traumatic—"

"Get out," I snarled.

"I'm only trying to—"

"Get out!" I shouted, leaping to my feet. And the colonel and the doctor stumbled over each other in their haste to comply.

The next few weeks passed in a blur. I ate. I drank. I watched vids on the tablet, drowning myself in a sea of misery, beginning with the initial news reports after the aliens arrived and following their trail of death and destruction through the world to the moment they all collapsed. And when that became too much, I reread *Robo Mecha Dream Girl 5* from the beginning. I got through the entire series twice before I got bored and turned to another manga, but it couldn't hold my attention. Not after what I'd been through. Not even *RMDG5* had the same allure it once held. I'd clung to that image of Yumiko and her mechs for so many weeks when I was weak or on the verge of giving up. But now, with so much in my own past, it seemed to ring hollow. I didn't identify with the struggle anymore. I only saw death and pain in the carefully drawn panels.

And in between, I told my story. I told it to Trace again, once alone, once with some Omnistellar bigwigs who would have terrified me out of my wits only a few months ago. I told it via vid call to an international security council based in Kiev. I told it to people I didn't know and didn't care about until I'd gone numb from the retellings and could discuss my friends and family dying in front of me as calmly as I discussed brushing my teeth.

They didn't let me see any of the others, but they said they were all in the same facility, all isolated, all safe. "All chipped?" I asked, and they ignored me. They ignored anything I said that didn't respond to their direct questions. After a while, I realized it was easier to keep my mouth shut.

Through it all I had no real hope I'd ever see daylight again. This was Omnistellar, after all, and I'd betrayed them, broken their precious regulations. It was too much to hope they'd learned from their mistakes, from the disastrous results of letting the aliens loose on Earth, and Trace didn't have the authority to keep me out of prison.

And still I didn't care. Because every time I tried to muster the energy to worry about anything, two faces swam in front of me: Alexei and Rune, their sacrifices so big and bold and so completely unsung by a corporation that didn't consider them anything other than *anomalies*. Besides, if I got out of here, I'd have to face Cage. Cage, who knew I'd left his sister to die. I spent hours staring at a blank tablet and wondering if I could have done something to stop her. To convince her. To take her place. If there had been any way to change Rune's path, to prevent her sacrifice. And every time, I came up blank. Only one thing became clear: Rune had known what she would have to do, known it long before we reached the facility. We should have known it too. Only direct contact kept the console powered. Only power exploded the missiles. If I'd realized sooner, maybe I could have thought of something.

But I hadn't, and every day I tortured myself with that thought.

Then one morning, Colonel Trace and two armed guards showed up and hustled me out of my familiar room, down a corridor, and into a public meeting area. Trace grabbed my arm as I was about to leave. "The chip won't be removed," she said sharply. "By you, or anyone. If you try to deactivate it, we'll know. Do you understand?"

I blinked. "You're releasing me?"

"You'll be given citizenship with any corporation you want—except Omnistellar. That door has closed."

I gaped at her in disbelief. This was all happening too fast. My brain, sluggish and unused for weeks, wasn't catching on. "Why? How?"

She sighed. "If you must know, someone leaked the story of what you did to the press." A slight smile played on her lips, smothered before it could grow, but enough to give me a hint about who that "someone" might be. "The people still hold some power here, Kenzie, and they weren't willing to see the group of you executed or locked in prison after saving us all. Public opinion toward anomalies has softened." Her face softened too. "My son was fighting the aliens when they disappeared. He probably would have died without you. I've done what I could. I got you your freedom. And I've made sure that Lin Hu will always be remembered as the girl who saved us."

I clenched my jaw so tightly the pain echoed through my skull. "Her name," I growled, "is Rune."

"Either way, her sacrifice won't be forgotten." Trace examined me. "I don't expect you to be grateful. I don't expect you to appreciate how much effort this took. At least, not now. But one day, I hope you'll understand that not everyone's against you." She smiled thinly. "I've even managed to obtain a small financial reward as an expression of the intercorporate community's gratitude. Obey the laws, and it will be like all of this never happened."

I laughed shortly. Like it never happened? There were some pretty gaping holes in that idea, too large to bother pointing out. "And my friends?"

"Same deal. For all of them, even Mia Browne, who actually bit the guard who came to release her this morning."

I smiled. "Good for her."

Trace shook her head in bewilderment. For a moment she looked like she wanted to say something—to express amazement at my transformation, maybe, or apologize, or maybe even to mention my parents. But she didn't. She just turned and walked away.

Dr. Marshall James, who'd been lurking behind her, pressed a small silver disc into my hand. My heart sank. A new comm device. Something I'd never even considered living without, and now it felt strange and cold in my hands. "I took the liberty of programming my contact information," he said. "If you need me, need anything . . ."

I snapped my fingers shut around it. "Thanks," I said, but I wouldn't be contacting him. Not because I wouldn't need therapy. I would. We all would, to get past this. But wherever I found it, it sure as hell wouldn't come from Omnistellar.

Squaring my shoulders, I went to face the much more difficult task of reuniting with my friends.

They were all gathered in a brightly lit, clean waiting room, waiting for me. I stood in the doorway awkwardly, gathering my nerves. I didn't dare meet Cage's eyes. All the bravado and nonchalance I'd built up dealing with Omnistellar faded as I stared them down. I wanted to apologize, wanted to explain, but what words would ever be enough? How could I tell them I'd let Rune sacrifice herself? How could I tell Cage? He would never speak to me again, and I didn't blame him, couldn't . . .

Suddenly, Cage lurched to his feet from the couch where he was sitting. He descended on me in five sweeping steps, and I actually retreated, but I wasn't fast enough. He caught me in his arms and pulled me close, folding me against him, holding me so tightly I blamed his grip for the tears spilling from the corners of my eyes. "Cage," I whispered, "Cage, I have to tell you . . ."

"No, you don't. Omnistellar told us everything. We've all heard your story."

I buried my face in his chest. "Do you hate me?"

A long silence, far too long. Then he pulled back and smiled down at me, still Cage with his flashing eyes, although there was a shadow there that hadn't existed before. He stroked his hands over my face, drying my tears. "Rune made her choice," he said. "You both tried to tell me I couldn't keep her safe forever, that I had to let her make her own decisions. Well, she did." He choked on the last word and raked his hand over his face, as if physically wiping away his grief.

"I could have stopped her," I said, and this time I didn't even resist the urge to cry.

Cage blinked hard but couldn't stop his own tears in response. "No," he said. He tried to say something else, but the words were lost. He pulled me close again, and we clutched each other in desperate, lonely belonging, maybe the only two people in the world who would ever miss Rune with this gaping, desperate awareness that part of us was gone forever.

No one said anything for a long time. At last my tears dried. I pulled away from Cage and wiped the sleeve of my shirt across my eyes. He was doing the same.

"She saved us all," said Imani quietly from behind him.

I glanced at her and then at the rest of my friends, gathered together. Jasper's face was grim, and Reed had his arms wrapped around himself and looked sad and lost, but he gave me a quick smile. Legion still lingered to one side, but somehow that no longer seemed to separate them. It was more just what they were accustomed to, drifting together, not pulling apart. Priya gave me a sympathetic nod, and Hallam forced a smile. Matt, his fists clenched at his sides, met my gaze with a despondency that matched my own. Only Mia held herself separate and didn't look my way. She stared at her feet without moving. Would she ever be the same again without Alexei? Without Rune? Would any of us?

But they were still there. We'd lost so much. Lost so many. And yet here we were, safe and strong and together. That had to count for something.

Cage drew a deep, shuddering breath and set his jaw. Misery, grief, and agony slid over his face, settling there, then vanished beneath the mask he always wore. "I know, Imani," he replied, and he sounded almost normal. "She did save us. And maybe someday, I'll forgive her for it. In the meantime, I'm not going to waste time being angry at the people I have left." He caught my chin in his hand and pulled me in for a fierce, possessive kiss, one that absolved me, leaving me with the lingering awareness of grief without blame.

Or at least, without *his* blame. I wasn't sure I'd ever stop blaming myself.

. . .

A couple of hours later, Cage, Mia, Hallam, and I stood on a hillside outside the Omnistellar base, cries and laughter bubbling around us as everyone reunited below. Imani's parents took one look at her and swept her into their arms, soothing her babbled explanations and tears as they led her away. Now they sat in a shaded corner, talking quietly. Reed was nearby with his moms, who kept touching his face as if they couldn't quite believe it was him standing in front of them. Matt had his arms around what must be a younger sister and was talking to his parents. Our eyes met over his sister's head, and he gave me a quick nod of acknowledgment—forgiveness, maybe, or, if not that yet, at least an awareness that our grief was shared.

Priya turned out to have a husband and a toddler, much to my amazement, and they, too, were nearby, talking and laughing with reckless abandon. That left only the four of us without anyone or anything to call our own, watching from the sidelines. Presumably my aunt, uncle, and cousins were still somewhere on Earth, but they either hadn't been notified of my presence or hadn't shown up. I wasn't sure I blamed them. I had wondered if we might see Anya, who Trace assured me was alive, but she was nowhere in sight, presumably still on Mars, and still blissfully unaware of what had happened to Alexei. I supposed I would have to find her at some point to tell her the truth. She deserved that much.

"So," I said to Cage, my fingers threaded through his, "what now?"

"I was offered corporate citizenship," he said, a mocking note in his voice.

Mia snorted. She was more or less herself again, although something deeper than grief lurked behind her gaze. "Me too."

"I think we all got the same deal." Hallam shrugged. "We aren't taking it. Priya, Matt, and I are forming our own team. Not bound to any corporation this time. Totally freelance." He hesitated. "I think I can speak for them when I say you're welcome to join us."

I glanced at Cage. A few months ago that would have sounded like a nightmare. Now . . . "Maybe," I said softly. "We may need some time to think first."

"What'd you have in mind?" Cage asked.

I smiled. "I'd kind of like to see Taipei." I fingered the lump on my arm where the chip lurked. "Of course, I won't be able to understand anyone. . . ."

"Well, we've dealt with that problem before." Cage's fingers drifted unbidden to his own arm. "Mia? What do you say? Want to take a holiday?"

She smiled faintly. "No. Thank you, but no."

"Come with us?" Hallam suggested.

"No. Again. Thank you, but no."

"Then what will you do?"

She shifted her weight, eyes darting back and forth as if already looking for an escape. "I don't know yet. But I can't be around anyone else. Not right now."

Cage ran a hand through his hair. "Mia . . . I know what you're going through. Rune . . ." His breath shuddered in his chest, as it always did when he mentioned her name. My own heart clenched, and I turned away, blinking rapidly at the sun to hide my tears. Behind me, Cage went on, his voice unsteady. "Sometimes I wonder how many of them died because of me. Choices I made. Plans I came up with. For what it's worth, I won't forgive myself in a hurry."

Mia shook her head. "I'm not blaming you, Cage. It's not about that. I just . . . I was never much of a people person. Maybe I've been around others too long. I need to be by myself, at least for a while."

Cage examined her for a long moment and then did what I would never have dared, releasing my hand and stepping forward to hug Mia. She stiffened for a moment but then, although she didn't actually hug him back, she relaxed, going so far as to tip her head onto his shoulder. "We love you," he told her quietly. "Stay in touch, okay?"

"I will." She bent and shouldered her backpack, flashing me a quick smile. "And you stay away from Omnistellar."

"No worries there," I said, glaring at the opulent building in front of me. I still hadn't figured out what I wanted to do, but if it spit in Omnistellar's face, I would probably be on board.

"Sorry about everything, Kenzie. Take care of yourself." Mia nodded at the others. "Say good-bye for me."

"We will."

As she strode into the distance, Hallam, Cage, and I sank onto the grass. I ran my fingers through it. Grass, real grass, even if it was carefully engineered to look perfect. And it was alive because of us. Because of Rune. "Rune," I said out loud, softly.

"Rune," Cage agreed, laying his hand over mine.

Something popped to my right, and I pivoted to find Hallam lazily hefting a can of beer. "To Rune," he declared. "She saved us all. May she rest in peace with a thousand smoldering alien corpses at her dainty feet."

"Where the hell did you get that?"

Hallam took a long sip and grinned. "I have my secrets." His face grew serious. "Your sister was something special, Cage. I hope you know that."

"I always knew. I just don't think I ever really appreciated it." Cage stretched out in the grass and reached up for me. I took his hand and curled against him, blinking into the midday sun. We were actually, finally free, free of Omnistellar and aliens and monsters. Prisoners only to these chips in our arms and our own guilt. And as for those, well . . .

I rolled my head to scrutinize Hallam. "They chipped you, too?"

He seemed unconcerned. "Uh-huh."

"And that can limit your . . . cybernetics?" Was that the right term? I didn't think "robot parts" would go over well.

"Nah, they can't do anything about that without killing us. But we were all anomalies to start with. The doc said you have to be, for the enhancements to take. And so . . ." He gestured lazily. "The chips."

"And I'm guessing you have a way to get rid of the chips without alerting Omnistellar?"

He took a long drag of his beer and belched before answering. "Sure. You want in?"

I smiled at Cage. "What do you think? A pit stop before we head to Taipei?"

Cage flexed the muscles under his shirt and gave me his new, slightly sad smile. "Why not? After, well . . . who knows?" He hesitated. "I've been thinking. What Rune did . . . I don't want her to be forgotten. And I don't want Omnistellar's version of her to live on as a hero, either."

I made a face. I'd already seen the vids celebrating Lin Hu, the Omnistellar heroine who'd saved us all on the corporation's behalf. Trace had made sure she wouldn't be forgotten, all right. I'd spent an hour in angry tears after seeing the first vid. Cage had destroyed his hotel room in a fit of rage that almost got him thrown right back in prison. "No," I said quietly. "What did you have in mind?"

"I'm not sure yet. I mean . . . there are still lots of anomalies in prison. Sanctuary might have been destroyed, but I'm sure they've started something new. We might have turned the tide of public opinion in our favor for a while, but Omnistellar is already working the narrative, strengthening their position, consolidating power."

I considered that. "Rune . . ." I choked on her name. Cage looked away for a moment, blinking rapidly. Drawing a deep breath, I focused on the sound of Hallam loudly slurping beer beside me. Hard to grieve with a noise like that. "Rune would want them to be free. That's all she ever wanted, I think. For everyone to be free. To live their lives. To know warmth and happiness and love."

"Maybe we can find a way to make that happen." Cage pulled me back to him and gave me a weak smile, his sister's ghost reflected in his gaze. "Who knows?"

I curled against him and let the warmth surround me. Who knew, indeed? But somehow, after everything that had happened, I didn't think I'd be content to lie back and enjoy the warmth for long. I was choosing to stay down this time, at least for a while. But there wasn't a chance in hell that I wouldn't get back up again.

ACKNOWLEDGMENTS

A FEW YEARS AGO I SAT DOWN AND WROTE the acknowledgments for *Sanctuary*. I thanked literally everyone I could think of, mainly because I had no idea if I would ever get to write one of these again. Now I'm writing my third set of acknowledgments, but the list of people to thank hasn't gotten any smaller. If anything, it's grown.

Thanks goes first and always to my family: my mother, Audrey; my father, Lanny; my brother, Chris; my sister, Kim; and my nephew, Emmett, who is not old enough to read this book but is old enough to enjoy seeing his name in print. My wonderful family by marriage—Erin, Liz, and Brian—have supported me every step of the way. My husband, Dan, moved across the world with me and then spent half of his time in another country supporting me while I wrote this book, which would not exist without him.

Books don't exist without readers, and I am truly, profoundly grateful to the readers who have loved *Sanctuary*, including readers and groups like the To Be Read and Beyond

Facebook group, and especially my amazing students (and former students) at the Canadian International School in Tokyo and at St. Patrick's Fine Arts in Lethbridge. Every time I see you at one of my events, every time you send me a message or tell me you loved my book, it just melts my heart a bit more. Soon it will be a puddle of goo, and it will be your fault. Keep at it.

I'm blessed with the most supportive friends and family. Timanda Wertz, Nathan Gilchrist, Sarah Taylor, John Harland . . . all of you who supported me—thank you. The staff at CIS and SPFA—thank you. Honestly, I couldn't do this without you.

Books aren't created in a vacuum, and this book wouldn't exist (or at least wouldn't be very good) without the help of my tremendous agent, Caitie Flum; Liza Dawson; Mackenzie Croft; my incomparable editor, Sarah McCabe; and the amazing designer, Sarah Creech, and cover artist, Jacey.

This is the end of Kenzie's journey. Thank you all for coming on it with me. Thank you for reading. Thank you for imagining. I will miss these characters, these stories, but I know there are always more to come, and I hope you'll be there with me for that journey as well.